More Praise for *The Starboard Sea*

"Amber Dermont has conjured up a preppy hall of mirrors, filled with hauntingly complex characters, grand houses and borrowed art, privilege and paybacks, and friendship touched with malice. *The Starboard Sea* blends propulsive mystery, lost love, and mournful coming-of-age into something layered, wise, and completely riveting."

—Michelle Wildgen, author of
But Not for Long and *You're Not You*

"*The Starboard Sea* is a beautifully layered novel with an authenticity that takes the reader beyond the clichés of rich preppies and exposes a world that is vivid, compelling, and heart wrenching. With it, Amber Dermont establishes herself as an exciting new American talent."

—Mark Jude Poirier, author of
The Worst Years of Your Life and *Goats*

"In a series of seemingly effortless strokes, Amber Dermont's *Starboard Sea* has brought to life one of America's great literary outcasts. Set adrift in a storm of his own making, Dermont's Jason Prosper takes us on a journey into the darker depths of our human capabilities. Damaged and dangerous, by turns as despicable as he is lovable, Prosper's voyage is a treasure from a writer of dazzling gifts."

—Holiday Reinhorn, author of *Big Cats*

"Amber Dermont illuminates the bizarre and insular world of boarding schools in her debut novel, *The Starboard Sea,* and her young narrator, Jason Prosper, is captivating. His is a unique voice, searching and full of heart. *The Starboard Sea* is sharp, funny, smart, and vastly entertaining."   —Victoria Patterson, author of
Drift, a Story Prize finalist, and *This Vacant Paradise*

THE
STARBOARD SEA

AMBER DERMONT

ST. MARTIN'S PRESS
NEW YORK

This is a work of fiction. All of the characters, organizations, and events portrayed in this novel are either products of the author's imagination or are used fictitiously.

THE STARBOARD SEA. Copyright © 2012 by Amber Dermont. All rights reserved. Printed in the United States of America. For information, address St. Martin's Press, 175 Fifth Avenue, New York, N.Y. 10010.

www.stmartins.com

Library of Congress Cataloging-in-Publication Data

Dermont, Amber.
   The starboard sea : a novel / Amber Dermont. — 1st ed.
      p. cm.
  ISBN 978-0-312-64280-8 (hardcover)
  ISBN 978-1-4299-5097-8 (e-book)
  1. Young men—Fiction.   2. Self-realization—Fiction.   3. Male
friendship—Fiction. I. Title.
  PS3604.E75455S73 2012
  813'.6—dc23

2011041100

10 9 8 7 6 5 4 3

For my parents

*I wish to have no connection with any ship
that does not sail fast for I intend to go in harm's way.*

—CAPTAIN JOHN PAUL JONES

*You know
what you did. You know you know
what you did.
No one is hearing your ornate confession.*

—DAN CHIASSON, "Stealing from Your Mother"

THE STARBOARD SEA

ONE

On the morning I turned eighteen, instead of a birthday present, my father tossed me the keys to his car and informed me I was finally man enough to captain his Cadillac. It was early August. I was doomed to trade the final blaze of summer for the first days of school. Dad kept the engine running while I half-assed my way through packing, racing around our apartment stuffing boxer shorts and sport coats into duffel bags. Instead of helping me, Dad ordered our ancient doorman, Max, to ferry my luggage to the car. In his navy wool uniform, all epaulets, gold tassels, and brass stars, his kind face glistening with sweat, Max looked like the commander of a sinking ship. I told him not to worry, but Max was adamant. "Okay," I said, "but leave the heavy stuff to me." More than anything, I hated being waited on, but I didn't want to cause trouble for Max. We rode the elevator to the lobby and I told him, "For wearing that get-up in this heat, you deserve hazard pay."

"Don't worry about me," Max said. "I get paid to look this pretty." Max helped me load the car and wished me good luck. "It's your senior year," he said. "Enjoy yourself."

My mother was still on vacation in Maine. It occurred to me that the only soul in all of New York City I would miss would be my doorman. "Take care, Boss," I said and slid into the driver's seat.

Once on the road, Dad turned down the air-conditioning. I could feel the heat radiating off the dashboard as we cruised away from

Manhattan, weaving along the East River, headed for the coast of Massachusetts. Dad sat beside me in the passenger seat, alternating between the *Wall Street Journal* and *Forbes*. Every few minutes, he checked the road over his bifocals. "Jason Kilian Prosper, this isn't a race."

My father was tall, with a good two inches on me, three on my older brother, Riegel; the Cadillac was custom-designed with extra depth and legroom. A pair of life jackets could have been stowed in the space beyond his outstretched legs. Still, my father struggled for comfort. He lifted his left knee toward his chest, wincing when the bones cracked. His blue linen pants remained crisp in the damp heat. Even in pain, Dad sat composed and pleated, looking less like a dad and more like a member of the British House of Lords.

According to my father, I was "damaged goods." Selling me to another school wasn't going to be easy. This was the summer of 1987, the year of damaged goods: Oliver North and paper shredders, Gary Hart and *Monkey Business,* record-high AIDS, and a record-high stock market. That spring, Mathias Rust, just one year older than me, eager for a thrill, had evaded Soviet air defenses and landed his Cessna 172B in Red Square. That fall, the entire country would be riveted for two and a half days, as rescue workers in Midland, Texas, plotted to pull a baby from an abandoned well. And in the meantime, I had gotten myself banished from Kensington Prep and was about to start my senior year at Bellingham Academy.

"What's the drill?" I asked, breaking our silence. "Drinks with the headmaster? Nine holes of golf?"

Dad folded his newspaper into a tight, narrow column. "The headmaster is out of town. We're meeting with the dean. Dick Warr."

"I hope he lives up to his name," I said.

"Try behaving for once."

"I stopped behaving myself a long time ago." The needle fanned over seventy-five. Before Dad noticed, I decelerated, slightly.

"Just graduate." Dad scanned his newspaper. "Finish up for your mother. The poor woman. She doesn't like to show her face in public anymore."

"So *I'm* the reason Mom leaves the apartment in disguise. Go figure."

"Your brother never speaks to me that way." Dad cracked the side of my head with the *Journal*. His weapon of choice.

I don't think he meant to hurt me, but the impact and surprise caused me to swerve. The corner of the paper struck my right eye, knocking it shut and, for a brief instant, I let go of the wheel. Imagined us hitting the guardrail, the Cadillac embraced by an elbow of metal.

"Get control of yourself, for God's sake!" Dad pulled the steering wheel back in line.

For the rest of the trip, I half daydreamed and half drove, the car flipping forward and crushing Dad's body. Leaving me to surgically excise what little was left of my dad from the wreckage. Snapping his legs off cleanly at the knees. No blood. Just bones and sockets, white as a whale's tooth. On one knee, I'd scrimshaw the word "left," and on the other, "right." Neat and orderly. During long trips, the legs could be packed into one of those cases ventriloquists use to store their dummies. At last, Dad would no longer be in pain. His linen pants would drape and rest like opera curtains on the carpeted car floor.

"Pull over at the next rest stop. Time for me to drive."

Our near accident had been his fault. For some parents, having children meant full absolution from any future mistakes. My father wouldn't permit himself to be wrong. He shifted the blame of misplaced scissors, rising interest rates, and iceless ice cube trays all onto Riegel and me. Dad cheated on our mom and told our mom it was her fault he cheated on her.

My mother really had left our apartment in disguise. Decoyed in a rotating masquerade of ginger-haired wigs and cat's-eye sunglasses, she'd chased after my dad and his harem.

Mom and I had spent the earlier part of that summer at our cottage in Maine. Our mornings devoted to relaxing on wicker porch chairs, watching the Iran-contra hearings, mixing champagne with grapefruit juice. As the men on the TV bragged and lied, denying their accomplishments, my mother turned the sound to mute and spoke to me about my father's indiscretions.

"Of all your father's mistresses, my favorite was this knock-kneed Eastern European hussy he would lug around on business trips, this woman Gayla, a dozen years his junior. Called her his 'administrative aide.' Gayla the Flying Whore is what I called her. I followed them once on a nonstop to the Caymans. Your father didn't notice me in my red wig coming down the aisle to claim my seat in coach. He was preoccupied with his first-class hot towels, with brushing the white cloth against her neck. That woman took forever to get off the plane. Commandeering the aisle, prattling on to the flight crew while the rest of us cooled our heels. The way that woman laughed, with her teeth. I never laughed that way." My mother swept the champagne flute to her lips, then confirmed that she was ready to hunt a new breed of Gaylas. From under her wicker seat, Mom pulled out a hatbox, opened the top, and withdrew a mass of chocolate ringlets. "My latest disguise." She twirled the hairpiece on her fist and said, "When you were little, I caught you and Riegel with one of my old wigs. Remember? The hair all matted like a rat's nest."

"We used it to play tag. Chasing each other, then forcing the loser into the wig." Riegel had made up this game as a way of torturing me. A brittle net material covered the inside of the hairpiece, and my brother the bully liked to pull it over my nose and push the scratchy lining into my face. The suffocation became my own definition of blindness. Not an absence of light, but a prickling concealment. A rough and painful mask.

"I guess we both played games with the damn thing," Mom said.

Mom was wrong to tell me about Dad. To let me know that he cheated and to make me afraid of the ways he could hurt me. He was a swindler passing for a saint, and as I sat beside him in his big American luxury car, I thought, "Be careful, Dad. I'm on to you."

My father had his wild streak, but he drove his Cadillac slow and steady like a grandma rocking a baby to sleep. It took us all afternoon to reach our destination. We exited the highway and a wooden historical marker welcomed my father and me to the small Atlantic village of Bellinghem, spelled with an "e." Another sign, this one metal and posted just a few yards away, welcomed us to Bellingham Academy. It was impossible to tell where the school ended and the town began. A run of dorms resembled coach houses. Fenced roads between the dormitories felt like estate driveways. I'd been to Bellingham twice before for dinghy races. My sailing partner Cal and I had won our individual races but lost both regattas to the home team. They sailed high-performance Fireballs and had an ocean advantage over schools like Kensington that practiced on lakes with shifty winds. As I stared at the waterfront, the color and movement on the ocean created an optical illusion in my mind. The entire school appeared to float on water, like a life raft. I felt weightless. The rhythm of the waves reminded me of naval hymns, of songs about peril and rescue.

Most of us who found ourselves at Bellingham had been kicked out of better schools for stealing, or having sex, or smoking weed. Rich kids who'd gotten caught, been given a second chance, only to be caught again then finally expelled. We weren't bad people, but having failed that initial test of innocence and honor, we no longer felt burdened to be good. In some ways it was a relief to have fallen. To have fucked up only to land softly, cushioned, as my dad reminded me, "by a goddamn safety net of your parents' wealth." Bellingham offered us sanctuary, minimal regulations, and a valuable lesson: Breaking rules could lead to more freedom. Because the school catered to thieves, sluts, and dope fiends, it was understood that additional transgressions would be overlooked. If you could pay, you could stay. I comforted myself knowing that I'd lowered all future expectations. So long as I didn't torch my dormitory or poison my hall mates, I was free to take full advantage of the lax standards and leniency. But all this freedom would indeed cost me something: a stain on my reputation. I'd been Bellinghammed. It was almost as bad as winding up at Choate.

Dad parked in front of the Academic Center, a modern two-story building that clashed with its traditional surroundings. While the outside walls were dressed in silvery cedar shingles, the roof wore a crown of glass. A massive arch of shiny blue windows curved atop steel rafters. A giant dorsal fin. Either the building was masquerading as a fish or a fish was moonlighting as a building.

"Monstrosity," Dad said, slamming the car door. "How many donors does it take to screw up a building?"

"Looks like a barracuda," I responded.

All over campus, parentless students raced about wearing Vuarnet sunglasses and Hard Rock Cafe T-shirts. Happy delinquents newly freed from their families. A tribe of boys stood in a circle playing Hacky Sack. Each one wore a brightly colored woven Guatemalan belt tied around his waist like a signal flag.

My father took great pride in introducing me to the men in charge. His way of taking care of his son. We entered the Academic Center and found Dean Warr's office. Dad told me to wait in the lounge, so I slid into the bucket seat of a brown leather chair. At my father's request, I'd thrown on a blue blazer and a red tie decorated with dark blue sailboats. The tie was a gift from Ted Turner, commemorating the ten-year anniversary of his victory at the America's Cup. I'd swiped it from my dad. I looked entirely presentable except I'd forgotten to wear socks. My ankles stuck out all white and hairy, and I was worried Dad would notice, criticize me. In a few minutes, I heard laughter. The distinct sound of hands slapping backs. I stood up and pulled my pant cuffs down to my loafers.

"Dick, I'd like you to meet my son, Jason. Jason, this is Mr. Warr."

The dean had a broad back, a narrow waist. He smelled like limes and wore the school's colors: a maroon jacket and blue pants. The sport coat sleeves stopped short around his wrists. We shook hands. He invited me into the bright white light of his office. Dad waited outside.

The office had a view of some newly planted saplings.

"Your father tells me you're quite the sailor." He sat down behind his desk.

"When the wind is strong," I said and found a chair to sit in.

"I think we SeaWolves have a lock on the Tender Trophy this year." Dean Warr leaned forward on his elbows.

"That's tremendous, truly." I nodded, flashing my teeth and folding my left leg across my right knee. I covered the bare ankle with my hand.

"We'll get you set up with Mr. Tripp, the head coach."

The dean's facial expression reminded me of a clown's smiling face lacquered onto a plastic Halloween mask. I wanted to reach over, grab the mask by its bulbous nose, and snap the cheap elastic string against his ears. A reverse slingshot.

"Your father's an important man. He's shared his deep concern over your future. At Bellingham, we specialize in fresh starts, second chances." The dean raised both of his eyebrows but tilted his head, so it appeared that only the right brow was lifted.

"I just hope to graduate in the spring," I said.

"In the meantime, enjoy yourself. Our girls are grade-A fresh. Not like that monastery Kensington. I bet it can get lonely in those boys-only woods." Dean Warr continued smiling, his lip sat caught on his teeth like a crook on a barbed-wire fence.

I said nothing in response but wondered what my father had told this man.

"Good." He stood up. "No more questions."

Up to this point, I hadn't asked him any. I didn't move out of my chair, felt welded to it. "I was wondering if you could tell me how they named the school."

"After the town and the Bellinghem family," he said.

"But they're spelled differently. I noticed driving up. Thought there might be a story. Some history."

"The 'a' looks better on the letterhead." Still smiling, he opened the door of his office and checked his watch.

Dad and I said good-bye in front of Whitehall, my new dormitory. Before he had a chance to drive off, I decided to cost my family something more and reminded Dad that I needed an allowance. He slipped a leather folio from his sport coat, tore out a blank check, and signed it. "I trust you to fill in an appropriate amount." Dad told me to open a bank account first thing in the morning and then to call his current secretary, his latest Gayla, to report the exact figure I'd deemed necessary for my financial survival.

We scanned through the car one last time to make sure I had unloaded all my belongings.

"Do me a favor?" he asked. "Try to like this place."

"They're all the same, right?"

"Don't lose that check." He looked me over. "Buy yourself a pair of socks, and call your mother."

"Anything else?"

"Be sure to tell us if you need something."

I knew we weren't going to embrace, but it surprised me that my father didn't hold out his hand or pat my back or wish me one last happy birthday. He nodded once and settled into the driver's seat.

There wasn't much for me to unpack, but the thought of hanging blue button-downs in my closet and fun-tacking posters and tapestries to the bare walls made me feel claustrophobic. I decided to go for a walk.

I followed the local wind, the sea breeze, and made my way through the town center, passing a post office, a general store, a bank, and an array of restaurants and gift shops. Bellinghem was a one-street venue. Everything the town had to offer sat lined up in a neat shooting gallery. Oval-shaped wooden signs swung outside the shops. Names stenciled in gold leaf. The SINGING LIGHTHOUSE, the CHARMED DOLPHIN, the LOST MERMAID. I figured these businesses catered mainly to parents visiting their children on weekends. Quickly, I thought of my own store names in defense: the Toxic Oyster, the Slutty Sea Nymph, the Nauseated Fishmonger. I imagined a time in midautumn when my parents would drive up for the weekend. My mother would make us all wait while she picked out some overpriced silver knickknack in one of the gift stores. The three of us would then walk down by the waterfront, speaking only to point out different yachts in the harbor. In the evening, at dinner, Dad would order a bottle of his favorite Barolo and make sure that I had half a glass. This is how it had been at Kensington. Year after year. But no one in my family had mentioned any visits.

After a mile or so of passing saltbox houses, the road turned into a long camel stretch of sand. A groin made of orange and purple stones ran into the ocean and divided the beach into two sections. My best friend Cal and I had spent summers together in Maine hurdling and jumping off every big rock we could find. I always seemed to be drawn to jagged edges.

The high tide rushed in and washed over the break. That far from shore, only the sharp tips of the rocks were visible, and a strange figure stood a hundred yards out, surrounded by waves, with no discernible path behind itself. For a brief moment, I thought it was a cormorant. The tall black birds have no oil on their feathers, so they stand with wings unfolded, waiting for the sun to dry their plumage. But as I walked closer, I saw it was a person. Even closer, and I knew it was a girl. She had a bundle of curly hair streaming behind her. The wet feathers turned into the folds of a long, colorful skirt. Her arms rested at her sides. She belonged on the prow of an ancient vessel. I couldn't see her face, but I imagined it. I'd been to Greece and seen broken statues. A tour guide told me that the heads were removed because the Greeks felt they were too beautiful for the conquering Romans to see. Had even one of those faces survived, it would have been hers.

For a few minutes, I just stood and watched her. She never moved. The tide continued to rise, and I knew that she risked being trapped. Risked being washed out by a rogue wave. With the break flooded, there would be no way for her to walk back to shore. Even a strong swimmer could be pulled out into the rip.

I waded into the cool water, pushing out with slow, deliberate steps. Waves lapped against my pant legs and sprayed the edges of my jacket. The sand fell loose, collapsed, and tried to swallow one of my loafers. Unwilling to lose a shoe, I pulled away from the suction and gripped my toes tightly into the soles. Before continuing, I thought quickly and removed my jacket, holding it above my head. I walked, pressing down with only my heels. Shivering and strutting in delayed motion, I looked ridiculous. The girl stood farther out than I had judged, and just as I thought I was getting closer, the horizon changed. Expanding the distance between us.

"Hello," I shouted. "The tide's coming in."

She didn't hear me, or else didn't feel like responding.

"The break's flooded," I yelled even louder. "You'll have to paddle in." I was still a good hundred yards from her, but my voice echoed and rang out over the waves. "Hello. Over here. Can you swim?" If she couldn't, I'd need to dive in and carry her back. "If you'd just nod or something to let me know." Her face remained hidden, with only a hint of profile. A long, narrow nose and tall forehead. "I'm a strong swimmer. I can hold you." She offered no response. Maybe she was deaf, or foreign. "Do you want me to come out? Hey."

The "hey" got her attention. Just impolite enough. Just slightly menacing. I wanted to take it back and let her know I was concerned, not rude. She turned around quickly and looked to the beach. Then, like a gymnast preparing for a run of flips and tumbles, she skipped over the water in double time. From my view, she appeared to dance on the ocean. The rocks were arranged underneath her, just inches below the surface. Not the life-threatening flood I'd imagined. She hadn't been in danger. Not really. I stood, wet up to my hips, watching her reach shore.

Once she hit the sand, she hesitated and looked back. I took my jacket off my head and straightened my necktie. She smiled to me across the water, waved, and cried out, "Thank you."

"But I didn't do anything," I shouted.

"You have no idea." She waved again and started up the beach. Her voice didn't sound distorted or strained, but close, as though she was in the water beside me.

"Wait," I told her.

I tried to run and catch up but managed only to splash myself and drop my jacket. The only untouched part of me was the inside knot of my tie. I felt like a puddle.

The girl was safe and dry and gone.

Walking back to campus took some time, as I traveled in wet leather shoes that puckered and squeaked with the sound of warped windshield blades. I wanted to avoid being seen as this soaked bog creature, so I crept along behind trees and mailboxes, wringing out the drips in my jacket every few steps. Even wet shoes reminded me of Cal. He liked the barefooted feel of summer grass and heated pavement. His own feet had high arches that worked like suction cups, gripping better than the treads on any boat shoes. When we sailed together, he loved to hitch himself to the trapeze and move along the gunwale with just the skin of his feet holding him to the edge of the hull. I followed him always in damp sandals or sneakers.

Now that Cal was gone, the differences between us had become more evident. I'd heard that amputees had phantom pains, twitches and spasms, their bodies unconvinced that the limbs were removed, still flexing the elbows not there and extending the make-believe knees. I felt more like the severed arm or leg longing for its missing body. I was anxious for something to cling to. For years, I'd been happy to simply experience my life as an extension of Cal's. Another limb that picked up the slack. While knowing him, I'd always searched for similarities. For anything that might make us interchangeable. Cal and I looked alike. Both of us had wild brown hair that turned woolly when our mothers forgot to have it cut. Our bodies were trim and athletic. We were sporty sailors, lean and lithe, not larded or buff. We walked with the same crooked swagger and low bent knees. Each of us had a cleft in our chin, a weakness in the muscle that we thought made us seem tough. But there were differences. Cal had broken my nose by accident and joked that my face was asymmetrical, that he had caused my good looks to be a millimeter off. I had to agree that he was the movie star and I was the movie star's stunt double. My eyes were a dull slate gray, Cal's were magnetic. His eyes were two different colors. One was green. Not hazel or tortoiseshell, but a rain forest green. The other varied from misty gray to violet: his mood eye. My face received comfortable, comforting glances, but people stared at Cal. He commanded an electric attention. The only other physical difference between us was obvious at the end of a summer's day. Cal's skin tanned olive brown, and mine turned red with blisters. Cal belonged on a postcard from the Mediterranean. I, on the other hand, would always be Prosper the Lobster. At least, that's what he called me.

Each time in Maine was a vacation from the months we spent together as roommates at Kensington. In the summer, we sailed without a thought for competition. Read without worrying about exams. We drank Johnny Walker Red and smoked Pall Malls. Kurt Vonnegut smoked Pall Malls, and we liked him. Mornings, we would fill a deep and ancient cooler with roast beef sandwiches, hard-boiled eggs, and liquor thieved from our fathers' reserves. We sailed all day and slept out on my family's boat at night. In the late hours, we rested together, planned trips.

"As far down as Tierra del Fuego. Recreate Magellan's voyage." I massaged my neck with a beer bottle, rubbing the cold glass against my sunburned skin.

"You know, they named a part of the Milky Way after Magellan," Cal said.

"What, like a star?"

"A whole cloud of stars near the Southern Cross. It's some kind of phenomenon." Cal rested on his back and stared up at the night. He turned over on his side and looked at me. "You know, the tip of Orion's sword, it's not a star. It's another galaxy."

"A whole other galaxy?" I asked. "How do you know?"

"Celestial navigation. At night the stars are all real sailors ever need."

"Sea of Tranquillity," I said.

We were quiet for a long time, drinking our beers and waiting for the air to cool.

After changing out of my wet clothes, I made my way to the main dormitory, Astor, which housed the dining hall. New England boarding schools are a small, incestuous world. In theory, I already knew everyone I was about to meet. If I didn't know someone personally, I knew of him, or knew his grip on the social ladder. Knew if his dad was a friend of my dad. Knew what his mother had kept in the divorce. Knew if his apartment faced Central Park from the east or the west or not at all. Knew if he wintered in Vail or St. Moritz. Knew if he summered at all, and if so, was it the Vineyard, the Hamptons, or Tuscany. Knew if his nanny had a French accent or a French Creole accent. Knew if he gave a shit about money. Knew if he couldn't wait to self-destruct.

On the path from Whitehall, I ran into a friend from Kensington, Tazewell Marx. Taze the Dazed. He'd once bragged that he could fashion a bong out of anything: a Granny Smith apple, his roommate's oboe, the trophy cup Cal and I brought back from Nationals. Our sophomore year, he'd been expelled for making pipes in ceramics class and selling them at the Kensington Christmas Craft Bazaar. The headmaster's wife bought two for her ten-year-old nephew, when Tazewell cheerfully explained the pipes were "bubble pipes," for blowing soap bubbles.

On weeknights, dinner at Bellingham was jacket and tie. As I adjusted my dress coat, Tazewell sneaked up behind me and pulled down the sleeve. He pinched my biceps.

"What's this? A mosquito bite?" Taze let go of my arm and walked backward in front of me. He smiled with straight, expensive teeth.

I'd always liked Tazewell. His father had gone to Princeton with my dad. He lived on the West Side, three blocks down from the Museum of Natural History. In the settlement, his mother was awarded the vacation homes in Vail and Bridgehampton. Taze spoke Pidgin French, especially when wasted. He had thick dirty blond hair, an aristocratic face. Just the right combination of preppy and unkempt. One wrist showed off his grandfather's antique Piaget. The other wrist was stacked with colored bracelets woven from embroidery floss. The bracelets were faded and frayed. Together, the watch and the bracelets were proof that Taze belonged to our world. The sun and salt water faded the bracelets. The same sun and salt water tanned his skin and burnished his hair with blond highlights. Rest, play. No one ever returned to school pale. The jacket Tazewell wore was blue-and-white-striped seersucker. I owned one. Every guy I ever went to school with owned one. I think we inherited them from our fathers. We all managed to wear them about once a year. Regattas, dining clubs, lost days.

"I want you to meet somebody." Tazewell turned and called back to a large lumbering figure wearing a yellow necktie knotted around his head. He looked like a cross between a frat boy and a chieftain.

"Jason Prosper, this Sasquatch here is my best buddy, Kriffo Dunn."

The curves of Kriffo's forearms were visible through his sport coat. He pulled the yellow necktie down over his head and around his thick neck, keeping the tie loose, his collar too tight to button. We shook hands and my fingers disappeared inside his fist. He had short black hair, his cheeks like a pair of round strawberries.

"Very pleased to meet you." For a big guy, Kriffo had a gentle, almost mellifluous voice.

"I was psyched to hear you were coming." Tazewell walked behind me and tried to step on the backs of my shoes.

"Not half as psyched as your girlfriend." I stopped short. Taze ran right into me, and I elbowed him in the chest.

Kriffo laughed. The two boys made for an unusual couple. Tazewell, tall and trim, the handsome prince, always prepared to charm. Kriffo, the laconic and oversized knight-errant, willing to shield. I knew that Tazewell played soccer, and, for an instant, I saw Kriffo on the soccer field, geared up in a giant football jersey and shoulder pads, thundering down the sidelines, guarding his friend, and knocking down opponents. Kriffo's family owned a sporting goods empire. DUNN was emblazoned on lacrosse sticks, across kneepads, under chin straps, and on the backs of crash helmets. His family had its own catchphrase: "Tell your opponents, they're Dunn."

We entered the dining hall, a spartan room with long, dark tables, captain's chairs, and low-hanging brass chandeliers. The walls were covered with portraits of sour-faced elders. Taze and Kriffo took off in pursuit of other distractions, leaving me lost. The line I thought I needed to stand in didn't move and only seemed to get wider as more bodies filed in past me. I decided to force my way up to the front by saying, "Excuse me," pretending to know where I was headed. This didn't work. Students carrying trays of food seemed to be coming out on one side of the hall. I entered through this exit.

My New York sensibility kicked in. I felt myself hailing a cab. Cutting through a crowd of people, I reached over for a tray and silverware, then picked up a plate of chicken with roasted potatoes and a bowl of red gelatin. Just as I was leaving, a gangly boy wearing an apron and carrying a ladle accosted me.

"You . . . you can't do that," he stammered.

"What can't I do?"

"You cut. I saw you cut." The boy had a small patch of acne on his left cheek.

If I'd been smart, I would've kept walking. I would've ignored him completely, but now I was trapped.

"Look, I'm just hungry, that's all." Balancing my tray with one hand, I gestured with the other.

"Everyone's hungry," the boy said.

"Hey, Plague. You causing trouble?"

I swung around and saw Taze and Kriffo. For a moment, I worried that they were calling *me* Plague. Then I turned and caught the boy slowly backing away.

With his lilting, saccharine voice Kriffo asked, "What's the disease, Plague?"

"This guy cut everyone." Plague looked away.

"Jason." Tazewell put his arm around me. "I want to apologize. Plague is a wombat who sometimes forgets he's a wombat."

Wombat was a term we used at Kensington to describe the servers, cooks, and janitors who waited on us. It felt good to hear a familiar term I could identify. Part of me enjoyed being an insider. But another part of me hated the meanness, the smallness of the word. Wombat. The kid looked completely normal, even the acne on his face was nothing special, but he wasn't a student. A local kid paid by the school to serve us. I wondered what his real name was.

We—Tazewell, Kriffo, and I—sat on the far left of the dining hall, beside a wall of French doors that looked out onto the crowded harbor and an island across the bay. The only movement on the water was a single rower gliding by on a scull.

"Senior privilege," Tazewell told me. "Underclassmen can't sit by the windows. Hey, Race, don't you have a home to go to?" Taze picked up a roasted potato wedge and pitched it at a boy with shaggy orange hair. "Fucking day student. Fucking day flick."

"I missed you too, asshole," Race said. His orange hair had splotches of wine red in it. The fur of a bleeding fox.

"My good friend, Jason Prosper." Taze tipped his head toward me.

"I know this guy." Race Goodwyn held out his arm. "I competed against you in Tortola. This kid kept me sailing inside his wake. Cutthroat but smart."

I put my tray down and shook Race's outstretched hand. "I've never been to Tortola."

Cal had spent his final vacation there.

"Well, the guy sure looked like you. Do you sail?" Race asked. "I'm the captain of the team."

Taze spoke up. "Prosper is going to save the day. Win us the Tender."

I didn't like the idea that people were relying on me to win something for them. I wasn't even certain that I wanted to keep sailing. Since Cal's death, I'd developed a nasty habit of capsizing.

Race squinted at me. "So, Prosper, sounds like you're a cause for celebration. You want to crew for me?"

Before I had a chance to answer, a short guy with a big blond head approached our table. With his oversized head he looked like he'd managed somehow to stunt his own growth. He carried two dinner trays and placed one in front of Race.

"They ran out of Jell-O," the blond kid explained.

"Did they run out of silverware too?" Race asked.

"Eat with your hands," Tazewell said. "Like a man." Taze pulled off the remaining skin on his chicken and folded it into his mouth, laughing as he chewed.

"Stuyvie, this is Jason Prosper, my new crew," said Race.

"I'm Stuyvesant Warr," Stuyvie said. "Race's sidekick."

Stuyvesant Warr. Dick Warr. Faculty kids were the worst. They spent all of their time trying to prove that they weren't snitches, and then the first chance they got, they narked on everyone.

Race had the build of a sailor—slender, not overly muscular—but he was too tall to be swift footed, or at least he was taller than me. Together we'd be a cumbersome and awkward pair. I imagined the two of us tacking, scrambling across the boat and taking on water. Plenty of sailors believed in the classic hierarchy: The helmsman gave orders while the crew took orders. But Cal and I both understood that the roles were less about power and prestige and more about being right for the job. Still, I couldn't help toss attitude at Race. "Sorry," I said. "I'm a full-time helmsman."

Tazewell and Kriffo snorted, while Stuyvie looked down.

Race stared at me the way a patient father looks at a disobedient child. "Unlike you, Mr. Helmsman, I'm what you might call a good sportsman. I'd crew for a girl if it was the best thing for the team."

That night at dinner, my friends were all trying to act older, more confident, more aloof, and yet I knew or would soon learn their boyhood secrets. At twelve, on an Outward Bound trip, I had listened to

Tazewell, red faced and hysterical, cry for a good twenty minutes because he was frightened of riding a chestnut Tennessee Walker down a nature trail. Our guide eventually persuaded him to saddle up behind me. While the old mare kept her smooth four-beat walk, Taze clung to my waist with anxious, clawing hands. Kriffo's real name was Christopher. According to Tazewell, Kriffo spent his entire childhood insisting he was the real Christopher Robin. Kriffo, eighteen and gigantic, still tucked his pillows into faded pillowcases illustrated with cartoons of Piglet, Owl, and Eeyore. Kriffo would confide to me that all of the men in Race's family died in their forties from the same congenital heart defect. Race's dad spent his forty-third birthday with his son fishing for blues on their Boston Whaler, then, without warning, dropped his pole, grabbed his son's wrist, and collapsed. By the time Race taxied the boat to shore, his father was dead. Race asked his algebra teacher to help him devise a formula that would tell him the exact number of days he had left until his own forty-third birthday. I'd learn from Race that Stuyvie, the dean's son, had applied to Bellingham twice before finally being accepted. We all had our own private humiliations and heartbreaks. The trick was pretending we didn't.

Our dinner conversation stalled on how to improve the basketball team's chances that winter.

"I've been telling Stuyvie he's got to get his dad to start recruiting some brothers to help us out." Race raised his fist and mimicked the black power sign.

"Next time you come to the city, I'll drop you at 125th Street. You can catch a gypsy cab and scout for talent," Tazewell said.

"I don't know why Chester won't play." Race scrunched up a bunch of paper napkins. He played imaginary basketball, shooting his napkins over Tazewell's head.

"Chester's too good for us." Tazewell smiled. "He's waiting to go pro."

"No way." Stuyvie blocked a shot. "Dude can't even dunk."

Sitting across from us, at another table but within earshot, was Chester Baldwin. His father was a federal judge and Chester's family owned a summer cottage with tennis courts in Oak Bluffs on Martha's Vineyard. I'd met Chester on the ferry from Wood's Hole to the

Vineyard and accepted an invitation to play a few sets at his home. I'd never been in a black person's house before. The rugs were all cream colored, and I'd been asked to remove my shoes before entering the foyer. I stood in his living room, holding my racquet, desperate to hide the holes in the toes of my socks. On the fireplace mantel, there was a framed photograph of Chester as a little boy shaking hands with a thin-lipped Vice President Bush. On our piano, my mother kept a similar photo of Riegel and me meeting a red-lipped President Reagan.

While everyone at my table joked, I glanced over at Chester. A deliberate look, and Chester was prepared for it. He expected people to scrutinize his reactions. Holding my stare, he reached down and picked up one of the crumpled pieces of napkin that Race had thrown. Chester smiled at me. He balled up the napkin into a tight sphere, aimed, and shot the basket. The napkin ball landed in my water glass and quickly expanded. I looked at the glass, then picked it up and toasted Chester. He nodded his head.

"You know what we should really do?" Taze asked. "Go to Jamaica and bring back some Rasta men. Buy this school a greenhouse and get our ganja farmers to work their magic. You should see this new poster I have up in my room. Huge blowup of Bob Marley, kicking back, smoking a big spliff." Taze reached into his pocket and pulled out a flat metal cigarette case. "Speaking of which, let's hit the Flagpole."

We got up and headed outside. I started to pick up my tray, but Kriffo knocked my hand.

"Leave it. Gives our pal Plague something to do."

The Flagpole was a narrow stretch of lawn next to the seawall that served as the designated spot for illegal smoking and drinking. I thought it would have made more sense to hide in the woods or sneak off to the beach, but everyone seemed comfortable smoking under the cover of an oversized American flag. In the dark, I could see several orange embers pass back and forth between hands like swinging rows of Japanese lanterns. The cigarettes looked too big for our young faces.

"Brizzey," Tazewell shouted. "Move your sweet ass over here."

I'd forgotten about Bristin Abbington. She was from Greenwich and liked coming into the city for parties.

"Kriffo, are you going to let him speak to me that way?" It was nighttime and warm out, but Brizzey wore purple sunglasses with violet lenses and a fawn-colored fur coat that skimmed her knees. The coat was buttoned all the way up to the collar, and by the careful way that Brizzey shifted and teetered, I suspected she wasn't wearing anything underneath.

"You lighting up, or what?" As Race spoke to Tazewell, he reached over and ran his hand down the sleeves of Brizzey's coat. "Our naughty chinchilla," he said.

"It's *tanuki,* silly." She spun around and laughed. "Japanese raccoon dog. Very rare. I should probably be arrested for wearing it."

Bristin was the girl my mother wanted me to date. I'd kissed her first, at the Gold and Silver, an annual dress ball in Manhattan for the predebutante set. She'd talked Cal and me into going with her on a triple date. Bristin was my girlfriend for a while, I suppose, although we never really did much except listen to Beatles albums and make out on her little sister's bed. She would stop me whenever "Dear Prudence" came on, abruptly sit up, brush her hair, and try to hum or whistle. She never sang the words. If I was a shit to her, and I know I was, it's probably because she couldn't find the melody.

That night at the Gold and Silver, I did a lot of fondling and groping. I slobbered over all my dance partners like some wet and hungry puppy. None of this was discreet, but then everyone date swapped. That was kind of the point, I guess. You drank either vodka and orange juice or rum and Coke. You tried not to mix the two. After a certain blindness set in, you saw how many people you could mess around with. It was careless in the most deliberate way. Learning the fast art of infidelity. Most guys were proud and comfortable as they moved from date to date, but I felt clumsy. Like I was playing charades using somebody else's hands. On top of that, I lived in constant fear of running into one of these girls again.

"Brizzey knows Jason." Taze blazed a joint and tried to decide whom to pass it to.

"We went to the Gold and Silver." She opened the top two buttons of her coat, revealing a swath of tanned skin.

Girls like Bristin never let you forget that you messed around with them. They'll hold it over you, as though there's some residual source of pleasure remaining to be paid. The wind blew my hair across my face. I wanted to be in my room unpacking.

"The Gold and Silver is très juvenile." A girl in shiny black pajamas and pink ballet slippers strode over to us. She held a silver lighter in her hand and flashed the flame off and on as she approached.

Tazewell leaned over to me, his eyes glazed. "Diana's got a body built for two."

After four years of being co-ed, Bellingham still didn't have many girls. Demand far outweighed the supply, and the economics of the situation necessitated that the guys trade off with one another. All of the girls lived on the top floor of Astor Hall—the only place that was off-limits for guys. We weren't allowed to visit them in their rooms and I thought of the girls tempting us like so many Rapunzels, hanging out windows and letting down hair.

Diana had white eyelashes that glowed in the dark. She greeted Tazewell and Brizzey by kissing them on both cheeks.

"*Somebody* was in France this summer," Race joked.

"Ugly American." Diana stood in front of Race, lifted her hand to his chest, and slowly wrapped her fingers around his tie. She pulled him in close, and then, before any of us could stop her, she set the point of his tie on fire with her lighter. The material didn't flame so much as melt and smolder. Diana let go and jumped back.

"Crazy pyro bitch," Race yelled. He pulled his tie loose, whipping it over his head and casting the thin snake of material to the ground.

Brizzey clapped her hands and laughed. "Synthetic meltdown." Her laughter was infectious. With the exception of Diana, who calmly hid the lighter in her hand, stroking the igniter with her thumb so that a long lick of flame appeared to rise from her fist, we all began to laugh, not knowing why.

"Is someone going to control her?" Race unbuttoned his collar.

Tazewell sneered at Race. "Don't be such a dick wagon. Go home. It's past your bedtime."

"You know she started it." Race was already walking backward toward the pier. He hopped into a Boston Whaler and geared up the engine.

Kriffo explained, "He lives across the harbor, on Powder Point. Throws a great party, so we keep him around."

From there, things began to break up around the Flagpole. I was glad that I wouldn't be the first to leave, but I didn't want to wind up going to someone else's dorm and hanging out. Most of the senior guys lived in Whitehall, but they were all heading over to Squire to watch *Platoon*. My clothes still needed to be put away, and I had to throw some sheets on my bed if I didn't want to sleep on a plastic mattress. Classes were beginning the next day, and I wanted to check over my schedule.

As I crossed campus, I looked up and tried to find Orion. Celestial navigation was never my strong suit, and as I stood on the lawn in front of my new dorm, a sudden loneliness hit me. Cal was dead and I was at a new school, running around, wearing shoes without socks, and picking stars out of the sky. I stood there for some time, with my face up, not really searching for anything.

TWO

My dorm room was a large single. No roommate. I suspected my father probably had his hand in this, but as I slid across the hardwood floor, past a row of bay windows that looked out onto the harbor, I almost didn't mind Dad throwing his weight around. Best of all, I had access to a fire escape. My own balcony. At Kensington, Cal and I had chosen to live together in the same room for three years. A white oak stood outside our window, and at night we climbed down the trunk and sneaked into town. We went to an all-night truck stop, the Starry Diner, and loaded up on cheeseburgers and french fries with white gravy. We complimented the waitresses, no matter what they looked like, and they gave us large pieces of warm sugar cream pie. Other times, if we had something to drink, we would just hang out in the tree, passing Cal's pewter hip flask back and forth and swinging our legs beneath us. We picked out thin branches and dared each other to climb up on them. No one ever caught us, but one spring we came back from holiday and discovered that the tree had been trimmed back. The main branch that ran by our window was stumped in half. Cal took this measure as a personal affront. He demanded that we take action. The next afternoon, we jacked up one of the athletic vans, took two tires, brought them to a garage to have them removed from their wheels, and borrowed rope from the gymnasium. We suspended a pair of tree swings. One for each of us.

Pleased with my new room, I went to work hanging clothes on

wooden hangers and fitting sheets onto my bed. I tacked up a poster of the Star Child from *2001: A Space Odyssey*. The poster had been on display over Cal's headboard and was a constant source of tension. I thought the movie was unwatchable. Cal thought the movie was about him. He was the ape discovering tools, he was the computer who knew what was best, he was the mysterious monolith, he was the abandoned astronaut. The poster was the only wall hanging I'd taken from Kensington.

I tossed a shaving kit filled with miniature bottles of whiskey into the top drawer of my dresser. The whiskey probably wasn't enough to get me kicked out of Bellingham but, even so, I hid the black mesh case under a mound of socks. Then I pushed the bureau and mirror next to my closet. I'd almost left behind a Polaroid of Cal I'd snapped after a long day of sailing. When I took the photo, Cal was standing at the end of a pier with his wet suit unrolled to his hips. In the picture that developed, the white border cropped Cal's body at the waist. With no evidence of the pier beneath him or the clothes he wore, Cal appeared to hover above the water completely nude. I kept the picture hidden from my friend and used it as a bookmark. Now, as I stood in front of my dresser, I tucked the snapshot of Cal into the corner of the mirror, then I stretched out on my new bed, kicked off my shoes, and made a conscious decision to fall asleep, wearing my clothes and with the light still on.

I woke up to a man standing over me. A short guy, but solid and fit. His hair and eyebrows were the type of light blond that looked ridiculous on anyone other than a small child.

"I didn't realize you were sleeping. I'm Mr. Tripp, your house fellow." The man had his dinner jacket on but had removed his tie. His feet were bare. He smelled as though he'd just sucked down his second scotch on the rocks, before remembering that he'd been asked to introduce himself to me.

"I must have drifted off. Long day." I got up out of bed and looked down at his bare feet. My toes were hairier than his. He had slender feet and high arches. My feet were stubbier, flatter.

"I'll be your sailing coach." Mr. Tripp gripped my hand and patted my arm. "We have big plans for you. I know for sure I want you to skipper, to sail on our first team. Some of the other boys might have a problem with that in the beginning, but don't worry."

I continued to examine his feet. A good high school sailing coach has calculated the strengths and weaknesses of every skipper and crewmate on every team in his division. I suspected that Mr. Tripp already had notes on me and knew that Cal and I won ninety percent of our races with our closely timed starts. Already knew that we preferred triangular racecourses over windward-leeward courses. Knew that we trained on 470s. In terms of sailing, he understood more about how Cal and I worked than Cal and I ever had. My new coach had had the time to examine it all from a distance.

Mr. Tripp cleared his throat and walked over to the wall of windows. I was afraid that he'd caught me staring at his toes. At that moment, I should have told him that I didn't want to sail. That I didn't want people relying on me to win for them and that I never liked the company of racing sailors. Just a bunch of gearheads in life vests. But I sensed that Mr. Tripp thought he could teach me something. He pulled up the screen of the middle window and leaned out.

"You know, this fire escape leads right down past my apartment. Not that you would ever use it to sneak out or anything, but I thought you should know." He beamed and winked at me. Not a creepy wink, like most people give you, but a wink that told me he didn't mind a little messing around in his dorm, as long as no one caused him any trouble.

"Thanks for the warning. I'll only use it if I set myself on fire."

He laughed and said, "You shouldn't sleep in your clothes. That's how they get wrinkled. Okay, the waterfront, tomorrow afternoon."

I skipped breakfast and arrived the next morning early for class. The lecture hall was shaped like a fantail, elevated at the top, with semicircular rows of bolted desks descending to a stage. I dashed up a set of stairs and chose a seat against the wall by a pair of tall windows. From my backpack, I took out a notebook and wrote "Modern U.S. History" on the cover. Together, the first letters spelled out MUSH, and on the basis of this acronym alone, I decided that the class would be easy. There were a dozen or more students waiting. All boys. The only one I recognized was Chester. He sat at the other end of the room, against the wall and parallel to me. We nodded hello, and I considered changing my seat to be closer to him. Before I could move, Race and Stuyvie entered the class and sat in the center of the lecture hall.

"Hey, Prosper. Want to see Mr. Guy go ballistic?" Race left his backpack on the seat of his chair, walked over to the blackboard.

Stuyvie kept lookout for Mr. Guy, poking his giant head out the door. Race pushed up his sleeves and waved a large piece of yellow chalk. We all waited to see what Race would write. He started to draw something, then erased the lines with the heel of his hand.

"Incoming," Stuyvie warned and rushed back to his seat.

Race froze in place, his orange hair still wet from that morning's shower. Because he had to do something, and fast, he scrawled "DILDO" in large rounded letters. Just as Race sat down, Mr. Guy entered, locking the door to the classroom behind him. He wore a plaid wool vest with a matching bow tie. He looked elderly but well maintained. Agewise, I guessed he was in that strange meridian between my dad's age and my grandfather's. I wondered if he'd taught at Bellingham for most of his life. It was conceivable that he'd graded papers analyzing Wilson's Fourteen Points written by boys who would later shatter Japanese naval power at the Battle of Midway.

"Good morning, gentlemen." He studied our faces. "None of you look particularly rested, but I trust you enjoyed your summer holiday." His words were carefully chosen and his voice had a cultivated British accent. Right then, a boy's face appeared in the door's rectangular window. The boy twisted the knob and banged on the door. No one dared let him in. Mr. Guy opened his briefcase and sorted loudly through a stack of papers, ignoring the disruption. I noticed a small pink hearing aid in his right ear. The boy at the door gave one last knock before giving up.

I looked out the window just as a girl with long red hair pushed open the doors of Astor and raced down the front stairs. She carried a large leather bag and was headed straight for the outside of our classroom. The girl's hair was so fiery and bright that it hurt to stare at her.

Mr. Guy passed out the course syllabus. He turned to the board and saw what Race had written.

Mr. Guy didn't speak so much as sing the words, punctuating each one with a snap of his fingers. "What is the meaning of this? Is this a new word for us?" He continued his ratatat snapping. "One does not use a dildo unless one knows the meaning of a dildo."

Race fidgeted in his chair, leaned over, and whispered something to Stuyvie.

Mr. Guy stood in front of Race. "Leslie, could you possibly enlighten us?"

Leslie. I laughed to myself. Leslie was his name, not Race. I instantly liked Mr. Guy.

During this confrontation, I heard a tapping sound. Outside, the girl with the leather bag crouched down, trying to push the window open. Mr. Guy, addressing Race, stood with his back to us.

"Leslie, be of service to the class. Teach us the meaning of *dildo*." He sharpened his inflection but stayed calm.

"The meaning of dildo?" Race asked. "I don't know, Mr. Guy. You tell me."

Stuyvie's body rocked with stifled laughter.

I leaned over to the window and unlatched it. The room was warm, and I didn't think anyone would mind the fresh air.

"Young Leslie, is it not poor form to use a word one does not understand?"

I pulled the window open and gazed down at the curly-haired girl. She lifted up her bag for me to take.

"We would all like to learn the definition of this new beautiful word and add it to our burgeoning vocabulary. Accompany me, Leslie, to the board."

As Mr. Guy led Race over to the blackboard, I reached for the handles of the girl's brown tote bag. The dark leather felt soft and well traveled. I hid the bag under my chair. Chester glanced over at me, and I shrugged. Race glared at Stuyvie. The tops of Race's ears had turned bright pink. He dug his hands into the pockets of his trousers.

Mr. Guy and Race stood at the front of the class behind a table and a lectern.

"Bring me a dictionary."

Race ambled to the bookshelf, lifted the heavy text, and placed it on the table.

"Let's see, now," Mr. Guy said, putting on his glasses. "Our new word begins with a 'd,' unless that is, our Leslie here's dyslexic. You didn't mean to write 'bilbo,' did you?"

A few people snickered.

" 'Dilapidate,' 'dilate,' 'dilatory,' that last one means 'tardy,' by the way, yes, 'dildo.' Ah, the origin is unknown. Not from the Greek or even from the Latin. Circa 1598, though, so we have a bit of history here, ten years after the great Spanish Armada was routed by the British. You want to write the following on the board, Leslie."

Mr. Guy turned toward the blackboard and I could hear the girl outside grab hold of the window frame.

Mr. Guy spoke slowly. "An object serving as a penis substitute for vaginal insertion."

As he spoke, I could hear the girl climbing. Her feet against the brittle shingles. Out of the corner of my eye, I saw her arms flexing, trying to pull herself up. We were only on the first floor, but the window was a good five feet off the ground. She climbed, lifting herself quietly and holding on with tremendous discipline. I felt the strain on her face on my own face. She rose up and hung along the edge of the window like a hand puppet at rest. Careful to stay out of Mr. Guy's line of sight. As she leaned over into the classroom, I knew she'd be unable to land without crashing and calling attention to herself.

"Do you have it all written down now? Excellent. Let's use it in a sentence, shall we?" Mr. Guy paused. "Due to an error in judgment regarding his capabilities, Leslie was forced to supplement his own shortcomings by using a—"

Our shouts and laughter saved the girl. They were the perfect cue for her to enter, and we carried on long enough to cover the sound of her landing. Mr. Guy stayed focused on staring Race down. He didn't notice the girl slide into the chair beside me and pull her bag out from underneath my desk. Her knuckles were scraped and torn. She brought her hand up to her lips and brushed the blood away. I waited for her to glance over and thank me. She didn't. Scanning the classroom, I caught Chester's eye. He wasn't laughing at Race but staring at the girl and me. Chester shook his head.

For the remainder of the class, Mr. Guy went through the syllabus and explained what we would be covering that semester. The girl took notes using a thin brass fountain pen. Eventually, a long, dull buzzer signaled the end of the class period. She stood, gathering books and arranging them in the leather bag. I studied the print on her skirt, the unruliness of her hair. It was the girl from the beach. I'd only seen her in profile before. This time, she did not smile or thank me. She left the classroom quickly and headed down the hall.

Most of the girls I considered to be pretty had soft, rounded features. Small eyes. Creamy skin. This girl was different. Her features called attention to the high planes of her cheeks and forehead, the sharp angles of her lips and eyes. Unlike Bristin's or Diana's faces, which begged and invited "Admire me," her face had a quiet authority. A frontier quality that said, "I am not to be put on display. I am not here to be looked at." She stood tall. Had I not seen her crawling through a window, I might have mistaken her for a teacher. Even then, I was certain of her beauty, but I was also certain that a person could miss this about her.

It should have been the most natural thing for me to ask someone in the class about the girl, but it wasn't. She'd come in through the window like some sort of changeling, and no one had bothered to notice her.

I went from history to physics and then calculus. My father had drawn up a four-year plan for me, and I was sticking to it. The same courses he had taken as a boy. After prep school, Dad had gone to Princeton, as had my grandfather before him. My brother Riegel, who claimed to be smarter than all of us, would be graduating from Princeton in the spring. I used to be expected to attend as well, but, over time, my father had decided that I didn't have a chance of getting in. It was good enough that his eldest son had ensured the family legacy. A generational hat trick. Dad had given me college catalogs from schools like Hamilton and Union and Lake Forest. It made me sad to know that he had such little faith in me. Lake Forest College. L.F.C. Last Fucking Chance. At the time, I didn't care where I was headed, but I wanted an acceptance letter from Princeton. I wanted to show my father that I could belong anywhere.

After third period, there was a free block of twenty minutes on my schedule. I'd planned on hanging out in the Fishbowl, an atrium near the mailboxes. As I'd passed through the corridors, I'd seen other kids flopped down on sofas, hanging out in between classes. We weren't supposed to return to our rooms during the school day. I sat down on one of the sofas, but the main hallway became thick with students streaming out of the Barracuda. Everyone seemed to know where they were going, and everyone seemed to be going in the same direction. I got up searching for a friendly face and almost walked into a phalanx of wrestlers. I could tell they were wrestlers by the way their ears stuck out. Like they'd been pulled from clay pots into handles. I spun around and allowed the force of the crowd to carry me down the hall and out of the building.

Outside, I saw Diana in front of the Academic Center, the Barracuda, speaking to a man wearing a wrinkled plastic windbreaker over a dark business suit. I looked around and decided to ask her what was going on. As I approached, I realized that the man she was talking to was holding his face in his hands. Diana was yelling at him.

"Go home," I heard her tell him.

Keeping one hand over his eyes, the man reached into the side pocket of his jacket and pulled out a pale blue box with a white ribbon. "Breakfast at Tiffany's," I thought. When he offered the gift to Diana, she waved her hands in protest. He threw his arms around her and slid the box into the tote bag she carried over her shoulder. Diana shrugged him off, retrieved the box, pulled the white ribbon, and threw the gift at the man. The box landed on the pavement, and a square of cotton coughed itself out, along with a small, shiny object. Diana turned and saw me staring. Without any hesitation, she strutted up to me, grabbed my arm, and said, "Come on."

I craned my neck and caught the man kneeling over his gift, desperate to fit the cotton block back into the box.

"Who was that?" I asked.

Diana clicked her tongue. "No one."

"Was that your dad?"

"He gets on my nerves." Diana squeezed my arm and pinched me through my jacket.

We fell in with a group of students.

"Where are you taking me?"

"To Chapel." Diana bit her lip. "Tell me, is he still there?"

I glanced back at Diana's father. His hands were shoved deep in his pockets. He looked like he'd just returned from the wilderness, like he could use a shower, a shave, a haircut, a hug from his daughter. It scared me to see a grown-up this messed up.

"Yeah, he's still there. Did he surprise you or something?"

"It's always like this." She let go of my arm. "But I never see it coming."

The Chapel was built on a hill, separated from the lower campus by a two-lane road. Cars stopped on either side of the crosswalk as an influx of students proceeded to block traffic like a herd of lazy sheep. We marched into the building, bells echoing from a loudspeaker attached to a telephone pole. There was no bell tower.

Diana pointed me to a seating chart hanging in the vestibule, then took her place. I found my name and the location of my pew. With its tall wooden ceiling and concave walls, the Chapel's structural design resembled the frame of an inverted whaling ship. Rows of long benches, in a T-formation, ran down either side of the altar and along the center. All of the walls were lined with stained-glass windows. The images on them weren't religious scenes or saints but generals and monarchs, their identities stenciled in colored glass. I read off names to myself as I walked down the aisle. Alexander the Great, Julius Caesar, Marcus Aurelius, Attila the Hun. There was a lectern with a microphone, an organ, and an empty choir box. A plain wooden cross hung above the raised altar. Pepin the Short, Charlemagne, William the Conqueror, Richard the Lion-Heart, Henry the Navigator. Four straight-backed wooden chairs stood empty on the stage. The chairs had been upholstered with red velvet cushions. One of the chairs had a higher back and was also embroidered with a golden crest. Oliver Cromwell, Louis the Sun King, Napoleon, Admiral Nelson.

An older woman stationed herself at the organ and began to play what I soon realized was the theme music to PBS's *Masterpiece Theatre*. Everyone around me started singing. The only words I could make out were from the chorus: "We shall follow, follow, follow." The school hymn. Dean Warr and another, more diminutive man entered from the back of the Chapel. They proceeded down the aisle toward their velvet thrones. The short man fiddled with his green bow tie and waited in front of the gold-crested seat. His hair was dark but graying at the temples. As he stood with his chin out, singing the second or third verse, I realized that this man was another of Dad's old Princeton buddies. The headmaster himself. Jolly Raleigh Windsor.

Once the song finished, the students waited for Mr. Warr and Mr. Windsor to be seated, then followed their example. After a moment of surveying our sleepy faces, Mr. Windsor stood and approached the lectern. He adjusted the silver neck on the microphone and gripped the edges of the podium. His voice, bold and in stereo, ricocheted off the stained glass onto his audience. A well-served squash ball.

"How many of you are afraid of the dark? How many of you have woken up in wet sheets? Have any of you cheated on a quiz, or borrowed money fully aware you'll never pay it back? How many of the Ten Commandments do you know? Of those you know, how many have you broken?" Jolly Raleigh stared at us accusingly, then lowered his voice. "I slept with a night-light until I was twenty-five. I'm proud to tell you that I was a high school junior when I finally stopped wetting my bed. Commandments? By the time I graduated, magna cum laude, from Princeton, I had dishonored my mother and father. Forged my best buddy's signature on checks. Eloped with my best buddy's high school sweetheart. Lied for the thrill of lying, and so often, I had forgotten when it was I'd lied. The real question is, am I ashamed of any of this? The answer: not even a little." The headmaster paused dramatically. He cleared his throat and raised his voice again. "Shame,

I have come to realize, is a scourge. The scourge of cowards. I'm going to let you in on a secret: Everyone—your parents, your teachers, your government, your closest friends—has either disappointed you, or will. It is our duty to forgive them, to not ask too much of them, for in return, they will not ask too much of us. So, you have cheated, stolen, lied: What else is new? You think that makes you horrible or special? What makes you horrible is if that's *all* you've done. I've made my living through hard work, decisive action. The woman who eloped with me and I still have a happy marriage. I gave my mother three beautiful grandchildren and purchased my father a Mercedes SL convertible for his sixty-fifth birthday. I have outgrown my youthful indiscretions—I have atoned for them, but I do not regret them. The trials and missteps of my life, I'm proud to say, helped me become the decent gentleman you see before you."

I shifted around in my seat, desperate to share a grin or knowing look with anyone. The guy to the right of me was conked out asleep, and the guy to my left was preoccupied scratching his balls.

"I want nothing less," Mr. Windsor concluded his speech, "than to be impressed by each and every one of you. If not during your time at Bellingham, then later, when you make your first Wall Street million, discover a vaccine, or run the Boston Marathon in two and a half hours. Be sure to notify the *Bellingham Alumni Newsletter* of your achievements. I'd like you all, when you retire to your rooms tonight, to figure out how you will make this happen. Ask the question, 'How might I distinguish myself?'"

(When I later asked Diana what she thought of Mr. Windsor's candid lecture, she told me that the headmaster gave the same motivational speech every year. A copy was available on tape at the Bellingham Bookstore for seven dollars. Parents and alums could also buy a Chapel kneeler embroidered with the line, "Shame is the scourge of cowards.")

"I'd like to close this morning's services," Mr. Windsor said, "by announcing plans for the construction of two new dormitories made possible by a generous family donation. I am extremely proud to report that the trustees have voted for the dormitories to be named Windsor

House and Prosper Hall. The groundbreaking ceremony will be scheduled for later this semester." He smiled and returned to his throne.

My father hadn't mentioned anything about endowing dorms. I felt myself becoming a cliché. The boy in trouble. The wealthy father. The school in need and willing to offer refuge. The organ player chimed in with a recessional march, and everyone stood as the headmaster and dean walked down the aisle together. I waited for my turn to file out of the Chapel.

Dean Warr stood outside together with the headmaster greeting their congregation. "Jason! Why don't you come and say hello to Mr. Windsor?"

The headmaster shook my hand. "I'm sorry I missed your father." He squeezed hard. When I returned the pressure, he squeezed harder, and then released his grip.

In the background, I could hear the church bells.

"Dad sends his best." I folded my fingers behind my back and rubbed the joints.

"I hope he'll be here for the groundbreaking ceremony." The headmaster pursed his lips. "I'd like to invite you to my house for dinner."

I thought it was funny when people told you that they'd like to do something but then didn't actually do it. At that moment, the bells turned from a steady chorus to a repetitive, skipping static. The bells continued to skip. The source of the broadcast was nothing more than a record player. A needle skittering over black vinyl. Jolly Raleigh pretended not to notice.

"Well, then." He looked me up and down. He turned his back and continued to greet students.

I was amazed that the headmaster wasn't more discreet. And I was even more amazed that my father would allow our name to be attached to anything so public, but I supposed that if he was going to pay for a building, he wanted due credit. My father believed that if a person could throw money at a problem then there was no problem. He'd been given the challenge of finding me a new school and he had solved it without much fuss.

Cal and I had once resolved to someday donate a dormitory to Kensington. The only requirement for this generous gift was that our school would have to name the building Squalor Hall. That way, when people asked students where they lived, they'd have no choice but to respond, "I live in Squalor."

Unofficially, I was already on the sailing team. All I had to do was show up that afternoon. Officially, I still had to prove myself and try out. The wind was calm but the sun beat down brightly as I went to the boathouse after classes. I'd changed clothes in my dorm room and was wearing a hi-tech long john–style neoprene dry suit with a hip-length neoprene life jacket. Soon everyone would be wearing this type of suit, but there I was, showing off. Mr. Tripp wore shorts and a long-sleeved shirt with NEW YORK YACHT CLUB running down both arms. "Race, you'll be Jason's Argonaut," he said. "Your task, boys, is to find the Golden Fleece." I was the helmsman captaining our Fireball. Race was my crew. Race had on red waterproof sailing pants, thermal underwear, and a body harness that fit around his chest, waist, and groin. He would use the harness to attach himself to the trapeze. "Nice suit." He grinned. "No, seriously, where did you snag that?"

We rigged the boat together. I loved the ritual and ceremony of stepping the mast, fitting the mainsail first and then the jib. Of literally making the boat. Tweaking it in reference to the wind in anticipation of how she would sail. Together, Race and I made sure that every batten was secured in its pocket, that the clew was secured to the end of the boom, that the halyards were secured to the head of the sail. We made sure everything was safe.

The funny thing about sailing accidents is that it's rare to read or hear a real description of what went wrong. In the most severe cases there are no survivors to tell the story. In more minor accidents, people are too worried about lawsuits and insurance to ever be completely honest. Our boat, like most racing boats, had a center mainsheet system. As helmsman, this meant I had more control over the shape of the rig but less freedom to move across the boat when tacking and jibing. I had to use a dagger grip to simultaneously hold the tiller extension and the mainsheet. Quickness was the key. I had to be quick to move across the boat, quick to communicate to Race. Race's main job, as crew, was listening to me and doing everything to keep our vessel stable.

We launched the boat and took her out past the water garden of ignored moored yachts, out deep into the bay. That afternoon the ocean was a dark plum color. Sparkling mirrors of light reflected the sun's rays. For a tall guy, Race was nimble and sure-footed. We went farther and faster than any of our teammates. Race and I worked well together. He pointed to a shipbuilding marina on the far side of the harbor. "My grandfather built all that," he said. "And now it's mine."

Most people when they first start sailing make the mistake of trying to angle their boat directly into the wind. To sail directly into the wind is impossible. The closest you can ever come is a forty-five-degree angle, but you're always aiming for the power of that engine. Race and I zigzagged along, chasing the invisible wind, drenching ourselves in salt spray, and increasing our speed. "Faster, faster," I thought. We were only competing against ourselves. Race had hooked himself into the trapeze, and the two of us were cruising at a quick clip. I realized that before the day ended, we'd need to capsize. We'd need to practice righting the boat together. Need to make sure that we could work efficiently and be a team. I figured I would end our cruise by capsizing us close to shore in shallow water. Coach Tripp motored by in a launch. Using a bullhorn, he told us to alter to a downwind course. I called, "Ready about!" to signal that Race should prepare to tack. He answered, "Ready." I released the mainsheet from the jammer, moved the tiller extension forward and up, and Race unjammed the jib sheet. I called out, "Hand-a-lee," and pushed the tiller away, keeping my arm straight. I'd done this thousands of times. Race was supposed to come in and release the trapeze. But we were traveling too fast. It is so easy to be wrong. As Race tried to come in, the wind overpowered the Fireball, forcing Race to lean too far back on the gunwale. Our boat heeled excessively, tipping over and filling with water. The Fireball flipped, spitting me out. The boat failed to right itself and the hull stayed exposed above water like a turtle's shell. I went underwater briefly, then bobbed up. Race was still hitched to the trapeze wire. He did not rise to the surface. Coach Tripp drove his launch closer, and I called out to him and waved. I stripped off my life jacket and dove under the boat in search of Race. His head had somehow slipped into a bundle of knotted rope hanging off the boom. He was snared and dangling underwater like a worm baited to a fishing line. The ropes, the noose choking him. Race struggled and pulled at the ropes, only tightening their grip around his neck. His red hair fanned and haloed around his head. He kept his eyes shut and didn't seem to know that I was beside him. Seeing me might cause him to panic and hold me under. I swam behind him. Though I was terrified, I knew exactly what to do. I popped back up to the surface, found my life jacket floating on the water, unzipped the pocket and pulled out a Swiss Army knife. It's not easy to cut rope underwater. Harder still when holding your breath, and when the person whose life you are trying to save is thrashing about in front of you. I held on to the rope, cutting it from the mast, hoping to pull Race to the surface in time to snag the tight tangle away from his neck. I had to leave him once, in order to retreat to the surface for air. Coach Tripp was still in the launch. "There's rope knotted around his neck," I said, holding up my knife. "I've cut one loop." I dove back down before I had a chance to hear Coach Tripp's response. Diving, I thought, "This is the first day of my senior year." Slick as a seal in my neoprene suit, I thought of Cal, of how he'd died. I slit the final rope, unhooked Race from the trapeze wire, and clutched him in my arms against my chest.

I was not a cause for celebration. Accidents are always the captain's fault. It was my fault we were going so fast and my fault that we tacked too soon. True, I had saved Race's life, but my carelessness, my inattention, had almost killed him. Everyone at Bellingham would know me, know who I was, by dinner. Would they consider me the hero or the fuckup? All I had wanted was to be anonymous.

Coach Tripp and I hauled Race up onto the launch. Race had never lost consciousness, but he had red burn marks around his neck and was coughing furiously, spitting water. On our way up to the surface, he elbowed me in the gut and tried to punch me. A reflex of fear and confusion. "Let's rush him to the infirmary." Coach Tripp wrapped a brown wool blanket around Race's shoulders. "Christ, kid," he said to me, "too much drama. What are you going to do for an encore?" He handed me an identical Army-issue blanket, the wool scratchy in my wet hands. My dry suit had kept me warm underwater, had enabled me to perform valiantly.

I held the dangerous necklace of rope in one hand, the Swiss Army knife in the other. Someone would need to tow our Fireball back to shore. The knife was the real hero. Later that night, I would give it to Coach Tripp to give to Race. I heard Race ask, "Coach Tripp, what happened?"

I had failed spectacularly, and in doing so I'd protected myself from ever having to fail again. I didn't want to sail with Race, or anyone who wasn't Cal. Glancing around the water one last time, I made a decision to remove myself from the world of teams. I would stop choosing sides and holding allegiances. I was through playing.

THREE

You never sail with one wind. Always with three. The true, the created, and the apparent wind; the father, son, and Holy Ghost. The true wind is the one that can't be trusted. The true wind comes in strong from one direction, but then the boat cuts through the air and creates her own headwind in turn. The apparent wind is the sum of these two forces. A combination of natural gusts and the forward movement of the boat. The sails create their own airflow, constantly forcing a skipper to reevaluate the angle of travel. Handling the apparent wind requires finesse. Imagine carrying a candle and walking through a house after a storm. The electricity is down, the only light shines from the flame, and the wick will blow out if unprotected. Every move creates a wind. Every move brings the risk of extinguishing the candle. A sailor knows how to create shelter, cupping his hand in front of the melting wax, so that the flame will stay straight and lit.

I didn't establish an apparent wind. Not at Bellingham. Didn't disrupt or engage the social clime. The accident with Race shook my confidence. Convinced me that I was a danger, a failure. Through my carelessness, my recklessness, I'd nearly killed my crewmate, and I couldn't blame Race for his dislike or mistrust. A few days after the accident, someone sneaked into my room and left a noose of rope dangling from a hanger in my closet. Though I was startled, I understood how Race would want to send me a message. "Be careful, Prosper. Watch your back." Those first weeks, I left my room only for meals and classes. Skulking across campus while my former teammates sailed. Locking myself in dead air. I avoided social contact, then felt disappointed and lonely when nobody noticed my absence.

The tedium of boarding school life set in and took hold of my imagination. Two or three hours would pass unaccounted for daily, while I stretched sideways on my bed or sat at my desk staring at the empty spaces on my Princeton application. I'd already filled in the name and address. The only thing left to complete was the essay section: "What has been the most significant event to influence your life?" A good question, one with an obvious answer.

I found Cal's body hanging from a hot-water pipe that ran up the back wall and along the ceiling in the room we shared at Kensington. It was a Sunday in April. A week before Easter. Cal looked as though he was in the process of dressing for church. He wore a white collarless shirt, unbuttoned at the neck, and tan pants. His feet bare. His eyes still open. A chair, my chair, on its side underneath him. We kept some lines of rope around as practice tools. We'd challenge each other to invent new sailor's knots.

"That's a triple lather snake bend." Cal tossed me a tangled mess. "Figure it out."

"Looks like you twisted your grandma's underwear." I untied the jumble and designed my own hitch. "Now that's a royal thunder wench rig."

"Looks more like a royal pain in the ass."

We could go back and forth like that for hours. Pausing in between knots for conversation.

"I'm glad we got to choose each other," Cal once said.

"Choose what?" I asked.

"Being friends." Resting his elbows on his knees, he stretched his arms flat and open in front of me. Veins tightened and flexed from his wrist to his biceps. Solid muscle. "If you were my brother, I'd still like you, but it wouldn't mean as much."

"I know what you're saying." Sometimes when I looked at Cal, I felt myself blur and fall into the weight of his arms. "It's weird," I said, "but if it ever came down between you or my brother, Riegel. Like a life jacket question?"

"You'd throw it to me?" Cal asked.

"Without a doubt." I nodded.

"Don't tell Riegel."

In the last semester of our junior year, Cal used a coil of nylon eight-plait rope to tie a noose. Taking our game one step further.

When I found Cal dead, I didn't go for help. I captured and understood the entire scene in the frame of an opened door that I quickly closed in front of me. Calmly, I went to the library, the chemistry lab, and the lake. I was lying flat on the bottom of a canoe in the Boathouse when ambulance sirens interrupted the quiet spring campus. I waited for someone to search me out and messenger the news. No one came. I shifted my weight and rocked the canoe, hoping to draw attention to my hiding place. At the time, it didn't occur to me that I was unimportant. That Cal, dead and gone, mattered more than me, stretched and cradled in a canoe. I stood up in time to look out a window and catch the sight of his body being carried on a stretcher. Hidden under a long white sheet. Later, I would be told that an underclassman had knocked on our door, looking to play a game of roof Frisbee. I would listen as this boy, this finder whom I did not know, recounted to a group of mourners that he'd only opened the door because he'd thought he'd heard a voice call out to him.

I wonder about that voice. A few days before his death, I stopped speaking to Cal. We'd done things. Touched each other. At night, alone in our room, we'd pretend to wrestle. Rolling and bracing our chests and legs in tight formation. Cal would pin me to the floor. He'd bite my neck, scratch his teeth against my chin. He'd mask his palm over my eyes. Bring his open mouth onto mine. Wet blackness deeper than I'd ever given or received. He'd shift his hands down my thighs and, because our bodies were so much the same, Cal knew just how to apply the right grip of pressure and quickness. Exactly what I would have used on myself. That familiarity made everything stronger. I knew instinctively how to touch Cal, and I felt affirmed and confident. For months, we slept together on his single twin mattress. In the morning, we'd leave the bed and say nothing. I'd think about him during the day, waiting for classes and sports and then dinner to end. Looking for any excuse to go to bed early. I made myself sick with eagerness. One night Cal noticed me undressing and said, "You're so giddy." I flung my copy of *O Pioneers!* at his head and left for the bathroom. Brushing my teeth and brooding. "Enough," I thought, but I didn't hold out, not for long. The physical closeness seemed like the most natural extension of our friendship. Then, one Saturday morning, my father, arriving on time to take me for a driving exam, discovered his son, nude as far as he could ascertain, in bed with another boy.

He yelled, "Get up," pitching a plastic binder and a small desk globe at the wall above us. My father kicked a floor lamp and left the room, slamming the door.

"Did you know he was coming?" Cal asked.

"I guess so." I was amazed that Cal could speak, and more amazed that I was capable of a response.

Cal stood up from his bed and put on a pair of shorts.

"He didn't see anything," Cal said. "There was nothing to see."

I got up, picked a towel off the floor, and wrapped it around my waist.

"I need to take a shower," I said.

"We were tired and fell asleep talking." Cal stripped the sheets off of his bed and tossed them in a pile at his feet. "Tell him that."

"He won't say anything." I looked at Cal.

He folded his arms like the wings of a bird and turned his back to me.

When I returned from my shower, Cal had left and taken the sheets with him.

In the weeks between my father's visit and Cal's death, I hurt my friend in ways that frightened me. I thought of writing down these scenes, submitting them to Princeton. But, as it was, there didn't seem to be any chance for acceptance.

My accident with Race left me uneasy around Tazewell and Kriffo. I didn't avoid them, but they didn't exactly seek me out either. Both guys kept busy with afternoon practices and away games. In the dining hall, I'd see them eating with the soccer team or strategizing with football jocks. I felt like an afterthought.

More than anything, I was afraid that Taze and Kriffo had helped Race string that noose up in my closet.

There was no privacy in Whitehall. No locks on bedroom doors. Our parents paid thousands of dollars for housing but the school didn't even bother to give us a room key. Anyone could come into your place while you were gone, tie all of your laundry together, tuck leaking cans of sardines into your coat pockets, fill your shoes with shaving cream.

A few nights after I found the noose, someone banged on my door and shouted, "Fire, fire!" I recognized Tazewell's voice and straggled out of bed, half expecting to find a bag of flaming shit outside my room. But the door wouldn't open. I didn't smell smoke but I did hear laughter. I went back to sleep. In the morning, it was easy enough to climb down my fire escape and back into Whitehall. The guys had locked me into my room by stretching a rope between my doorknob and the knob on the broom closet across the hall. For a moment, I thought of leaving my door locked that way and spending the rest of the school year entering and exiting through the fire escape. Turning this stupid prank into the gift of privacy.

I had a genius for both tying and untying knots. It was nothing for me to pull apart the loose mess that Tazewell had left behind. But as I crouched down in my sweatpants, unraveling the jumble of cord, I felt like I'd been demoted. I wasn't a cool untouchable upperclassman, just some friendless frosh. It bothered me that Taze would choose Race over me, but it bugged me even more that I cared. I'd known Taze for almost as long as I'd known Cal. The three of us had been friends. Even if Tazewell was nothing more than a stoner prick, a high-class jerk, an asshole, I'd taken it for granted that we were loyal members of the same tribe of assholes.

Near the end of August, I was relieved, grateful even to return to my room after a late evening nap in the library only to find Taze stretched out on my bed, a six-pack of Heineken sweating beside him.

"You shanked, my friend." Tazewell kicked his sneakers over my comforter, shedding a line of sandy dust. Dressed entirely in black with a knit hat covering his blond hair, he looked like a restless eel waiting for his skin to recharge.

"Shanked how?" I asked.

"You get cut and vanish, just like that." He took out a key chain, clicked a church key over the bottle cap, and handed me a beer.

The bottle felt cold and soothing in my hand. I worried that I was being set up for something. Hiding my fear, I took a long pull off the beer, then brushed the dirt from my comforter.

"As I was never actually on the team, I couldn't, technically, be cut."

"I'm just capping on you, that's all." Taze cracked open his own beer. "Thought you might like to venture out this evening."

"It's twenty minutes until lights-out." We were both being overly casual, drinking cheap imported beer, but I wasn't sure about breaking curfew.

"What are you? A narc?" Tazewell swung his shoes off my bed. "I own this dorm. Wear something black."

If Tazewell was setting me up for a final round of hazing, I could either take my licks or confront him. I decided to play along and see where the night took us.

"You going to brief me at least?"

"I've lined up a Suzy Nightlife for you."

"A what?"

"Some action. I figured it was about time you broke out of your shell." Tazewell rummaged through my closet and took out a charcoal pullover. "Put this on and let's jam." He took his beer and left my room without waiting to see if I'd follow.

I threw on the sweater and opened my window, ensuring that I'd be able to sneak back inside.

It hadn't taken me long to realize that curfew at Bellingham was more of a suggestion, not a hard-and-fast rule. The school failed to employ any nighttime campus patrol and students signed in not with their house parents but with other students. On my hallway, the proctor was a senior named Yazid Yazid, an international student whose family owned the largest tractor corporation in Saudi Arabia. Yazid had a killer British accent, a closet full of bespoke Savile Row suits, and a well-heeled cannabis habit. He wore his thick brown hair in a frizzy high-top, twisting his Afro into curly springs that shot out from his head like exclamation points. "I'm so nice," Yazid Yazid would say, "they named me twice."

Yazid had been forced out of his luxe London boarding school for smoking hash. If I'd had to guess, I'd have imagined that Yazid was probably the wealthiest kid at Bellingham. His family had purchased a giant parcel of land two towns over, converting a fallow field into an actual airport all for the convenience of flying their son home to Riyadh. Yazid held private hookah parties in his room and lectured extensively on what he termed the "hashish system of value"—his ranking of countries based on the quality of their cannabis crop. "Pakistan," Yazid told me. "Pakistan is the shit."

I had some interest in working out a friendship with Yazid, not just for his drugs but mostly because he seemed cool and untouchable. Like he didn't have a care in the world. I cared too much about everything. Maybe I wanted to study Yazid and learn how to care a little less.

The one thing Yazid resented was being given the active responsibility of hall proctor. To avoid any real work, Yazid kept a fresh sheet of paper tacked to his door. We could initial the check-in list at any point during the evening. Every night before lights out, Yazid turned the paper in to Coach Tripp as proof that all of us were asleep and accounted for even if none of us was asleep or accounted for. Tazewell called Yazid "Prince Yaz" to his face and "the Assassin" behind his back. Yazid had nicknamed Tazewell "Boyat" and Kriffo "Sharmuta." He promised that these were Arabic terms of respect, but I wasn't so sure.

Yazid was busy wearing giant headphones and beating a pair of drumsticks against an electric drum pad. I waved, wrote my name on Yazid's sign-in sheet, and left the dorm.

While the New Boathouse actually held the crew shells and team equipment, the Old Boathouse functioned as a clubhouse. As we walked into the night, Taze explained his plans to paint "Class of '88" on the Old Boathouse roof. When I asked him why we were going to paint this rather lame graffiti, he countered, "Because I'm a maverick. We're mavericks."

"Then why don't we paint 'Mavericks' on the roof instead?"

"Then no one will know who painted it." Tazewell chugged a beer, then smashed the glass against the asphalt. "It has to be 'Class of '88.' That way, the whole world will know it's us. Otherwise, some lame-ass sophomore will claim credit."

As pranks go, it was pretty innocent, not at all what I expected from Tazewell. Toward the end of our freshman year at Kensington, Taze was the only one of us ballsy enough to seek revenge on the seniors for all of their dickish hazing. On his own dime, Taze bought thousands of crickets from some pet shop and released the critters inside the seniors' dorm. "A plague on their house," he joked. What made Taze's prank especially diabolical was that he did it during finals week. The seniors couldn't study or sleep with the dorm buzzing from all those crickets hacksawing their legs together.

The rest of the gang waited for us in the dark, swinging paint cans and brushes. Race stood in the middle with a long metal flashlight. He shined the beam at our faces.

"Fuck off, Race," Tazewell said.

Race took a playful swing at him. They grappled. I could still see the rope burns and bruises around Race's neck. We'd barely exchanged words since the accident.

"Cut it out, you two." Diana wore a black minidress and velvet headband, with a pack of Marlboro Reds tucked down into her cleavage.

She made me want a cigarette.

Diana held her same silver lighter by her side, snapping but not igniting the cartridge. "We have to be careful," she warned.

"Listen to Tough Girl here," Kriffo said, carrying two buckets of paint in one hand and a bottle of Southern Comfort in the other.

Tazewell let go of Race. "Is anyone up top?"

"We waited for you," Kriffo answered.

"Onward, then."

I followed Tazewell and asked, "We have a ladder?"

"Ladder? We don't need no stinking ladder. Build our own human chain." Tazewell leapfrogged onto Kriffo's back. He stood on his friend's shoulders, grabbed hold of the gutters, and pulled himself up onto the roof. "Who's next?"

Race climbed onto Kriffo's shoulders, went up, and then helped Di, Brizzey, and another girl I didn't recognize. The girls carried paintbrushes and lifted cans up to Tazewell. Everyone smelled like cheap beer. I went last.

"How's Kriffo getting up?"

"Big guy's afraid of heights. It's cool, though. He'll be lookout." Tazewell opened a paint can with Race's new Swiss Army knife. "Jason, I'd like you to meet Nadia. Her mother's Yugoslavian, but she's a Southern belle, a Georgia peach. Directly descended from *Gone With the Wind*." He motioned to the girl who stood holding a paint roller, staring at her own feet.

Nadia looked significantly younger than any of us. Her brown hair fell just below her ears. Her body petite and boyish. If she'd been wearing a baseball cap, I'd have mistaken her for somebody's kid brother. Brizzey and Di ignored Nadia and sat beside Race on the peak of the roof, drinking beers.

"You three going to help out?" Tazewell asked.

"Roof's old," Race said. "Might collapse with all of us walking and working."

"Useless." Taze threw a foam paintbrush at Race's head. "All right, Jason and Nadia, you can be the eighty. I'll be the eight."

I turned my attention to Nadia. "How'd you get shanghaied into manual labor?"

"Diana, she's my protector," she paused, "my proctor. She said it would be fun."

I started to paint, and Nadia pointed toward the edge of the roof.

"Could we start there?" she asked.

"Sure. You're the boss."

Nadia and I crawled across the rough shingles. She stayed quiet, keeping her head down. When we got close to the gutters, she leaned over the side and heaved.

"What's going on?" Kriffo shouted.

Nadia let go and slid diagonally. I grabbed hold of her wrist.

"Sorry about that, Kriffo," I called down. "There's some weird birdshit up here we've been trying to scrape off."

"Your birdshit landed in my goddamn hair," he fumed.

I leaned over to Nadia. "Are you all right? Do you want to leave and get some water, maybe?"

Nadia opened her eyes wide. She nodded her head. I brought her down to the far end of the roof, away from the others.

"I'm going to jump." I tilted her chin up. "All you have to do is hang off the edge, and I'll catch you."

I jumped, falling hard and straining my left knee. I looked up at Nadia. She blinked.

"Your turn," I whispered.

She knelt close to the edge, folding her arms and rocking her body. I gestured for her to slide toward me. She bit her lip, turned, and stretched out flat against the roof, dangling her feet first, then her legs. Holding on to her sneakers, I eased her down. Her calves stiffened from my touch. I reached around her waist and told her to let go of the roof, but she kept her grip tight.

"It's okay," I said. "I have you."

She clutched the roof like a gymnast afraid of her dismount. Her arms finally trembled under the strain, her elbows unlocked, and I gently pulled her away from the Boathouse.

"Do you want to go to the infirmary?" I asked.

"No," she said, closing her eyes. "I'm very, very stupid." Nadia crouched on the ground beside a bush of scrub pine. I wiped the corners of her mouth with the sleeve of my sweater.

"What were you drinking?" I asked.

"Beer, oh, and vodka I guess, with some juice, or . . ." She vomited. Her shirt label cropped up the back of her neck. I read, "Size Small." If I had wanted to, I could have cradled her entire face in one hand. A freshman. I tucked the label back into her collar.

"Look, it's way after lights-out. We're going to have to sneak you inside." I had no idea how to do this.

"Can't I just . . ." She held on to the grass, her eyes rolling white, like those of a dead fish.

I couldn't leave her there. I knew that even if it got me into trouble, I needed to take care of her.

"Come on. I'll help you."

Wrapping her arm around my neck, I lifted her, and began walking over to Astor. My plan was to carry Nadia up a fire escape. I didn't know the layout of the dorm, but I hoped that once I made it to the third-floor window, someone would help me sneak her inside.

Cradling Nadia in my arms, I tripped up the first few metal stairs. Small as she was, Nadia still felt heavy enough to throw off my balance. I tried to put my feet down softly, but the wrought-iron staircase echoed and vibrated beneath me. The window at the top of the fire escape was open and the shade drawn. I leaned Nadia against the railing and pushed the window up. The shade snapped.

The girl from the beach and from that day in history class, the seabird and the sprite, appeared in front of us, seeming for a moment to be nothing more than a lunar face and a pair of hands.

"I'm sorry," I said. "She's been drinking."

Without waiting for an invitation, Nadia leaned into the open window. The girl looked at me. I gave Nadia a boost and helped her swing her legs around. The girl guarded Nadia's head and brought her through. I hesitated before joining them both inside.

A strong scent of ripe citrus filled the room. The girls spoke quietly to each other, while I stared at a row of lit candles set in green glass holders. Some of the flames had blown out with the draft from the opened window. Debris from a séance. Piles of books balanced and crept up one wall beside rows and rows of bookshelves. The girl seemed to have her own private library. Above the shelves, a half dozen pairs of men's tap shoes hung from their laces, suspended in midstep. The remaining candlelight cast shadows, leaving a pattern of dance steps, foot tracks behind the heels.

The girl said, "If you could carry her down the hall, we can clean her up and put her to bed."

I lifted Nadia to my chest while the girl led me down the dark corridor to a shared suite. Together, we woke up Nadia's roommate. While the two girls changed Nadia's clothes, I left and returned with a cold washcloth and a large glass of water.

After swabbing Nadia's forehead and adjusting her pillows, the girl resigned her post as night nurse, instructing the sleepy roommate to stay awake and make sure that Nadia slept on her side. "You need to learn how to take care of each other," she said, then motioned for us to leave.

We crept back down the hallway and I said, "You were great. This isn't a big deal, but—"

She put her finger up to her lips and made a sign for quiet. Ms. Alvarez, the Spanish teacher, had an apartment at the end of the hallway. The girl didn't want to get caught with me. We went back into her room. I nearly tripped over a pair of oranges that had spilled out from a wooden crate. The girl picked up the oranges and placed them on her nightstand. Beside her bed were several scattered paper plates with bread crusts and a jar of peanut butter. Without looking at me she said, "Most guys just drop the girls on the fire escape." She picked up two of the plates and folded them into a trash can. "You're the first to actually come in and help."

"I never had the opportunity to practice much before. My last school was all boys. When we broke curfew, all we had to do was climb up this ancient white oak." She didn't seem interested in my past or having me around in her present. The girl continued to straighten up her room, throwing out another plate, tightening the lid on her jar of peanut butter.

"This is some room," I said. "Those shoes are wild."

She walked over to the hall and adjusted one of the heels. "They're Fred Astaire's," she said.

"Like a brand name?" I asked.

"No. They're his actual shoes. He died this past summer."

"What, did you inherit them or something?"

"Sort of. He gave them to my mother. Years ago. They were friends. I think he might have loved her. Men are always falling in love with her."

She became quiet again, and I felt it was time for me to leave.

"I'm Jason, by the way."

"Aidan," she said.

"Isn't that a boy's name?" I asked.

"My father named me." She gathered her long hair together and tied it into a loose knot. "Aidan means fire."

"Why did you stop coming to history class?"

"I convinced Mr. Guy to let me study with him one-on-one." She relit some of the candles that had blown out.

"Wish I'd thought of that," I said.

"It's time for you to go."

"Yeah. Luckily, I have a fire escape, too."

"I bet your fire escape sees a lot less traffic."

Halfway out her window, I paused. "I'm not a bad guy," I said.

"I have my own suspicions about you." Aidan leaned down to face me and spooled a loose curl of hair around her index finger. "I spend most of my afternoons at the beach. In case you're interested."

I felt, for the first time since early spring, a connection to someone or something. I climbed quietly down the stairs as she closed her window and pulled down the shade.

The next day, I waited impatiently for classes to end so that I could follow Aidan to the breakwater. I liked the feel of her company. The wildness of her hair and the strange shadows on her wall were unlike anything I'd ever known. She worried me, intrigued me.

I sat through last period and ran back to my room to change before finding Aidan. On my way to the beach, I passed by Tazewell, Kriffo, Race, and a dozen other guys taking an afternoon run. Tazewell trailed behind me, kicking my heels. He reminded me of a reoccurring muscle twitch I had under my eye. A spasm I couldn't get rid of.

"You work fast," he said.

"How so?" I adjusted the heel of my sneaker.

"With Nadia. You must have been something else. Diana said the poor girl couldn't make it out of bed."

"Heard she was having trouble walking," said Kriffo, sidling up beside me.

"Nothing like that. She felt sick, and I carried her over to Astor."

"Just thank Diana when you get a chance. Di is one of a kind. She's a goddess." Taze spat, spraying Kriffo on the cheek. "Not only did she pick her out, she primed her for you."

"Hey, Spittles," Kriffo snapped. "You better watch your aim."

"Diana got Nadia drunk?" I asked.

"You think someone would volunteer for you?" Taze smirked.

The guys began to chant military-style, and I followed along. As we passed by the girls' field hockey team, Race, coming up behind me and running to the front of the pack, hollered out: "Why do field hockey players look funny when they walk?" He skipped a beat. "They-use-their-hockey-sticks-for-cocks!"

The girls didn't respond. Race tried another. "I don't know but it's been said, Bellingham girls give wicked good head."

Diana waved in our direction and sashayed in her field hockey skirt, trying to organize her teammates to call back. As the pack passed by, the girls shouted, "Fee-fi-fo-fum, Bellingham guys can't make us come." Diana and Brizzey catcalled and flipped up their skirts. The roundness of their bottoms curving out from black panties. Their skin still firm, still tan. Their black and gauzy panties. I wondered if I'd ever made Brizzey come. She was phony, bitchy even, but that just made me want her more, made me want to prove myself to her.

"Don't hold back. Show us your tits." Tazewell cackled.

We headed toward the water, down Front Street. I kept pace with my friends, past the gift shops and restaurants. Halfway to the beach, on the opposite side of the road, Aidan strolled alone.

"Let's cross," Race called out.

The pack held tight together and closed in on Aidan. Kriffo whistled, directing the guys to surround her.

"Hey, Hester, where you been hiding?" Tazewell asked. "You shouldn't be out unescorted."

"Care for a serenade?" Race ran circles around her, and everyone else followed him in messy loops.

They engulfed her. Aidan stopped and folded her arms across her chest. She was tall enough that I could see her over their circling bodies. She stood rigid and straight as a maypole.

"We've got a song for Hester." Race led the chant. "Take my big brown stump, stick it down your throat, and suck it, suck it, suck it."

The boys repeated the chorus over and over. "Suck it, suck it, suck it." The words passed quickly among them, like a precision soccer drill.

Aidan didn't move. She just waited, taking their abuse.

"Cut it out," I shouted, running across the street. Before I could get to Aidan, I heard a strange noise. A bleating sound. A long, extended sheep music.

"Baaah. Baaah. Baaah." Aidan defended herself with a shrill, feral animal call.

Collectively, the pack seemed puzzled, as if unable to determine where the noise was coming from and why. They stopped circling and chanting and stared at Aidan. She continued to smile, bleat, and bellow. The guys left her behind, running off and laughing. They didn't look back. Didn't notice that I failed to join them.

I stood across from Aidan, chewing on my tongue and breathing heavily from the short run. She turned and stared straight at me. "Oh, look. Another raptor, circling."

Aidan started back toward campus, with the harbor on her right side. She walked past saltbox dormitories and a pair of tennis courts. We stayed parallel to each other. Every time a car passed in the road, I worried that I would lose her. I skipped sideways just to hold her in my sight. Aidan kept her head down and her shoulders hunched. I moved like a distant moth hovering by a screen door, unable to reach the porch light.

She finally crossed over to my side of the street. "Don't follow me," she warned.

"Let me apologize," I offered, making an effort to stay a few steps behind her.

"No." She straightened her posture and walked up the cement path that led to the library. As she entered the building, I decided not to hesitate and followed her inside.

The ground floor was divided into a reference section no one used and a fiction/nonfiction room no one visited. Aidan bypassed the lobby, trailing up the stairs and to the second floor. I waited at the bottom of the staircase. When she reached the top, I clutched the railing and bounded up the steps, two at a time. The yearbook staff and school newspaper had their offices on the second floor. I'd been up there once already; most of the rooms were locked. Aidan used a key strung on a silver beaded chain around her neck to open a door that led to more stairs. I caught the door before it closed and continued to follow her. At the top of a narrow staircase, I found myself inside a reading room. There were two large overstuffed leather chairs, three walls of built-in bookshelves, and, to my surprise, a grand piano. Instead of choosing a chair, Aidan sat down on the windowsill, her back to me, and gazed out at the harbor.

I'd never met a girl this quiet, this determined. She sat at the window, leaving me standing without any acknowledgment from her. I walked over to the piano, took a seat on the bench, and began to play. Nothing really at first. Just notes and chords. Aidan gave no indication that she even heard me. I decided to break the moment and sing.

With Paul Simon's insights about the crap people learn in high school as my anthem I banged out "Kodachrome." Aidan didn't join in, but as I continued praising the benefits of a lack of education, I saw her fingertips tap in time to the music. Encouraged, I broke into a furious piano solo, before remembering that I was in a library. When I looked up from playing, Aidan stood in front of me.

"Hope these walls are soundproof," I said.

"They're pretty thick."

"Do you play?" I asked.

"No. My hands are tiny."

"Is this your private study?"

"Mr. Guy put me on key permission." Aidan rubbed her palms over the outside lip of the piano. Her fingers were thin and childlike for someone so tall.

"What's Mr. Guy like? Tazewell told me he's a closet pervert."

"Well, Tazewell would know, wouldn't he?"

"Sorry. That was stupid." I looked down and continued to play. "I haven't been speaking to many people lately. I think I've forgotten how."

Aidan went over and sat on one of the chairs. Curling her legs and stretching her skirt down over her feet. She closed her eyes.

"Why did they bother you back there?" I asked.

"I can't imagine the movies inside their heads." She spoke with her eyes closed.

"You said your name was Aidan, but they called you Hester."

"Race's attempt at a literary allusion." She picked up the key that hung like a charm on her necklace. Running it back and forth along the silver chain.

I shook my head and looked down at the piano. The keys were real ivory, but I could tell where a few had been replaced and covered with yellowing plastic. I stroked each off-colored note and began to improvise medleys of old songs my mother had taught me. "I Remember You," "All My Tomorrows," and "You Stepped Out of a Dream," then crescendoed with a number Riegel had insisted I learn: Mötley Crüe's "Home Sweet Home." Aidan listened as I tried to make up for Tazewell's serenade.

"You're very sweet," she said. "And completely ridiculous."

The politeness in her voice told me that I'd done enough and that she would be okay on her own. It was my signal to leave. I didn't want to. "Can I ask you," I started, "why you stand out on the rocks?"

She smiled. Sat up straight. "For the ocean. The one good thing about this place."

"Why do you stay here if you don't like it?"

She stared hard at me. "I grew up on the West Coast. The water makes me feel safe. It's a constant." She put her hand to her face. "Have you ever wondered how the oceans were formed?"

"They weren't just always there?"

"I figure it must have rained. Incredible storms for hundreds of thousands of years. Raining all the time."

"I guess," I said. None of this had ever occurred to me. "I sail," I said, and instantly regretted it.

Aidan glanced at her watch. "You should go to dinner."

"Join me." I stood up.

"Sorry, no." Aidan looked out the window at the darkening sky.

"You don't eat, do you?"

"I know how to take care of myself."

"I don't believe you." I closed the piano cover and stood up to leave. "You know, I'm going to make it a point whenever I see you to be like the ocean. You can look to me for relief."

Aidan said nothing, and I left her on her own.

FOUR

We gathered on a green skirt of lawn for an all-school photo. A four-tiered section of bleachers had been arranged in a horseshoe formation to hold the three hundred or so Bellingham students who had lasted through the first weeks of school. Positioned in front of the stalls was an old-fashioned camera set up on a tripod. Tinks, the headmaster's secretary and our impromptu photographer, marshaled orders, flashing a strobe over our faces, taking light readings, and fixing the camera's exposure. Mr. Windsor stayed cool under the red shade of a Japanese maple.

"We want to do this fast while the sun is still with us." Tinks, with her gin-and-tonic lockjaw, looked like a candy cane in her bright pink-and-mint-striped dress. "You know the routine. Seniors in back standing tall, then the juniors, then sophomores. All of you freshmen will have to sit down on the grass."

"The grass is wet," one of the freshman girls said. I recognized Nadia's accent.

"Do as you're told," Tinks said. "Your clothes will dry. And, please: no fidgeting."

We rushed onto the steps like a frenzy of fire ants. Below me, I saw Nadia lifting the hem of her floral-print dress, arranging herself awkwardly on the wet ground.

"Freshmen, please keep your feet flat on the grass." Tinks tapped the tips of her shoes. "We have no wish to photograph the scuffed-up soles of your clogs and loafers. Sophomores, fill in the gaps, but don't block the person behind you. Remember, this is not just any snapshot. One day, this photograph will be the only proof you'll have of having been here. The pose you strike today will be the pose your grandchildren, as they walk through these halls, will know you by." Though Tinks was a much older woman, there was something strangely sexual about her. Like a favorite nursemaid who might spank you and call you naughty. "You"—she pointed to Aidan, who stood beside Mr. Guy— "go join your class up top. Chop-chop." Tinks flashed the light meter near Aidan's face.

Momentarily blinded, Aidan hesitated before climbing up onto the stall. She saw me, began to move in my direction. Someone started the wave, raising wild arms and pushing Aidan forward. She braced herself against my leg. I helped her up beside me.

"Tip-top," Tinks announced. "It's posterity time. Now, the camera will start on the left, sweeping slowly across your pretty faces, until it glides over to the right side. Stand still. Scratch your nose, and you'll show up as a big blur."

"Wouldn't be so bad," Aidan said, "to be faceless."

Shouts broke out as Tazewell and Race cut across the quad in a swift gait. They looked identical in their black Wayfarers and garish red-and-yellow sport coats. As they came closer, the yellow splotches on their jackets turned into sunfish, while dancing hula girls shimmied across the bellies of their comically enormous neckties.

"Tastes great," Tazewell and Race yelled.

"Less filling," the bleachers volleyed their response.

"Tastes great."

Less filling. Tastes great. Thus, the banter continued. Bellingham Academy: everything you always wanted in a prep school and less.

Aidan gazed down behind her. We were a good ten feet from the ground.

"Don't jump," I said.

Tazewell pushed through the bleachers.

"You weren't going to start without us." He and Race joined Aidan and me on the far end, forcing us inward.

"Hey, Hester," Race said, "move over."

"You're going to like this, Prosper." Tazewell slapped my back.

Tinks stood behind the camera and shouted, "Don't forget to smile." She pulled a crank device and started the camera.

I held still as the lens slowly captured me. Smiling straight ahead, I heard a sound to my right. Tazewell and Race jumped from the bleachers, catching Aidan off balance. She twisted around, her arms swimming above her head. I reached out to her but Aidan fell back clumsily onto the grass below. As the film rolled, Tazewell scrambled and ran out across the lawn in a wide arc around Tinks and the camera. Race trotted unseen behind the bleachers. They both wanted to appear in the picture twice. Twinning themselves. I wished I'd thought of it. While the camera glided over posed faces, cheers of encouragement broke out for Tazewell. I cheered too. Aidan held her knee and looked up at me. I sprang off the top stair. Soon there was whistling followed by applause.

"I think they made it." I knelt down beside Aidan.

She reached for the metal frame of the bleachers and pulled herself up.

"Are you okay?" I asked.

"Same routine. Every year." She shook her head.

Students stomped against the stairs and filed past us. Tazewell flew by, twirling his sunglasses and shouting, "Live, and in stereo!"

Mr. Guy came around the corner and touched Aidan on the arm. "Ready?" he asked.

Aidan nodded.

Mr. Guy tilted his head and studied me. "Mr. Prosper, are you aware that the dress code specifically regulates that all gentlemen maintain a haircut above the collar line?"

"My mother likes it long," I said. "Breaks her heart when I try to tame it."

"I'm sure she wouldn't mind if I introduce you to my barber." He turned his back to me.

Aidan bowed to Mr. Guy.

As I returned to the Barracuda, Stuyvie and Race accosted me. Greeting me with smug, shit-eating grins.

"Did you see that, Prosper?" Race slapped my shoulder. "First time in three years someone's beat the camera. Beauty. Total beauty."

"Sure you made it in time?" I asked.

"Of course I made it."

Stuyvie dug his hands down into his pockets and adjusted his underwear.

"Looked pretty close to me," I said. The three of us walked up the cement stairs that led into the Barracuda. "That girl, the Hester Prynne girl, what's her story?"

"So *that's* your type." Race loosened his tie.

Stuyvie spoke up. "Guess Prosper has a little thing for bad girls."

"I don't have little things," I said. "I'm curious, that's all."

We stood together by the Barracuda's glass doors. Race kept his Wayfarers on as he spoke. I couldn't see his eyes, so I couldn't tell for sure whether or not he was lying.

"She's not a beast or anything. Nice hair. Who knows what kind of body's hiding under those gypsy skirts she wears. The thing is, Hester's damaged goods. She's tarnished. Just like the real Hester." Race snapped off the hula girl tie and rolled it up.

"The whole point of *The Scarlet Letter* is that Hester hasn't really done anything wrong," I said. "She's punished for no good reason. It's supposed to be ironic."

"Dude, I'm not here to argue metaphors." Race smirked. He cleared his throat and lowered his voice. "The girl was kicked out of school for seducing her art teacher. She forced herself on him. Then she went crazy. Tried to kill the guy when he stopped nailing her. It was a megascandal. Made some papers."

"It's true," said Stuyvie. "I read Hester's files." He gave me a long, sideways look. "I read all of the files in my dad's office. Even the confidential ones. Even the ones the teachers aren't permitted to see. My father lets me take a peek at everything."

Stuyvie stared at me and winked.

"So what is it you know?" I asked.

"She held a shard of glass to the guy's neck. Threatened to slit his throat. Some art project." Stuyvie seemed scared and excited at the same time. One of his eyelids was twitching. "Cops arrested her, tossed her in jail. You've *got* to see the mug shot in her file. She looks deranged."

I listened with interest, more intrigued than ever. Aidan had a past. I liked this about her. The real story of how she'd landed at this school was probably more fascinating than anything Race or Stuyvie could imagine or read in a manila folder. I thanked them both for warning me.

Late that afternoon, I found myself sitting alone on the seawall kicking my feet against the cement, watching the sailing team practice. The prevailing winds ran southwest, carrying canopies of white scalloped clouds over the choppy waters. Out in the harbor, Coach Tripp piloted around the Fireballs on his silver launch bullhorning orders, critiquing maneuvers. In the distance, I thought I saw Race and his new crew.

I'd always believed that I was at my best when out on the water. Now I wasn't so sure. Maybe I wasn't careful enough or maybe I'd been any good in the first place only because of Cal. When we'd sail off Northeast Harbor, Cal would insist on searching out storms, the coastal weather defined by danger. "We need to learn how to handle the wilds. Test ourselves." Cal wanted a competitive edge, and at Kensington we were one of the rare teams to play the squalls, using the rough winds to make a charge for victory. As a team, we loved taking risks, but Cal had an alertness, a feel for what could go wrong. "It's the waves we need to worry about, not the winds," he'd always say, and he was right. Winds could knock a boat around, but a wave could seize a ship and blast her open. I knew how to read the wind, but Cal was an expert at appraising the waves.

I was thinking about the last time Cal and I sailed together, when I suddenly felt a shadow over me. I turned and saw Aidan.

"Thought that was you," she said. "You look so calm. Didn't want to interrupt."

"Watch this." I pointed to a dinghy attempting to jibe around a buoy. The winds were flukey and in one brief instant the sails went from full breasted to flat chested. "They're going to capsize." Sure enough, the dinghy broached to windward and the boat began to oscillate, sinking into a death roll. The mast and sails collided with the water as the skipper and crew dumped overboard, legs and arms akimbo.

Aidan gasped. I assured her that the sailors would be fine, though it took the pair several attempts before they righted the boat.

"Did you cast a spell?" Aidan asked. "How'd you know that would happen?"

"I always know about the wind."

Even on land, I never stopped being a sailor. I clocked the wind gradient, how the speed of the wind increased the higher it rose off land or water, and constantly measured the air against surfaces, considering how I would angle and trim my sails.

"What's your trick, Prospero?" Aidan brushed her hair back off her face. She had on a shapeless, oversized sweater, black tights. A long black scarf wrapped loosely around her neck. She sat down near but not directly beside me, tucking her knees inside the ugly rust-colored sweater, clasping her arms around her legs.

Aidan's body carried a sense of caution. Like she might spring up and leave me at any moment. Her perfume drifted downwind, some mixture of large and small white flowers, the kind my mother always bought for Easter. Gardenias and lilies of the valley.

"I have no tricks, just my powers of observation." I pointed out to the bay. "Waves are one indicator for what the wind's about to do. See how the water looks as though it's been scarred. Like a cat ran its claws over the waves. Now watch: The wind's going to build first in small gusts, then larger puffs. You can see it take shape over the water until finally"—I signaled to a dinghy that was stalled in a lull—"the wind will hit that sail and send the boat bowling forward."

When the dinghy took off as I'd predicted, Aidan clapped. "So it's not just luck," she said. "You don't aim your boat in one direction and hope for the best."

"It's not enough to know where the wind is. You also have to anticipate where it's going to be."

For me, sailing was as much a language as a sport. The nomenclature key to communicating with a crew. I tried to explain the basics to Aidan. She nodded as I described the difference among a beat, a run, and a reach. "If you're beating, you're sailing as close to the wind as possible but not so close that you end up in irons. Too much wind can actually slow your sails. When you're on a run, you're sailing away or downwind."

"Like the wind is chasing you," Aidan said. "And you're running away."

"Yeah, like that. A reach is all the angles in between beating and running. From there, things get more complicated because you could be on a beam, a close, or a broad reach."

Aidan raised her hands signaling that I was confusing her, telling her too much.

"Maybe," I said, "it would be easier if I just showed you. I could take you out sometime."

"Boats scare me." Aidan pulled at the hem of her sweater, releasing the silky yarn from its weave. She loosened the scarf around her neck. "Those little numbers out there look like all they want to do is sink."

"Actually," I said, "what a sailboat really wants to do is fly. The wind doesn't just push the boat forward but actually lifts the sails like an airfoil. Like the wing of a plane. If the angle of attack is just right and the camber of the sail full bellied, a boat can soar right out of the water and into the air."

"So why aren't you out there sailing?" Aidan asked.

It occurred to me that she hadn't heard about my accident with Race. I liked that she didn't know. She made me feel exempt, protected from my mistake. "Oh, I'm just taking a break from it all."

We leaned back against the lawn staring up at the flagpole. I used the waving American flag as a telltale to teach Aidan how to see the wind and predict its movement. First I had her study the different stages of unfurling, how the flag went from being at rest to twisting and snapping and finally to a full billow. Then I showed her how the wind would travel from the flag to a stand of red cedars, rustling the needles and branches before singing against a wind chime hanging on the headmaster's porch.

"That's really something," she said. "A person can actually read the wind."

"Don't be too impressed."

"Who said I was impressed?" Aidan flashed a small smile. "I bet you've taught me everything you know."

"Almost everything," I said.

"I bet you'd like to be the wind," she said. "Bet in your next life you'll return as a typhoon."

"Not a tycoon?"

"No. You'll be a windstorm."

"And what are you going to come back as?"

Aidan thought about it for a moment. "I'd like to be a light meter."

"A what?"

"A light meter. Like a photographer uses. Tinks had one this morning." Aidan snapped an imaginary photo of me. "I'd like to be able to measure and know for certain whether people were giving off light or taking light away."

"You're strange," I said. "But I think I like that about you."

Out in the harbor, the sailing team began to head in to shore. I didn't want to be there when they landed. Didn't want Race or Coach Tripp to think I'd been watching them. That I was missing out on anything. "Sorry," I said to Aidan. "I have to go."

We both got up to leave. I rushed off to Whitehall and assumed Aidan would head back to Astor. But when I turned around briefly, I saw Aidan uncoiling her black scarf from around her neck. She held each end of the scarf above her head, the silk capturing the wind, arching above her like a parachute. Aidan released one end, kiting the scarf. The wind swirled around her for a moment before Aidan let go completely. She was an excellent student. The light silk caught a thermal and rose, sailing above the water. A dark black bird against the blue sky.

Nothing more than coincidence and serendipity brought Aidan and me together, but something unspoken held us close. After our first few encounters, I always knew where to find her. She became like the weather to me. On bright days, she studied on the beach, and when cloud streets turned into autumn storms, I knew she'd be locked in her library tower. I fell into a habit of finding her.

We didn't speak much at first. Mostly, I watched her study. I sneaked food into the library for her. Cider and gingerbread. Cranberry muffins. I hadn't seen her at the dining hall, and from the stray oranges and jars of peanut butter in her room, it was apparent that she didn't eat well. I would steal apples for her, place tea biscuits beside her.

"Why did you change schools?" Aidan asked.

We were in the library. Aidan had just finished reading *The Grapes of Wrath*. She rubbed her eyes and twisted her hair on top of her head, knotting the coil. Then she stretched her arms above her head in a V.

That simple motion of stretching reminded me of something Cal had done once. Sometimes, the whole world can come down to a single gesture.

"How did you end up here?" she asked me.

I shrugged, looked away for a second or two, and she asked me again, a third time, more emphatically.

"My roommate," I said, "my best friend, actually, he died at school."

"What was his name?"

"Cal." I coughed. "Cal," I said again.

"How did Cal die?"

She asked so plainly that I realized no one had asked me the question before. Not directly.

"You know, I'd like to tell you," I said. "I really would. But I'm afraid whatever I'd say right now might be untrue. And I have no interest in possibly lying to you."

She bit down on an apple. "So tell me something else. A story about Cal."

I thought about it for a moment. "He stole a motorcycle for me once. A 1964 Triumph 500. All chrome with a black body."

"How'd he steal it?"

"He never said. Usually he'd burst from trying to keep a secret, but in this case he was just too proud of himself. Loved keeping me guessing. We were only sophomores then, and we had been disqualified, unjustly, from a regatta in Connecticut. The coach refused to flag a protest. The rest of the sailing team still had to compete, so Cal and I went off together to explore the town."

"Come on," Cal said. "Lunchtime."

"I hope you have money. I'm hungry."

"I'm flush," he said, patting his wallet. "Grandma's convinced that every month is April, so every thirty days, she mails me five crisp Bennies."

We ate at the first restaurant that met Cal's requirements: wide booths and roast beef sandwiches.

"You think Coach would reconsider a protest?" Cal pressed down on his sandwich and licked a flood of mayonnaise. "We totally gave way on that approach. Plenty of room. It's like there are rules and you learn them and you use them to win. Then someone notices that your coach is a wuss and decides to wreak havoc over your life."

"It's not that bad."

"I don't understand how you can be so"—he searched for the right word—"blasé," he said. Cal finished his potato chips and began eating mine. "What's wrong?"

"Didn't feel like sailing today. Almost relieved when they disqualified us."

"That's crazy talk." He reached over to another table and picked up a white cloth napkin from a place setting. After carefully wiping his face and hands, he looked up at me. "Your dad was supposed to come. Wasn't he?"

I hadn't been too upset about my father not showing. Not really. Happened all the time. But when Cal looked up, some switch inside of me turned on. Before I could stop myself, I began to cry. No sound. Just several round drops of mercury out of a broken thermometer. Cal didn't say a word. He slid out of the booth. I tried to pull myself together before he returned. The more I tried to control myself, the more I couldn't. Cal slowly and deliberately maneuvered across the dining room, gathering all of the white linen napkins from their place settings. Before any waitress noticed, he brought the cloth stack over to our booth and flourished the pile in front of me. Almost every napkin in the restaurant spread out over our table. Cal picked one up and held it out. I took my new handkerchief, blew my nose, and wiped my eyes.

"It's just a game," Cal said.

We left the restaurant and made our way back to the school. I was worried about the sailing team leaving without us, but Cal lagged and hummed to himself.

"Look at that." He pointed to a gas station and sprinted across the street in front of a truck.

I waited for traffic to pass and joined him on the other side. Cal bent down beside a motorcycle.

"What is it?" I asked.

"It's a classic."

"A 1964 Triumph." A short man in oversized coveralls came out of the garage. He looked like a bird washed up after a tanker spill, as though years of overturned oilcans had leaked together, forming a dripping, shapeless figure. He slid over to us, holding a rag in his hand and polishing a ratchet. "Fixed her up clean," he said.

"Sure would like to take a ride." Cal inspected the motorcycle, careful not to touch the body. "See how she handles."

The grease man smiled. "Bike's not for sale. Not for your joyriding either."

Cal put his arm around me and patted my chest. "My associate here is rated third on the pro-am motor circuit. The man's a legend."

Our new friend gave me the once-over. "He doesn't look like a legend."

"A spin around the block." Cal ran his hand down the leather seat.

"She's a show pony, not a racehorse." The man appeared to shrink in the sun, his coveralls growing long over his shoes and arms. He squinted his eyes and returned to the shade of his garage.

Cal stood in front of the bike, unwilling to surrender.

"Maybe if you'd said I was rated number one," I offered.

"The man's not a fool."

We walked back to the campus. Our teammates had showered in the guest locker room and stood together collecting their gear. I went in, picked up my duffel bag, and headed out to the sports bus, where I promptly fell asleep in the backseat. When I woke up, we were already on the road.

I'm not certain when I noticed Cal missing. The bus felt too quiet. No one was arguing with Coach or asking the driver to change the radio station. I stood up and walked down the aisle. No Cal. Not stretched out napping or leaning back with a magazine. He wasn't on the bus. We'd walked by a train station on our way into town, and I could only figure that Cal had decided to head home for the weekend. I kicked the seat in front of me, annoyed that I had been abandoned. I wanted to ask Coach but knew that Cal had probably left without permission. I had no intention of ratting on him.

A mile or two from Kensington, I heard a buzzing. A fly-in-the-ear sound at first, then a swarm of mosquitoes, and louder, a wasps' nest. I turned to look out the back window and saw Cal riding the motorcycle. No helmet or sunglasses, even. Just his hair plaited back by the wind. I pounded on the glass and waved. He smiled. He must have been going sixty miles an hour, but it was as though he managed to stand still in time and smile. And then he did the most amazing thing. He took his hands off the bike and lifted them both up over his head. In victory. The hero on his Triumph. No one has ever looked as beautiful to me. With that one gesture, in that single moment, he was the definition of perfection. That was when I knew.

"What did you know?" Aidan asked.

"I knew he was the best friend I would ever have."

Aidan leaned in and stared. "That's all?"

"I thought that was a pretty big thing."

"It is," she said, "a hugely big thing, but it sounded . . ." She started to tie her hair back in a knot. "Sounded like there was more you meant to say."

I stood up and, for the first time since we'd started these afternoon visits, I didn't wait for Aidan. I left on my own.

After dinner, I wanted a cigarette. I went down to the Flagpole, hoping I'd be able to find a smoker, but it was dark and cold. At first, I thought I'd struck out, but then I saw someone sheltered on the beach down by the seawall. Lighting up.

I took the stairs down to the beach and shouted into the wind, "Hey, can I bum a smoke?"

"A what?" Coach Tripp turned around and exhaled.

"Busted." I laughed.

"Who?" he said. "You or me?" He reached into his breast pocket and pulled out a pack. "You're welcome to it, but I will have to report you."

I couldn't tell whether he was kidding or serious. I waved him off.

"I know I'm not much of a role model, but the rules, such as they are, are still different for you." He held the cigarette down by his side and flicked the ash. "Haven't seen you around."

"Been studying a lot."

"It made me sad to see you quit the team. That thing with Race was just a freak of nature. You know, it's funny," Coach said. "Most ship-wrecks happen within sight of land. You're part of a long tradition. Sailors who screwed up before they make it out of the harbor."

"Well, when you put it that way." I laughed. "I know Dean Warr told you to look out for me. Sorry I disappointed you."

"Even before the dean said anything, I was psyched at the prospect of coaching you. You know, I saw you and your friend at Nationals. Took notes. You two had a real synergy."

"We grew up sailing together." I ran my hand against the rough seawall.

"From what I saw, he seemed like a nice kid. It's hard," Coach Tripp said, "when someone does the tragic thing Cal did. Easy to blame your-self."

"Dean Warr told you more than I thought." I rubbed my hand, hoping to feel some of my skin scrape off.

Coach Tripp flipped open the cigarette pack and held it in front of me. I took one. He struck a wooden match and lit the tip.

"I was out the other morning, alone," Coach Tripp said. "The winds calm. The sun breaking over the water. Birds quiet. Sailed right into this mass of green fog, moist, lush air. Washed my eyes green. I lost all sense of direction. I forgot that I wasn't a novice. Actually thought that I might have drifted off. Thought I was trapped for good in some strange ether."

"What happened?" I asked.

"Nothing. I just kept her steady." He stubbed his cigarette out against the seawall. "Fell out of the fog." He paused to look at me. "I always fear I'm going to turn into one of those ghost ships. Like I'll disappear and some stranger will find my empty boat."

"The Flying Dutchman," I said.

"No, that's just folklore. I mean disappear for real. You ever hear of the *Marie Celeste*?"

I shook my head.

"She was a famous phantom ship, a giant brig who sailed out of New York only to be found near Gibraltar with no crew to speak of, her food supplies untouched, her sails at full mast. Couldn't have been a pirate attack because all of the valuables were still on board."

"What do you think happened?" I asked.

"Not sure I want to know. I enjoy a good mystery. Makes me happy that there are so many things I don't understand. That's part of why I like the ocean so much. All of that water makes me feel small and uncertain. You learn more about yourself when you're afraid."

It had never occurred to me that being scared or unsure could be good, useful, even.

We smoked another cigarette and talked about the wildness of the Atlantic, how the strange currents of the Gulf Stream forced a sailor north before he could travel east. Coach Tripp told me about a summer he'd spent fishing for swordfish in the dangerous shallows of the Flemish Cap. A lot of prep school teachers were rich kids. Guys struck sick with nostalgia for their own prep school glory days. I hadn't figured out if Coach Tripp was one of these casualties or not. He loved sailing but not in a yacht club way. He actually cared about the history of sailing, how the trade winds helped determine empires. Coach hoped to recreate all of the famous early voyages. Like the Phoenicians, he wanted to cruise through the Pillars of Hercules and down the coast of Northern Africa. He'd studied charts and understood how Leif Ericson had navigated from Norway to Cape Farewell in Greenland and then all the way to the coast of Canada and the Bay of Jellyfish. Coach was a smart guy. I could learn something from him.

"Can you teach me about celestial navigation?" I asked.

"Sure," he said. "It's one of my minor obsessions. We should go out sailing sometime. Just the two of us."

"Yeah," I said. "I'd like that."

We finished smoking. Coach pointed to the dorm, and, without a word, we began to race along the beach, then up the seawall's staircase and onto the grass. Dashing hard, fast, we stayed about even until we hit the path to Whitehall. Coach Tripp stopped short, smoothed down the front of his jacket, and fell behind. I continued to run straight up to my room and into bed. I slept well that night because someone had been kind to me.

FIVE

I'd made it through an entire day without visiting Aidan. Sitting in my room. Face-to-face with the blank essay page on my Princeton application. I'd used the word "beautiful" to describe another boy. I knew how it must have sounded to her. I also knew that it was exactly what I'd meant, exactly what I did not want to mean.

Aidan said nothing when she saw me back at the grand piano. I was still in dress code. A blue suit jacket and my favorite tie: yellow silk with small navy medallions, my mythical family crest. Aidan had made me a copy of her key, and I arrived before her, placing an apricot and a box of cinnamon graham crackers on what I took to be her favorite chair. Aidan entered wearing a black sweater that fell below her waist and flowed into a long skirt that covered her shoes. She sat down in the empty seat, across from my gifts, opened a blank book, bound in marbleized paper, and began to write.

"What's in the book?" I asked.

"My journal," she said. "Don't you keep a journal?"

"I did. Once. At least I tried to. The stuff I put down was so dull, I decided that if anyone else read it, they'd think I was the most boring person in the world."

"Boredom is actually the most plentiful substance in the universe," Aidan said.

"I started making stuff up, just to sound more interesting. Stories about sailing mostly. Like a captain's journal. Sudden storms. Sea snakes. Pirate battles. Islands of sea grass."

"What made you stop writing?" Aidan swept strands of hair off her face.

"Cal found it. He copied some pages and plastered them around campus. Cal knew me better than anyone. Knew how to get a rise out of me."

"So if Cal were here, what would he tell me about you?"

"Like how would he embarrass me?"

"No. I don't want to hear anything goofy or mean. What would Cal say to convince me that you were one of the good guys?"

I didn't have to think too hard to recall Cal's favorite story about me. "Here's the thing you need to know about Jason," he'd begin before highlighting what in his mind was my singular achievement. I told Aidan how Cal and I had gone to grade school in the city together. "We had this teacher who gave out gold stars for every book report we did. I'm not talking tiny stickers but like these really big stars she cut out of foil. If you got enough of them you could trade them in for prizes. Stuffed animals and calculators. She even had this really nice desk globe, you know, the kind where the ocean is all black. That was the grand prize. Anyway, there was this kid in our homeroom, Paul Sullivan, a really sweet kid, you know. Everything made him happy. A pink eraser, pizza at lunchtime, indoor recess, you name it. Paul would just smile and clap and hug everyone. He was so fucking happy. Sometimes seeing him like that made me want to cry, I guess because I knew I'd never be that excited about anything. Poor kid had Down syndrome. Our teacher told us not to treat Paul any differently, but then the teacher did this really messed-up thing. She wouldn't let Paul do any book reports so he could never earn any stars. The only time he'd get anxious or flap his arms and cry was when she'd hand out those stupid stars. Maybe I just wanted to make up for our teacher's stupidity. I read a lot of books and did a ton of reports, and at the end of the year, I gave Paul all my stars. I didn't tell anyone, I just did it. Then Paul went right over and told the teacher he wanted that globe. It was worth the most stars. She probably never thought anyone would earn that many. I remember Paul spinning the globe at his desk. I was nine years old and it was the first time I'd done anything nice for someone. Of course, Cal found out and blabbed to my mom."

I paused and looked at Aidan. She smiled.

I said, "That's what Cal would tell you about me. 'Jason's the nice one,' he'd say. 'He'd give you all his stars.'"

"So you were Cal's hero." Aidan folded her arms and tilted her head.

"No," I said. "It wasn't like that. We were just pals." Telling the story made me feel embarrassed. Like I was full of fake humility. Cal had been less impressed by my generosity and more impressed by the fact that I hadn't bragged about what I'd done. "You kept it to yourself," he'd said. "That's what makes you special." I neglected to tell Aidan how for the remainder of grade school, I did my best to avoid Paul or how I always felt uncomfortable when he would run over to hug me. I leaned back and tried to touch the back of my head against the wall, but I lost my balance and braced my hands on the piano bench for support.

"You all right?"

"Fine." I nodded and pointed to her journal. "I've told you my story. Now you tell me what's in there?"

"Flotsam and jetsam. Scattered thoughts."

"Unscatter some."

"I don't know. You think I'm bright, but there's so much I can't do. I can't paint, or draw, even, but I love art." She opened her journal. "My art teacher at my old school told me this story about Cézanne, about why he painted so many apples. It's a silly thing, but I like to understand people through their obsessions. Like you with your sailing." She paused and smiled at me. "Anyway, Cézanne grew up with this writer, Émile Something. Zola?"

I wasn't sure whether I recognized the name.

"As a little kid, Émile was chubby and awkward," she said. "He was a target for bullies, until Cézanne befriended him." Aidan stopped and breathed. "Cézanne protected Émile. By way of thanks, the young writer brought the young artist a basketful of apples. Red tops and yellow bottoms." She stood, walked over to the other chair, and picked up the apricot I'd left for her. "I guess in our case, the roles are reversed. You defend me, and you bring me snacks." She tossed the apricot in the air and caught it. "Have you heard any stories about me? Have you asked anyone?"

I lied and said I hadn't.

"The first thing I wanted to know about you was why you came to Bellingham," she said. "Almost everyone comes here with a story. Mine always seems to change. Kriffo and Race tell people I'm a slut. Stuyvie's convinced that I'm a homicidal maniac. Once, I was peeing in a bathroom stall, when I heard Brizzey tell another girl that I'd given myself an abortion. In their minds, I've broken every taboo." She turned and faced me. "I wish you knew me before I came here." Aidan laughed. "I was fearless." She turned her back to me and looked out the window.

She rolled the apricot over her mouth. Bruising the fruit and attempting to bite into the skin with just the softness of her lips.

"Who hurt you?" I asked.

"Sweet Boy." Aidan offered the words to me. "That's what I'll call you from now on. If someone reads my journal and asks, 'Who's Sweet Boy?' you can tell them."

"Seabird," I said. "That first day I saw you out on the breakwater, I thought you were a cormorant."

"Mr. Guy's right." Aidan looked down. "You need a haircut."

She stood at the window and finished the apricot. A small fruit, but Aidan took her time. I wanted to know what the apricot juice tasted like in her mouth. I liked wanting to know this. When she finished, she placed the pitted heart of the fruit on the windowsill. I pushed back on the piano bench and walked over to her. From the window, we could see the waterfront. The harbor decorated with sloops. Close to shore, the sailing team practiced maneuvers with Coach Tripp riding at a distance in a launch. The sun would set shortly, and I knew that the sea breeze would die down as the evening air cooled. I moved in close to Aidan, keeping a hand's distance between our bodies. My chin parallel to her cheek.

"I'm going to summon a storm for you," I said.

Aidan spoke in a feathery voice. "Will the ocean rise?"

"We'll play in the rain together." I brushed my neck against her hair.

My chest steadied itself against her back. For a moment, I felt that Aidan might lean in for support. Instead she turned and faced me. I'd thought of her with unblinking eyes, moving always, across the pages of opened books with rapid precision, but as she stood in front of me, her eyes looked slow and watery. I capsized into them. The sides of our noses touched. Her body stayed tense and rigid. I caressed her, searching for a response, rolling my tongue lightly, but deeper inside. She answered with her teeth. Kissing me with their sharpness. Scratching them along my lips. Defending herself with small bites. Our mouths together felt decidedly wrong. Hers, rough and agitated. Mine, lost but hopeful. The word "mistake" surged up along my spine, snapping my head back, swiftly, and away from her.

Aidan didn't move. I half expected her to flee from the room. She creased her forehead. My lungs filled with shallow breath. Anxious for air, as though I had just been submerged for several minutes under frozen water. Aidan moved her eyes over my face, across my chest, and then away from me. I looked down at the discarded apricot pit.

"Your teeth," I said. "They're sharp."

Aidan placed a hand over her mouth, horrified. I started to apologize but she pushed past me. I heard her kneeling on the floor, collecting books and dropping pens into her leather satchel. I wanted the texture of that worn leather to be the smoothness shared between us. Aidan stood in the middle of the room. I held my back to her and listened as she closed the piano cover over the keys and left.

In the harbor, I searched for Swedish boats. Half-ton cruisers that would keep a sailor, alone at sea, comforted by their sturdy construction. Weight and heaviness promising security. I'd never thought of sailing on open waters without a crew. Cal and I had planned to see the world together. I'd touched Cal on impulse, just as I'd done to Aidan. Cursing them both like characters in a German fairy tale. Pricking fingers on silver needles. The first time I kissed him, we were standing in front of a mirror in the entryway of my apartment. It was fall break of our junior year. Cal was leaving the next day for Anguilla. I was staying behind to have my wisdom teeth removed. The two of us were just talking and joking when Cal told me that he wished I could come with him, and instead of agreeing, I leaned in and kissed him. A solid kiss on the mouth. As we broke away, we both caught ourselves in the reflection. Two tall boys. Two red mouths. I could feel the strength of his body vibrating against me, and I knew that with one swift wrestling move, he could pin me to the floor and hurt me for what I'd done. He didn't. To be with someone who is stronger than you. To have him relinquish his strength.

Without looking down, I picked up the apricot pit and placed it in my mouth, holding it under my tongue. The outside felt hard and scabrous. I ran the pointed tip along the bottom of my gums, until a shallow pocket of blood formed. I took the wooden shell between my teeth, splintering the edges and releasing an added bitterness. Holding the mixture loose in my mouth and rolling it over my tongue and palate like a rock polisher rinsing pebbles. As I swallowed the blood and saliva, bits of broken seed scratched down my throat. The heart of the fruit bulged from my cheek, reminding me of Kriffo's chewing tobacco. Unable to spit or throw the seed out a window. Unable to reject the sharpness of Aidan's kiss, I took the seed from my mouth and placed it in my breast pocket.

Every weeknight, after dinner, we had two hours of study and then a free hour before curfew. During that time, couples convened in the first-floor parlor of Astor, flopped on couches, bounced on chairs, sprawled across itchy wool rugs, then got down to the business of making out. Table lamps were turned off, but the two main chandeliers ran on a timer and wouldn't go black until quarter of eleven. That gave fifteen minutes for the real nasty stuff. Sucking off. Humping. Tazewell called this ritual "milk and cookies." The dining hall staff actually set out vanilla wafers and glass pitchers of chocolate milk. According to Brizzey, who'd previously invited me to snack with her, the whole thing had been Tinks's idea. Once girls were admitted, she'd determined that there'd be less temptation to sneak off campus or into each other's rooms if there were a time scheduled for intimate exchanges. "They don't mind us screwing around," Brizzey claimed. "They just don't want us doing it in our own beds." The faculty took turns monitoring the make-out sessions, usually departing moments before the great blackout occurred, then returning at eleven o'clock to detangle bodies and send boys home.

My plan was to sneak up to Aidan's room while the lights on the first floor of Astor were out. The main staircase ran right off the parlor and up to the third floor. I'd seen Ms. Alvarez, the Astor dorm parent, in Whitehall hanging out with Coach Tripp, so I knew I'd have time to sprint up the stairs, find Aidan's room, and apologize. I didn't want Aidan going to sleep still mad at me. There was also the possibility that I wanted to try kissing her again.

I timed my parlor entrance with the setting chandeliers. For a moment, I stood and watched puffy male lips smack little girl faces. Arms and legs like a muscle of boa constrictors twisting and tightening around an opossum. A haze of sweat and steam hung over the air. I can't say that there was sex in that room. Sex to me meant privacy, not a thrashing scrum of bodies fighting it out in the dark. But I liked this public display. The liberty one had to roll and writhe. To make strange liquid sounds with spit and tongues. Unashamed, unabashed. I admired the athleticism. Kriffo sat in an upholstered armchair with a miniature girl on his lap. He ran a hand along a white flash of her thigh. I saw his fingers disappear under the shade of her skirt. With my own dirty mind, I conjured up a department store Santa. Being naughty or nice. I grabbed a pocketful of cookies prior to mounting the stairs.

I didn't knock. I heard muffled crying and entered, bracing myself.

Aidan wasn't crying and she wasn't alone. She sat on her bed wearing only an oversized T-shirt. She clutched her arms around another girl. Both of them turned to me, surprised and jolted. Here was Diana, bleary-eyed and dressed in silk pajamas.

"What are you doing here?" Diana asked.

This was a good question. I pointed to Aidan.

"No." Aidan stood, pulling her T-shirt down over pale legs.

"Him?" Di squinted. She blew her nose with a balled-up tissue, then rose and whispered something to her friend.

I'd stumbled onto a secret. Aidan touched Di's cheek, held her hand, and nodded. Words were exchanged in low, cooing voices. And me, I merely stood there, waiting. I didn't understand any of it.

Diana's face was red. Not blotchy or swollen but warm and sad. She looked so old to me then, the way a tired mother must look to her child. I watched her peck kisses over Aidan's eyes. On her way out, Di said good night to me. Aidan sat on the middle of her bed with her legs folded. She glared at me.

"I thought you'd be alone," I said.

"What difference does it make?" Aidan spoke in a controlled voice. "You don't belong in my room." She sounded like Mr. Guy did when humiliating Race.

"I wanted to apologize for being a jerk earlier."

"I'd rather not talk about that." Aidan reached back for a pillow and held it in her lap.

"We don't have to." I took a few steps toward her bed. "I'm sorry."

I shuffled my feet and looked for a place to sit. There was one straight-backed chair, but the seat was covered with books. The only other place was beside Aidan on her bed. The more I hesitated, the smaller her bed seemed. Alice in Wonderland small, and I felt every inch of my six-foot frame.

"I was surprised," I said, "to find someone here with you. I'd rather you existed only when I was around." I made a decision and sat at the foot of her bed.

"We used to be roommates," Aidan said quietly. "Sometimes she likes to talk."

"She confesses her secrets?" I asked.

"I'm a good listener."

"Sounds pretty one-sided." I relaxed and moved farther back onto the bed.

"What about our friendship?" Aidan tossed me a pillow. "I listen to you talk about Cal. How beautiful he was."

"That 'beautiful' comment," I said. "I didn't mean anything by it." I folded the pillow, placed it behind my neck, and propped my back against the wall.

I closed my eyes and let a few moments pass by.

"Jason," Aidan said, "you're drifting."

"I should probably go." I stood up and shook out my legs.

"If you're caught leaving my room, I'll be in trouble. It's the one thing they still punish us for."

"Are you offering me sanctuary?"

Aidan glided from her bed and turned off the lights.

"I'll leave early." I took off my jacket and tie and stepped out of my shoes. I began to unbuckle my belt but decided to keep on the rest of my clothes.

Aidan raised the sheets and slid over against the wall. There was room for me in her bed, but I picked up the extra pillow and stretched out onto the wood floor.

"Are you comfortable?" she asked.

"My punishment for this afternoon." I used my jacket as a blanket.

Aidan whispered, "You surprise me, Jason."

"Just trying to distinguish myself."

"Jason," she said softly, "I'm sorry my teeth are sharp."

I didn't want to hear this. Unlike Aidan, I wasn't a good listener.

"I think I'm going to fall asleep," I said.

I rolled over onto my side and studied the dance shoes on the wall. Black-and-white patent leather. Imagining Fred Astaire in top hat and tails. Spinning and tapping a straight black cane. Smiling with a face full of sharp teeth and charm. My dreams turned to home movies. Scratchy film of Aidan balanced on Fred Astaire's shoes. Fox-trotting on his feet. I slept.

Aidan woke me during the night. She sat up in bed, beating the air with her arms. Kicking the sheets and pillows aside. I went to her. Wrapping myself around her chest and bringing her back down to the mattress, whispering quietly into her ear. We slept in that tight hold. Aidan always hid her body in loose and unflattering clothes. I was surprised to feel the thin arches of her ribcage and the slender curve of her waist. I didn't run my hands over her body. Instead, I held her close. My face buried in her hair. Just enough room for the two of us.

I left early in the morning, before Aidan had a chance to rise. She slept with her lips pouted and her mouth opened slightly. I put on my jacket, touching the breast pocket to feel the dried apricot seed, then made my escape through the window.

I jetted down the metal stairs, dismounted, and crossed through a small parking lot on my way to Whitehall.

"Late night?"

Turning to my left, I saw Plague. Sitting on the hood of a blue Chevy Malibu, a triangular sign advertising Lighthouse Pizza crowning its roof. He bit into a chocolate doughnut, chasing it down with a swig from a bottle of cola.

"Jump-start your morning," I said.

"You giving it to one of those muffs?" Plague asked.

I pointed to a white bag perched beside him on the car. He stared at me, then offered me the bag. I took a powdered doughnut.

"Thanks."

"You have a lady up there?"

"Not really."

"They act all uptight, but I bet they put out just the same." Plague stuck his finger in his mouth and ran it down along his gums, licking and uncaulking the chocolate cake.

"No comment," I said.

"Like you'd tell me, anyway."

"Does it bother you"—I chewed—"the way you're treated?"

"How do you mean?" he asked.

"The name-calling, the put-downs."

"It takes a whole lot more to get to me." He jumped down from the hood of his car.

"I guess it would."

"You and your friends," Plague said, "are a joke. Like right now. I could turn you all in. Have the lot of you thrown the hell out."

I brushed powder off my fingertips and spoke calmly. "You think they'd believe you? Over me?"

"I have no reason to lie."

"What's your real name?" I asked.

He seemed taken aback. "What do you mean?"

"Your real name can't be Plague," I said.

He frowned, as if needing a minute or two to remember. "Leonardo. Leo for short." He pulled out a gold chain with a medallion. "You know. Like the lion."

I looked at the golden animal's head and smiled. "That's a good name for you."

"My girlfriend," he said. "She gave me the necklace."

Without any prompting, he took out his wallet and showed me a picture of himself seated on a picnic bench with a small dark-haired girl on his lap.

"That's Cheryl." Plague stared at the photo. I felt as though I was intruding on an intimate moment.

"Time to go to work." He picked up the white bag and rolled down the top.

"A bit early for pizzas," I said.

"No, that's my other job. Now it's time to make pancakes for you fools."

"Don't spit in the batter."

"That would be the least of it." Plague walked away with his shoulders hunched, swinging the satchel of doughnuts.

"Leo," I called out. "We're cool. Right?"

He looked back at me and saluted.

That afternoon, I ran into Aidan outside Mr. Guy's classroom.

"Good," she said. "I found you." She grabbed my hand and hauled her leather bag over her shoulder. "Come with me."

"Where are you taking me?"

"To the Salon."

We raced through the Barracuda's Fishbowl together and Aidan pulled me into the girls' bathroom. She locked the door. The room was small with only a sink, a mirror, and a toilet. She removed a towel from her leather bag and wrapped it around my neck.

"What's going on?" The towel was thick and white and felt good against my skin.

"I want to see what you look like beneath this mane." Aidan turned on both faucets, running her fingers through the stream and adjusting the hot and cold taps. She opened a bottle of shampoo and placed it on the sink. "Lean forward," she said.

I bent over at the waist and stuck my head down into the basin of the sink. Aidan circled her fingers along my neck, drowning the warm and cold water into my hair. She rubbed shampoo between her palms, lathering a pink peppermint lotion. My scalp tingled like Christmas candy on a cold tongue. It felt good to be touched, and I wanted her to work the massage from the crown of my skull toward my neck and my shoulders, then downward, the route of my spine. As the water licked my ears and dripped down my cheeks, I thought again about kissing her. Aidan turned the water off and pressed the towel plush around my head.

"I can't believe I'm letting you do this," I said.

Aidan unsheathed a long, thin pair of scissors. "Sit." She pointed to the toilet seat.

I sat, and she began to snip away. Hair fell in dark curls onto the linoleum floor.

"Don't look down." Aidan held my chin straight.

"Shouldn't you be preserving a lock of my hair?"

"Are you kidding? I could make a wig." Aidan held her face within inches of my own, her breath cool, her stare controlled.

Her eyes were a dark russet, but up close I noticed that within the iris of her left eye a bright splinter of gold gleamed like light bouncing off the sharp tip of a needle.

"One of your eyes," I said, "has this crazy fleck of gold."

"It's a piece of broken glass." Aidan tipped back on her heels. "It's lodged in there. Here, feel."

Aidan took my fingers in her hand. She closed her eye and ran my fingertips over the soft skin of her eyelid, pressing down on the hard, small granule of glass.

"Does it hurt?" I asked. "How did it get in there?"

She sliced the scissors open and closed, a silvery sound. "I don't want to talk about that. Not today."

Aidan continued to trim my hair. I was happy just to sit in silence and let her work. We both had our secrets and I didn't want to overreach.

"You know that song," Aidan said. "'It Had to Be You.' I always thought the line went, 'With all your false I-love-you-stills.'"

"It's 'With all your faults, I love you still.'"

"I know that now," Aidan said. "You sang it one afternoon."

A piece of hair landed on my nose. I blew it up and away, but the itch remained. Aidan slid me around and trimmed the back. Finally she snapped the towel from my neck and rubbed my hair dry. "Take a look," she said.

We stood together in front of the bathroom mirror. She'd managed to keep my hair long and curly, but neater.

"Well done," I said.

"Now I can be seen with you." Aidan collected furry mats of hair from the floor. "Hair is destiny," she said. "The right look can change your life."

I held up the shears and began clipping them dangerously close to her head.

"No one cuts my hair," she whispered.

"I'm glad to know that."

As she busied herself sweeping up the mess, the pink arch of her ear peeked out from her long red curls. In that moment she looked like an elf or, even more, like a boy. How strange and rare it was to see the top of a girl's ear. I reached out to touch her, but my hand flew back from a spark of static electricity.

In the weeks that followed, Aidan and I spent hours together walking on the beach. We'd play this game where I would stroll several yards in front of her and sing. She loved the way the wind carried the lyrics back to her, claimed that some words arrived before others shuffled out of order. She believed that the wind composed its own music from my voice. "You're like one of those Sirens in the *Odyssey,*" she claimed.

"That's right. I'm luring you into shore only to have you crash against my rocks."

I kept offering to take Aidan sailing and she kept insisting that boats frightened her. I tried to reassure her that despite all dangers, I would keep her safe.

"I know you mean well," she said, "but for now, let's stay on land."

When the tide was out, Aidan and I would sit on the breakwater and I'd school her on the art of sailing. She was surprised to learn that despite thousands of years of history and advancements in high-tech navigational instruments, sailing still wasn't an exact and measurable science. "A compass may point north, but the metallic needle is swayed and influenced by the boat's own magnetic field."

"So north isn't really north?" Aidan asked.

"Not when you're sailing. True north becomes compass north, and the degree of deviation must be drawn and plotted on a curve." No matter how precise the instruments, how frequently adjusted, I had to admit to Aidan that certain aspects of sailing had no firm guidelines.

Like deciding when to reduce sail. Knowing when fast is fast enough. An overcanvased boat will strain and broach, rolling windward out of control. Reefing the main and reducing the headsail requires athleticism. Challenging a crew's unity and strength. Striving to keep the areas of each sail in proportion. A wardrobe of sheets to select from. Mizzen, genoa, lapper, spinnaker. The skipper commands the crew and forecasts the need for change, basing his decisions on intuition and experience. The art of interpretation.

Though I didn't set out to conceal it, Aidan and I kept our friendship private, hidden, even. We hadn't known each other long, but there was an intensity, an immediacy to our feelings for each other. What made me like her? Her pain. Her mystery. I was drawn to her because she reminded me of Cal. I was drawn to her because she reminded me of myself. I couldn't tell you what she saw in me. She certainly didn't expect that I would add to her hurt. She could not have known the harm I'd bring.

SIX

Among the many tricks I learned from him, Cal taught me the secret to counting waves. He believed that if a sailor paid close attention and knew when to begin counting, he could track waves and predict their size and duration. Cal was convinced that in a series of waves, the seventh wave would always be higher than the sixth. The seventh wave would give a sailor an extra charge. A sailor just had to know when to start counting. "The first wave always looks like it's going be a killer but then it breaks early, drops out, and doesn't deliver. When you see one of those, that's when you start counting." We spent hours looking for that first wave in order to hunt down our seventh, knowing that longer swells traveled faster than short wind waves. What Cal liked best was to spot waves during an oncoming squall. We both understood that it was always best to sail directly into a storm. Never away. When riding into colder water we could feel the surface air cool, the wind slow and back down. Together we'd calibrate the rise, as gale forces cause the edges of crest to break into spindrift.

Cal and I often talked about what we'd do if we sailed into a hurricane. Revolving winds greater than sixty-three knots. Exceeding force twelve on the Beaufort scale. Beginning as shallow depressions. Settling on a path, then altering their set course without warning. Rotating and building into a warm core with the release of latent heat and rain. A solid wall of cloud. Cal thought that with the right boat, we'd be able to heave to and take the brunt of any storm's beating.

I'd been at Bellingham for just over two months when a hurricane was predicted to ride up from the Caribbean, miss the Keys, strike Hatteras, and land finally on Cape Cod. A late-season storm, making a slow surge up the Atlantic coast.

The storm inspired Race to organize a hurricane party at his home on Powder Point. I had no interest in spending a night at Race's house, but Race didn't invite me. Tazewell did.

The note Tazewell left on my door said, "Come see me."

My dorm room was big, but Tazewell's was a penthouse. A corner room with a private bath and four windows. When I came in, Tazewell was sitting on his own full-sized bed, not the regulation Bellingham cot. A tackle box filled with safety pins and embroidery floss opened in front of him. Dressed only in teal gym shorts. His naked chest puffed out like a proud peacock. A pile of lacrosse sticks sat like kindling on the floor. Kriffo's last name, "Dunn," repeated in silver letters up and down the lengths of all the shafts. I picked up a stick, scooped up a balled-up pair of socks, and cradled the dirty laundry.

"Got something for you," he said. "Give me your wrist." Tazewell held out a woven bracelet, similar to the ones that decorated his right arm.

"You make this?" I asked.

"Took me over a week." He slipped the cord around, tied a reef knot, and turned my wrist over to admire his own handiwork. "Used seven different colors. Call it my cat's-eye design."

"It's incredible." I ran a finger over the intricate pattern. Both the tight weave and Tazewell's choice of blues and greens reminded me of Cal, his changing eyes.

"Damn right it's incredible." He closed his tackle box. "I'm a fucking artist."

"You really made this for me?" I asked. "Thank you."

"Been feeling bad about not hanging out." Taze picked up another lacrosse stick and shoveled up two paperback novels. "Why don't we make these books look read? Let's crack 'em."

We volleyed the novels back and forth, bending the covers and denting the pages.

"Hurricane party this weekend. You in?"

"Where at?" I asked.

"Race's. The storm's supposed to hit on Saturday, so plan on signing out for an overnight. Say that you're visiting Riegel at Princeton for a college preview. They never check college stuff. I mean, let's be real, they don't check much of anything here." He snatched up a cream-colored paperback. "So are you game for a party?"

"Race doesn't want me at his house."

"It's a party. More people the better." Tazewell shot *The Awakening* over my head.

I reached back and made the catch, saving a desk lamp from *The Awakening* and obliteration.

"Nice," Taze said.

I spun around and accidentally tossed the book out a window that was open only a few inches.

"One-in-a-million shot," he told me. "You know when you do something unconscious like that. Then you try again, for show, and it's impossible? I dig that."

"Dumb luck," I said.

The door swung open, and Kriffo entered, holding a rolled-up newspaper like an ice cream cone. The side of his cheek bulged out at the jaw and he spit brown tobacco juice into the wrapped paper.

"Dumb fucking luck," Kriffo echoed. "Just heard about some serious bad luck."

"What's the word?" Tazewell asked.

"You know that freshman, Skinner?"

"Sure. A little guy," Tazewell said. "Does cross-country."

"That's the one." Kriffo spit. "Guess his roommate found him choking his chicken."

"Choking?" I asked.

"He was spanking it, Prosper." Taze gestured, meaningfully, with his hand. "So is Skinner packed? Is he out of here?"

I put down Tazewell's lacrosse stick. "They'd kick him out for that?"

"No one's telling him to leave," Kriffo said, "but you can't exactly live that shit down. One thing to do it. Another thing entirely to get busted."

"The Skinman rides tonight." Taze reached for his lacrosse stick, rubbing his hands over it and howling.

"The horny little homo." Kriffo spit and missed his mark. Black liquid tobacco drool punctuated the dimple on his chin and trickled down one of his ironed shirt cuffs. "Couldn't keep his hands off himself."

"Remember Dewey Altman?" Tazewell asked me.

I nodded. Tazewell began to tell Kriffo about this epic masturbator we both knew at Kensington. "Dude would sit on his right hand till it fell asleep, then he'd jack himself off with it. Claimed it felt like someone else was doing the work."

I laughed. "Yeah, Altman called it giving himself 'the Stranger.' "

"Did it work?" Kriffo asked.

"I guess so," I said without thinking.

"Oh, so you tried it Prosper? You're a closet Skinman?" Tazewell asked. "Are we going to sneak into your room some night and find you humping your favorite pillow?"

"You must think I'm cute, now, don't you Tazewell, if you're making plans to sneak into my bedroom some night."

"Bitch." Tazewell dove and grabbed me by the knees. He picked me up, threw me back onto his bed, and straddled me. His groin was in my face. "You want some? Want some Tazewell magic?" He loosened the drawstring on his shorts.

Tazewell's balls were pressed up against my chin. His naked chest covered with a light sweat that smelled like ivy on brick. As Tazewell looked down on me smiling and laughing, I felt myself stiffen underneath him. I tried to overpower my erection with thoughts of Nancy Reagan. Nancy Reagan on a surfboard. Nancy Reagan pitching horseshoes. Nancy Reagan holding a lacrosse stick.

"Prosper," Tazewell began, "I want to see if you swallow."

"I'm going to have to hose you two down." Kriffo hit Tazewell on the head with his newspaper, spraying brown juice.

Tazewell rolled off me and went over to his bureau. He took out a cigarette, opened the window, and stood by it, smoking.

I sat on the bed with my back against the wall and one of Tazewell's pillows covering my waist and groin. I looked to Tazewell. To Kriffo.

They were just boys. Tall and strong, older looking than most, but still boys. They thrived in the world of games and rules. When someone slipped, they knew how to drag him down with a nod to each other. Down with a well-chosen word. They liked the world that had been created for them and wore this world, with cocksure pride, around their wrists. A birthright of confidence.

They were my friends, and I wished to be effortless with them. I wanted to register the same strength they did in the way I laughed or held chewing tobacco in my cheek. We were alike enough, the three of us, and yet my every gesture felt like a compensation.

I stood up to leave.

"Don't forget about the party," Tazewell said. "And don't dream about me too much."

I held up the bracelet. "Now that we're engaged, it's hard not to."

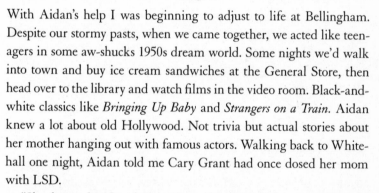

With Aidan's help I was beginning to adjust to life at Bellingham. Despite our stormy pasts, when we came together, we acted like teenagers in some aw-shucks 1950s dream world. Some nights we'd walk into town and buy ice cream sandwiches at the General Store, then head over to the library and watch films in the video room. Black-and-white classics like *Bringing Up Baby* and *Strangers on a Train*. Aidan knew a lot about old Hollywood. Not trivia but actual stories about her mother hanging out with famous actors. Walking back to Whitehall one night, Aidan told me Cary Grant had once dosed her mom with LSD.

"She dropped acid with Cary Grant?" I asked. "The guy in all those Hitchcock films?"

"Archie promised Mom it would help her see more clearly. That was his real name, Archibald Leach." Aidan pressed her lips together and looked off into the night. "He's gone too. Just like Astaire. An end of an era." Aidan wasn't bragging. These stories slipped out only to be followed by long periods of silence. Like most people who came from privilege, Aidan was guarded about her family's connections.

I was happy to listen, to not ask for more, and to slowly piece together her life.

That night, Aidan followed me back to my dorm. She was having trouble sleeping and I'd promised to lend her a bunch of dreamy music: Leonard Cohen, Nick Drake, and even a recording of me singing Christmas carols with the Kensington Choir. "My rendition of 'Silent Night' will send you right to sleep."

Girls were allowed in the lobby of Whitehall, but Aidan had never gone inside. She wanted to see what she'd been missing. As we approached the dorm, we were both hit by the strong smell of pizza. Aidan asked, "Does Whitehall always reek of sausage and onions?"

We entered the dorm only to find Chester Baldwin in the lobby, his head bowed, his arms crossed at his chest. An older man with a graying ponytail stood beside two towers of pizzas, the boxes leaning perilously on a coffee table. The delivery guy kept insisting that Chester owed him money. "Somebody ordered these pizzas," he said, "and somebody's got to pay for them."

Chester admitted to ordering one pizza but not the twenty he was being charged for. It was a classic prank. One of the Whitehallers had probably heard Chester phone in his order, then called back and added to it.

"Can we help?" Aidan asked Chester.

"Do you have two hundred bucks?" Chester didn't even look at us as he spoke. He didn't expect us to have an answer.

Aside from seeing each other in the hallways and nodding hello, neither Chester nor I had made any effort to become friends. Chester woke up early, ate all of his meals alone, and went to bed before curfew. He didn't hang out with anyone. This was my opportunity to change things between us. I told the delivery guy, "You know this is a lame prank. Cut my pal some slack. There's no need to extort funds."

"Are you guys running some sort of scam?" the guy asked. "Or do you just think you deserve everything for free?"

"Wait right here," I said. Chester and the pizza guy both looked at me like I was nuts. They were in a standoff. Neither guy was going anywhere. Aidan smiled, curious to see what I would do.

I knew I had at least a hundred dollars in my room. I grabbed the cash, then knocked on Yazid Yazid's door. "Want a pizza?" I asked. I promised to sell him one for ten bucks. He gave me the money. I knocked on a few more doors and hit up a few more stoners. Kriffo, who never stopped eating, was the only guy on my hall who refused to pay for a pizza. I figured he was the one who'd set up Chester. "Let me know if there are any leftovers." Kriffo winked. I almost didn't care that Kriffo was such an obvious prick. I was happy and high from trying to help someone out of a jam. By the time I made it down the hall and then back to the lobby, I had a serious wad of cash.

The delivery driver unwrinkled the stash of bills and examined them while Chester and I watched. Aidan added twenty dollars of her own. I kept smiling at Chester, but he just looked at me like I was a stranger. When the pizza guy was done counting and recounting the money, he nodded and left. "Thanks for screwing me on my tip," his final salvo.

"What a douche," I said to Chester.

"It's not his fault," Chester said. "The guy didn't want to get stiffed." Chester went over to the stack of pizza boxes and opened the top box. "I'm not even hungry anymore," he said.

"You should eat something," Aidan said. "You earned it."

Chester shook his head. "I'll pay you guys back tomorrow."

"No need," I said. A bunch of Whitehallers came downstairs to collect their pizzas. They tore through the boxes. Meanwhile, Chester went upstairs empty-handed. I thought I'd done something nice but I couldn't help feeling like I'd failed.

Coach Tripp stopped by my room later that night carrying a small black case and a set of charts and maps, *A Sailor's Guide to the Stars.* He unfolded one of the larger maps and said, "We'll start with all of the major stars and work our way through the constellations. You've got to know what you're looking for before you can navigate by starlight."

The star finder maps were printed in a fading blue and gold. They reminded me of the dingy ceiling of Grand Central Terminal. My dad had explained how the dirt and grime from trains and smokers obscured the once shimmering stars. "Used to look like heaven," he'd say. "Now it's just filth."

Coach Tripp rested the black case on my bed and opened it with care. "Have you ever used one of these?"

I knew enough not to reach for the sextant. The brass contraption looked heavy but it was a delicate instrument. The double mirrors were easily disturbed and misaligned. If I dropped it, I risked bending the arc and rendering the sextant useless. It wasn't the sort of heirloom a father could hand down to his son. A sextant was something you earned the right to own for yourself. A real sailor bought his own brand-new sextant and took care of it like it was his lifeline, his most precious possession.

Coach Tripp held the sextant up to his eye. "Haven't used her since the Newport Bermuda Race."

"My uncle Roland had a swank sextant like that. All brass," I said. "He's the man who taught me how to sail. Great guy."

"Your dad didn't teach you how to sail?"

"My dad gets seasick eating fish and chips."

Coach laughed. "Well, your uncle Roland probably taught you that you never want to become too dependent on some computer or satellite for your location. With a little basic math and this"—he held up the sextant—"you'll never get lost at sea."

The two of us climbed out onto my fire escape and looked out at the harbor. "It's great to be this high up," Coach said.

"Yeah. It's like we're in the crow's nest on some tricked-out schooner."

The night sky was bright with stars. We could still make out the horizon line. A sailor needed to measure the stars against the horizon, but when it was too dark to separate the night from the ocean, the stars would be nearly useless. "Aries is the first star in the zodiac. All of the other stars are fixed in relationship to Aries." Coach reviewed how to take a sight measurement and how to use the measurement to calculate position. I knew the basics of sighting stars, but Coach Tripp explained how the position of the stars was plotted not using latitude or longitude but declination and right ascension. "It seems like the stars are fixed in the sky, but they do move, and you need to know how to account for those adjustments." He made everything sound simple and clear, and I realized that Coach was actually a good teacher. He'd promised to look out for me and even though I wasn't on his team, he was making good on his promise. It was a nice gesture, but I worried that Coach Tripp was reaching out to me only in the hope that I would rejoin the sailing team in the spring. I promised to study the maps and charts.

We talked about the impending hurricane, and I asked if Coach had ever sailed into a squall.

"I don't go in for that sort of adventure," he said. "I like to play it safe. Plus, I've never owned my own boat. Wouldn't feel right putting someone else's yacht at risk." Coach Tripp told me that he'd grown up in Cleveland, Ohio. "Not in Shaker Heights either." His dad had worked for some tire company. "Middle management," Coach said, "the worst thing that can happen to a man. To wind up in the middle." Coach had grown up sailing Lake Erie on borrowed Lasers and Larks. "I did what the rich kids did." Coach smiled at me. "Always trying to blend in. Now you know my secret."

Coach Tripp was a striver. He'd wound up at Bellingham because he didn't know any better. He saw a beautiful school by the sea and figured he'd be lucky just to be a part of it. I told him his secret didn't change anything, but I knew Coach had given up a little of his power.

Before he left my room, I asked, "Do you still want me to be one of your SeaWolves? Are you hoping I'll join the pack?"

Coach Tripp placed the sextant back in its velvet case and locked the box.

"Look, Jason," he said, "I'd love to coach you. But it's your talent to squander."

SEVEN

The more time I spent with Aidan, the more she opened up to me. She was shy about her childhood not because it was modest but because it was so oddly glamorous.

On the morning Aidan was born, three wise and dutiful men arrived at the Beverly Hills Cedars-Sinai Medical Center to claim her as their own. Aidan's mother had actually warned several different admirers that they might be new fathers. "She was unmarried. Gorgeous but in decline. An overfathered baby, one more lapse in a lifetime of lapses in judgment." Aidan's mother had been, on various occasions, an heiress to a Simi Valley orange grove fortune, a merry prankster on the Grateful Dead's tour bus, a Whisky a Go Go go-go dancer, Jane Fonda's stand-in during the filming of *Barbarella,* a studio executive's mistress, and, finally, a producer on an Academy Award–winning film. "You know that song 'Hotel California'?" Aidan asked. "That's my mom."

I wasn't certain how a person could be a song, but Aidan made this music seem possible. The details of her mom's misadventures might have made for serious late-night gossip, might have served as powerful social currency. Instead, this backstory embarrassed Aidan. Extracting information took patience and restraint on my part. East Coast wealth and social status had long failed to impress me, but West Coast scandal and intrigue left me a little starstruck.

"Don't you miss it?" I'd ask Aidan. "All that Hollywood sunshine?"

"It's like hating the color yellow," she'd say, "and living in a golden age."

Two of the men who showed up at the maternity ward were competing real estate developers, business rivals who upon seeing each other exchanged insults, threatened lawsuits, then fled. The third man stayed. He was the actor, Robert Mitchum.

The night before Race's party, Aidan and I camped out in the mildewing basement of the library's video room watching tapes of the miniseries *The Winds of War.* I was supposed to be taking copious notes for a Mr. Guy research paper on cinematic misrepresentations of World War II. As the film flickered with inaccuracies, an intrusion of silver beetles swarmed around us. Aidan kept snatching the insects from my polo shirt and charming them onto her wrists only to have the beetles fly off and attack the television screen. Aidan toyed with her beetles while I heckled Jan-Michael Vincent and Ali MacGraw as they pretended to fall in love. Then Mitchum showed up, stoic and kick-ass in his navy dress blues, promising his blond lover he'd leave his wife, abandon the war.

Aidan had painted her nails an intense shade of cobalt, turning her already pale skin ghostly and diaphanous. She tapped the small TV screen with her fingers and said, "He was almost my father."

I thought she was kidding. It seemed unlikely that the evil star of *Cape Fear,* Marilyn Monroe's laconic lover in *River of No Return*, and the scariest man in the world in *The Night of the Hunter* could ever be anybody's father. The fact that I could rattle off Mitchum's credits impressed Aidan. In truth, I studied leading men, tough guys, heartbreakers, princes among thieves. Maybe I felt I needed to. I also didn't reveal that with my cleft chin, broken nose, and almost handsome face, I knew Mitchum's films only because I'd always secretly hoped someone might tell me I looked like him.

Aidan traced Mitchum's profile with her blue fingertips. "The first photograph ever taken of me was in his arms. Old enough to be my granddad. Mom claims she never met a man who loved his wife more. Didn't stop her from sleeping with him."

Aidan had certain suspicions about her father's identity but no definitive answers.

"If you don't ever know where you come from," Aidan said, "it's impossible to know what you're supposed to be."

I paused Mitchum and his wars. The room grew dark and the beetles turned into flashing fireflies.

"We have swarms of lightning bugs in our orange groves," Aidan said. "In springtime they star up the white blossoms like Christmas garlands." Aidan knew the names of every orange. Her mother the citrus heiress had taught her daughter how to tell the difference among blood, Valencia, navel, and satsuma, but she wouldn't teach Aidan anything about her dad. The only detail her mother had ever revealed was that her father, who refused to give his daughter his last name, had insisted on choosing her first. Aidan knotted and unknotted her hair. "I almost don't care anymore. Figure if I stop caring entirely, she might tell me who he is."

"I've met my dad," I said. "I'd prefer the mystery."

The tiny Yankee warden who ruled the library neglected to escort us out at closing, locking us in with the silverfish, the ancient sets of Britannica. The fireflies followed us upstairs as we explored the building in search of unlocked exits. We dared each other to climb a column of freestanding bookcases, scaling the tall shelves like they were our own stand of sequoias. When we reached the top, we perched opposite each other kicking our feet against the unread books. I hated seeing Aidan sad, lonesome for a father who hadn't welcomed her into his life.

"You need some fun," I said. "Come with me to Race's party tomorrow night. We'll get trashed, then trash his house."

Aidan smiled. "When he was young, Robert Mitchum was arrested for drug possession. Film studios usually protected their stars, but he actually went to jail. That happened a long time ago, before he met my mom, but it made me think maybe he really was my dad." Aidan jumped down from the shelf, her gypsy skirt parachuting out as she landed hard on her knees. "I can't go to any party."

Aidan roamed the dark library, thieving books into her leather bag. I followed her into a storage locker stuffed with abandoned slide projectors, leaking mimeograph machines. The room reeked from the cloying purple duplicator fluid. "You can get high off that sweet scent," Aidan said. "I'm a former powder girl. But there was a time when I'd inhale anything."

I knew a fair number of guys who seemed destined for a lifetime of waking and baking, of spending minor fortunes on epic bongs. Knew girls who emptied blister packs of amphetamines when they wanted to slim down and embezzled their moms' Klonopin when they wanted to calm down. Then there were the rehab cases, sick kids who promised to destroy their own privilege, who hoped to construct a cage just small enough to contain themselves. But it wasn't all illicit times and overdoses. With cash, self-control, and the right careless spirit, there was plenty of fun to be had. Once during a deadly dull charity auction for the American Heart Association, Cal and I each snorted two snowy rails in the bathroom of the New York Racquet and Tennis Club. We bailed on our parents, sneaked into the squash courts, and swatted handballs for hours, stopping only when we noticed each other's palms bleeding.

"Drug stories don't interest me." Aidan narrowed her eyes. "Especially not my own. But if you want to, you can ask me anything."

I told her how I'd heard from Stuyvie that she'd seduced a teacher, then attacked him. That she'd been arrested. "Stuyvie insists you were tabloid news. Claims you're famous."

"I prefer infamous." Aidan laughed. "Or maybe I just wish I were that glamorous. The truth is I had a crush on someone who wanted to help me get straight. As a thank-you, I broke all of the stained-glass windows in her house."

Her house. I didn't say anything. Just hoped that Aidan would continue. She left the storage closet and I followed.

Aidan found a fire exit and decided to chance that the door wouldn't be alarmed. It wasn't. We could have walked back to our dormitories, waved good-bye, entertained our proctors with our excellent excuses for being late, but neither of us wanted the night to end.

"Let's go down to the harbor," I said. "I want to show you something."

The fireflies lit our way to the dock where earlier in the day I'd noticed Coach Tripp battening down a classic Nautor's Swan 36. The moniker *Solitude* stenciled on her white transom in thick black cursive. The sailing team usually kept her moored out in the harbor, but with the storm threatening she'd been nestled into a slip along the academy's main finger pier. This baby yacht had real history—one of the first and finest fiberglass racers ever built. A museum piece of science and engineering. I tried to explain its significance to Aidan—how this yacht constituted a marriage between Finnish boatmakers and American naval architects, how the founding designers at Sparkman & Stephens had grown up cruising in this very harbor, but Aidan knew nothing of sailing.

"What did they make boats out of before fiberglass?" she asked.

"Forests and steel," I said.

"Oh." She laughed at herself. "My first dumb question. Feel free to make fun of me." She climbed into the cockpit and I joined her.

"We can sleep here." Aidan gripped the wheel. "I love waking up in the cold air."

I didn't want to sleep. More than anything I wanted to listen to my friend talk about her past. The cabin door was unlocked and I went belowdecks in search of blankets. I found four white billows of sail silk and brought the sheets up to Aidan. We sat across from each other on the cockpit's opposing teak benches, our capes of silk warm and thermal against our skin, the boat lullabying in the light waves. My eyes struggled to adjust to the dimness. Though she sat just a few feet away, I couldn't see Aidan's face.

"Tell me what happened," I said. "Why did you break those windows?"

"Has anyone ever stopped paying attention to you?" she asked.

I nodded, weighed down by the memory of Cal's final days, though I was the one who'd stopped paying attention. Not Cal. I was the one who'd allowed a flood of silence to swell between us.

"I thought I mattered most to someone." Aidan shook her head. "But being nice to me was simply her job." Aidan described the first time she saw her art teacher, Hannah Florent. "She wore a wife beater, jodhpurs, a welder's mask. She was wielding a blowtorch. I watched her forge horseshoes for this Abyssinian the school allowed her to stable. She was wild."

I wasn't sure who was wild, the horse or Hannah.

Though Aidan wasn't much of an artist, she began hanging out in the studio hoping that Hannah might notice her. "I'd come to class all hyped up on this shitty baby laxative cocaine. Then I'd tinker with the heat settings on the kilns, open all the supply drawers, decorate my toenails with acrylic paints, knock over cans of turpentine, and threaten to light the spill on fire. The only way Hannah could settle me was if she sat beside me and focused all of her attention on keeping my hands busy. I was lousy with love for her."

Aidan described Hannah's long chocolate hair. How she kept the layer above the nape of her neck shorn. How when she wore her hair up in a ponytail, Aidan could see this soft bristly trapezoid of fuzz. "Her horsehair, I called it. When I was good she let me run my fingers over and through it. Hannah said she could always tell when I was high because when I was high I always seemed to know exactly what I wanted."

My eyes had adjusted enough to the darkness that I could see Aidan grin.

"Then," she said, "there was the sad matter of Hannah's husband."

Colin Florent refused to be entertained by Aidan's schoolgirl crush on his wife. "He considered me a threat to his marriage. Some marriage." Hannah too had a history with drugs, had kissed her share of women. She'd given up both for her husband, the lacrosse coach and head of admissions at Miss Lilly Tate's School for Young Ladies. "Miss Little Tits" I remembered Cal calling it.

"I wasn't the only one with an infatuation." Aidan waved her hand as a constellation of fireflies sparked between us. "My first night in Miss Lilly's dorm, I heard the older girls on the floor above me pushing their beds together. Almost everyone had a girlfriend."

"Girlfriend, boyfriend." I closed my eyes and paused before finishing my question. "Which do you prefer?"

Aidan said nothing. Maybe she'd drifted off to sleep or maybe she hadn't heard me or perhaps she understood that in my own way, I was telling her something about myself. Then she yawned and stretched her arms.

"I'm exhausted," she said.

"Me too," I said. "Good night."

I rested there in the darkness trying not to breathe too loudly. I didn't dare move or even take off my shoes. Just timed the fireflies as they flashed at one another, trying to decode their mating signals. I heard Aidan rise. She paced along the companionway to the foredeck before returning to the cockpit. Then she sat down on my bench facing away from me.

"Hannah designed and built those stained-glass windows herself, the ones I broke. She'd made them for Colin. Abstract images in reds and blues. Fire and ice. It wasn't easy to destroy them. I mean literally, the first bricks I threw just bounced off the glass." She turned, looked at me, then rubbed her eyelids. "It's hard when you have that much love inside of you, so much it just explodes."

I imagined pulling Aidan down on that teak deck. Stripping off her clothes. Taking pleasure in the way she moved. Even in all that darkness I could see her beauty. Still, I couldn't claim it for myself. Instead, I decided to hurt her.

"You loved someone," I said, "who was completely inappropriate. Does she even speak to you anymore?"

Aidan caught a pair of fireflies. She held them for a moment before pinching the beetles between her fingers and tweezing away their light. I sat up, confused by this small show of cruelty. Before I could ask why she'd killed them, Aidan raised her hand. With her fingertips, she rubbed the phosphorescence onto my bottom lip. Then Aidan leaned over and placed her mouth against mine. Her kiss this time calm, restrained. When she pulled back, her own lips shimmered green and gold. My mouth stung with the sharp bite of lemon.

"Don't worry." Aidan stared at me. "Neither of us has anything to prove."

I swiped the back of my hand against my mouth, brushing away the firefly light.

"Maybe"—Aidan's lips continued to burn and glow—"I just like you because you remind me of Robert Mitchum. With your cleft chin and your curly hair. You look like him when he was young and in trouble."

"What sort of trouble?" I reached out, clasping Aidan's wrists, bringing her closer. We'd come to need each other and I decided to push our attraction as far as Aidan would allow. She'd just told me about the father she didn't know, the woman she'd loved, alerted me to her own addictions, her temper. I could see that spark of gold glass in her eye and I understood now where it came from, what it could lead to. I wanted to be part of what she desired. Contrary to what Aidan believed, I had everything to prove.

EIGHT

Earlier in the week, following Tazewell's suggestion, I'd phoned Riegel at Princeton and left a message warning him about a party I had to go to. That he'd be my weekend alibi.

Since leaving for college, my brother had become a near stranger to me. We were never close, but when I was younger, on the weekends when we were both home, Riegel and I would wake up early and challenge each other to competitive morning sprints through Central Park. We'd run, taunting whoever fell behind. The loser would spring for street vendor snacks, treats our mother never allowed. Walking back to the apartment, Riegel would suck the rocky salt from his pretzel and disclose one of his guilty secrets. My big brother stashed his rotten behavior with me for safekeeping as if confessing his sins to a child absolved him of any crime.

Riegel and I had the same cleft chin, but my brother had a rough potato face, a doughy body. His sweat turned almost instantly into a sour yeasty stench. Yet more than anyone I'd ever encountered, Riegel exuded a profound self-assurance. "Entitlement," our mother called it. In Maine, Riegel would dive off rocky cliffs just assuming the water below would be high enough to contain him. If we went skiing, he could be counted on to sneak off trail without consideration for the rush of snow that might avalanche in his wake. Because of his confidence, Riegel could sidle up to any bar and instantly be enclosed by a clutch of admirers.

With minimal effort, my brother had fingered his way through the *Social Register.* Drunken debutantes regularly appeared before me at Dorrian's armed with berating messages for my cheating brother. "Tell him I hate him," they'd slur before penciling down their phone numbers. "Tell him to call me," they'd insist. These girls had platinum hair and smelled like lavender and gin. They deserved better than Riegel Prosper, but I could not have turned these girls off even with Riegel's dark truths: his ritual of shoplifting his Mother's Day gifts, his affair with his best friend's underage sister, the abortion he paid for with our dad's American Express.

More than girls, my brother loved wealth. "The problem with our parents' money," he liked to claim, "is that there isn't enough. Not for the two of us to share." When Cal died, Riegel tried to cheer me up by disclosing his own dubious involvement with an upstart hedge fund. "I'm roaring with the Asian tigers. Plan on putting our trust funds to work."

Having left Riegel a long, convoluted phone message, I hadn't expected to hear back from him. So I was surprised that Saturday morning to return to Whitehall and find my balding older brother wearing a tuxedo and playing floor hockey with Yazid Yazid in the hallway outside my dorm room.

"Dude," Riegel said, his red face glazed with perspiration. "I just totally hat-tricked." Earlier that morning I'd woken up belowdecks in the Swan's forecabin berth, shivering, confused by my surroundings. I called out to Aidan, but she was already gone. Before slipping off and leaving me, Aidan had placed a book on my bare chest, a stolen library copy of Joshua Slocum's *Sailing Alone Around the World.* Slocum had circumnavigated solo for three years on his sloop *Spray.* The first man to conquer all of the world's waters on his own strength and company. Flipping through the brittle pages, I remembered reading Slocum's adventures together with Cal—we were fascinated by the cranky sailor's antics with pirates and shipwrecks. Slocum's book had even inspired my own fake captain's journal. Cal had once asked me if I thought I could do it, sail alone around the world. "Sure," I said. "But why would I want to do it alone when I could sail around the world with you?"

Cal's eyes lit up. "That's the right answer."

I noticed in the book that some long-ago reader had underlined one of Slocum's bits of wisdom: *I once knew a writer who, after saying beautiful things about the sea, passed through a Pacific hurricane, and he became a changed man.*

The hurricane was supposed to hit today. I was looking forward to the storm and wondered if I'd be able to convince Aidan to go to Race's party with me. I wasn't sure how to interpret Aidan's leaving me Slocum's book. Our night together had left me uneasy, though Aidan had done everything she could to reassure me.

"Take me sailing," Aidan had insisted. "I'm ready to be out on the water with you."

I cupped Aidan's face in my hands. "Can you swim?"

"I'm a regular mermaid."

While I ushered Riegel into my room, Yazid insisted on a rematch. "Your big brother is a high-sticking, cross-checking motherfucker."

I nodded in agreement.

Once we were alone, I asked Riegel, "What's with the tux? Did you get hitched? Some lucky girl invite you to prom?" I wondered if everything was okay.

"Thanks for the garbled phone message," he said. "Had a trip planned to Boston. Figured I'd swing by on my way back and surprise you."

"What were you doing in Boston?" My brother always drank dark and stormies, and I could detect last night's rum and ginger beer on his breath. His black tie fell loose, unknotted around his neck. He looked and smelled like some down-on-his-luck lounge singer. I snapped the tie off and said, "You hate Boston."

"I loathe Boston, but you know . . ." Riegel snatched the tie back from me, tucking it inside his breast pocket. Surveying himself in my mirror, he ran a hand through his thinning blond hair. "I go where my investments take me."

I knew all about my brother's investments.

After Cal's death, I cracked up, acted up, and finally, with just a few weeks left in the semester, got caught cheating on a precalculus exam. I'd told Aidan all about this during our late night on the Swan. I described Kensington's mercenary Honor Code. How the dunce kid I cribbed from, Spenser Macauley, self-righteously narked. "You should have copied off someone with the correct answers," Spenser insisted, not understanding that I wasn't looking for answers, just hoping for a way out. I'd suspected the dean might refuse to cut me any slack. He seemed eager to punish me, to confirm to the school and to all my Kensington classmates that I was the one responsible for Cal ending himself. At least that's how I read the dean's ruling to kick me out. Leaving his office, the dean warned me, "Cheaters never prosper."

Dad was stunned when he couldn't pull the necessary strings to keep me enrolled. The best he could manage was to cut a deal ensuring I'd receive full credit for that final semester so that I could graduate elsewhere on time. Driving away from Kensington, my dad turned to me and I steeled myself for a lecture, for more fatherly admonishments. Instead he said, "Let's go get some ice cream." And we did.

I sat out the remainder of that spring at home in Manhattan. My bedroom had a view of the reservoir, and I murdered time gazing out at the boatless, placid water. Every morning I'd choose a different detail about Cal and attempt to vaporize it from my memory. *Today, I forget how Cal enjoyed flaring off bottle rockets indoors.*

I shuffled around the penthouse in an old terry cloth robe, a souvenir I'd stolen from the Greenbrier during a long-ago family vacation. Mom greeted my return home with a prescription for some choice tranquilizers and I kept the pills safe in the bucket pocket of my robe— the orange bottle my one beacon of hope. *Today I forget how Cal borrowed my sport coats and returned them with holes punched in their pockets.*

Neither of my parents was interested in having me interrupt their daily routines. Dad traveled a lot that spring, and if I saw him it was only very late in the evening and only to say good night. Mom left the apartment every morning by ten, eager to have her hair done, happy to enjoy an alcoholic lunch with a rotating cast of *Mayflower* matrons.

I got so used to being alone that one morning, when I was startled out of sleep by a loud rumble of voices, I actually hid briefly in my closet before finding the courage to investigate. I pulled a polo mallet out of an old umbrella stand, swinging my sporty weapon at invisible intruders until I determined that the voices originated from the formal dining room. No one in our family ever went into that room. Everything in there was fragile and famous. Mom had emphasized the significance of these heirlooms. We had Philadelphia Chippendale, an Augustus Saint-Gaudens bronze, a Miró tapestry, a tangled red-and-black Calder mobile, a seventeenth-century Japanese scroll. But the item of greatest value in our entire home, the thing to save in case of fire, was a John Singer Sargent full-length portrait of our great-great-grandmother.

As a portrait artist, Sargent was notorious for making rich people more attractive than they actually were, and my great-great-grandmother was no exception. Sargent, the original airbrush artist, had given this homely socialite a chin she didn't have, corrected a lazy eye she did have, and shaved a good thirty pounds off her waist. Now she hung in our dining room, a priceless beauty.

The noise in the apartment grew louder, and I hoped to hear something domestic, something that would reassure me that Mom had ordered the carpets cleaned, the candelabras dusted. Then came a racket that could be understood only as the criminal clamor of a multimillion-dollar painting being heisted.

With my polo mallet poised to brain any and all art thieves, I stormed the dining room and was summarily clotheslined by a phantom forearm. I buckled onto the floor sputtering for breath while Riegel and a half dozen of his Princeton buddies stood over me, a blur of madras and Nantucket Reds.

Riegel kicked my ribs with the blunt tips of his loafers. "Shake it off," he instructed before lifting me to my feet. He greeted me with a hug, feeling up the prescription bottle in my robe. While I panicked for air, Riegel picked my pocket, scanned the label, and whispered, "Valium is for suburban hausfraus. You need Thorazine." He popped two pills and introduced me to his college pals. Hairy-legged men in Bermuda shorts with navy sport coats and striped ties. A fraternity eager for a hazing. Then my brother turned to the enormous, spike-haired Asian man whose strong arm my chest had already encountered. "Jason," Riegel said, "this is my boss, Hiro."

Hiro was busy deaccessioning our great-great-grandmother from her perch.

"Hiro?" I asked.

"Yeah," Hiro said. "Like Hiroshima."

"Oh." I blinked. "I'm sorry."

Even in my Valium-induced stupor, I was able to summon a degree of concern for the Sargent. As Hiro excused himself to escort the Princeton princes from our apartment, I punched Riegel on the shoulder and mouthed, "What the fuck?"

"Business meeting." Riegel picked up the mallet and gave it a few practice swings. "Reeling in some new clients. Young blood, old money."

My big brother was using our dining room as a boardroom. "Why'd you take down the Sargent?" I asked.

"Hiro's an art lover. Didn't believe me when I told him we had a Sargent. Now he owes me lunch."

Hiro managed the hedge fund where Riegel interned. He seemed to be using my brother's social connections to bring in new investors. Hiro strode back into the dining room, overhearing the last bit of Riegel's spiel. "It's a real Sargent, all right," Hiro said. "Total beauty."

While Hiro admired our art collection. I stood back transfixed by his wingspan, his arms thick and boundless. The ropy veins in his neck like taut sailing lines. *Today I forget how the veins in Cal's neck and arms bulged after he bench-pressed.*

Hiro waxed on about Sargent's technique. The way the artist loaded up his brush with clumps of color and painted in spontaneous flourishes imitating Velázquez. "Aristocrats and tycoons—you were nobody until Sargent painted you. Nowadays critics fault him for being too stodgy, but for his day, he was a real revolutionary. Look at the way he turned your grandmother into some sort of gypsy."

Hiro had a point. With her gold-fringed scarf and wild red hair, our great-great-grandmother looked more like a dancing beggar than an heiress. Riegel cracked his knuckles and said, "Art is still one of the best long-term investments a person can make."

When Hiro finally left, I said to Riegel, "Never seen you so eager to impress."

Riegel waved me off. "Hiro's already impressed and it's making Dad nervous." Riegel smiled. "Dad always thought I'd graduate and start slaving away for him. Now he knows I have other options."

"You'd really leave the family business?" I was blissfully ignorant on the subject of our parents' wealth. Knew little beyond the impressive fact that Prosper Investments had not merely survived but had famously profited from the 1929 stock market crash. "I never thought you'd abandon the family fortune."

"More like misfortune these days." Riegel laughed. "Our ship is sinking."

Overhead, the Calder mobile turned almost imperceptibly. The Sargent towered in the space between us. I wrapped my arms around the gold frame. "Help me hang this back up," I said.

As my brother stood in my Bellingham dorm room staring glassy-eyed and sleep deprived at the picture of a half-naked Cal tucked into my mirror, I wondered about his supposed investments. "So," I asked again, "what exactly were you doing in Boston?"

"Went fishing." Riegel lightly slapped my face. "Now I need you for bait."

The weather that late morning was sunny and mild. The literal calm before the actual storm. "See those clouds," I said to Riegel, "those are prehurricane clouds, all thin and straggly. Nimbostratus."

"You and your weather patterns." Riegel shook his head. "Breathe in that salty air. This school reeks of seagulls and malfeasance."

My brother had parked his hunter green Jaguar next to some visiting parent's red Alfa Romeo, the flashy car the color of fake blood. We caught Tazewell and Kriffo goofing off inside the two competing convertibles, each guy in his respective driver's seat.

"Make yourselves at home." Riegel motioned for Taze to climb out.

"Hey, Riegel." Tazewell patted my brother on his back. "Sweet ride. Is that a legit car phone?"

"Comes in handy." Riegel knew Tazewell's older siblings Maxwell and Linkwell. I imagined he'd already hit them up for Hiro's hedge fund. "You taking good care of my brother?" he asked.

"We're throwing him a bash tonight." Kriffo pulled at the pouncing jaguar hood ornament and asked, "Jason are you ready to get bashed?"

"Take it easy, big guy." Riegel triggered his fingers and Kriffo let go of the jaguar.

Just then Chester Baldwin jogged by in a pair of white shorts and a blue T-shirt. He held a small yellow Walkman and wore the headphones with the metal halo resting low against the back of his neck. Chester had slid an envelop of cash under my door. I'd slid it back under his with a note asking him if he wanted to play tennis sometime. As he ran by in a blur of sporty orange sneakers, I waved but Chester failed to notice.

"Don't worry, Jason," Taze said. "Chester's going to DJ our party. He's probably picking out tunes. You're coming right, Jason? Race will be disappointed if you don't show." Tazewell gave us directions to Race's house.

Riegel looked at me. "Guess I better have him back in time for the festivities. You guys need me to buy any booze?"

My big brother was just trying to help me out, but with his showy sports car, his shiny tux, his offer to corrupt minors, he seemed like somebody's sad stepfather—a little too eager to be cool. In the bright daylight, I noticed a streak of dried ketchup on his tuxedo shirt, saw a stain of sweat yellowing his collar, a pile of fast-food garbage decomposing on the car floor by the passenger's seat. Riegel wanted to appear Ivy League genius and Rat Pack slick, but he was a regular mess.

"We're taking off." I hopped in the car, kicking a Styrofoam container under the seat. "But I'll check out Race's tonight."

"I'll be sure he gets there." Riegel gunned the engine and saluted good-bye.

We weren't even out of the parking lot when I spotted Aidan. Still wearing the same clothes she'd slept in, she carried a pair of plump tangerines, one in either hand, her blue fingernails gemlike against the orange skin. She seemed to be headed back down to our Swan. "Aidan," I heard myself shout. I asked Riegel to stop the car.

I'd never seen Aidan run before. She ran like a girl, jutting out her neck, windmilling her arms, and kicking her legs to the side. In that moment I imagined what she must have looked like as a little girl playing hide-and-seek among her grandfather's orange trees. I made a note to myself that I would tease her later about her running. Tease her sweetly.

Aidan dropped the tangerines onto my lap and leaned across the passenger's seat to shake Riegel's hand. As Aidan stretched over me, her T-shirt dipped, exposing her bra. Though I looked away, I caught my brother darting his eyes over her breasts. I couldn't blame him. Her breasts were worth lingering over. Aidan must have noticed his glance. Instead of placing a hand over her cleavage, she leaned down even more, challenging Riegel to take a second look.

I had no sense of where Riegel and I were headed, but I wanted to invite Aidan to join us. Riegel was likely to be impressed by her. His attraction might translate into goodwill toward me. Before I had a chance to mention her tagging along, Riegel interrupted, insisting he and I needed to spend some time alone. "We've got some family business," he told Aidan. "Tremendous to meet you."

The ocean breeze began to shift and I could feel the nor'easter making its way up to our shores. Aidan took a step back from the car and asked, "You still going to Race's?"

I nodded. Aidan shook her head.

"Find me before you go," she said. "And eat those tangerines. We don't want you catching scurvy."

As we pulled away, I turned and watched Aidan wave good-bye.

Riegel smacked my head. "Cool it, Orpheus. It's bad luck to look back."

I faced forward, explaining how I'd wanted to invite her along.

Riegel nodded. He took one of the tangerines from me and bit into the skin, peeling the white pith away with his teeth. "Teenage girls are a total gift. Soft, scared, and eager to please. You'll never have it this good again."

With the convertible's top down and the wind belting our faces, I realized that I hadn't been off campus since arriving at Bellingham. "Thanks for liberating me," I said. "Been feeling claustrophobic."

"No problem. We're family. We look out for each other."

We drove along the coast past waterfront mansions and fried-fish shacks with plywood boards sheeting the windows. Spray-painted signs warned, CLOSED FOR THE SEASON. I kept watch over the weather, waiting for rain.

"See all those mansions?" Riegel yelled against the wind and waved his arm toward an impressive row of gabled homes each with a railed widow's walk on the roof. "Those were built with whaling money. There was a time when these little harbor towns were the richest kingdoms in the world. Total Gold Coast." Riegel's hair whipped in the breeze.

I rested my Tretorns up on Riegel's dashboard and he slapped them away.

"Show respect," he said. "That's bird's-eye maple."

A buzzer went off, a loud warning ring that jolted me from my seat, knocking Aidan's tangerine from my lap. Riegel steered with one hand while answering the car phone. He barely spoke. Just listened and agreed. Cal's mother, Caroline, had once made up a deck of vocabulary flashcards, encouraging us to quiz each other in preparation for the SAT. Cal's favorite word was "abrasive." He'd misuse it every chance he could, inserting it into sentences where it didn't belong. *"This ham and cheese sandwich is mighty abrasive." "That's some abrasive foot odor." "I'm going to get abrasive on this ancient history exam."* My favorite word was "incongruous." Leaning forward to capture the rolling tangerine, I whispered, "Riegel's car phone is to incongruous as Riegel's tuxedo is to ridiculous." When he secured the phone back in its slot, I said, "That thing's a tad nouveau riche."

Riegel shrugged. "It may be flashy, but it's the future." He patted the phone box like it was his favorite pet lap dog. "Promised Mom and Dad I'd take you out to lunch."

"Was that them on the phone?" It hadn't sounded like our parents.

Riegel ignored my question. "We have a little drive ahead of us down the coast. Before lunch, we need to stop over in Padanaram. Go see the cousins."

"Did Mom put you up to this?" I asked.

"Come on," Riegel said. "You love Ginger and Dill."

We called Ginger and Dill Thatcher "the cousins," but they weren't blood relatives. Our mother carried a torch for their dead father, our faux uncle Roland Thatcher. The two had long ago enjoyed a failed courtship, then managed, despite their jealous spouses, to stay friends. Roland was the first to take me out sailing, the first man to show me the ropes. Gliding across Apponagansett Bay, he'd tell me stories about his ancestors fighting the Wampanoags during King Philip's War. Roland was the real Yankee deal, a descendant of Pilgrims and revolutionaries, still lording victory over the redcoats. I was twelve when Roland dropped dead at the Connaught in Mayfair. My father joked that the British had finally wrested their revenge.

Riegel cleared his throat. "I'm trying to help out the cousins, but they seem dubious. Ginger asked for you specifically. You're her tiger and all that."

My brother explained that he'd brought me along to reassure Ginger. "Whatever she asks, just tell her everything will be okay." I hadn't seen Ginger in almost two years. Not since she'd dropped out of Brown and skipped off to Morocco with her French tutor. The last I knew of Dill, he'd failed his Series 7 exam for what seemed like the seventh time and finally given up on becoming an investment banker. Without their father to figure things out for them, Ginger and Dill had both stalled out, faltered.

"Plus"—Riegel winked—"Ginger has something she wants to show you."

"So the cousins are back living with their mom?" I asked.

"Yeah," said Riegel. "That woman's still ruining their lives."

A historic landmark plaque posted on the front gate of the Thatchers' seaside estate explained how on this site Roland's long-ago descendants had tortured some Tories and helped create America. The enormous shingle-style mansion hovered above the water like a silvery luna moth readying for its final landing. The house boasted not one but two turrets—a large round tower with a screened-in sleeping porch and a smaller, narrower turret with a spiral staircase that led to an observation deck. From up there you could see the terraced lawns, all emerald turf, slope down and abruptly alter into ocher marsh grass, then salt-and-pepper sand. Instead of gargoyles, the gutters were decorated with sea monsters. Their large spouting mouths had terrified me when I was little.

The house had survived in my happy memory through the joy of sliding down its mahogany banisters, skimming in stocking feet across its marble floors, and the dark thrill of coasting between the cellar and attic inside the vestigial dumbwaiter. During one summer visit, Dill had lured, then trapped, me inside that dark tunnel. He was disappointed when I didn't seem to mind.

Though the Thatchers could still claim a postcard view of the harbor, I saw the house now for what it was: a crude maze of additions, rambling uneven hallways, low-ceilinged rooms, patched and peeling wallpaper. I could hear the ancient plumbing whistle and drip. In the entryway, Riegel picked up a giant broken tooth of plaster that had decayed from the collapsing ceiling.

Ginger popped her head out from behind a hidden door. The house was filled with false walls and secret staircases. "You're here to rescue me from the impending deluge." My fake cousin waltzed into the foyer in a canary yellow evening gown, her face puffy, her domed belly straining against the satin bodice. Ginger was pregnant. I felt a sudden rush of love and sympathy. She ignored Riegel and greeted me with a wet kiss smacked straight on the lips.

Ginger had long scarlet hair but no freckles. I slung my arms around her bare burnished shoulders, her pregnant belly firm between us. I half adored Ginger. She was the closest thing I'd ever had to a sister. In truth, she sailed as well as I did, though I'd never heard her receive credit for this talent or for any talent beyond her ability to maintain a glowing year-round tan. Ginger liked to claim that she was probably part Native American. She'd whisper and wink, "One of my ancestors was held captive by a brutal, sexy tribe."

Unless Ginger invited questioning, I didn't feel that I could ask about the baby inside her or the man who'd put it there.

"Where's Dill?" Riegel asked.

"Despairing in the east parlor." Ginger motioned for us to follow her. "Dilly's bidding farewell to the Renoir."

———

The east parlor was nothing more than a medium-size sitting room with a view through the French doors of the Padanaram Harbor Club. Outside, a coterie of groundskeepers were strapping crosses of duct tape against the windows to keep the glass from blowing out from the storm's winds. Like Riegel, Dill wore a tuxedo, his tie stiff around his neck. He sat spread-legged on a faded blue velvet sofa studying a large painting of an impressionistic seascape showcased in an ornate gilt frame. Staring at the painting through bloodshot eyes, Dill seemed determined to dive into the canvas.

Though I was stunned to find Ginger pregnant, somehow I was even more surprised that Dill had grown a beard. He looked like a sea captain, like the ghost of his father.

"Jason, darling, how do you like Dilly's beard?" Ginger spun around in her evening gown, flashing a swirling layer of ruffles under her skirt. "The Thatcher men all have weak chins. Not like the Prosper boys. I told Dill the beard would make him scratchy but distinguished. What do you think?"

"Yes, Jason," Dill said, "what do you think? You've been brought here for your opinions." Dill leaned the Renoir against the sofa's rolled arms. In the painting, the sky and the ocean were the same palette of blue and gray, and it was only the power of the brushstrokes that defined the horizon and distinguished air from water.

Riegel slapped my back. "Jason has always been a voice of reason."

"I'm a little hurt," I said. "You pretend to want my opinion but you three Cinderellas didn't even invite me to last night's ball."

"Oh, it was decadent." Ginger clasped my hands. "Riegel knows how to stalk his prey. But we missed you. I insisted Riegel play fetch. Told him we wouldn't do anything without your approval. You're my tiger. Remember? Tiger, tiger burning bright."

"Ignore her, Jason." Dill left the sofa, striding over to the French doors. He motioned to one of the workers outside to reenforce the duct tape. "Ginger's hunting for a husband. Still hoping to make a good marriage."

Ginger picked up the painting, propping the frame atop her pregnancy. Her mountainous belly seemed to fill the entire room. "I could be Jason's bride," she said.

"No," said Dill. "You're not cut out to be a wife. You've no manners. You didn't even offer our guests a glass of water or a place to sit."

Ginger handed the frame to Riegel, the cresting waves in the painting matching the sea outside. "Here's some water," she said to my brother. She perched on the sofa, fanning out her dress's yellow skirt. "Jason, come sit on my lap."

Once he had the painting in hand, Riegel turned to Dill and said, "Let's get this wrapped up, shall we?" Riegel nodded for me to sit with Ginger, then quick-stepped it out of the parlor. Dill followed.

I sat down beside Ginger. She smelled oddly of cigarettes and talcum powder. "How is your mother?" I asked.

"She's very fit. Every morning she goes to the beach. Swims a mile out and a mile back. Dilly keeps hoping she'll catch a riptide and wind up in the Bermuda Triangle."

"And how are you? All of you."

"There is more of me, isn't there?" she said. "I'm like a Russian nesting doll. Want to see something?"

Before I had a chance to answer, Ginger lifted her dress, pulling the soft layers of silk and the crinkly tulle back to reveal the full hemisphere of her ripeness. The belly skin pulled tight, a dark purple line bisecting the middle of her stomach. She had on flesh-colored panties and I could see the bristle of red pubic hair through the nylon. The whole display, the enormous mound of life, struck me as obscene and I was about to tell Ginger to lower her dress, to hide herself, when I saw the outline, first of tiny toes, then of the entire sole of a miniature foot kicking up from inside of her. I flinched.

"There's a baby in there," I said. "For real."

"I'm telling you, Jason"—she pointed to where the foot had been— "I've never felt more alive."

We sat like that for some time before Riegel stomped back in, impatient, jangling his car keys. "We're going to be late," he said, as though we had some pressing appointment.

Dill had disappeared and Ginger escorted us out to the porch, begging me to stay. "We can watch the waves swallow the veranda."

Miriam Thatcher, Roland's widow, appeared on the porch, three groundskeepers trailing behind her like courtiers. When she spoke, her voice carried the sound of a velvet rope being lifted.

"Well, our little mausoleum should be safe enough. The shutters are all latched, the French doors secured, and we sandbagged around the foundation." Miriam removed an impeccably clean pair of suede gauntlets, passed them back to one of the men, then ordered the others to move the rattan deck furniture inside.

The old matriarch was painfully thin, her clavicles jutting out from her pink-and-green paisley dress. My mother always made fun of Miriam's taste in clothing. "She looks like Lilly Pulitzer just threw up on her." Miriam wore her gray-blond hair in a girlish bob. She'd been overseeing the lawn work in handmade Belgian loafers, gold anchors embroidered on the tops of the shoes. Though the mansion was falling down around her, she'd done an impressive job of preserving herself. My mother would have been jealous.

Riegel and I gave perfunctory pecks on cheeks and apologized for having to leave so quickly.

"No," said Miriam. "You're smart to go."

"The house looks great," I said. "Just as I remember it."

"It's been some time since we've seen you boys. The funeral, I imagine. I was so sorry to hear about your parents." Miriam smiled at me. "Please give your mother our best."

I looked at Riegel for some sort of explanation—what was there to hear about our parents? But my brother just skipped down the steps and warmed up the car. I promised Miriam that I would convey her respects to my mother, my tone painfully formal.

Miriam held on to the balustrade, a widow staring out at her harbor. "I imagine your mother's still pining after Roland. But you know"—she turned and looked at me—"those two were never right for each other."

Roland and my mom used to drink rum punch and smoke cigars while I sailed the three of us around Buzzards Bay, the briny sea air mixing with the almond smoke from their Cohibas. Mom called Roland "Bear" and he called her "Goldie." I liked how relaxed Mom was around Roland. How she forgot to fuss over me.

I looked at Miriam and wondered what she missed most about her husband. Just then Dill shot out of the house. I said good-bye to Miriam and walked with Dill over to the Jaguar, the white gravel rough and unsteady beneath our shoes. I noticed the Renoir, wrapped in plastic, tucked behind the front seat.

"Why can't you put it in the trunk?" Dill asked.

"It won't fit," Riegel reassured him.

"At least raise the top." Dill leaned against the Jag and said to Riegel, "Promise me I'm doing the right thing."

Riegel said, "If I'm wrong, you and Ginger can have my scalp."

I was excited for Ginger, glad to have seen her. Holding the remaining tangerine Aidan had given me, I wondered what she might think of Ginger and her giant belly. "What did Miriam mean?" I asked Riegel. "What's there to hear about Mom and Dad?"

"I'm afraid you've mistaken me for someone who listens to nattering old biddies." Riegel's car phone rang again but this time he didn't answer. "We're late," he said. "I know I promised you lunch, but I also need to go to this museum. The Whaling Museum. It's over in New Bedford. My American lit professor insists I check out an exhibit on Melville."

"Melville," I said. "I distinctly remember your taking great pride in being illiterate."

Riegel checked his mirrors and changed lanes. "True. I still find it much easier to critique novels I've never actually read. I enjoy making wild assertions without any accountability."

I thought of Tazewell flinging paperbacks around his dorm room.

"But I'm close to failing this class. If I could, I'd pay some geek to write the paper, but the prick professor makes us turn in all these drafts and pass these oral defenses. I've got to nail down a grade-changing essay on *Moby-Dick*: the whale hunt as metaphor for religious revivalism— whatever that means."

Here was my brother, downgraded to student just when he felt ready to become a captain of industry. Riegel looked over at me and smiled. "Plus, I figured you'd get a kick out of the Whaling Museum. You always loved that high seas stuff. You and Cal were like Ishmael and Queequeg."

From a distance, New Bedford looked as shimmering and prosperous as it must have appeared to Melville when he first set sail from its port for the South Pacific. Once we exited the highway, the downtown revealed itself to be a labyrinth of abandoned factories, condemned mills, empty warehouses with broken windows. We drove by a strip club called Harpoons located right next door to a pet crematorium. New Bedford had seen better days.

I didn't feel like wasting time on dead whales. I held the tangerine up to my face and thought to myself, "I miss Aidan." It wasn't that she'd replaced Cal, but the difference in feeling was that missing Cal had proved useless. He was gone. Missing Aidan gave me hope. If Cal was my past, Aidan was quickly becoming my future. Being away from her for an afternoon made me even more grateful for her friendship and the simple certainty that I could count on seeing her again.

We continued down to the waterfront. The marshy shoreline, littered with rusting ship containers and derelict scallop boats, was more of a junkyard than a harbor. Toxic steam rose off the surf in spectacular mist, blanketing the air with a sulfurous stench, making me wish the convertible's top were drawn closed. We passed a series of fish-processing plants and I wondered what it was like to work inside one of those places, wielding a knife, slicing guts, breathing in the salty fumes. Any fish pulled out of the local waters risked being poisonous.

Riegel couldn't stand the harbor stench either. "What died out there?" He depressed a button, raising the Jaguar's top, then reached across me to the glove box and slipped out a hammered silver flask. He knocked back a long swallow, pulled a pack of Camels from his inside pocket, and lit up a cigarette.

"They say those will kill you." I smiled.

"Here." Riegel tossed me the pack. "Smoke up."

I examined the box, searching along the camel's leg for the subliminal naked man. Cal had shown me this trick, the hidden man's giant erection some sort of incentive to inhale. I tapped a cigarette on the bird's-eye maple and Riegel handed me a lighter, our father's initials engraved in the gold. I didn't even know our dad smoked anything beyond the occasional cigar.

To prove my fraternal loyalty, I'd given Ginger my word that whatever scam Riegel was running wasn't a scam. She wanted to know if I'd met Riegel's boss, Hiro. If he could be trusted.

"So what sort of deal did you work out for Ginger and Dill?" The smoke from the cigarette burned down my throat, setting off a coughing fit. I took a sip from Riegel's flask and spilled rum down my chin.

"You've got a smoking and a drinking problem." Riegel shook his head.

"Seriously." I continued to cough, my voice straining. "I need to know what I just signed off on."

Riegel pulled a toothpick from his pocket and stuck it between his lips. "You ever wonder why people buy art?"

I started to answer when Riegel cut me off and said, "It's all about class. People buy art so they can feel like they've escaped the middle class."

The car filled up with smoke. Riegel cracked the window and explained that he was interested in something called value creation. "Hiro's a computer genius. Works with derivatives, complex financial instruments."

"What's a financial instrument?" I asked. "Like an expensive banjo."

"You're as bad as Dad. He doesn't even understand how computer trading works. He still believes it's a bank's job to make money for its investors." Riegel explained that a derivative was an option. An investment in an opportunity, a scenario, a possible disaster or beneficial outcome. The hedge fund he worked for traded mainly in exotic, not vanilla, derivatives. "We deal in intangibles. The stakes are high but so are the rewards. Hiro gave me the challenge of bringing in new clients. I wanted to help out Ginger and Dill, but those two are cash poor." Riegel detailed how he'd negotiated a special circumstance for Ginger and Dill. "Instead of money, they're investing the Renoir."

I was dubious. "If they need money, why don't they just sell the painting outright?"

"Selling a painting can be expensive. They want to avoid a major tax event. We're using the painting as collateral. It's like I'm turning their Renoir into an ATM. Plus, Hiro's high on sporting a minor masterpiece in his office." Riegel tossed his cigarette butt out the window.

"Can you believe your big brother came up with an unprecedented market opportunity?" Riegel hit the steering wheel, blasting the horn. "Ginger and Dill secure a little financial freedom, Hiro gets his art trophy, and I receive a sweet commission."

"What's my cut?" I asked.

Riegel smiled. "Now you're learning."

The Whaling Museum was housed in an enormous brick building. The main exhibition hall featured the world's largest toy ship, a half-scale model of a whaling bark big enough to climb aboard and explore. The museum had been built around all eighty-nine feet of this black-and-green bark, the three white masts nearly skimming the dome of the vaulted ceiling. A ship in a bottle. A boat in a building. On the bow, the billethead was decorated with dark flares of wood trimmed with golden eagles. I had to hold myself back from clawing up the ratlines on the lookout for imaginary whales. The double top-sail rigging intricately strung with miles and miles of hemp lines and metal chains. Riegel was right to believe that I would enjoy this sort of thing. For the first time in a long while, I felt like a little kid.

In an even more cavernous gallery, two fully articulated whale skeletons flew suspended from the rafters. The yellowing bones a stark constellation against the celestial blue ceiling. I thought of our family's Calder mobiles, those floating metal plates imitating these skeletal remains. From the label signage, I discovered that the whales were a mother North Atlantic Right and her unborn calf. The mother had beached ashore, sick and disoriented. The baby dying inside of her.

I followed Riegel into a painting exhibit. He kept yawning, the purple circles deepening under his eyes. It occurred to me that he needed a nap, that after an evening of dark and stormies, he might not be able to drive me back to school.

"I thought there was some secret to this." Riegel pointed to a series of etchings that depicted the whale hunt from first sighting to harpooning to the flensing.

"What sort of secret?" I asked.

Riegel stood in appraising silence, then said, "I guess I thought there was some trick to capturing a whale, but the whole thing was pretty primitive. The sailors just pulled up in these tiny dinghies and stabbed the whales with their blades. I mean, once you struck with the harpoon the whale could take off, could drag an entire boatload of men down." Riegel nodded to an oil painting of a whale doing just that. "There was no secret, no special technique. Why would anyone sign on to do this?" Riegel asked. "To take that sort of risk?"

"For the payday," I said.

Riegel nodded, money a language he understood. He tapped the front of a glass case. "Check it out."

Behind the glass, mounted on a simple black frame, was a ship's log, a registry of all the sailors who had boarded the *Acushnet* on January 3, 1841. There in the middle of the page was the name and signature, "Herman Melville." He would later jump ship in the Marquesas, wind up living with a tribe of cannibals. The museum's brochure mentioned that Melville was born into a rich family but became downwardly mobile and died penniless and forgotten. Seeing his name on the ship's registry touched me, made me want to round Cape Horn in his honor. I would take Aidan sailing. Teach her about the water.

Riegel whispered, "I heard Melville was a queer. That he wrote *Billy Budd* for some dude he wanted to screw." Riegel strolled off, then turned on his heels and said, "I'll be in the gift shop."

I took my time. Studied every whale's tooth. Learned about spermaceti, that it wasn't sperm at all but rather this crazy wax found in the whale's head that was used to make candles and lipsticks. Then there was the ambergris—whale shit or vomit used to scent the kind of fancy perfumes my mother always bought in Paris. I wasn't going to leave that museum until I felt like an expert.

It's possible that I would have made Riegel wait for hours, but a security guard approached and told me that the museum would be closing early.

"It's storming something fierce," he said. "You ought to get on home."

I found Riegel in the fetal position on a bench outside the gift shop. If he had happened upon me asleep and defenseless, he would have stirred me awake with a wet willy, licking his finger and sliding it inside my ear. I tapped the bottom of his shoe and he startled.

"There's thunder and lightning," I said.

Riegel claimed that he was merely resting his eyes. He got up and the two of us began to walk down a marble corridor and out of the museum. Just as we were about to exit, Riegel turned around, ran back to the bench, and picked up a brown shopping bag. "Here," he said to me. "Belated birthday present. Open it later. Happy eighteenth. I promise this will be the best year of your life."

Maybe Riegel was a little hungover or simply tired, but just like my father had on our way to Bellingham, Riegel gave me the gift of driving his car. The Jag took the slick corners like it was on rails, and I couldn't imagine piloting another vehicle and loving it the same way. By the time we neared school it was evening and a true darkness had descended, and not just with the setting sun and the hurricane sky. Riegel's mood had turned. He kept dialing phone numbers on the car phone and grew frustrated over being unable to connect to anyone.

I said, "I thought that thing was the future."

"Yeah, well," Riegel said, "the future is full of things that don't work." He rubbed his neck and said, "I still have a long night ahead of me." Riegel sniffed at his own underarms. "Wish I'd brought a change of clothes. I too reek of seagulls and malfeasance."

We neared the exit for the town of Bellinghem and Riegel cleared his throat. "Sorry we didn't make it out to lunch or dinner, even, but look, here's the thing," he said. "Dad's been living at the St. Regis."

"Like the hotel? Why would he be doing that?"

"I know," Riegel said. "If Mom kicked me out, I'd stay at the Plaza."

I wanted to understand if what my brother was telling me was a temporary matter or something serious, something I needed to worry about.

"They're separated for now," he said. "Mom wants a divorce and Dad seems willing to give her what she wants."

"Are you kidding me?"

"I hate to tell you this on an empty stomach, but you and I need to protect our interests."

"What interests?"

"I've seen a lot of kids get fucked over by their parents' divorces. I'm insisting one of them keep the penthouse. You better be sure there's money in place to pay for your college."

It didn't make any sense that I was hearing this news from my brother or that he would be so focused on giving me the kind of information and advice I didn't want. I nearly missed the exit and Riegel had to yell at me to turn.

"Why are you the one telling me this?" I gripped the wheel and signaled, barely making the off-ramp.

"Mom and Dad felt it would be best if I broke it to you. They wanted me to reassure you that their separation has nothing to do with you or what you've put them through."

Nothing to do with me. What I've put them through. I didn't respond. Despite the rain, I'd been driving pretty fast on the highway, the speed obscuring the sounds around me. Now that I was on the surface streets, I slowed and could hear the tight traction of the Jag's wheels on the wet road. The rain drilled the soft car top. The windshield wipers strained. The entire car had filled with a thick cloud of humidity. I could barely breathe.

"You're probably going to hear gossip," Riegel said. "Divorce news travels fast. Ignore it like you did that stuff with Cal."

"What 'stuff' with Cal?"

"Look, I never believed any of it, but you must have known what people were saying."

Just ahead of us, I saw a police car's flashing red and blue lights. A row of white sawhorses gleaming with orange reflectors barricaded the road.

"Shit," Riegel said.

I slowed, stopped, and waited. A police officer approached the car and I opened the window prepared to hear the obvious: "The road's blocked." The cop wore a vinyl rain poncho and what looked like a plastic shower cap over his hat. His thick mustache drenched with rain. "Where are you headed?" he asked.

"My little brother's a student at Bellingham." Riegel tapped me on the shoulder like I was his property.

Right there, in front of the cop, I wanted to punch my brother in the jaw. Wanted to be arrested, to be found guilty. I still had a lot to say to Riegel. I couldn't believe that he had waited all day to give me the news of our parents' divorce. That Miriam Thatcher knew before I did. Couldn't believe that he had dragged me around on his errands. That he'd had the nerve to bring up Cal.

"What do you want to do?" Riegel asked. "Still want to go to your friend's house?"

I'd forgotten about Race's party. The idea of getting high on someone else's dime sounded like the right and necessary medicine.

With a little too much hopefulness in my voice, I asked the cop, "Could you drive me out to Powder Point?"

"The causeway's flooded," he said. "The only way out there is by boat."

I nodded at the police officer. "How close can you get me to school?"

"Some trees are down, power lines too, but I know the back roads. I can drive up near the dorms."

I agreed to go with the cop, then rolled up the window to say good-bye to Riegel. "Will you be okay?" I asked.

"I'll either fall asleep at the wheel or I'll be fine," he said. "Don't have to make it all the way to Princeton. I can stop in the city. Check up on Mom."

"Maybe I should go with you."

Riegel blinked, and I understood that he had other plans in the city. If he made it home, it would be late and consoling Mom wouldn't be his first priority. I took a long look at my brother and saw something of my own future in his tired face.

"You know that girl I introduced you to this morning," I said. "She's my girlfriend. Her name's Aidan. She's from California. You can tell Mom all about her."

"Mom will like that." He smiled.

In order to change seats, Riegel had to slip out of the car and into the rain. I remembered the gift he'd given me and reached over to the backseat to grab the bag. Then I saw Aidan's tangerine still untouched and tucked it into the bag as well. I waved good-bye to the Renoir.

The officer insisted I sit up front. "No tossing you in the back. Don't want anyone to see you and get the wrong idea."

In the brief run to the car, I'd managed to get myself drenched. I felt the upholstery soak up the water. With his thick mustache and relaxed demeanor, the cop resembled the television actor Tom Selleck. I caught myself about to hum the theme from *Magnum P.I.*

"My name's Jason." I rubbed my hands in front of the heater. "Thanks for helping me out. I appreciate it."

"Officer Hardy." He had a strong nasal accent and emphasized his *a*'s and *r*'s as though the two letters were unhappily married. He began to drive, turning down a dirt road I'd never noticed before, shooting out into the woods. Branches smacked and scraped the windows and sides of the car.

I lost all sense of where we were. I asked Hardy if he was from Bellinghem. He nodded. His silence made me nervous. I found myself jabbering on. "You must get sick of us preppies invading your town. Bet it's a relief when we leave for the summer. Bet you'd get a kick out of tossing us all in the clink."

"Actually," Hardy said, "I'm a fellow SeaWolf. Class of '72."

"Really?" I knew I sounded surprised and felt shitty for what my tone implied.

Hardy picked up on it. "Yeah. And for the record, I don't enjoy arresting anyone."

"Town and gown," I said.

Hardy looked me over. "You must be a city kid."

I told him that I was indeed from New York and then, just to hear myself say it and to make Hardy feel a little sorry for me, I told him that my parents were divorcing. "My brother dropped it on me like it was nothing. I feel bad for my mom. My dad's a whole other story."

"Divorce is always hardest on the kids." Hardy turned around an impossibly sharp hairpin curve.

I asked Hardy if he had any children, and he nodded. Then, maybe realizing that his silence could be mistaken for meanness, he said, "I have a son. He lives in Providence. With his mother."

We came out of the woods and onto a service road that ran behind the infirmary. Hardy got a call on his police radio. He answered, speaking in numbers and code.

When he got off the radio, he said, "Every wannabe sailor is calling for his hourly update. Like I'm supposed to Navy SEAL my ass out to the harbor just to see if some cabin cruiser is taking on water." Hardy stopped the car on the road near Whitehall. "Here." He gave me a cellophane rain poncho. "I know you're already wet, but this should protect you out there. Be careful. Look out for power lines and go right straight to your dorm. And one more thing." He stared down at me. "Don't blame yourself for your parents' mistakes."

I shook his hand and thanked him.

"Tell Windsor I took good care of you," he said. "Tell him he owes me one."

Even though I wanted to see Aidan, wanted to tell her about my day and have her make sense of it for me, I took Officer Hardy's advice and set out directly for Whitehall. I merely had to cross the street and cut through the lawn, but the rain, salty and frigid, lashed out from every direction, piercing my skin, blinding my sight, the darkness impenetrable. Nothing was illuminated—no streetlights, no lamplight in the dorms. The only brightness flickered from the whitecaps on the waves. The plastic poncho Hardy had given me suctioned tight against my clammy skin, sealing in the water. My Tretorns sank down in the lawn mired in muddy turf. As I neared the harbor, the wind walled itself off, the gale pushing me back. I felt vulnerable, exposed to the raw elements. Every step was awful, dangerous. I loved it. For a moment, I imagined myself on some soldier's mission, clutching the soggy paper bag close to my chest like it contained top secret instructions. I hollered into the night, channeling my own hurricane, howling my anger. The storm still intensifying. The eye, the central calm, yet to pass.

A dead quiet hung over the dorm. Someone, probably Coach Tripp, had lit a row of stubby candles in red glass holders and placed them on a coffee table in the entryway. I grabbed one and fumbled my way upstairs and to my room.

I needed to do a lot of things. Needed to get out of my wet clothes, needed to take a hot shower, needed to call my mom, needed something to eat, needed to find out what Riegel had given me as a present. The pay phone in the hallway had no dial tone. Mom would have to wait. I hadn't spoken to her in days, and I wondered if she knew about the storm, if she was worried. My stomach growled, though I hardly needed any reminding that I was starving. It was after eight, the dining hall long closed. I thought the tangerine would upset my already upset stomach. I tapped on a few doors in search of food or company, but no one answered. My best option seemed to be the shower. Even with the power outage there had to be some last supply of hot water on reserve. As I stripped off my sopping-wet clothes, I had to contain my envy at the thought of Tazewell and Race smoking premium pot and goofing around. Then, like a bolt, it occurred to me that I had nearly a dozen miniature bottles of whiskey hidden away in my dopp kit. I opened the top drawer to my bureau and felt for the mesh case until I found a small glass bottle. Twisting the narrow cap open, I pursed my lips around the glass neck and let the warm liquor strike the shivering cold from me.

At Bellingham, if you wanted to jerk off, you didn't do it in your own room. There were no locks on the doors and ever since Skinner had been caught choking it, guys were air raiding rooms, swinging open doors, and snapping Polaroids. If you wanted to beat off, you did so in the shower stall the farthest away from the entrance. The Alcove, I heard Kriffo call it. The Alcove was just an open stall raised up and tucked behind the other curtained showers. It was an unspoken rule in a world of negligible decorum that once the water in the Alcove was turned on, the luxury of privacy was guaranteed. Socially sanctioned masturbation. Anyone who sneaked back to the Alcove while the shower was occupied was instantly dubbed a perv, a peeper, and was subject to a different kind of beating.

The other benefit of the Alcove was that it smelled relatively clean. The constant stink of mildew and shit hung over the other showers no matter the time of day, but the bathroom was especially offensive in the mornings and late evenings. Kriffo would come back from breakfast or dinner and take these nuclear waste craps. I once heard Yazid Yazid stand at the sink and complain, "Morning and night, Kriffo shits on my toothbrush."

I called out "Hello," my voice reverberating off the tiled walls. No one was in the bathroom. I'd left the red candle burning on my dresser and had to paw around for a place to put my towel. Once I made my way to the Alcove, I turned on the faucet and leaned into the hot spray of water. I didn't have any soap or shampoo, but I didn't want to get clean, just wanted to soak under the steam long enough to warm up and maybe a little longer to get off. My body ached. I felt a surge of tension that needed release and so I began stroking myself, quick to get hard, aware that this was the last sure pleasure I could give my body. I thought back to this morning, of Aidan leaning down and of Riegel staring at her breasts. Thought of what had happened with Aidan last night, how long ago it now seemed, how unprepared I was to deal. I'd actually told her the truth about Cal and why he'd killed himself.

Aidan probably figured I'd blown her off, left for Race's without checking in, and I was mad at myself for not going straight to see her. I tried to picture what she looked like at that moment. Saw her in a white nightgown slick with rain, the cotton and lace plastered against her body. Felt myself grow harder still. Then I began to hear a strange but familiar electronic music, the percussive beats sound tracking through my head. The theme from *Magnum P.I.* I held on to the picture of Aidan's nearly naked body, but other images strobed through my imagination joining Aidan. First Tom Selleck in a Hawaiian shirt. Then Officer Hardy holding a pineapple. They were joined by Magnum's buddies: the black helicopter pilot and the ugly sidekick with the Brillo hair. Finally, I saw the old guy on the TV show, the one with the British accent. Higgins. Saw a close-up of his mustache, his mouth puffing on a giant cigar. The more I tried to get rid of this Higgins, the more alive he became, and then suddenly he was speaking to me, saying, "Do it, old chap. Rub one out." I came loudly, my chest heaving.

Cal had loved that stupid show. I needed more whiskey.

I hadn't heard Chester Baldwin come into the bathroom, but when I left the shower, he was there brushing his teeth. A flashlight on the sink's counter beaming up at the ceiling.

"Hey," I said. "Thought you were playing DJ at Race's party."

Chester spat into the sink. "What?" he asked.

"Race's party," I said. "Isn't that why the dorm's empty?"

"I wouldn't know." Chester took a swig from a bottle of mouth-wash.

I decided to ask Chester if he had any food in his room. "Bet your mom sends you care packages."

"As a matter of fact," he said, "I have a box of homemade cookies. They're delicious. I'd be a fool to share them."

I said, "No need to be abrasive."

Hungry and defeated, I went back to my room. I stood naked in front of the window watching the storm, the bracelet Tazewell had braided for me the only thing on my body. The water had tightened the knot-ted rope, and as I tried to loosen it a little, I realized that the only way I'd ever get that bracelet off would be to cut it from my wrist. I pulled on a pair of pajama bottoms, sleepy from the shower. Cal claimed that jerking off made him more awake, more alert, but the minute I came I felt sapped of all my strength. Defenseless like Samson. I was already under the covers when I heard a knock and saw Chester appear in the doorway. "Here." He held out a metal cookie tin, then placed it at the foot of my bed. "There are some oatmeal raisin and peanut butter sand-ies. I ate all the brownies." Chester was about to leave when I asked him to sit down.

"I've got some whiskey if you're interested." I slipped out of bed and gave him one of the tiny bottles.

Chester held up his flashlight and laughed. "Thought you'd pull out some single malt. Not these airplane freebies." Chester handed back the bottle, reminding me that he was an athlete in training.

I was impressed by his restraint.

"Whiskey and cookies," I said. "The perfect snack treats." The cookies were salty and buttery. They should have been savored, but like a pig I scarfed down half the tin, crumbs scattering over my bare chest. I opened another bottle of Jim Beam.

Chester narrowed himself along the foot of my bed, leaning his back against the wall, his long calves spilling over the lip of the mat-tress. He was tall and slender but muscular. Most tennis players over-worked their upper bodies, but Chester was perfectly proportioned.

His legs as strong as his arms. I could hear him breathing, could smell the cinnamon from his mouthwash. In history class I often sat near Chester, staring at his profile, surprised by his seriousness. He looked like the kind of guy who'd read all of the books in the library and found most of them wanting. He had closely cropped hair and high cheekbones, but he also had these long curly eyelashes that made him seem delicate, childlike. The one physical detail that might have detracted from Chester's appearance was an odd scar on his jawline, a coin-sized patch of skin that bubbled up like a blister. He was always holding his fingers over it, concealing the scar. Sitting alone together, I nearly reached out and touched that patch of skin. Curious whether it was rough or tender.

I asked Chester how he'd been, and he told me that he'd gone undefeated in all of his tennis matches. "Haven't dropped a set all season."

Chester was a rarity, one of the few students who'd come to Bellingham on their own accord. The tennis team was highly ranked, Chester the star. "I should come out and watch you. Learn from the master."

"You could do that," he said. "Listen to the wind. It's whistling graveyards out there."

Outside, the hurricane rattled and raged. Earlier, I'd heard a windowpane somewhere in the dorm blow out and shatter. Chester held his flashlight up under his chin. "Got a question for you. Is it true . . ." He paused, considering whether or not he should ask me, then asked me, "Is it true that Race almost bought it on your watch?"

"I fucked up," I said. "But I also saved him."

"Too bad." Chester drummed his fingers over the lid of the cookie tin. "Was there a moment," he asked, "when you thought to just let him drown?"

With Race's accident, I'd relied on instinct. There was no thought of right or wrong. My actions all part of some survival mechanism, as though my own will to live had been redirected toward keeping Race alive. I told Chester, "I can't bear to see anyone in pain."

"My dad, he's a judge, he once had to witness an execution. Mom says Dad didn't speak for like a week afterward." Chester paused.

"Sorry to get all morbid," he apologized. "Must be because the power's out. All this darkness descending. Ever find that there are things you can do or say at night that you couldn't manage during the day?"

"I guess so." I sank my head back onto my pillow and stared at the red-glassed candle. Red navigation lights were supposed to prevent night blindness. A long time had passed since I'd sailed through darkness, and though it was dangerous to sail or even be anchored during a storm, I knew that on a night like tonight Cal would have convinced me to go out on the heavy seas. That he would have placed us both squarely in harm's way.

"Do you play chess?" Chester asked.

"I know how the pieces move but I wouldn't say I'm any good."

"I could teach you." Chester smiled.

"Chess with Chester." I was officially drunk, slurring my words.

"Been looking for someone to match wits against. You seem like a worthy opponent." Chester took an oatmeal cookie from the tin. "You know who's actually got skills? Diana. She and I used to play."

Chester looked down and away from me. He and Diana were similar. Both guarded and private about their loneliness. I assumed Chester and Di had done more than move bishops and rooks. I said, "Diana's the original queen."

Chester laughed, flicking his flashlight off and on. "That girl wore me out."

"What do you mean?"

"I did everything right with Diana, and it didn't matter." Chester swung the bright beam around the room like his own anxious searchlight. "My mom says it's my fault for caring. She always tells me, 'If you hug a lamppost, you can't blame the lamppost if it doesn't hug you back.'"

Once the cookie tin was empty, Chester rubbed his eyes. "You still think I'm, what's the word you used? Abrasive?" Chester laughed. "Where'd you get a word like that? From your grandma?"

It was Cal's word. He'd used it in all of his nonsense sentences, but he'd also used it to describe my skin after a week without shaving. He'd rubbed his hands against my cheek and told me he liked how the roughness felt against his own skin. Weeks later, he'd used the same word to describe how cruel I'd become.

"Look," I said. "I'm sorry."

Chester got up to leave, and I was sad to see him go. Though I'd done little in all these months to reach out for any sort of friendship, though I didn't deserve access to his mother's recipes and care, Chester had gone out of his way to make everything comfortable between us, easy, even. I wasn't sure how to show my gratitude.

"Thank you," I said.

"Do you hear that?" Chester asked.

The weather had gone quiet. I ran over to the fire escape, threw open the window, and motioned for Chester to climb out onto the wet railing. The breeze outside was calm, the rain had stopped, and the air smelled cleanly of night.

"Is it over?" Chester asked.

"No. It's the eye. We're right in the center of the storm."

NINE

Sunday morning I slept late. When I finally woke, my head felt like someone had wrapped a thick, wet flannel blanket around my skull and squeezed tightly. My body achy, my mouth cottony, my sheets and skin itchy from cookie crumbs. The bed was littered with empty whiskey bottles, and I lurched over to my bureau to hide the evidence. I flipped a light switch. Nothing happened. The power was still out.

Opening my windows, I could tell that it was a brilliant day. Hot and sunny as though the storm had scrubbed the sky a deep blue, washing away the clouds, carrying off the seabirds. I left Whitehall curious to survey the storm damage, hoping I'd run into Aidan.

The ground floor of the dorm was flooded with several inches of standing water. I slipped off my shoes, rolled up my khakis, and sloshed through.

Outside, the storm surge had pushed the ocean up beyond the seawall and onto campus. The waters had yet to recede. A moat of rain and ocean puddled around the dorm. I kept my shoes off as I waded into the swampy lake. A school of thin speckled fish, probably cod, floated belly up on the surface. Similar moats of standing water encircled nearly all of the buildings along the harbor. Poseidon had struck his trident, summoning his flood, turning Bellingham into a temporary Atlantis. The destruction blatant and impressive.

By the Athletic Center a grove of pitch pines had dominoed across the parking lot, obstructing entry to the gym. A once soaring silver oak had timbered, crushing a fleet of sports vans. Swirling winds must have sheared off the top of a red cedar, leaving just a few branches of juniper needles. The rickety roof of the Old Boathouse had survived and still proudly exclaimed CLASS OF '88, but the Barracuda had lost its sharpest glass-and-metal fin. The glass reduced to shards and the steel frame twisted as though a shark had taken a bite out of our Barracuda. Everywhere I looked I saw shingles, roof tarpaper, windscreens, leaves, and debris. What I thought were dozens of trash bags scattered across the road turned out to be knotted clumps of brown seaweed. No one had bothered to take down the American flag and the canvas flapped, its frayed edges in tatters, the flagpole bent several degrees off its foundation.

Saddest of all, the Swan, Aidan's and my hideout, had been driven hard against the seawall. The storm surge had smashed the baby yacht, towing it wildly along the embankment, ripping a large gash in its red hull. A pile-up of lesser yachts had pinned the Swan against the seawall, forcing the Swan upright, vertical on its transom. A whale at the summit of its breach.

I figured that the dining hall might be closed for business, but I knew the school had to find a way to feed us. I jogged over to Astor to check things out. The closer I got, the more noise I heard. Someone in Wee House, the boys' freshman and sophomore dorm, had propped a boom box inside an open window and was using all of its battery power to blast Bob Marley's *Legend*. The groove for "Could You Be Loved" started up: *"Don't let them fool ya, or even try to school ya."* Cal had this theory that all dorm room windows were programmed to play Bob Marley's greatest hits.

The front lawn of Astor had been staged as a kind of storm relief center. Cafeteria workers grilled hot dogs and burgers on an assembly line of outdoor grills while students waited to be fed. It looked a little like a carnival set in the middle of a catastrophe. Raleigh Windsor bustled around in boat shoes barking orders at anyone who would listen. Four gleaming black armored bulldozers stood at the ready, YAZID YAZID TRACTOR decaled in red letters with golden Arabic scrawled underneath. Prince Yaz held court in the open cab of a minidozer showing Brizzey and Nadia the controls. Across the street at the headmaster's house, a pair of large striving elms had uprooted much of the lawn, revealing a complex, gnarled root system. Yazid's machinery was about to come in handy.

I shouted up to Yazid, "You know how to work that thing?"

He waved back. "I'm dangerous with a lorry."

On my way to grab some food, it occurred to me that I should ask Nadia to hunt down Aidan. Though rules were pretty lax at Bellingham, for a guy it wasn't always easy to see a girl right when you wanted to see her. With Aidan I'd come to rely on habit and prearrangement. In daylight, I couldn't just saunter up to her room, but I could put out the word that I hoped to meet up with her.

I went back and motioned for Nadia to climb down from the tractor's cab. Brizzey smacked her lips and asked, "Why so bossy?"

I ignored her.

Nadia's hair fell over her face in stringy bangs—a failed attempt to conceal a blister of acne on her forehead. She had on cutoff jeans and a red-and-white-checkered cowboy shirt, the kind with snaps, the kind that could be flashed open with the flick of a wrist. We hadn't really spoken since her drunken night and I wasn't even sure how much she remembered. She looked up at me expectant, smudges of black eyeliner drawn under her lids. Brizzey had the same thick lines drawn under her own eyes.

"Do me a favor, when you go upstairs," I said. "Tell Aidan I want to see her."

Nadia blinked. In her Southern drawl she said, "But I'm right here. Don't you want to see me?"

I guessed that Nadia was attempting to flirt with me. The ends of her shirt were tied in a knot at her waist and I could see the milky skin of her belly. "I'm like better now," she said.

I wasn't sure what Nadia meant or how I was supposed to respond.

She fixed her bangs, flattening the hair over her forehead, covering her zits. "I can hold my liquor a lot better. Peach schnapps and orange juice, that's my new drink. Just thought you should know." Nadia swung back up onto the bulldozer full of bluster.

She'd clearly been studying Brizzey. There must have been a lot of pressure for the girls at Bellingham to pigeonhole themselves. To be the smart girl or the slutty girl or the girl who could hold her liquor. To remake oneself in other people's image, trying on new masks just to see if they fit.

The cafeteria had emptied its refrigerators. Sausages, burgers, and chicken breasts sizzled on the barbecue grills, white coals smoking from the grease. Bowls of pasta salads sweated in the sun. The day was turning into a street fair. I ate a cheeseburger while waiting on line for something to drink. Leo, whom I no longer thought of as Plague, busied himself refilling carafes of red bug juice. I smiled and nodded and was surprised when he turned his back and ignored me. Leo must have thought twice about his snub, because as I walked away with my drink and lunch, I heard him shout my name.

"Jason," he said, running after me. "Got a question for you."

Just as I turned to speak with Leo, Tazewell, his eyes pink, his hair a dreadlocked mess of shaggy blond, appeared at my side. He looked like a Viking with a hangover. Taze snapped his fingers and told Leo to fuck off. I nodded to Leo, hoping he'd understand. Trading one snub for another.

Tazewell wore a tight blue R.E.M. concert T-shirt. I could hear Michael Stipe's plaintive wail. Stipe sang like a man in need of someone's arms around him.

I said, "I'm impressed you like those guys."

"My favorite band," Taze said. "Have you heard their new album? Fucking inspired." Tazewell promised to play some songs for me later.

Kriffo stumbled by in a large white tent of a shirt with the question WHO'S THAT GIRL? printed on his chest in purple pastel script. Before I had a chance to ask, Kriffo explained in his soft voice, "My housekeeper went to a Madonna concert. As a joke, I told her to get me a T-shirt. Had to pay her sixty bucks for this thing."

"Guess the joke was on you," I said.

"We should go see the Butthole Surfers," Tazewell said. "We'll buy a T-shirt for your housekeeper and make her pony up some cash." Tazewell snatched the burger from my plate. "We've been deputized." He took a bite, chewing and speaking. "Jason, you want to go play hero?"

Raleigh Windsor, in his reckless wisdom, had decided that it would be okay to allow Yazid to tool around campus in his father's shiny black machine. Tazewell wanted to join in the fun and asked to ride along.

"Why don't you boys help clean up some of this debris." Windsor ordered the groundskeepers to use the other tractors but gave Yazid the green light to help out any way he saw fit.

Yazid didn't have the requisite skills for operating the tractor's controls, but it didn't stop him from driving all of us over to the Athletic Center. Taze, Kriffo, and I rode on the footboard of the tractor, balancing and holding on like we were circus acrobats. We set our sights on removing the pitch pines from in front of the blocked entrance. Yazid had a clawlike device on the back of his tractor, a "ripper," he called it, and demonstrated how it worked, attacking the trees, shoveling them off the ground and piling them over onto the middle of the parking lot, digging up the asphalt in the process. When it was my turn, I sat up in the dozer's captain's chair, the open cab rumbling and bucking as I practiced shifting backward and forward, then finally pushing the blade on the bulldozer through the needles and branches, the gasoline exhaust mixing with the fresh fragrance of pine. Once the entrance was unblocked, Tazewell disappeared inside the Athletic Center.

Since there wasn't much room on Yazid's bulldozer, Stuyvie had been forced to drive over in a green golf cart. He had on a Bellingham polo shirt and was pretending to be in charge. "We can't just leave the trees in the parking lot." Stuyvie stood with his hands on his hips. "Windsor wouldn't like it and neither would my dad."

Yazid and Kriffo jumped off the bulldozer. Stuyvie had turned their fun into a chore. Yazid and Kriffo weren't interested in actual manual labor. Playing with the dozers ceased being fun.

The Athletic Center's double doors flashed open and Tazewell busted through dressed in a vintage leather football helmet and shoulder pads. I recognized the gear from one of the trophy cases that lined the gym's hallway. The helmet and pads had been worn in some long-ago Bellingham championship. Tazewell tossed an old pigskin in the air.

"Enough with the groundskeeping. Let's play hurricane ball." Taze snapped the football to Kriffo, then led us all into the dark Athletic Center.

Light streamed in from the high windows. The building smelled of bleach and ripe teenage bodies. I felt the wreckage of sharp broken glass under my feet.

"Found these cases smashed," Tazewell said. "The wind pressure from the storm must have done it. Might as well take advantage."

Several trophy cases had been shattered open. Silver bowls and bronze cups tipped on their sides. The wind an unlikely perpetrator. I imagined Taze was probably to blame.

The trophy cases held retired jerseys from nearly every decade. Taze wanted to play football but he didn't want to get his R.E.M. T-shirt dirty. He was too lazy to walk back to the dorm and change. "Pick out your own gear," Taze ordered.

Once dressed, we looked like a time line of football history. Tazewell modeled an old-school Walter Camp lace-up blouse. Kriffo was all Knute Rockne in his knitted wool sweater, a gold Bellingham "B" budding on his chest. Short and stocky, every shirt Stuyvie put on was too big. "You look like that Hail Mary midget, Doug Flutie," Kriffo snarked. Though he claimed never to have seen a game, Yazid donned a classic maroon silk jersey and threw perfect spirals channeling the golden arm of Johnny Unitas. And me, in my polyester vest, I wanted to be Joe Montana talking trash and delivering the goods.

Back outside, Tazewell split us up into teams. "Me and Kriffo against Jason and Yazid."

"What about me?" Stuyvie asked.

I noticed that Stuyvie had a trail of scratches along his left cheek, as though a cat had swiped his face.

"You can referee." Kriffo laughed.

"Touch or tackle?" Stuyvie asked. "What are the rules?"

"There are no rules."

That about summed up our afternoon. Our friendly game of touch turned quickly into a high-stakes war of tackle. The four of us carved up the wet turf into rough zigzagged furrows, doing more damage than any storm could have imagined. We played full force, drilling the ball, talking smack, shouting "ass clown" and "d-bag." Every time Stuyvie made a call against us, Yazid instructed Stuyvie to "Unfuck yourself."

"What does that even mean?" Stuyvie finally asked.

"Americans are born stupid," Yazid said. "You tell one another to go fuck yourselves like that's a bad thing. Most people enjoy fucking themselves."

"I dig it," Tazewell said. "But then I have dual citizenship."

Though all of us were primed to unfuck one another, it turned out that hurricane ball was my game. After making the first touchdown for either side, I fielded an interception and scored once again. When Kriffo finally caught a pass and raced toward the goal line, I galloped toward him, dove, and grabbed his knees. The giant fell, blasting the earth, spraying mud. For just a brief moment, I held Kriffo's legs, warm and pulsing beneath me. Felt my strength connected to his defeat.

"Prosper nailed you," Stuyvie hooted. "I've never seen anyone take the Big Man down."

That was all Kriffo needed to hear. He stayed on me for the rest of the game. Bearing down. Riding me hard. Throwing elbows and stiff arms, taunting me in his little-girl voice. Calling me his bitch. I told him that I dreamed about being his bitch, then sprinted down the field, jumped up, and cradled one of Yazid's long bombs. I was faster than Kriffo. He couldn't catch me, couldn't tackle me.

Tazewell decided to cover me instead. I ran a bootleg on a fake to Yazid only to have Taze blitz. Hoping to save the play, I tossed a lateral to Prince Yaz right before Taze swept my legs, sending me flying. As I landed on my back, my jaw snapped down and I bit my tongue. The blood salty in my mouth. For a moment, I couldn't feel my arms.

I stayed on the grass, spitting blood, until Kriffo came over and offered me his hand. He pulled me up, then reached down and tapped my sack. I doubled over. "Just making sure you didn't lose your balls." Kriffo smiled.

I smiled back.

When Riegel claimed that there had been rumors about Cal and me, I began to fear for my future. I was afraid that Tazewell had heard the gossip and was waiting to spring some charge or accusation. The minute Kriffo swatted my balls, I stopped worrying. There was no way someone like Kriffo would touch another guy if he suspected the dude was anything other than straight.

It was always weird to me that guys played grab ass or snapped towels in the shower as a way of saying hello. Tapping testicles struck me as just plain creepy. But here was the funny thing: Right after Kriffo helped me to my feet, I noticed a bulge in his shorts. Kriffo had an erection. Watching Tazewell tackle me had done something to him. Though I briefly considered taunting him, no one said a word as Kriffo reached down into his pants to calm his excitement.

Finally Yazid broke the silence and asked, "Who's winning?"

The anarchy of the day took my mind off of my parents and their troubles. I was grateful for this, happy to be raising hell with my friends. This was a raw physical kind of pleasure, the kind I hadn't experienced in ages. Not since Cal and I had ripped up the golf course at Kensington with his stolen Triumph. The only thing that might have bothered me at that moment was if Aidan had seen me. Allowing myself to have a good time with these guys made me feel like I was betraying her somehow. I planned on keeping our scrimmage a secret.

After a particularly brutal hit from Kriffo, Yazid called it quits. His woolly hair a crown of wild spirals. Stuyvie had done a shitty job of keeping score and no one could agree on a winner.

"What should we do with the tractor?" Stuyvie asked.

"Just leave it. I'm sure someone will clean up the mess." Yazid saluted us good-bye.

"But I never got my turn to drive one." Stuyvie ran his hand along the tractor's body, tracing the gold Arabic letters.

We watched Yazid walk off, his stolen jersey tossed over his shoulder.

"I don't get it," Tazewell said. "How do you make a fortune off of tractors? Are there like lots of farms in Saudi Arabia?"

I said, "There's lots of sand and oil."

"So?" said Kriffo.

"So," I said, "you've got to move a lot of sand to get to that oil."

We weren't sure what to do with the dirty jerseys and were going to abandon them on the field when Stuyvie offered to put them in his family's wash and sneak them back into the trophy case. Stuyvie and I seemed to be the only two concerned about the broken glass in the Athletic Center, the messy pile of tree branches, and the torn-up asphalt in the parking lot.

Walking back to Whitehall, I asked Tazewell and Kriffo about Race's party, whether it had been a memorable blowout.

"Not especially." Taze stuck a finger in his ear and dug around. "It was kind of lame, if you want the truth. Not much of a turnout. A lot of kids went home yesterday. Guess their parents were worried about the storm." He pulled his finger out of his ear wiped his nail on Kriffo's arm.

Kriffo reacted quickly, smearing mud on Tazewell's back. The two began to tussle, slapping each other. They'd perfected this kind of mock-violence, playful, almost friendly.

"Was Race pissed I didn't come?"

"He definitely noticed you weren't there." Taze gave Kriffo one last slap.

"I had this family thing I had to do and it took longer than I expected." I was disappointed but relieved that no one really seemed to care about my absence.

Kriffo asked, "Think we'll have classes tomorrow?"

Stuyvie came scampering up behind us. "No way," he said. "My dad told me we won't have classes until the power comes back on and even then it will take awhile for things to get back to normal."

The power wouldn't be restored until early Thursday morning, but by Tuesday night phone service was back and I waited in the hallway for a chance to dial my mother on the pay phone. I had zero interest in calling Dad, but I wanted Mom to know that I was all right. I needed to find out how she was handling the divorce. "Would you like me to come home?" I asked.

"Yes. Return to me so we can run away together."

I played along. "Where should we escape to?"

"The islands. Dominica, Martinique, St. Lucia," Mom said. "You can sail us into Marigot Bay. Like Doctor Doolittle on his giant pink snail."

"Dad will go crazy," I said.

"Your father's busy hiding his assets. Silly man. In St. Lucia, we can visit our cacao plantation."

"We own a plantation?"

"*I* own a plantation. Don't tell your father." Mom described the rain forest in St. Lucia. The smell of cacao being roasted and ground into chocolate. "Real chocolate isn't sweet. Most people don't know that, but then again most people don't know anything. My grandfather left me the farm. Among other treasures."

I asked Mom how Max was doing. "Max who?" she asked.

"Max, our doorman."

"Which one is he? Is he the chubby one, or is that Freddy?"

My mother called all of the doormen in our building Freddy. None of the doormen in our building were named Freddy. "You like Max," I said. "He's your favorite. You should date Max and make Dad jealous."

"You may be joking, but come Christmas, those doormen make a king's ransom in tips. I'm sure Max could keep us all afloat."

Mom and I plotted our escape to the Caribbean. She waxed on about the turquoise waters and coral beaches. We both preferred the pink sand to the rough black volcanic rocks. I told her a story about Cal. Once when we were sailing, Cal asked me why the water didn't stay light blue when he cupped it in his hands. "It gets all clear. The blue just goes away." It was the kind of question a child would ask. Cal must have been fifteen at the time, but he wasn't embarrassed. He trusted me. Knew I wouldn't make fun of him. I explained that it was the white sand reflecting the sunlight that gave the water its color, not the water itself. "But the sand's not blue," Cal said. "That can't be right."

"How funny," Mom said. "Cal was such a sweet boy. It's good to hear you talk about him. We should talk about him more often."

Mom was still friends with Cal's mother, Caroline, but she never mentioned her to me. We joked a little more about running away together and beginning a new life. To cheer my mother up, I gossiped about Ginger's pregnancy, lied about Miriam's appearance—"She looked sick"—and exaggerated the hard times that had befallen the

Thatcher estate. I also mentioned that I was worried about Riegel. "He's up to no good."

"Spare me your brother's details," Mom insisted. "You need to learn that you shouldn't tell your parents everything."

We ended our phone call with my mother telling me that she wished my father would simply keel over. "I'd prefer to be a widow," she said. "Widows are much more glamorous than divorcees. I suppose I shouldn't say all of this to you, but I have no one else. You're the only one who listens."

Talking to my mom left me a little depressed, exhausted. I decided to sneak out of the dorm late that night and visit Aidan. We hadn't seen each other since Saturday morning, and the passing days had made me less and less certain of where we stood. Maybe Nadia hadn't bothered to convey my message, or perhaps Aidan was avoiding me. I'd gotten so antsy that I'd actually called the pay phone in Aidan's hallway asking to speak with her. I didn't recognize the voice that answered and the voice that answered checked and informed me that Aidan wasn't in her room.

There was the slight possibility that Aidan had gone home with someone. Since the Academic Center was a mess and since so many parents had brought their kids home, Windsor had canceled classes for the week. We were free to stay on campus, but Windsor had joked, "Try not to catch cholera." I hadn't seen Diana either and knew there was a chance the two of them had run off to New York together.

I'd wandered around campus on Monday and Tuesday just looking for Aidan, hoping she was hiding out in our library. When she wasn't there, I worried that she was sick. I'd felt myself coming down with a cold and thought that maybe she was in bed nursing a fever. I sat in the library and played piano, amusing myself with my best Joe Cocker rendition of "You Are So Beautiful." I realized that I'd never given Aidan any real compliment. Never told her she was beautiful, though she'd heard me call Cal beautiful. That night on the Swan we'd promised each other that we'd have some sort of romance. Something unprecedented. "We don't have to be like other people," she'd said, and I'd believed her.

Coach Tripp had handed out slender metal flashlights to all of the guys in the dorm, a practical keepsake commemorating the Great Blackout of '87. I waited until after curfew before tucking my new flashlight into my belt and scaling quickly down the fire escape. When I hit the bottom of the fire escape, I paused in front of Coach Tripp's window, wondering if he'd heard me. That afternoon I'd helped him squeegee water from the ground floor of Whitehall, and Coach had nearly cried over the lost Swan. "I loved that little yacht," he said. "Completely irreplaceable." He'd also extended another offer for me to sail in the spring. "No pressure," he promised. "We'll make it fun for you." I told him I'd think about it.

Scuttling like a crab across the grounds and past the harbor, I noticed light shining from within the water. The storm had warmed the Atlantic, agitating a bloom of plankton. The entire bay lit up with phosphorescence, the water glowing from within, a blazing grand ballroom. With every lapping wave the light pulsed turquoise, then emerald. I loved this trick. Wanted to swim in the phosphorescence, even though I knew this particular type of plankton was toxic. By day the shore would be covered in a poisonous red tide. For the moment, though, it was as if the ocean had swallowed a swarm of fireflies. I felt Aidan's kiss on my mouth.

Quietly, I inched up Aidan's fire escape, realizing that I'd spent the better part of my adolescence sneaking in and out of windows. I feared Aidan might be asleep, that she might not hear me knock on the glass, but when I reached the top her window was open.

I stuck a leg inside the room and down onto her wood floor, nearly slipping and landing in a split. The floor was wet in places, as though she hadn't bothered to clean up after the storm. Aidan wasn't in her room. I figured she might be down the hall with Diana or off brushing her teeth, or maybe she'd sneaked out to Whitehall and was standing under my Star Child poster looking up at the photo of Cal. That would have been perfect.

I shone my flashlight around her walls. Aidan didn't have any of the traditional prep school posters. No obligatory John Lennon peace signing by the Statue of Liberty. No golden kissing Klimt or Salvador Dalí dreamscape. No lame hippie tapestries. In addition to Fred Astaire's tap shoes, she had a series of photographs of her own feet framed and hanging above her bed. Aidan had told me that she'd taken the pictures to mark all of her favorite memories: swinging from a tree house her grandfather had built, at the kitchen table in her mother's Malibu home, barefoot on her backyard beach, standing on line waiting for a hot dog at a place called Pink's. "I like to take pictures of my feet to remind myself of where I've been." Her feet doing all the smiling for her.

The longer I waited, the more I felt like I was trespassing, but I decided just to relax. Aidan trusted me and I had to believe I could sit on her bed and wait for her. Aidan kept a pile of leather-bound books on her nightstand. I opened one and saw her loose, curly handwriting. Her journals. Flipping through the pages I caught fragments: "hurt myself," "complete disappointment," "end it all." This wasn't the Aidan I wanted to know. I closed the book. On a shelf, I found a photo album. I picked it up and began riffling through the heavy black pages wishing she were there to tell me who the different people were. The first pages were all sepia portraits of married couples. The album then shifted into faded Technicolor snapshots featuring girls in miniskirts and men on surfboards. I tried to pick out Aidan's mother. I turned toward the back of the album and flipped open to a picture of a pregnant woman in a bikini sunbathing by a swimming pool. The woman looked like my fake cousin Ginger and not just because she was pregnant. It was more the way she stared out over her sunglasses defiant and seductive. I knew instantly that she was Aidan's mother, and I suddenly understood how a pregnant woman could be the sexiest and most desirable thing a man could want. I couldn't fathom my own mother allowing a photograph like that to be taken. Maybe that was why Dad had left her. Maybe he had his reasons.

On the opposite page was the picture I realized I'd been looking for: Aidan's baby photo with Robert Mitchum. I hadn't doubted the truthfulness of her story, but it made me tremble a little to see it confirmed. Aidan was just a chubby blanket and a blurred face. The actor himself almost unrecognizable in thick black glasses, but there was his signature swoop of hair and his rebel good looks. I knew that I was kidding myself into believing that I was a young Mitchum. Cal was the one who really bore a resemblance. Cal was the movie star. I was the stunt double. I felt the bridge of my nose where Cal had broken it. If she'd been given a choice, Aidan would have been wise to pick Cal over me. He would have thrilled in the curves of her body, the softness of her skin, would have loved her sharp tongue and quick wit.

Aidan had told me a story about Mitchum. Right after he was released from prison a reporter had asked him what being locked up was like. Mitchum claimed that prison was just like Palm Springs only without the riffraff.

"Bellingham's like Palm Springs," she'd said. "Full of riffraff."

"Yeah," I said. "Prep schools might as well be jail."

"Obviously," she said, "you've never been to jail."

I wondered about Aidan's mug shot, the one Stuyvie claimed to have seen. It occurred to me that Aidan and I could have fun sneaking into the dean's file cabinet and performing our own background checks. Maybe I'd break in there myself and steal her file back for her. There were so many adventures I wanted to have with Aidan. We had the beginning of something I didn't feel compelled to name. Maybe it would be a romance, maybe a friendship, but all I wanted was the pleasure of discovery, the joy of being swept up inside knowing her and allowing her to know me.

As the night passed, I began to worry about Aidan. I was blinking tired and poked my head down the empty hallway wondering if she'd fallen asleep in someone else's room. Perhaps she was up counseling Diana, or maybe they really had run off together, skipping town until classes started up again. I felt a little jealous of their friendship and decided to leave Aidan a note asking her to meet me that afternoon at the beach. I tore a sheet of paper from a sketch pad and left my message on her desk. Casting my flashlight's beam over Aidan's tap shoes, I saw that one of them had writing on the insole. I was never any good at reading other people's cursive handwriting, but I could clearly make out Fred Astaire's autograph. Aidan didn't have a father, but she had something better: a mythology of father figures.

On my way back to Whitehall, I passed the Swan still pinned upright, its mast mired in oily water. The Swan was one more casualty of my confusion. One more thing I'd touched only to see destroyed. That evening on the Swan, I'd joked with Aidan that having a girl on a boat was considered to bring the crew bad luck.

"But then why do ships always have those naked women carved on the front?"

"The masthead, you mean," I said. "Well, a woman can be on a ship if she bares her breasts. Naked women calm the seas and bring everyone good luck."

This was an old superstition, but Aidan took it as a challenge.

"If that's the case . . ." Aidan stood, pulled off her tights, and stripped off her sweater. She stood on deck long enough for me to take in the fullness of her breasts, the flatness of her stomach. Then she turned, arched forward, and dove from the Swan.

I followed her, the two of us skinny-dipping in the harbor, barely able to see each other's naked bodies in the dark. Aidan floated on her back, claiming her superhero power was buoyancy. She tucked her arms behind her head, crossed her feet at the ankles.

"No one floats as well as I do." She laughed. "I don't need to paddle or kick. I can just stay on my back and enjoy the stars."

The sky was bright with constellations. The warm waves licked our bodies. I could see Aidan's breasts round and white. I thought of water lilies.

"You'll need a superhero name," I said. "We can call you Bellatrix, the Amazon star. She's one of the brightest. Sailors use her for navigation."

"The stars are like a map to sailors, right?" Aidan splashed lightly in the water.

"Yeah," I said. "And they're also a clock."

"A star clock," Aidan said. "I like that."

Recalling Coach Tripp's lessons, I explained how the stars provided position and measured time. During the day it was enough to rely on the sun and horizon. But at night, so long as the horizon was still visible, a sailor used whatever was most brilliant: Sirius, Canopus, Arcturus, Polaris. I tried to describe a sextant to Aidan, the way the double mirrors provide a steady image on a rocking boat. "The best thing about taking a sight reading is that you have to forget all that stuff about the earth revolving around the sun. In order to stay on course, a sailor has to believe that the universe revolves around him. You and your boat are the fixed point. The heavenly bodies just rise and fall circling around you."

"I always wondered why sailors were so arrogant." Aidan flipped over on her belly. "You guys actually think you're the center of the world."

On Wednesday I woke up just in time to miss the brown bag lunches the cafeteria kept pawning off on us. I couldn't bear another peanut butter and grape jelly sandwich. At first I thought I'd walk into town and pick something up at the General Store. Then I decided that what I needed to do first was go for a run. My body felt restless. Weeks had passed since I'd bothered to exercise, and though I'd held my own on the football field, I was worried about getting soft. I stopped by Chester's room thinking he might be up for a workout.

Chester also had a single. His room was half the size of mine, and to compensate for the compactness, he'd lofted his bed up onto stilts and placed his desk in the narrow space below. The room smelled like musky cologne, the kind children give their dads for Father's Day. Chester's desk was impressively organized with actual folders and file cabinets. A plastic caddy held pens, highlighters, scissors, a ruler, and tape. The bed was neatly made, the blankets tucked, the comforter straightened, the pillows actually fluffed. In his closet, I could see shirts tightly folded, stacked like gold bars. His room looked as tidy as a mother would have left it for her son on the first day of school. I thought of my own mess, how I was content to sleep the entire semester on the same dirty sheets. How I'd sooner throw out clothes than wash them. My parents were paying a service five hundred dollars a semester to clean my belongings and I hadn't once bothered to drop off a bag of laundry.

Despite being smaller, Chester's room had more interesting architectural features: built-in bookshelves, a plaster rosette blooming in the center of the ceiling, dark wood paneling, and a large bay window with a cushioned seat. When I entered, Chester was stretched out over the window seat's gold velvet cushion wearing a white polo shirt and a pair of orange Bermuda shorts. The light shone on his shoulders as he read *The Sun Also Rises*. Mr. Guy had informally assigned the book. He'd been trying to make a point about World War I and the Lost Generation and was stunned when almost no one understood what he was referencing. "Don't they teach you anything anymore?" he'd asked, as though he wasn't the one responsible for our education. Mr. Guy had rambled on about Hemingway and the human condition, acting like he and Ernest had gone to Boy Scout camp together. I'm not sure what got into me, maybe I wanted Mr. Guy to stop talking, to stop chastising us, but I mentioned *The Sun Also Rises,* how it was one of my favorite books, how you could learn a lot about what it must have been like to go to war, to be wounded and unable to return to your former life. How Jake's impotence and expatriation were a metaphor for his guilt. Mr. Guy put his hand on my shoulder and told me that though I was wrong about my interpretation, at least it was comforting to know that one of his students was semiliterate. I regretted opening my mouth. Now seeing Chester with the book I'd recommended, I felt a surge of pride. Maybe it had been worth it to speak up.

"You're quite the overachiever," I said.

It took Chester a moment to recognize me, like he was trapped inside the pages of the novel, lost at a zinc bar in Paris. He paused to take me in, then looked down at the book. "So you really like this?" Chester closed the paperback and held it up.

I nodded. "One of my favorites."

"Yeah, I guess I can see why you like it so much. It's about you in a way, right?"

I smiled and shook my head, unsure of Chester's question.

"What I mean," Chester continued, "is that the world must have seemed familiar to you. You could be Jake, Lady Brett's like Brizzey,

Bill might as well be Tazewell. Made me start looking for myself. Do you remember the section with the black boxer?"

I told Chester that the things I remembered most were the passages on fly-fishing and bullfighting and the final line, "Isn't it pretty to think so."

"Well, there's a section where Bill tells this story about a boxer he helped rescue. Bill calls the man a 'wonderful nigger.'" Chester looked at me. "Is that a phrase people use?"

"What do you mean?" I asked.

"I mean"—Chester smoothed his polo shirt across his chest—"is that a phrase people use? Are you familiar with it?"

"That book was written a long time ago." I crossed my arms over my chest.

"True." Chester blinked, his long eyelashes fluttering. "Don't get me wrong. I'm not surprised to see the n-word. I just never expected to see the word 'wonderful' in front of it. Got me wondering. What does it mean to be a wonderful nigger?"

"People were different back then," I said. "The way they spoke." I could hear the inadequacy of my own words. "Hemingway was writing for a different time."

"And what time was that?"

"I mean . . ." I shifted back and forth from leg to leg. "I don't have to tell you what people used to be like."

"Used to be, huh?" Chester worried the scar on his jaw. "So what would Hemingway have thought of me in my tennis whites?" Chester rose up and popped the collar on his shirt. "There's another phrase here." He shuffled through the book and showed me a page. "'Awful noble-looking nigger.' Is that what Ernest would have called me?"

I could feel myself blushing. I knew this wasn't something to shrug off. Chester was dead serious. He tossed *The Sun Also Rises* facedown on the window seat and walked over to his bookshelf. I tried to think of something to say. I pivoted and followed Chester. "Look, I'm sorry."

"Sorry I'm being abrasive again?" he asked. "Or sorry you knocked on my door? Don't worry, you just walked in on me thinking aloud."

Chester was giving me an easy out if I wanted to take it. I knew that I shouldn't. "We could bring it up to Mr. Guy," I said. "Talk about it in class. I'm happy to admit that I didn't read the book carefully. That there were things I missed."

"I've got a recommendation for you." Chester found what he was looking for on his bookshelf. He carefully handed me a book that said "Advance Copy" on the cover. "I'm one of the few people in the world who has this."

The book was called *The Motion of Light in Water*. I flipped it open and saw an author photo of an older black man with a wiry beard.

"The writer, Chip Delany, he's a family friend. Grew up in Harlem with my dad. Chip's very careful about the words he uses. Why don't you borrow it and tell me what you think."

I didn't know when I would find the time to read the book and I hated taking something that obviously mattered to Chester knowing that he was so careful with his own belongings while I was so careless with mine. In the corner of the room a small metal folding table held a chessboard, the plastic pieces arranged in midstrategy. I wondered who Chester's opponent was, or if he was playing against himself. After one night of hanging out together, I'd thought we'd have a casual friendship, but now I understood that I owed Chester something more.

I thanked him for the book and asked if he wanted to go for a run. "I need to get back in shape. I'm turning soft." Chester picked up a racquet and explained that he had tennis practice. Even though Windsor had suspended classes, athletics were still running on schedule. We made a plan to play tennis later on in the week.

I was about to leave his room when Chester called me back.

"Jason, you know what sucks? Up until that 'wonderful' moment, I really liked *The Sun Also Rises*. I did. But now I feel awful for ever having liked it."

Whether he'd meant to or not, Chester had given me a lot to think about. He had problems and concerns I couldn't even begin to imagine. I wanted to be his friend. One day in the library, Aidan had mentioned that she thought Chester was probably the strongest person at Bellingham. "What he has to go through, none of us can imagine." At the time, I was skeptical. I argued that Chester was just as privileged as we were, that he'd grown up with every advantage she and I had, but Aidan said, "No. Tazewell and Kriffo went after Chester like he was something they wanted to break." I explained that guys hazed one another, that it was harmless, that it would ultimately lead to a lifelong bond. "They're war buddies," I said, confident that I knew what I was talking about.

I didn't bother to stretch my hamstrings or warm up for my run. After two miles, the insides of my thighs burned, my calves were cramped, and I had a stitch in my side from breathing sporadically. It wasn't easy, but I powered through the pain and managed to do an eight-mile circuit. It felt good to sweat in the cold, biting air, and I headed into town hoping to grab some snacks for Aidan and myself. Figuring we could have an impromptu feast on the beach.

All of the leaves had blown off the trees. I loved the rustling sound of charging through a pile of dried leaves, but these leaves were soggy from the storm. I kicked my way through a wet patch of maple foliage, the pointed leaves clinging to my sneakers like small golden hands.

The General Store had its own generator, and all of the refrigerated cases were freshly stocked. I heard the owner, Eddie, an older man, his hair a shoe-polish black, tell another customer that he felt guilty about the brisk business. "Just doesn't seem right to profit from a disaster." The owner asked me how I was doing and gave me a free sample of apple cider. There was more to this town than the school. This was the sort of place where people strove to be nice to one another. The type of place where you could raise a family. It had never occurred to me that I would live anywhere other than New York, but I understood how people could enjoy a small town, the familiarity, the safety.

I picked out a pair of clementines, then grabbed a block of cheese, a box of crackers, and some sparkling grape juice. Eddie joked about carding me. I was mad that I'd given my army knife away to Race and asked Eddie if he had any plastic knives or paper cups. He nodded and packed everything up. I'd slipped a twenty-dollar bill into my sock before setting out for my run but when I reached down to peel it away, the twenty was gone. I'd probably lost it to the wet maple leaves. I apologized to Eddie and was about to put the groceries back when a voice behind me said, "Just put it on my tab." Turning around I saw Race holding a jug of milk.

"That's awfully nice of you," I said, "but totally unnecessary."

Race shrugged. "It's no big deal. All my friends at school charge snacks to my mom's account. Isn't that right, Eddie?"

Eddie said, "Mrs. Goodwyn is very generous."

Race and I stood out on the sidewalk together. He had a fading shiner on his left eye, the green and purple bruises shadowing his face. Someone had punched him hard. "What does the other guy look like?" I asked.

"The other guy was just born ugly."

We both laughed.

Race said, "Next time we have a party, you've got to see Kriffo dance. When he gets drunk, he thinks he's Iggy Pop. He clocked me in mid–fist pump. Total accident, but dude doesn't know his own strength."

We chatted for a few minutes, casual and relaxed. Race complained that Coach Tripp had paired him up with a freshman. "The kid can't crew for shit. Slows us down around every marker."

We talked technique and I realized that Race knew his stuff. I asked him, "Back when I was at Kensington, did we ever sail against each other?"

"I was wondering that myself." Race shifted the milk from arm to arm, bouncing it like a baby. "We must have. I've kept pretty good records on my stats. I'm being recruited, you know. Tufts, BC. Even have my eyes on the Olympics. Ever think about competing at that level?"

"Might take the fun out of it for me." Cal and I had considered the Olympics or even going pro, but we'd both decided against turning sailing into a job.

"I guess I like training more than you do." Race opened the lid on the jug of milk and took a swig.

I said, "I think you like competing more than I do."

Race wiped milk off his mouth, then stuck his hand in my grocery bag, pulling out one of the clementines. He brought the fruit up to his face, breathed in the skin, and waved good-bye.

———

The houses closest to the beach had been badly damaged by the storm. Not much effort had been made to clear away trees or to fix windows, and I had to imagine that most of these houses were second homes, vacation cottages. My mother had once told Riegel and me this story about a friend of hers who lived in Newport. "Poor Celia," she'd said. "She lost two of her houses to hurricanes. Still has the farm in Rhinebeck, and it's a lucky thing that she has the ranch in Jackson Hole and her home on Jupiter Island. Otherwise, I just don't know what she would do." Riegel and I both dropped to our knees with laughter. The phrase "Poor Celia" became code for us. A shorthand for outrageous privilege.

Some of the longtime teachers at Bellingham owned houses near the beach, but none of theirs had a view. Mr. Guy's came closest. He had a small brick bungalow on a corner plot. The only brick home on the street. Aidan went there sometimes to meet with Mr. Guy and discuss her independent study. She thought Mr. Guy was the best teacher at Bellingham, the only one who'd really dedicated his life to the school.

A power line had collapsed on his front yard, but Mr. Guy's house seemed to have otherwise survived the huff and puff of the storm. As I walked past, I noticed that a van from the electric company was parked in the driveway. I waved at Mr. Guy as he and another man argued with a fellow in a yellow hard hat. Mr. Guy gave me a quick nod. He was probably even more grateful for the days off than his students.

Just as the road dead-ended into sand, a pair of police squad cars guarded the entrance to the beach. Officer Hardy leaned against the shiny black hood of his car, the sand coating the heels of his black boots. He seemed surprised but happy to see me.

"Jason from New York," he said. "Glad to know you're safe and dry."

We shook hands and I asked what was going on.

It was low tide and he pointed to three yachts beached along the salt marsh and tidal flats. A team of men in orange coveralls stretched thick bales of canvas straps out onto the sand.

"Some big shots are paying ten grand apiece to have their boats airlifted to dry dock."

"Airlifted?" I asked.

"By helicopters. The boats are too heavy to be pulled out and too damaged to go back in the water. Should be a good show."

I'd never heard of such a thing. Of rescuing sailboats by flying them in the air. This was something I wanted to see. I scanned around for Aidan, hoping to share in the spectacle. Hardy pointed to my grocery bag. "You got any snacks for me?" I offered him the box of crackers and he said, "I'm just joking. You're a nice kid, though. You'd hand your lunch money over to a bully."

Handing over anything to a bully had more to do with fear than kindness, but I didn't bother correcting Hardy, just took his statement as a compliment.

After days without a bird in the sky, the seagulls had returned. Their slender white bodies circling overhead. I watched as the gulls swooped down, flashing the black tips of their wings. I told Hardy, "You call a group of seabirds a wreck. Kind of perfect, isn't it?"

"Those scavengers are just looking for a meal. Smells like something died out here."

A stench of rotting fish and spilled petroleum overwhelmed the shore. I thought of New Bedford. Of the polluted waters and the fish-processing plants. On the beach, a dried-up horseshoe crab decomposed in the sand, its sharp tail skewered on a brittle bed of seaweed. The horseshoe's body a tough brown helmet, another casualty of the storm.

Officer Hardy and I had a view across the harbor of Race's shipyard. I imagined the yachts were headed there. Hardy pointed to the shipyard and asked, "You know Leslie Goodwyn?"

"You mean Race? Yeah, I know him."

"His family's going to make a killing off our little maritime disaster."

I always vowed that if I owned my own yacht, I wouldn't be some weekend warrior. I'd take good care of her. Especially during a storm when it was smart to put her in dry dock or moor her in a sheltered harbor. But if caught out at sea in a hurricane, I knew I'd be able to keep her safe. Using a parachute anchor as an underwater sail, Cal and I had practiced a tactic called heaving to. Instead of slowing down a skydiver in midair, the parachute anchor expanded underwater, keeping our boat steady during the blow. Together, Cal and I could have saved these beached yachts not by running them under bare poles but by trimming our sails and positioning the yacht right into the wind. The parachute anchor created a vortex street of water and held the yacht in place. Like hitting Pause in the roiling ocean. A seemingly impossible task. Cal would have been disgusted by these shipwrecks. Knowing that all of this destruction could have been avoided.

Another cop stood farther down the beach. He shouted out to Hardy and pointed up at the sky. "Look at that. Here comes the cavalry."

Like a shining flock of Canadian geese, three hefty Sikorsky helicopters tracked across the horizon in V-formation, silver fuselages nosing their way toward the yachts. Hardy and I jogged along the beach, hoping for a better view, our hair and clothes blowing wildly in the helicopters' downdraft. The rotator blades sliced the air, sending ripples along the surface of the water. Loose grains of sand funneled up off the beach, stinging our faces. Around us brown columns of cat-o'-nine-tails beat against plumes of sea grass. As the copters whirled above, the men in orange coveralls scrambled around hulls, over foredecks, and behind exposed keels, positioning the straps of canvas.

I tried to identify each yacht by size and design. There was a high-performance Shannon 50 Ketch whose white hull had been cracked open like an eggshell hit hard against a counter. I imagined the Shannon planing continuously in strong winds, lifting up onto its bow wave and skimming the surface of the water. Beside the Shannon, a 51 Formosa PH Ketch had crushed a boggy field of marsh grass. The Formosa was so heavily constructed that it would have made a perfect around-the-world cruiser. Joshua Slocum would have balked at the luxury. But my favorite of all the beached yachts was an Alden 54. A real offshore thoroughbred. With an Alden, Cal and I could have committed some serious passage making. Setting off from Martha's Vineyard to Bermuda on the first leg of our circumnavigation. From Bermuda, we'd sail to Saint Martin, down to Panama, and out to the Galápagos. With Cal, there would be no coast hugging. Only the bluest open ocean. I watched the yachts being readied for flight and turned to Cal, who wasn't there and said, "That Alden's begging for the South Pacific."

Officer Hardy looked at me. "I used to think about buying a boat," he said. "But I'd be better off flushing my greenbacks directly into the ocean."

Overhead, the helicopters staggered their positions, treading sky, maintaining a stationary midair pose. One by one, each copter uncoiled a vein of thick wire cable. The descending steel shone against the swimming pool sky and, for a moment, I imagined that the cables were giant zippers waiting to be unzipped. Opening out onto another dimension. On the beach the workmen gathered the wide straps of heavy canvas and secured the wire cables to a complex series of metal hooks cinched within the canvas. While the copters hovered above, the workmen slipped the straps under the hulls, fore and aft. A signal was given, and soon the copters climbed higher, winching the yachts, cradling them in their slings.

Colonies of acorn barnacles and hairy patches of orange algae had ravaged the yachts' blue-and-white hulls. With their cement-colored caps and sharp flared bodies, the barnacles looked like ugly, unwanted stars. It was funny to me that the owners would spend so much money on a rescue mission when these yachts had long been neglected. They should have been dry-docked and scraped down ages ago. The boats so dramatic and elegant when floating on the ocean were being consumed beneath the waterline, the barnacles thriving, forming a rough honeycombed crust, suffocating the yachts. "Poor Celia," I thought. The ocean was full of life, but when you tried to put your own life into it you wound up with barnacles, feathery webs of algae. In the summertime, Cal and I would scrape down our Catboat, singing lines from *The Rime of the Ancient Mariner.* Just when the Mariner realizes that his shipmates have perished, that he himself is cursed, that his only companions will be the schools of tormenting sea creatures surrounding his boat, he says:

> *The many men, so beautiful!*
> *And they all dead did lie;*

And a thousand thousand slimy things
Lived on; and so did I.

I pointed up at the hulls covered in algae and barnacles. "A thousand thousand slimy things," I said. Cal would have known what I was referring to, but Officer Hardy just said, "What a waste."

The helicopters hoisted the yachts high above the marshlands, ascending deep into the Atlantic sky. In a brilliant feat of engineering, the helicopters rose, the fuselages hidden amid the white surf of clouds, leaving only the yachts to dangle below the mist. Three ghost ships suspended by sunlight, their shadows darkening the ocean. I felt the gravity and weight of these yachts and their pull on the sturdy helicopters, but I also felt a soaring lightness as though I myself were being carried above the water. I thought of my family's Calder mobile, of the whale skeletons hovering from the museum's ceiling, of the Renoir seascape. All of these images converged into the form of these flying yachts and their hidden helicopters. Aidan would have loved the sight. In a moment like this, there were so many beautiful and uncommon things worth saying. Aidan would have said them all, stealing this spectacle from the men who'd paid for it, making it her own.

The noise from the whirring helicopters obscured the sound of the workmen in their orange jumpsuits waving at us, urging the officers to come down to the beach. I was the first to hear the men shouting and I led the way across the tide pools to the marshy sandbar.

The men huddled in a ring like cautious worshippers at some ancient ceremony. I had to press my way inside their circle. A woman had been pinned beneath one of the yachts, the massive boat crushing her body. Her face was shrouded in red hair, a cluster of broken barnacles crowning her head. Her naked chest and torso nothing more than a patchwork of lacerations and bruises. A rough of matted sea grass covered where her legs should have been.

"Mermaid," one of the men whispered.

The woman's arms stretched above her head resting on a slab of driftwood. Her fingernails painted cobalt blue.

The sound I made was a keening cry, and it was only the sharpness of my voice that broke the spell Aidan's body had cast over the men. Before I had a chance to dig down and free her from the wet sand, Hardy dragged me away from the beach and placed me in the back of his squad car.

TEN

I felt the waves of this new truth, this new loss crash over me, and I did the most unremarkable thing. With my fingertips, I dug into and peeled the clementine, the one Race hadn't taken. With great focus, I flayed the peel off in a single orange curl. I did all of this listening for an ambulance's siren, but when the ambulance arrived it was silent. The ambulance driver drove onto the beach and parked on the marsh blocking my view. After I removed the rind, I tried to fit the curly shell back around the orange, attempting to restore the skin. I would have no appetite. Not for a long while.

I figured that Hardy had put me in the backseat to prevent me from running out, from seeing Aidan being unburied and placed on a gurney. But locked in that car, sequestered behind a metal grate, I felt a surge of guilt. I wanted to confess my own crimes. How I'd hurt Cal, how I'd let us both down. I thought my remorse might save Aidan. I wasn't ready to accept that she might be gone. I needed her to be alive.

It wasn't long before Officer Hardy returned to the car and insisted on driving me back to school. "You knew her?" he asked. "Was she a student?"

I nodded. "Is she going to be okay?" I understood that she wasn't, but I needed to hear the hope in my own voice.

Hardy stole a look in his rearview mirror. "There wasn't much we could do, son."

What I wanted was to go to the hospital, to sit with Aidan. I had no desire to flinch or back away from this moment. I wanted complete access to whatever pain or mystery was attached to that scene on the beach. Hardy wasn't hearing any of this. He drove me to my dorm and asked me to spell Aidan's name. That was all he wanted to know. I wrote it down for him on a scrap of paper. "She doesn't have a father," I said. "Her mother does stuff with films and oranges."

"Films and oranges?" Hardy repeated.

"In California." I could hear myself not making sense. My shoulders began to shake. My chest expanded and I felt as though I were drowning.

Office Hardy looked away. I heard him open the glove compartment. He pulled out a crushed roll of toilet paper and unspooled a makeshift handkerchief. He handed me the tissue. "I'm sorry," I said. "She was my only friend. This can't be happening."

Some random freshmen from the JV soccer team saw me get out of the back of the police car. Hardy waved the boys along and said, "Nice cleats." I felt too old for this boarding school world, like I was living in my own past. Hardy asked if I was going to be okay. "Do you need to sit with someone?" I told him I'd be fine, though I wondered how I would even make it up to my room without smashing my fist into a wall or some innocent face. Hardy warned me against saying anything. "I know you're upset, but let's not turn this into gossip," he said.

"We were supposed to meet each other," I told him. "On the beach. That's why I was there." I held up my stupid bag of groceries.

"Look, son." He put his hand on my shoulder. "Just try and forget what you've seen."

And because I was always so good at following orders because I *would* give my money to a bully because I still wasn't certain of what I had witnessed, I said nothing to anyone and waited for someone with authority to tell me what to do next.

There was a windstorm that night. No rain. Just blustery wind. I thought Officer Hardy might return to check up on me. He didn't. I stayed in my room waiting for Windsor or Dean Warr to visit and invite me to their homes or at least send word that they wanted to meet with me in their offices. But I didn't hear from Windsor or Warr.

Scared, confused, and alone, I called my mom. There was no answer. I thought about leaving a message, then remembered her words, "You shouldn't tell your parents everything." Riegel had accused me of dragging Mom and Dad through unnecessary pain over Cal, of threatening their marriage. It was possible that in order for me to become an adult, I needed to learn how to be alone with my grief. I would spare my family the details of this loss, this sadness. In truth they hadn't been much comfort where Cal was concerned.

I tried cleaning my room, throwing all of my dirty clothes into a knapsack. The worst part of that night was that I knew I would wake up the following day. My face would greet me in the mirror. I would walk down hallways and into rooms and my name would be called and I would hear the call and answer. I would go on. The linear progression of time would rule and I would be caught in its mornings and afternoons. The nights would come and I would feel alone. When Cal died, I thought time would cease to recognize me. Thought that I would step into some new dimension. I realized how innocent I'd been and how much worse it was now to know the unsettling truth about grief. I heard the wind outside and knew that the weather was changing, that it would be winter soon, that I would need to wear a wool coat.

Mostly I spent the night wondering what had happened to Aidan, refusing to believe she was dead. I saw Aidan in her ugly rust-colored sweater surrendering her black scarf to the wind. I saw her standing on her rocks and felt her thin body sleeping next to mine on her narrow bed. Then I saw the two of us naked in the water, the same awful water that had taken her away from me.

On the same day Aidan was found on the beach, a baby in Texas had tumbled down a hole and got trapped in a well. News from the outside world usually didn't penetrate our campus bubble, but when the electrical power returned on Thursday morning, all anyone wanted to do was watch TV and the only thing on TV was coverage of this little girl in Texas. Baby Jessica the newspeople called her.

A group of guys sprawled around Whitehall's TV room and placed bets on whether or not the baby would make it out of the well alive.

"They can hear her. She's like talking to them."

"She can't talk. She's a baby."

"How stupid do you have to be to fall down a well?"

"She's not stupid. She's a baby."

No one spoke of Aidan or seemed aware of what had happened.

Word came down on Thursday night that Windsor was calling an emergency Chapel meeting for Friday morning. Chester walked in on me tying knots and asked me what I thought the meeting was about. "Are we supposed to have some prayer vigil for the baby in the well?"

I'd been avoiding Chester. He was the one person I was tempted to confide in, and I didn't want to risk saying anything about Aidan. In my grief and denial I believed that there was still a chance that Aidan was alive. That saying anything about her half-buried body was a form of betrayal. I stared at the scar blistering Chester's jaw. He'd been picking at it, making it worse.

Chester looked at the hunter's bend and jury rig knots I'd been making. "How did you learn to do that?"

"A trick of the trade."

Knots are a form of control. The halyards, sheets, painters, and lines all run because of knots. I schooled Chester on the parts of a knot: the live end, the standing part, the bight. Showed him how the live end of the rope holds all the action, it is what a sailor uses to make his knot. The standing part is the section of rope under tension and the bight is the bend. "Then there's the bitter end. The terminus of the rope. The funny thing about a knot," I said, "is that it actually weakens the rope."

"What do you mean?" Chester asked.

"When you tie a piece of rope, you take away some of its strength. Most of the time you're using the knot to connect two things to make them safer. But when a rope eventually breaks, it always breaks at the bight."

Chester picked up two coiled ends of rope and practiced the bowline knot I'd shown him. He tightened the knot and placed his hand inside the small loop. "So binding something together doesn't make it any stronger."

"No," I said. "Not in the long run."

At Chapel on Friday, I felt a strange electricity in the air. Usually everyone went right to their seats, but that morning students just jammed the entryway lingering, chatting. Though I'd put on my jacket and tie, almost no one else was in dress code. Stuyvie and Bristin were snuggled together. She had on a pair of tight jeans, her ass flat and heart shaped. Even Stuyvie hadn't bothered to put on a blazer or tie. He'd taken to wearing a necklace of bleached white shells, something that would have looked natural on a pothead like Taze but that looked cheap and ornamental around Stuyvie's thick neck. I heard Bristin say to Stuyvie, "Diana's freaking out. But then she's always freaking out." Stuyvie nodded. If anyone knew about Aidan, it was Stuyvie. His father would have told him. I pushed past the two of them, and Stuyvie called out to me. "We're playing football again this afternoon if you're interested."

"Yeah, maybe," I said and headed to my seat.

The Chapel was barely half full. Most of the students wouldn't be returning until classes began again on Monday. Since the power had come back, the kids who'd remained on campus had become restless. Without daily duties or boundaries, we were all on the verge of some sort of social mutiny. I was certain that Windsor was going to make an announcement about Aidan and I braced myself for the impact the news would have.

Windsor marched down the aisle in a charcoal suit and gray tie. There was no organist or music. Windsor simply mounted the stage. Clutching the sides of the pulpit, he spoke into the microphone. "Haven't I always been honest and forthright with you? Always willing to deliver bad news. What I have to say is difficult but necessary. A young student has chosen to take her own life."

A murmur rolled over the audience. The question, "Who did it?" repeating. I was confused. This wasn't the announcement I'd anticipated.

I swept the faces of my classmates, searching for reactions. Everyone looked generically surprised: hands covering mouths, eyebrows raised. Mr. Guy shielded his arm over his face like a visor shading his emotions. I saw Nadia scan the room, taking an accounting of the missing.

"Before we ask why she did this, I would argue that there is no satisfactory answer. We are better off not asking. Though we mourn this loss . . ." Windsor paused. He touched the lectern, lifted a piece of paper. He was reading off note cards. "I believe that it is more important for all of us to consider the precious nature of life." He paused again. The note cards had been shuffled out of order and it took Windsor a moment to reorganize. "At this moment there is a child in Texas struggling to live. Instead of dwelling in the mire of our own senseless tragedy, I would like all of us to bow our heads in a moment of silence for this child."

In front of me, Kriffo slunk his shoulders down and lowered his head. I did not bow mine. Almost immediately someone coughed, interrupting the silence.

I looked up at the windows, at all of the important men of history parading by in stained glass. An image of Admiral Nelson played guardian angel over me. Whoever assembled the stained glass had chosen to portray Nelson with both arms. This seemed like a lie. When I was twelve, I did a book report on the Battle of Trafalgar. Even then, I was a sucker for stories of naval battles, convinced I was born in the wrong century. I could still remember stuttering in front of my class, terrified to describe how Nelson beat Napoleon, how he won but still wound up dead. I imagined Aidan shattering the stained glass. Restoring Nelson's missing arm.

I'd assumed Aidan's death was an accident. She'd gone for a walk on the beach. The storm had excited her imagination and she'd stood out on the wet rocks just like she'd done so many times before. Some slip or misfortune had led to her catastrophe.

Windsor cleared his throat. He reached into his jacket, pulled out a red bandanna, and blew his nose, bringing the moment of silence to its necessary conclusion. It bothered me that Windsor hadn't spoken Aidan's name or given her an appropriate tribute, but what really angered me was the conclusion he'd jumped to: that Aidan had killed herself. Cal had taken his own life, in part because I'd pushed him there. But with Aidan, things were different. We'd been making each other happy. I refused to believe she'd taken her own life.

Windsor stood and with a quick wave ended the ceremony. He made his way down the aisle leaving behind his school of mourners.

Friday night and everyone was up in Yazid's room getting high. Tazewell knocked on my door, inviting me to join in the fun. Taze carried an electric hot pot steaming with neon orange macaroni and cheese. He sat on my bed and handed me a fork. "My specialty," he said. "One of the cafeteria ladies hooks me up with heavy cream. Makes the sauce extra cheesy."

It was a nice, small gesture of friendship, and I helped Taze finish off his snack.

"It's weird." Tazewell licked his fork. "How Aidan wound up like the lady in that novel."

"What novel?" I asked.

"The one we played lacrosse with."

I remembered the two of us beating up on *The Awakening*. "You didn't even read that book."

"Yeah," Tazewell said. "But Kriffo told me the lady, the main character, she like walks into the ocean at the end. They shouldn't make us read books like that. Bad influence."

"I guess." I was surprised that Taze had anything thoughtful or sensitive to say about Aidan's death. He made me wonder if Aidan had indeed read the novel. She'd promised once to write up a list of all of her favorite books, her favorite films, her favorite works of art. She kept lists like this in her journals. I wondered what would happen to her journals, her photographs, and Fred Astaire's tap shoes.

Taze invited me to drive up to Cambridge the next morning for the Head of the Charles Regatta. "Kriffo's parents are sending a car for us. We're going to rage."

Before I had a chance to decline, Taze smiled. "No excuses, Prosper. You're going."

Tazewell left, and I decided to skip Yazid's party and to speak with Coach Tripp. He had an open-door policy and I needed his counsel, needed to speak with an adult. I knocked and he didn't answer, so I decided to let myself in. His apartment was messy. Sailing gear strewn about his living room. A pyramid of orange life jackets littering his kitchen table. The jackets themselves were dusted with mildew and the entire apartment smelled like a mossy, wet forest. I called out Tripp's name and thought I heard a reply coming from his bedroom.

The light in his bedroom was on but Coach Tripp was fast asleep, fully dressed, on top of his bedcovers. I haunted over him listening to the deep timbre of his snoring before calling his name. When whispering didn't wake him, I shook his shoulders. He bolted upright and grabbed my arms, convinced I was an intruder. He flung me down, tackling me across his bed. Coach Tripp wheezed in smoky gasps and brought his face close to mine. For a moment I thought he might kiss me.

"It's Jason," I said. "I need to talk."

Coach cleared off a space on his sofa and told me to sit down. He gave me a glass of ginger ale. Before I had a chance to say anything, he let me know that he'd been worried about me. "Windsor said you were there when they found the girl."

Though I didn't tell Coach about sleeping out on the Swan, I did explain that Aidan and I were close. That when I'd last seen Aidan on Saturday, she was happy.

"Look," said Coach, "she was very troubled, a history of drug abuse."

I shook my head. "She was over that."

Coach walked to his kitchen table and began clearing off the life jackets, tossing them in a black garbage bag. "From what I've been told, she'd tried to kill herself before. I can't get into all of it. There are privacy issues. You've got to understand that this is a very delicate situation for the school."

"Four days passed and no one noticed she was gone."

Coach tied the neck of the garbage bag. "I'm not going to make excuses, but with the storm and with so many people going home, I'm afraid your friend got lost in the shuffle."

I took a sip of ginger ale then heard myself say, "We were dating. She was my girlfriend. We were making each other happy. I noticed she was gone. I just never imagined." I shuddered to think of my own ineptitude, my own cluelessness.

Coach took the garbage bag out into the hallway, leaving me alone in his apartment. On that first night at Bellingham, Coach Tripp had visited me in my room, waking me up. He'd seemed so excited that night, so eager to welcome me aboard.

When Coach returned, he asked, "Do you know how old I am?"

I shook my head.

"I'm twenty-four. That probably seems ancient to you. But I graduated from college just a few years ago. I don't make enough money to own a car." He paced around his apartment. "I'm not cut out for this sort of thing. Windsor summoned the faculty into the Chapel this morning. Had a stranger give us a twenty-minute lecture on grief counseling." Tripp held my gaze dead on. "With your experience, you probably know more about this stuff than I do."

Coach Tripp appeared small and defeated. I felt like it was up to me to make him feel better. "I'm not asking you for anything," I said. "I just don't think Aidan would hurt herself."

He came over to the sofa, crouching down in front of me. "I shouldn't tell you this," he said, "but they found a note in her room."

I flinched, thinking of the note I'd left her. *Come meet me at the beach.*

Coach Tripp rubbed his face. "I don't know what happened to the girl. I'm not even certain I know who she was, but she left a letter. She just decided to walk out into the storm."

I thought of the first time I saw Aidan out on the groin of rocks. How I'd imagined she might be courting some sort of danger. Maybe my first instincts about her were correct. Maybe I didn't know her at all.

As I left Coach Tripp's room, I heard someone say, "She's alive." I shot down the hallway toward this voice. "Who is?" I insisted. "Who's alive?"

I ran into Kriffo and he said to me, "They pulled that baby out of the well. Safe and sound. It's a miracle. Best of all, I just made a hundred bucks."

I'd become used to living without electricity, become accustomed to the blackout. Even when power was restored it didn't occur to me to turn on my lights at night. I stayed in the dark, keeping myself numb with sleep, dreaming about the little girl in the well, wondering whether she'd grow up to remember being trapped in the dark. I kept thinking about the note Coach Tripp said they'd found. There was no note in Aidan's room the night I sneaked in to visit her. Maybe I'd missed it, but there was nothing visible on her desk or bed. I hadn't signed my own note and I worried that it had been mistaken for a letter from Aidan. I tried to construct some sequence of events, some logic or order that would help explain how Aidan had gone from handing me a pair of tangerines to drowning herself. I feared our night on the Swan had led her to walk out onto those rocks and into the ocean. She'd told me about her crush on Hannah, how they'd kissed. How Hannah had realized her mistake. "But it wasn't a mistake," Aidan said.

"Maybe it was just an infatuation." We were belowdecks and I sat beside Aidan, running my fingertips over the soft, pale skin of her arms.

Aidan said, "Hannah was older and married and my teacher. I know how ridiculous that all seems. But I don't regret the feelings I had for her. She was extraordinary and I wanted to be a part of her."

"But isn't it possible that you misjudged her? That you just imagined her to be some sort of savior?"

"Sure," Aidan said. "But that's where all my love resides anyway. In my imagination. Most people's lives are failures of their own imagination. Not mine. I fantasize about my dad, my mom, even. Hardly anyone I love is real to me."

I pinched Aidan's arm and she flinched. "I'm real," I said. "And so are you."

As promised, on Saturday morning, Tazewell pounded on my door and told me to haul my ass out of bed. The Head of the Charles started early and went all day. Our crew team had probably left before dawn, but Taze and Kriffo weren't going into Cambridge to admire the rowers. The regatta might have been a longstanding tradition, but it was also an excuse for public intoxication, public urination, hotel parties, random hook-ups. Cal and I had always gone together. We'd spend the morning tooling around Harvard Square collecting party invites from pretty pony-tailed girls who promised us pot and the chance to fool around with even prettier girls. All day long, we'd drink warm keg beer, maintaining a low-grade buzz. In the evening, we'd switch to smoking weed and head into Boston, wandering the narrow cobblestone streets and brick sidewalks of Beacon Hill in search of the ultimate party. The more we'd smoke, the stupider we'd get. Stupid enough to dance with strangers. We'd bounce like pogo sticks to The Jam's "Town Called Malice" while girls with historic last names like Adams, Beecher, Burr, Fayeweather, Foxwell, Pickering, Saltonstall, and Winthrop decided which one of us was worth making out with. The entire day carried with it a predictable spontaneity. Like a wave, a party would swell, peak, and then calm. We'd move on to the next rowhouse until finally we'd cross through the Commons and Public Gardens, winding up at some stranger's suite in the Ritz-Carlton trying to feel up girls from St. Paul's and St. Mark's.

Taze insisted he had a killer day planned. I was barely awake and not interested in leaving campus. "Thanks for the invite," I said. "I'm just not up for it."

"Well, then get up for it." Taze studied himself in my mirror, raking his fingers through his thick hair. "Since when did you become Captain Buzzkill? You used to be fun. You and Cal were the two coolest guys I knew."

Taze and I had never spoken about Cal's death. Since my arrival at Bellingham, neither one of us had even mentioned Cal. The three of us had grown up together in New York, had gone off to Kensington together, smoked pot for the first time together, shared a history, a boyhood. One summer, we'd even spent two weeks in Wyoming doing

NOLS mountaineering training, surviving the Wind River Range on rainwater and granola. I wasn't the only one who'd lost a friend.

"Cal loved a good time." Tazewell looked at me.

I felt this hurt pass between us. "You miss him too?" I asked.

"Of course," Taze said. "He was our brother."

When Tazewell left the noose in my closet and locked me in my dorm room, I blamed his meanness on my accident with Race, but maybe the meanness had more to do with losing Cal. I'd been selfish with my grief. Unable to see that Cal's friends felt their own sense of loss. Tazewell was reaching out to me. I needed to make things right between us.

I climbed out of bed and got dressed. "Okay," I said. "Let's go."

Kriffo's parents had sent a white Mercedes sedan along with a driver, an older guy with slicked-back silver hair. "This is Gus," Kriffo said. Gus nodded and opened all of our doors. Taze and I sank into the white leather seats while Kriffo rode shotgun. "Thought your dad was sending a BMW." Tazewell played with the electric windows. "Not this pimpmobile."

"Your dad would have sent bus fare and a subway token." Kriffo collapsed his front seat onto Tazewell's knees.

Tazewell slapped Kriffo's head. "My dad would have sent a Bimmer."

For me, the Head of the Charles always signaled the end of something, the last great day outdoors before winter descended. It was warm enough that Taze, Kriffo, and I all wore long khaki shorts and untucked polo shirts in slightly different shades of blue. We looked like spectators.

On Kriffo's urging, Gus drove to a McDonald's drive-through. Without asking anyone what they wanted, Kriffo ordered two dozen greasy breakfast sandwiches and challenged all of us to an eating contest. "Whoever slams ten Egg McMuffins first wins." It was never made clear to me what would be won, but as I bit into the first of three McMuffins, I felt myself begin to wake up. Kriffo belched, tossing the waxy wrappers at Taze and me. Taze kept repeating, "They should call it 'The Give Me Head of the Charles.'" He laughed like he was the first guy to ever have made this joke.

"We need to find a dude named Charles," Kriffo said. "Make sure Charles gets blown."

I asked Taze, "What's the game plan?"

"Don't worry. The party will come to us."

Staring out the window at the passing trees, I told myself I was just along for the ride.

Gus dropped us off in front of The Charles Hotel. "Promised I'd say hi to Bok," Tazewell said. "We do this quick, then we're Audi 5000." I didn't know who Bok was but I assumed he was one of Taze's drug dealers. We rode the elevator up to a penthouse overlooking the river. When the elevator doors opened, we walked out into a cocktail party, and a much older crowd than I'd expected. The men at the party were a mixture of tall, leathery yachtsmen and short, rumpled Henry Kissinger types. One of them probably was Henry Kissinger. The women were decades younger than the men. Second or third wives with perfect peroxide hair and graceful malnourished bodies. Tazewell led us through the room, striding across the carpet with great purpose, a kid in shorts muscling past grown men in thousand-dollar suits. Kriffo and I helped ourselves to Bloody Marys garnished with monster stalks of celery. Outside, teams of eight-men sculls sliced effortlessly through the water.

At the center of the room, a man with salt-and-pepper hair commanded the kind of attention reserved for heads of state. Taze called out, "Hey, Bok," and the man excused himself from his cluster of admirers, greeting Taze with a hearty slap on the back. The man asked after Tazewell's father, then drew Taze in close and begged him to come to Harvard. The man insisted, "Princeton's not all it's cracked up to be."

Tazewell didn't bother to introduce Kriffo or me. I didn't care. No matter how important this guy looked, he was no more important than the dozens of important men my own father had introduced me to. I turned to Kriffo, who was busy sucking down his second Bloody Mary.

"Who are these geezers?" I asked.

"That's Derek Bok," Kriffo said.

I stared blankly.

"You know." Kriffo snorted. "The president of Harvard." Kriffo walked over to the bar and pilfered several Amstel Lights, sliding the brown bottles into the deep pockets of his cargo shorts.

Tazewell continued to nod and smile as the president of Harvard urged him to ditch Princeton and come to Cambridge. I thought of all the valedictorians, National Merit Scholars, and debate team geeks who'd sweated over their Harvard applications. None of those over-achievers understood that their real competition for admission was not a genius with a 4.0 but a kid whose most glorious achievement was his recent second-place finish in an Egg McMufffin eating contest.

Taze said good-bye to Bok and nodded at Kriffo and me. "Sorry about the nursing home," he said. "Let's bail."

The streets of Harvard Square were crowded shoulder to shoulder with college students and prepsters pretending to be college students. On our way to the riverbank, the food trucks selling meat-on-a-stick distracted Taze. Kriffo bought us all kabobs. We arrived at the Weld Boathouse in time to hear the drunken crowd erupt into a taunting chorus of "Safety school, safety school" as teams from Dartmouth and Brown rowed by.

All along the Charles River, welcome tents were set up so graduates from every major prep school and college could cheer on their teams. I kept my head down as we passed by the Kensington contingent. Deerfield and Groton had kegs so we crashed and mingled. When we finally made our way over to Bellingham's tent, we were all pretty buzzed. Race and Stuyvie called out to us and asked where the hell we'd been. Both guys sported brand-new Bellingham sweatshirts. Something about the brightness of the white lettering made Race and Stuyvie seem eager and self-promotional. "Great day to be out on the water, right, Prosper?" Race squinted into the sun.

"Any day out on the water is a good day."

Taze pulled me aside and said, "We need to ditch these clowns."

He took off, promising to return, leaving Kriffo and me to explain how we'd gotten to Cambridge.

When Stuyvie asked about our plans for the evening, Kriffo acted noncommittal. "Not sure what Taze has in mind." It was a sad fact that outside of Bellingham, a guy like Kriffo wouldn't have been friends with a guy like Stuyvie.

I turned away from everyone and watched the rowers. Race was right. It was a great day to be out on the water. Sunny and cool with warm breezes. Guys who rowed crew were usually smart, intense athletes with serious discipline and a deep sense of camaraderie. The best rowers were giants with infinite arms and legs, and the best crew teams had identical giants. I was close enough to the water to hear a coxswain bark out orders as an eight-man team rowed a set of power strokes in unison. Cal would have loved that harmony. "That's fucking perfection," he would have said. I disagreed. I thought crew jocks looked like machines. Their precision didn't seem human to me.

A sharp beeping horn disrupted my moment of peace. Taze and a guy I'd never seen before, a pudgy kid with a curly nest of dirty blond hair, pulled up in a white golf cart with the words HARVARD SECURITY decaled on the hood.

"Get in," Taze told me.

Kriffo and I hopped onto the back of the cart, ditching Race and Stuyvie.

"It's not a party," I said, "until someone steals a golf cart."

We escaped down Memorial Drive, gunning our golf cart through foot traffic. Our driver, Howie Cakebread VI, or "Cakes," as Taze called him, was taking a gap year between graduating from Bellingham and going off to college. "Working on my music," Cakes said. "Been studying guitar with Livingston Taylor." Cakes tried to convince us that Livingston was more talented than his big brother, James Taylor.

"Livingston has a much purer sound. Way smoother than James."

"If he's so talented," Tazewell cracked, "then why is he stuck giving you lessons?"

In one deft gesture, Howie Cakebread lifted his right hand off the steering wheel and pushed Tazewell out of our fast-moving cart. Taze landed hard but, to his credit, didn't drop the beer he'd been drinking. He got up, ran at full speed and vaulted onto the front of the cart, turning himself into a human hood ornament.

Kriffo laughed and handed me one of his stolen beers. I thought if I could just maintain my buzz, I could manage to not so much have fun, but to not care. I kept thinking *you're just along for the ride*.

We drove up to an enormous four-story red brick building I assumed was a Harvard dormitory. It turned out to be Howie Cakebread's river house. We ditched the golf cart on the lawn and followed Cakes inside. As the front door swung open, "Sympathy for the Devil" spilled out. A party was already underway. Thick-necked sportos and tweedy girls drank heavily under a high domed ceiling. Cakes ignored his guests and led us out to a garden courtyard where more guests swirled around, dancing to the music, waving lit cigarettes above their heads. In the center of the courtyard was a large black-tiled swimming pool. A green and red pedal boat decorated with a huge white swan floated on the surface of the water. The swan looked like something out of a fairytale but it also looked vaguely familiar.

Kriffo whispered to me, "Cakes stole that swan boat right out of the Public Gardens. Total badass."

A guy wearing madras patchwork pants and a blue sport coat kicked a soccer ball at Cakes, who kicked it back, then introduced us to his friend. Adriano looked like he could have been a professional soccer player. He had sandy brown hair, bright green eyes, and spoke with an accent I couldn't place. He seemed to be living with Cakes at the river house. "Adriano's getting his MBA," Cakes said. "His dad is the lawyer for Brazil."

Cakes booted a herd of hippies off a banquette of cushy chaises and the five of us got down to getting high. He loaded up a super bong and soon all our eyes were glassy and red. Cakes took out a beautiful Gibson guitar and began murdering "Sweet Baby James." I stared at Adriano, wondering how his father could be the lawyer for an entire nation.

Tazewell kept heckling Cakes, telling him he sucked. In turn, Cakes tossed the Gibson aside and pummeled Taze. The two tussled, pounding each other into the cushions. I rescued the Gibson and began strumming and singing "Suite: Judy Blue Eyes." Laughing through the opening, *"It's getting to the point where I'm no fun anymore."* The song was long but I tore through it, faking my way around the Spanish lyrics. Cal, who couldn't carry a tune, used to joke that he could throw any instrument at me and I could master it. "You should do something with that talent of yours," he would say. The most I'd done with it was maybe keep Aidan entertained. I looked out at the black swimming pool and thought of Aidan breathing in dark water.

I played a couple of Bob Dylan songs and Adriano nodded his approval. "You're very good," he said. "Did you study?"

I smiled. "Never had a lesson."

Cakes took the Gibson away from me. He cleared his throat and spat out into his pool. "I know you. You're that guy."

I looked at Tazewell and Kriffo for some sort of confirmation. They both shrugged.

"Which guy?" I asked.

"That guy," Cakes said. "Trust me, I know who you are." He held up his guitar and walked away.

Maybe the pot was making me paranoid, but I felt like Cakes was threatening me. He seemed angry and unstable.

"What's his damage?" I asked Tazewell.

"Cakes is a good guy. You shouldn't have upstaged him like that with the guitar."

"He was bragging like he could play. Who takes a gap year to study guitar and can't even play a chord?"

Taze looked at Kriffo for some sort of approval and Kriffo nodded. "Cakes is taking time off because his sister is sick. It's pretty bad."

"That sucks." I shook my head. "How old is she?"

"They're twins," Kriffo said. "She looks just like him. Ugly as sin but cool as shit."

The afternoon drifted into early evening. Tazewell and Kriffo spent hours chatting up Dana Hall and Milton Academy girls, trying to convince them to go skinny-dipping. I pedaled around the pool on the stolen swan boat, wishing I'd stayed at Bellingham. I wanted to sneak back into Aidan's room and search for clues. Better still, I wanted to go back in time to the first night we'd spent together and have Aidan return to me. I kept losing the best pieces of myself.

I wandered around the house through the library, the dining room, the sunroom. Cakes had a stellar music room with a tricked-out Pearl drum kit. Off the kitchen, I found a parlor that was empty except for an oxygen tank and a tall bronze sculpture of a headless, armless man. The sculpture scared me. Even without a face or arms, the statue felt more human, more alive than I did. I ran my fingers over the indentation of the artist's signature, "A. Rodin."

There was some talk of driving into Boston for dinner and hooking up with Adriano's sisters who were staying at the Ritz. I felt lightheaded and sleepy from the pot, and would have happily sprawled out on one of the cushioned chaises and fallen asleep.

Cakes had other ideas. "This party's dying. Time to ditch."

There were still plenty of people hanging around, but Cakes didn't bother to kick anyone out of his house. The four of us left together. Adriano promised to meet us later. Outside, our driver, Gus, was waiting. He'd managed to swap out the Mercedes for a sleek black BMW. I was impressed.

"Nice car," Cakes said. "Are we doing a drive-by shooting later?"

I smiled at Kriffo and said, "Everyone's a critic."

We cruised into Boston, stopping off at Cakes's townhouse on Newbury Street just a few blocks away from the Ritz. We waited in the car as Cakes ran inside. All of us were underdressed for dinner at the Ritz. I was annoyed at the thought of Cakes changing his clothes, but he returned wearing the same frayed yellow button-down and torn cargo shorts. He'd wanted to stop by his house in order to pick up some black Sharpie markers. He gave one to each of us. "If anyone passes out," he said, "we totally get to billboard the guy."

Drawing on people's faces in their sleep was a total dick move, and I said so.

"Well then, you better stay awake," Cakes said.

Gus dropped us off at the Ritz. Despite our scruffy appearance, no one blinked when the four us marched into the hotel. Cakes treated the place like it was his living room. The doorman, the bartenders, the concierge, everyone knew Cakes. "Mr. Cakebread," the maître d' greeted us. "Your table is ready."

At dinner, we ate thirty-dollar cheeseburgers and twenty-dollar chocolate soufflés. We didn't talk so much as trade insults. Kriffo called Cakes "Fart Bag" and Taze called Kriffo "Fat Bucket." Cakes predicted Kriffo would brown his shorts before the night was over and Taze predicted I would be the first to pass out. It was mostly good-natured ribbing. Cakes stunned me by saying I played guitar well. "You lit up that Gibson," he said. "I haven't been able to make that kind of music with her."

Fernanda and Flavia joined us midway through the meal. Adriano's sisters looked like the result of the world's most successful genetic experiment. Each girl had caramel skin, full lips, bright blue eyes. Their straight hair fell like curtains of golden honey. As the girls leaned in to greet us with kisses on each check, I breathed in their perfume. They smelled like sunlight and champagne.

Kriffo tried charming the girls by speaking Spanish 101.

"Portuguese, you ignorant slob." Tazewell laughed. "No one in Brazil speaks Spanish."

Cakes pulled me in close. I expected him to whisper something off-color about the girls having blowjob lips or big tits, but he said, "They're perfect, right? Like goddesses."

I'd assumed Fernanda and Flavia were college students, but they turned out to be younger than all of us. Both girls went to Le Rosey in Switzerland. The school of actual kings. I could picture the girls sailing on Lake Geneva and skiing in Gstaad. They were out of my league and I was happy just to admire them. Instead of eating, Fernanda smoked Gitanes while Flavia kept leaving the table to make phone calls. Each girl wore a gold, diamond-studded *F* around her neck.

I was quiet during dinner. The waiters refused to serve us alcohol and it had been hours since I'd had a beer or taken a bong hit. I felt myself coming down from my high, sobering up.

Fernanda looked at me and said, "You are very shy."

"Maybe," I said.

"I like shy boys." Fernanda lit another cigarette.

"I'm shy too," Tazewell said.

"I'm downright bashful." Kriffo smiled.

"Forget it, Fernanda." Cakes put his arm around her. "Never trust a guy who's quiet. He's hiding something."

"And what are you hiding?" Fernanda asked me. "Do you have a girlfriend?"

Before I had a chance to answer, Tazewell interrupted. "Prosper lost his girlfriend. Tragic case. He's the one who found her. Couldn't save her."

"This is true?" Fernanda leaned forward, grabbing my arm.

Maybe Tazewell thought he was doing me a favor, thought that Fernanda would pity me and that her pity would lead to consolation. I lowered my eyes and looked away.

Fernanda put down her cigarette, reached her hands out, and clasped my face. She was a beautiful girl, but I didn't want her pity. Even so, as I stared at her perfect mouth, felt her warm hands, I knew that later on that night, Fernanda would kiss me.

Cakes sensed this too. When the waiter dropped the bill off on a silver tray, Cakes slid the charges over to Tazewell and said, "Hey, matchmaker, you take care of this."

The girls had a two-bedroom suite with a view of the Public Gardens. Though the hotel wouldn't serve us alcohol in the restaurant, they were happy to send liquor up to the room. First we raided the mini-bar. Then we ordered a stash of top-shelf liquor.

Within moments of being in the suite, teams of crew jocks began flooding the room.

"This party's a total sausage factory." Kriffo insisted Flavia call up more girls.

I didn't want to pass out and wind up billboarded with insults scrawled all over my face, so I switched from rum and Coke to just Coke. I anchored myself to a gold silk sofa. Dozens of people partied with us in that hotel room and all of them spent some small time with me hanging out on that gold barge. A very drunk Fernanda cozied up to me. "Everyone wants to kiss me," she said. "But I want to kiss you." Her lips felt as soft as they looked. I kissed her back and out of the corner of my eye, I caught Cakes watching us. Our makeout session was cut short when Flavia pulled Fernanda away. The girls spoke to each other in some urgent mixture of French, Portuguese, and English. In the meantime, Adriano showed up and offered me cocaine. I passed on the drugs and nodded as Adriano told me about his classes at Harvard and various investments and market opportunities. I told him, "You should meet my brother, Riegel."

The air in the room grew thick with smoke and sweat. People were getting anxious. It was that point in the evening when everyone either wants to have sex or wants to break something. I pushed past a group of kids playing quarters and opened a window. Staring down at the Public Gardens, I could see the pond where tourists rode on the swan boats, but the swan boats were gone, retired for the season. I wondered how Cakes had managed to steal one. He was a strange guy and I couldn't say that I liked him, but I was sad to hear about his sister. We all carried some private loss with us. This was something I'd learned, something I was trying to deal with. I turned around and saw Cakes standing near me, staring out a different window.

"Hey," I said. "You know, I'm not that guy. I'm not the guy you think I am."

He turned to me. "I saw you with Fernanda. You're totally that guy."

I'd lost track of Kriffo and Tazewell in the scrum of partygoers but late into the night, both guys came up to me and told me we had to bail. "What's up?" I asked.

They brought me to the suite's master bedroom and opened the door. Two figures in white bathrobes were passed out together on a king-sized bed. Fernanda and Flavia would have looked like sleeping beauties except for the fact that someone had drawn a moustache above Flavia's lip. Someone else had drawn an arrow on Fernanada's cheek pointing to her mouth and written, "Insert here."

"Cakes wants to bail. He doesn't want Adriano thinking he did this."

I looked at the girls and wondered how they'd gotten into their robes. "How could you?" I asked.

"Trust me," Tazewell smiled. "We've done a lot worse."

I went to the bathroom, ran a washcloth under the water, then returned quickly to the room and tried to wipe off the marker. The girls roused a little but neither woke. The marker faded slightly. It was going to take more than water to clean off the stain. The guys just stood around and watched me.

"Come on," Kriffo said. "The car's waiting."

I tried to find Adriano but he was nowhere to be seen. We left the hotel. I thought Cakes would return to his townhouse on Newbury Street, but he asked to be driven out to his country home in Concord. It was totally out of our way, and I was surprised when Kriffo agreed. Though Cakes gave Gus directions, we mostly drove in silence. Every few minutes someone would say, "What a crazy night," and the rest of us would murmur our agreement.

We drove by Walden Pond, then turned off the main road and into the woods. Cakes's house was an imposing white Colonial. I thought we'd just drop him off, but Kriffo and Taze insisted on going for a swim. I didn't want to be near the water. While Kriffo and Taze went up to Cakes's room to borrow swimming trunks, I waited down in the kitchen. The house was rustic and homey. Cakes told me to help myself to some food, but the refrigerator only held a carton of milk, a jar of mayonnaise, and several boxes containing glass vials of something that looked like medicine. I closed the refrigerator door and a thin, bald girl appeared before me.

"There's no food," she said. "There's never any food in this house."

Cake's sister had large bulging eyes and gray, papery skin, but Kriffo was wrong about her being ugly. She looked like a spoiled child's favorite doll, one that had been carried around and worn out.

"Don't worry," she said, "I'm not a ghost."

We stood there together in the kitchen for a moment. I introduced myself and she told me her name was Grace. She asked about the regatta and the parties. She said, "You know, the Head of the Charles is a classic WASP mating ritual." Then she asked whether or not Cakes had hooked up with Fernanda.

I told her he hadn't but failed to mention that I had.

"He's crazy about her," she said. "But Fern's a phony. All those Le

Rosey kids are total Euro-trash. I should have gone and scared everybody away. Ruined their good time."

Kriffo may have been wrong about Grace being ugly but he was right about her being cool as shit. She did an imitation of Fernanda smoking that was dead-on. I couldn't stop laughing.

"Do you have a cigarette, for real?" Grace asked. "My brother hides them from me."

I wished at that moment that I had a cigarette for her. "I'm sorry."

"Could you tell my brother not to bother me tonight," she said. "I'm going to sleep."

I'd spent the day meeting people I'd probably never run into again. Though there was always the small chance I'd bump into Flavia or wind up at another party with Cakes, as Grace glided off to bed, I knew for certain I'd never see her again, not ever. Knowing this should have made me sad, but instead I wanted to run after Grace, to beg her to take me with her. I wasn't sure that I believed in any sort of afterlife, but it made me jealous to think that soon Grace would be with Cal and Aidan. I wanted to tell her about them both, to be sure she looked out for my friends.

I left the house and went out to the car. Gus was sitting in the front seat reading *The Economist*.

"It's been a long day," I said.

"No kidding."

I'd barely heard Gus speak. He had a deep, gravelly voice.

While Kriffo, Taze, and Cakes cannonballed into Walden Pond, I unloaded on Gus. Told him about Tazewell's meeting with the president of Harvard and the tour of Cakes's three different homes. I mentioned the stolen swan boat, the Rodin sculpture, the dying twin sister. I catalogued our entire adventure. At the end of it all, I expected Gus to say something that would help me make sense of my day. He cleared his throat and said, "Look, kid, I just drive the car."

We said good-bye to Cakes and drove back to Bellingham. Kriffo and Taze eventually fell asleep. As Taze snored beside me, I took out the marker I'd been given and considered writing "prick" or "douche" on his forehead. For Cal's sake, I'd wanted to make amends with Taze-well. But as we approached Bellingham, I thought back to that mountain-hiking trip Taze, Cal, and I had taken to Wyoming. I remembered how Tazewell had gone down the wrong trail and gotten us lost, how he ate the last of our food supplies, and left our sleeping bags out in the rain. In my rush to preserve our friendship, I'd forgotten that at the end of that trip, Cal had turned to me, pointed at Tazewell, and said, "Never again."

The next morning, Chester woke me up to play tennis. It was a gray, sunless day, the hazy light reflecting off the green painted court. I was surprised that I didn't feel hungover. Mostly, I just felt flattened and stiff. I wasn't much competition for him, and though I could tell that Chester was a little annoyed, he seemed committed to making the game fun, giving me pointers and taking it easy on me. I stupidly re-sented him for not playing his best. He asked me how well I knew Aidan, what I thought of her suicide.

I told him that she was a friend and was surprised when he called her selfish. "That was a shitty thing to do to her parents," he said. "I mean, I couldn't do that to my mom no matter how bad things got."

"Did you know Aidan?" I asked. "Do you know the first thing about her?" I smashed the ball across the court.

"Nice rally," Chester said. "You play better when you're pissed off."

"You know," I said, "she thought really highly of you."

"That's funny." Chester served into the net. "I don't remember her making much of an effort to be my friend. Can't recall her even speaking to me."

It began to rain lightly. I told Chester how Aidan had admired him, had talked about his strength. "She said you had to put up with a lot of hazing."

"Is that what she called it? Hazing? That's a bit of a sugarcoat."

"That's my word, not hers."

Chester told me that I kept missing the ball because I kept drop-ping my head.

"Every time you look down to see the ball, you jerk your arm and miss making contact with the center of your racquet."

"That's Tennis 101," I said.

"Yeah, well, it doesn't mean you aren't doing it."

The rain began to come down in thick sheets. Chester didn't want to risk playing on a slick court, didn't want to injure himself, and so we called it quits. We stood under the clubhouse's awning while Chester adjusted the strings on his racquet, realigning the squares.

I asked Chester, "So, if you weren't hazed, what did happen?"

Chester zipped his racquet into its leather carrier. He slipped on a red track jacket and said, "You don't want to know what those guys did to me."

At that moment I realized that I did want to know. That I wanted to make something right. "Did you ever tell anyone?" I asked.

"I'm not a snitch," he said.

"Telling the truth doesn't make you a snitch." I only half believed this. Hazing had its own self-regulating code, one that required secrecy and compliance but also the tacit understanding that certain lines shouldn't be crossed.

Chester looked out at the rain. "My dad, he's built his life around the idea that there's this thing called justice. I know better. If I told Windsor or Warr, nothing would happen to Tazewell's crew. But my life would be ruined."

The tedium of boarding school could be broken down into stages of getting hazed and hazing. We took turns hurting one another not because we were mean or violent but because we were bored. "That's why they call it boarding school," Cal used to say. When Cal and I were freshmen at Kensington, we endured such noble traditions as having our bare asses beaten by belt lines of seniors, being forced to pound grain alcohol that may or may not have been laced with piss, having all of our textbooks glued shut, and being directed to sing and act out "I'm a Little Teapot" while wearing nothing but a jockstrap. One night a particularly dickish group of seniors busted in while we slept, held us down, and rolled each of us up into carpets that were then duct-taped shut and spun out onto the fifty-yard line.

Cal and I held different positions on hazing. He preferred pulling pranks like inflating a kiddie pool in the middle of someone's room and loading it up with Jell-O and rubber ducks. "I like something that's clever," Cal explained as he covered the floor and every flat surface of our hall proctor's suite with Dixie cups filled with india ink. It didn't take long to set up those cups, but it took hours for our proctor to remove them one by one. I remember all of those little white cups and that dark black ink, how Cal squirted lemon juice over his hands to remove the incriminating stains. He didn't even want credit for his pranks.

I admired his imagination, but this is where Cal and I differed. The whole time I was trapped out on that football field, suffocating inside that mildewy rug, unable to break free, I kept thinking, "I can't wait to get even. I can't wait to do this to someone else."

At dinner that night, I sat alone at a long table by the window. There were almost no boats left in the harbor and I was oddly relieved to see it empty. I thought about the Shannon, the Formosa, and the Alden, wondering how badly the yachts had been damaged. If they were worth fixing. The only relief I'd had surrounding Aidan's death was the realization that it had freed me, however briefly, from thinking about Cal. I'd been so overwhelmed by losing her that I hadn't had time to feel the loss of Cal. This was how people recovered from love affairs. Replacing one lover with another. But here I was replacing one death with another. Maybe Cal's suicide had prepared me for Aidan's. It was possible that I would never again allow myself to feel close to anyone. I wondered why I was still alive when the people I'd felt closest to were dead. It was true that I had hurt Cal and destroyed our friendship, but I was trying very hard to make up for the pain I caused. Aidan had been my hope for redemption.

I tore the paper napkins on the table into strips, then twisted the pieces into ropes and then knots. A simple clove hitch, a sheet bend, a figure eight. I created a tattered mess of confetti and was about to leave it all piled up on the table when Leo came by. He had on his white uniform. The front of the apron stained with something that was probably tomato sauce but that smeared red like blood. Made him look like he was a butcher. Leo carried a round tray and was busy piling up the dishes students had abandoned on the tables. I said hello, and in a quiet voice Leo said, "If you're not busy, I'd like to take you for a drive."

According to Leo, Powder Point had a split personality. All the homes on the south end of the island were stone mansions with spectacular waterfront views, private docks, and beaches. "You can't even see the houses from the road. You can only glimpse them if you're out on the water." Leo smelled like the dining hall, a not unpleasant mix of grease and garlic that filled up his Chevy Malibu. His cheeks were spotted with rubies of acne. "My mom's cleaned all the houses on the South Side. She claims in the summertime, the South Siders use these high-frequency ultrasonic gadgets that chase all of the mosquitoes and bats over to the North Side."

On the North Side, the homes looked like army barracks. They had views of scrub pines. We drove by a neighborhood of ranch houses and Leo pointed to a yellow house with green shutters. "That's my family's," he said. The home was the size of a two-car garage.

"Looks cozy," I said. "You have any siblings?"

"Three. Two brothers and a sister. I'm the firstborn."

It made me depressed to think of an entire family living in that small house.

Still, it was a strange comfort to drive around with no particular destination. Leo had invited me off campus, and because I was impossibly sad, I thought it would be a useful distraction. "Meet me at the Gas Mart," Leo had said, and I'd walked the few blocks into town so that no teachers would see me get into Leo's Chevy. If caught riding in a car, I might have received a few minor demerits, but Leo would have lost his job.

At the Gas Mart, Leo tossed me a can of Budweiser. He didn't take one himself. His Malibu was in cherry condition, and I figured Leo was too responsible to drink and drive, too worried about screwing up his car. I snapped open the beer and took a long foamy chug.

We drove in silence until Leo pointed to a plastic case filled with tape cartridges and told me to pick out some music. I slipped Bon Jovi's *Slippery When Wet* into the deck.

"I love these guys," I said.

Leo looked at me suspiciously, like I was pandering to his taste. "I would have figured you for a Depeche Mode fan."

Leo and I swapped opinions on Guns N' Roses and Def Leppard. We parted ways on U2 and the Smiths but agreed on the Beastie Boys. "It's a kick-ass time for music." Leo drummed his steering column. I riffled through his tapes and held up an incriminating Whitney Houston album. "What can I say?" Leo smiled. "My girlfriend, Cheryl, goes crazy for that shit." I cut loose on "Living on a Prayer," and Leo said, "Wow. You sound nothing like Jovi." Leo told me he played guitar and for a moment we were just two guys enjoying the glory of being young and loving rock and roll.

My mother always warned that you couldn't have too many friends. "People come in handy," she would say. Leo made me feel connected to a former life. He reminded me of the locals Cal and I hung out with up in Maine. Cool guys who sold us homegrown weed, who took care of our summerhouses in the winter, and whose best hopes involved lobster pots and freezing weather. Leo explained that he planned on graduating from Bellingham's kitchen to working at the Goodwyns' marina.

We'd been driving along for several miles. It was dark and there were almost no streetlights, but I could sense the landscape changing. The barrack houses disappeared as tall hedges sprouted up on either side of the road. Even the air smelled sweeter, like sugary beach blossoms. Every five hundred feet or so we passed a steel gate with a NO TRESPASSING sign. We'd crossed over onto the South Side of the island. "Some of the South Siders want to put up a gatehouse with an actual guard," Leo said. "They'd keep the whole world out if they didn't need someone to clean up after them."

I felt compelled to rock and disrupt this quiet neighborhood, so I opened my window, took another swig of beer, cranked up the stereo, and belted out, "You give love a bad name."

Leo pulled up in front of a wrought-iron gate. He turned down the music and said, "It's closed now, but on Saturday night, this gate was open."

A large gold "G" swirled over the center of the iron entry.

"Who lives here?" I asked.

"You don't recognize it? It's the Goodwyn place. Biggest house on the island," Leo said. "This is where I dropped her off. Your friend Aidan wanted to come out here to see you. I was the one who drove her."

Now Leo cracked open a beer. He looked straight through the windshield and told me that on Saturday, Aidan had approached him just before the dining hall closed and asked for a ride.

"Did you know her?" I asked.

"Not really. In the dining hall, you come to know people based on what they eat, but that girl barely ate anything. I hardly ever saw her at dinner. She was a pretty girl. I was surprised she knew my name."

I remembered telling Aidan the story of Leo catching me sneaking out of her room. That I'd asked his real name. "So what happened?"

Leo turned to me. He squinted his eyes. "What happened? That's what you need to tell me."

Leo had assumed I'd been at Race's party. "Your friend told me she needed to find you. I had a sense she was worried. The storm was pretty bad by that point. Zero visibility. That girl kept bouncing her knees and tapping her fingers on the window. The only time I ever saw a girl nervous like that was when Cheryl thought she was pregnant."

Leo finished his beer. We sat together in the darkness. He said, "I don't know what you guys did, but I need my conscience cleared. You've got to tell me what happened."

"I wasn't there," I said. "I didn't go to the party."

I made Leo describe how he drove down Race's driveway, how he parked near the house. "The power was still on at that point. The house lit up like it was Christmas. I offered to wait for her, but Aidan told me not to bother. I think she felt guilty. Worried she'd get me into trouble. She kept apologizing."

It was hard for me to listen, to hear and make sense of Leo's details. To put his story into a sequence. "What are you telling me?" I asked. "What did you see?"

"I never left the car. I saw her open the door and go inside. I sat in the driveway until the lights went out. Then the storm got bad. I worried about the roads flooding."

Leo cracked another beer, the foam spraying across the dashboard. He ran his hand over the leather, his fingers thick with calluses.

"Did anyone see you? Did you see who was there?"

He shook his head. "I should have gone in after her. Look, I don't know what happened. I'd like to believe that you weren't there. Cheryl told me I should confront you. She told me to drive you out here. Return you to the scene of the crime. This hasn't gone the way I planned. I was going to accuse you of all sorts of things."

It took my mentioning the police to convince Leo that I hadn't gone to the party.

"I know this guy," I said. "Officer Hardy. He's a good guy. You need to tell him what you told me."

Leo turned the Malibu around and began to drive back to Bellingham.

"If there's a chance that something happened at Race's, you need to come forward."

Leo said nothing. He continued to drink as he drove, raising the silvery can to his lips, belching with impressive resolve. We'd managed to go from pals back to strangers. On the stereo, Bon Jovi sang about being wanted dead or alive. Leo skidded into a blind curve, one hand on the steering wheel, fishtailing across the lane. I could taste the beer acid rising up in the back of my throat. The lingering aroma of garlic and grease made me cough first and then heave. I asked Leo to pull over. "I'm going to be sick," I said.

We were still on the South Side when I tumbled from the car. A security camera hovered overhead, taping me as I retched through the gates and onto someone's shiny black driveway.

Leo put the hazards on and shot outside to check up on me. "Get back in the car," I said. "I'll be fine." I spat and cleared my throat. A moment later, Leo held out a towel. I took it, wiped my mouth.

"Thanks for not throwing up in the Chevy," he said.

We drove back to campus with the windows open, the cold air lashing my face. I knew I had to convince Leo to speak to Hardy, but I couldn't even get him to talk to me. My entire body felt like a smoldering furnace being tripped from high to low. Palms sweaty, feet frozen. My imagination fueling my sickness. Aidan had drowned. This was certain. But how she'd slipped into the water was now unclear.

Leo pulled back into the Gas Mart and parked. We sat for a moment, then he said, "If I tell some cop that I was driving your friend around, I'm as good as cooked."

"It won't be like that," I promised.

"I'd be incriminating myself. Making trouble where there is none."

I said, "The truth is always dangerous."

"Well, that's just some slick thing to say." Leo twisted the empty beer can in his hands, the metal making a sharp, painful sound. "What do you know about truth or danger? You're just some dumb rich kid at a second-rate school."

"Third-rate."

Leo almost smiled. He scratched at his cheeks, bloodying one of his boils.

He was conflicted, but I figured I could sway him, convince him to come forward, so long as I didn't push.

"There's a right thing to do here," I said.

"No," Leo said, "there isn't. I don't know what happened to the girl after I dropped her off. When I drove you out to Race's tonight, I thought I wanted to know. Thought there was something to be gained by knowing. Figured you'd confess and we'd go from there."

If before I'd heard fear and compassion in Leo's voice, suddenly I heard something else: money. I slipped out of the car, then leaned into the open window. "What exactly did you have to gain?"

Leo didn't need to say a word. He'd taken a chance that I'd done something worth hiding and that I'd be willing to pay for my secret. He'd picked the wrong guy, but he'd also acted in opposition to his own character. He was shaking. "Forget this. Forget all of it," he said. "It never happened. I made a lousy mistake."

Walking back to campus, I unbuttoned my shirt, hoping the night air might chill the nausea out of me. My lungs filled with cold, my breath foggy. If what Leo had said was true, and I wasn't entirely certain that I could trust him, I needed to consider a new series of possibilities. With some keen urgency Aidan had gone to Race's home. She'd needed to see me. A gust of wind slammed against my body. My hand fell across my chest and though my skin should have been icy, my fingertips burned from my own radiant heat. I had a fever and needed to put myself to bed.

When I got back to my room, I saw the torn paper bag with Riegel's present. My plan had been to open it with Aidan. To tell her the story of my day with Riegel and for the two of us to tear into his gift. Though I didn't deserve any presents, I took out the box from the Whaling Museum. A black ribbon was tied loosely around a long narrow carton. Inside, a glass bottle rested on a wooden stand with a piece of cork stoppered inside the neck of the bottle. Where I expected to see a ship, instead the glass held a large ceramic whale. With a ship in a bottle, all a person had to do was rig the masts and then, once the ship was glued into place, raise the sails. I couldn't understand how a person could put a whale inside a bottle. The bottle felt heavy in my hands as I rotated it, looking for seams in the glass. There was a boat after all. A tiny dinghy with small faceless sailors balanced in the whale's shadow.

The sailors in the dinghy rowed with their backs to the whale, blind to their oncoming danger. During a whale hunt, there always must have been a moment when the hunt could have gone either way. When the harpooned whale might have plunged underwater and taken everyone in the dinghy down with her or when the harpooneer might have struck the perfect, life-ending hit. It was all I could do not to go to the headmaster's house and wake him up to tell him that my friends had been among the last to see Aidan. I wondered if the weight of my accusations alone would be enough to sink them.

————

On Monday, classes started again. I woke up sick and it took all my strength to climb out of bed and throw up in my garbage can. Lying on the floor, I noticed that there was something else in the bottom of Riegel's gift bag. The tangerine Aidan had given me. It looked as fresh as the day Aidan dropped it in my lap. I put the tangerine on my bureau, coughed up more bile, and decided to sign myself into the infirmary. After dressing quickly in a sweater and jeans, I walked down the hall, leaving my garbage can filled with sick in front of Kriffo's door.

In the hallway, I met Tazewell coming out of Yazid's room. He reeked of cheap air freshener and expensive weed. I nearly clocked him when he asked how I was doing.

"Not well."

"Yeah. You don't look so good."

"You look like shit," I said, a little too harshly.

"Yeah, maybe." He smiled. "But I never get sick. Nature's medicine."

Tazewell and his stoner routine. He leaned against the wall, obstructing my exit. "Man, it was so nice to have a week with no classes. Felt like we were in college. That reminds me, Kriffo's pissed at you."

"Why would he be mad at me?"

"You're going to Princeton, right?"

"I applied."

"Well, you and I are legacies, and they never take more than two students from here. Until you came along, Kriffo thought he had a shot. With his grades, he'll be lucky to get into Syracuse." Tazewell checked his watch. "We should be roommates."

Outside Whitehall, Nadia stood on the walkway, balancing her weight on one foot. She'd swept her brown hair off her face and back into a high ponytail. It looked funny, like a rooster's cockscomb. She wasn't wearing any makeup. She lightly touched my arm and said, "Her mom's here."

On her way to the bathroom that morning, Nadia had seen a woman, "prettier than any Astor girl," carrying boxes from Aidan's room. "I thought you'd want to know." Nadia was wearing a loose T-shirt and a long gypsy skirt. She tripped over the fabric as she walked with me to Astor.

"You look different," I said.

"Is that good? Or just different?"

"You look good without all that makeup."

Nadia pointed out a black Lincoln Town Car parked in front of Astor. We stood together for a moment, right by the fire escape, the one I'd managed to hoist Nadia up the night we'd sneaked into Aidan's room. Nadia was rocking back and forth on her heels.

"Wanted you to know, I never saw her," she said. "Never had a chance to give Aidan your message."

I nodded. Aidan had died on the night of the storm. She'd come to shore with the yachts. I'd spent days looking for someone who was already gone.

"I can't miss class." Nadia took a few steps backward.

We said good-bye and I was surprised when Nadia sprung forward, clasping her arms loosely around my waist, tucking her head against my chest, hugging me. She was so tiny and awkward. Too young to be away from her family. It was clear that she needed someone to look after her, but here she was looking after me.

As Nadia walked away, I shouted, "Thank you."

"But I didn't do anything," she said.

I called out, "You have no idea."

I waited around outside until a man in a brown suit and black sunglasses left Astor pushing a dolly stacked with boxes. A woman followed him. I recognized Aidan's mother from the photograph. She held a pair of Fred Astaire's tap shoes in one hand and a brown cigarette in the other. She was tall, almost as tall as me. She didn't look like any mother I'd ever seen. Her long hair was blond and copper like Aidan's, but where her daughter's was wild and natural, the mother's was perfectly sectioned into costly spiral ringlets. She wore a purple-and-green dress, and even though it had no formal waist, even though my mom would have called the outfit a muumuu, somehow Aidan's mother managed to look even more slender and slight. Her body lost inside all that fabric.

I don't know why, but I expected Aidan's mother to recognize me. Thought she might call out my name and rush toward me. I wanted to believe that Aidan had told her mother about us. As she approached, I could smell the clove blowing off her cigarette. Her hands ablaze with rings. Aquamarine and amethyst stones the size of a child's fist. She came closer and I could smell her perfume. Patchouli. Not the musky toilet water hippies bought at head shops. Her cologne was sultry and fresh. She smelled like California before everyone went west. When California was just an idea, just the ocean carrying its breath over land. I wanted her to take me wherever she was going.

I wasn't sure if the man pushing the dolly was a driver or something more, a bodyguard or boyfriend. He popped open the trunk and didn't see me as I approached Aidan's mother and introduced myself.

"I was your daughter's friend," I said, my voice hoarse.

Aidan's mother put her cigarette up to her lips. She inhaled, holding the smoke down deep in her chest, then exhaling with purpose. "Glad to hear my daughter had a friend."

While the driver packed the trunk, we sat together in the back of the Town Car sinking into the plush seats. I wasn't sure where to begin, what to say about Aidan, how to raise my suspicions. I couldn't imagine the pain of losing a child. Of no longer being a mother.

"Are you young for a teacher or old for a student?" she asked.

I smiled. "Student."

She held out a box of Djarum cigarettes and told me to call her Marieke.

"Marieke," I said. "That's pretty. I've never heard that before."

"It means star of the sea." She lit my cigarette. "But it's really just a fancy way of saying Marie. Aidan used to make fun of all the kids here and their silly East Coast names. Tizzey and Dizzey." Marieke reached over to the front seat and with one hand dug into an enormous leather purse. She immediately located what she was looking for and slipped either a mint or a pill into her mouth.

I took a long drag on the cigarette, the clove oil like candy on my lips. For a moment, I thought that if I made my eyelids heavy, my sight blurry, I could convince myself that it was Aidan and not her mother I was sitting beside. That Aidan had been returned to me. I wanted to tell Marieke that I was sorry for her loss, that I missed her daughter. Instead, I just kept smoking.

Marieke opened the window, flicking ashes, straightening her rings. I let the cigarette burn between my fingers. When Aidan first told me about her mom, I'd imagined meeting her in Malibu, quizzing her about Jerry Garcia and Jane Fonda. This was not the happy occasion I'd hoped for. I kept thinking about the film Marieke had produced. A story about an old man and his cat. I'd never seen the movie, but Aidan had warned me that if I ever met her mother, I needed to tell her how much I loved it. "It's an ego thing," she said. "Tell her it made you cry."

I feared that anything I said about Aidan would bore or annoy Marieke, afraid that at any moment she might finish smoking and be done with me. I was about to bring up Race's party when she stuck her head out the window and summoned the driver, then turned to me and asked, "Can you show me where they found her?"

We drove to the beach. Marieke had dozens of silver bangles on her wrists, the bracelets crashing against one another like cymbals. I kept thinking of the cat, not the one in Marieke's film but the one in Aesop's fable, the one the mice gave the bell to so they'd always hear her coming.

Aidan had said that when her mother was a young girl, she'd used her inheritance to finance her freedom, running away from home, flirting with young musicians and old movie stars. Positioning herself as muse, starlet, businesswoman. "She's not a bad mother, she's just not interested in mothering. When she's in a room, there's not enough air for anyone else."

The car windows were tinted brown. They turned the sky to smog, the sand to dirt, the ocean to mud. When we parked at the beach, Marieke leaned forward and asked the driver, "Is this what you thought it would look like?"

He said, "Ma'am, I didn't make a clear picture."

"I think it's rather ordinary." Marieke unzipped her tall purple suede boots and slipped out her feet. I wasn't used to noticing things like nail polish, but Marieke's toes were painted a familiar cobalt blue.

From her purse she removed a small cloth bag with a drawstring and said, "Show me what my daughter saw in this place."

There wasn't much to see. The yachts were gone. The sea grass matted down. The low tide had left behind pockets of brackish water. Dried beds of seaweed made the beach seem shabby, unkempt. I walked Marieke down to the sandbar, pointed to the groin of rocks. "That's where she was standing the first time we met." I paused, then asked, "Did she ever mention me when you two spoke?"

"Hard to say." The winds swirled around Marieke, her dress rippling against her body. I could see how thin she was. She had a flat chest, the buds of her nipples pushing against the silk. Marieke held up her hand and pointed to one of her rings. "Aidan gave me this little gem." A large green stone towered over her index finger. "We were watching the surfers climb the waves along Dana Point. Aidan found this piece of beach glass. She must have been ten years old. I had it made into a ring. See how the light shines through." She held the ring up for me to see.

The green stone glowed warmly from within, emitting a strong yellow nimbus of light.

I said, "Aidan was like a light meter. She could measure whether a person gave off light or took light. Your daughter was incredible."

"We all take more light than we give." Marieke asked if I wouldn't mind putting some sand in her little cloth bag. "I'm making a reliquary."

I didn't know what that word meant, but I squatted down and sprinkled dry sand into the tiny sack, slipped a pair of shiny yellow shells, jingle shells, Cal called them, inside before handing the bag back to Marieke.

"I'm not going to blame myself," Marieke said. "Mothers are always blamed when their children are hurt."

I tucked my hands into my jeans pockets.

"It's her father's fault," Marieke said. "I could never kill myself."

Without meaning to, I'd stumbled on to something. Marieke reached out and brushed a few stray hairs off my forehead. "What's your name again?"

"Jason."

"Jason, you'll have to forgive me. I'm feeling terribly lost. My therapist says I'm creating my own stages of grief."

Her perfect hair blew across her face. She reached up, gathering her curls together, tying them into a knot. Her bracelets chiming in the wind. An airplane flew overhead. Across the water, boats were being salvaged, ships were being built, money was being made.

"I really don't think it was a suicide," I said. "An accident maybe. But I think these boys, the ones with the silly names, they might have done something. There was a party and I don't know what I happened but I can imagine—"

Marieke shook her head and interrupted. "Until this morning, I was willing to believe anything. But your headmaster, he gave me the letter they found. I wish he hadn't. Now I know it wasn't an accident. Aidan wanted this. You have no idea how sick this whole thing makes me." She turned her back to me for a moment. Her body shivered. "I forgot how cold it gets," she said. "I thought my daughter would be safe here. Why did I think she'd be safe?"

Marieke twisted the ring off her finger. She held up the green glass to the light, showed me how the ocean had smoothed the surface, how a single bump in the glass looked like a wave. Then she knelt down onto the beach, her dress blooming around her. "I imagined setting up a memorial out here. Maybe making a cross out of driftwood. That seems foolish now." With her manicured hands she dug deep into the wet sand, scooping out piles of pebbles. When she finished digging, she dropped the ring down into the hole. She said something, a prayer maybe, performing her grief.

A hermit crab sidestepped around the gully. Marieke picked up the crab, its red body retracting inside its small brown house of a shell. She poked her finger into the opening where the crab had disappeared, and when the crab didn't pop back out, she dropped it down the hole. Marieke cast a handful of sand down after the crab. She buried the ring and the crab together. Like a child collapsing a sand castle, she patted down the wet beach. "There," she said. "Enough."

The letter complicated matters, but it didn't change the fact that Aidan had been at Race's. I tried to imagine what was in Aidan's note, what turn of phrase had convinced Marieke that her daughter had taken her own life. More than anything, I wanted to read the letter, but that was not an intimacy I could demand. Driving back to Bellingham, I struggled over bringing up the party again. It seemed cruel to force the issue. Instead, I reassured Marieke that Aidan had been happy these last few weeks.

"Sometimes," she said, "happiness is the boost people need." Marieke jangled her bracelets. "My therapist doesn't worry about her depressives until they begin to feel better. That's precisely when they summon up the energy to walk into the ocean."

I looked out the window. "When did you last speak with Aidan?" I asked. "How did she sound to you?"

Marieke had placed the tap shoes on the floor. She held up the black-and-white patent leather shoes and asked if Aidan had ever shown them to me. Then she leaned forward and showed the driver. He said, "Wow, Astaire had small feet."

Marieke turned to me and asked, "Do you want them?"

I did. I wanted something of Aidan's. Cal's mother had promised to give me his watch. An old Breitling with an enormous face and a marine chronometer. The kind of timepiece a sailor could actually use to determine longitude for celestial navigation. Caroline had meant to give me the watch at Cal's memorial service, but I saw her wearing it around her own thin wrist. It was much too big. It looked like it actually hurt her wrist to wear it, but she claimed she couldn't bring herself to let it go. "I'm sorry," she said, "but it's a comfort to me."

Marieke held up the tap shoes, offering them again. I said, "You don't remember, do you? You don't remember the last time you spoke with Aidan."

"I know it was a few weeks ago." She cleared her throat. "I just don't remember anything my daughter said." She held the tap shoes against her chest, then put them down between us.

"You shouldn't give them away," I said. "You'll regret it."

"They're ghost shoes," she said. "All they'll do is haunt me."

I left the tap shoes in the car, watched Marieke drive off behind tinted windows. She had a plane to catch, a life to return to. There were an infinite number of ways to mourn, and I figured that Marieke would try on as many as she could. For now she seemed resigned to her daughter's death. Maybe Aidan really was her father's daughter. Maybe she had inherited his fate.

Before Marieke left, she told me I was handsome. She held her hand up to my cheek and asked if I'd ever broken my nose. I told her it had been broken for me. "I bet you photograph well," she said. "That broken nose of yours gives you character. Be sure to take care of it."

"My nose?" I asked.

"No," she said, "your character."

I'd ditched my classes and failed to make it to the infirmary. I'd ridden in cars without permission, violated curfew, brazenly sneaked in and out of dorms, smoked countless cigarettes, imbibed all sorts of cheap liquor. Even for a school that catered to rule breakers, I'd broken an extreme number of rules. It wasn't clear that anyone would be looking for me or that anyone even cared about the rules I'd broken, but I decided to turn myself in, to go to the headmaster and tell him that I was having problems. I also thought that maybe there was some small chance that if I mentioned my doubts about Aidan's suicide, if I brought up Race's party and, without saying anything specific about Leo, suggested that Aidan had been out on Powder Point during the storm, then maybe Windsor would feel the need to do something.

I hadn't been inside the administrative offices since arriving at Bellingham. Tinks sat behind the reception desk barking into a red phone. A pair of eyeglasses balanced on the tip of her nose while another rested on the top of her head. I saw a third pair by the typewriter on her desk. Three different ways of seeing. In the background, two different phone lines were ringing and a small portable TV was turned on and flickering. Red banners flashed along the top and bottom of the screen as numbers scrolled by. A voice narrated film of a warship and images of oil platforms. Tinks nodded at me and held up two fingers, signaling for me to wait. I could hear the phones in Windsor's and Warr's offices ringing.

Tinks returned the phone to its cradle and it began to ring again. She flashed a quick smile. "You need help?"

I explained that I wanted to meet with the headmaster and she informed me that that wouldn't be possible. "Why are you out of dress code?"

"I'm sick," I said. "Caught that cholera Windsor warned us about."

"Quel tragedy." Tinks clucked her tongue and switched the glasses on her nose with the ones on her head. The phone rang again and Tinks answered and asked the person on the other end to hold. "You're Jason Prosper," she said, as though informing me of some crucial unknown fact. "We're going to need to speak with your father."

"What's going on?" I asked.

"Crisis control," she said.

"Does this have anything to do with Aidan?" I wondered if somehow the news of Race's party had leaked, if Leo had gone to the police.

"Everything's topsy-turvy. The stock market's crashing. We bombed some oil platforms and might be going to war with Iran. The dean can meet with you in an hour or so. In the meantime, let's try and get your dad on the phone. Maybe he can save us."

I hardly ever called my father at work, but when I did his secretaries usually put me straight through. Every number I tried was busy, and when I finally reached a person, she told me that my father was unavailable. "I'm his son," I said.

The voice on the other end said, "I'm sure he'll call you back."

Tinks looked up from her desk. "Couldn't reach him? Not as much pull as I thought."

"This crash couldn't come at a worse time." Dean Warr ushered me into his office. "Our endowment's going to take a hit. Have you spoken to your father yet? Will he come out of this with his shirt?"

"My father's divorcing my mother. I think she gets to keep all his shirts."

"Laughing to keep from crying," Warr said. "We're counting on your father for those dorms."

This was the second time I'd been pawned off on the dean. I wasn't qualified to talk about money. Riegel was right—I didn't really care about wealth. I could afford not to. "I'm sure everything will work out," I said, wondering just how bad this crash would turn out to be. If, at that moment, bankers were diving out of windows. "My father prides himself on weathering storms."

Warr's arms were small for his body, like a dinosaur's, a T.rex. He waved them in front of himself, declaring their uselessness, then got up from his desk. "Well, be sure to have your dad call us when he has a minute." Warr struck me on the back and began escorting me from his office.

We'd barely spoken, and already I was being shown the door.

"I wanted to talk to you about Aidan."

He nodded his head. "Terrible business. The mother was here this morning. The headmaster and I did our best to comfort her. Poor child was a lost cause."

"See, that's the thing," I said. "Aidan wasn't a lost cause."

Tinks came into the office with a stack of papers. She said, "The Dow dropped five hundred points, lost over twenty percent of its value. Tuition is due this week." Tinks looked at me and said, "You're still here?" She walked out without waiting for an answer.

Warr flipped through the papers Tinks had dropped on his desk. He half listened as I explained about the party, how I wasn't there but how I knew that Aidan had been out at Powder Point. When I finished, Warr looked up and asked, "Anything else?"

"I just don't think it was a suicide."

"You were sweet on this girl." Warr's lip caught on his dry teeth. "I'm glad to hear things are going in that direction."

It was a straight shot and I felt the blow.

"I'll look into this party matter." Warr nodded toward the door.

It was time to leave. "One last thing." My pulse quickened. "The party was at Race Goodwyn's house. I'm pretty sure your son was there."

It was a ballsy move on my part, but I figured I could risk it. Warr didn't need me, but he needed my father's money. If the world had in fact come crashing down, if the stock market had fallen, if we were headed toward a war, I was happy to lead the charge. Happy to let it all crumble.

In Whitehall that night, Tazewell kept playing the same R.E.M. song over and over again. The lyrics carrying down the hallway and into my room. The voice resigned but sincere: "It's the end of the world as we know it, and I feel fine."

ELEVEN

Parents' Weekend coincided with the Halloween Dance. I wasn't thrilled about seeing my dad or watching my classmates prance around as monsters and superheroes. Mom chose to stay in New York so that Dad could drive up in his Cadillac and bask in the attention surrounding the big Prosper Hall and Windsor House groundbreakings. Half a pine forest would need to be cleared in order to make room for the new dorms. I stood sandwiched between Dad and Windsor as we dug into the loamy earth with our ceremonial shovels. A photographer flashed his camera, and my dad said to Windsor, "Make sure I get a copy of this. I'm starting a bragging wall."

Dad looked surprisingly good. He'd lost weight and seemed relaxed, like he was on an indefinite golf vacation. "The St. Regis is agreeing with you," I said.

"Let's give credit where credit is due. The divorce was your mother's idea."

After the groundbreaking, Windsor held a reception for visiting parents at his home. His wife, Charlotte, played hostess, leading parents through the large white complex past the colonnade of what I knew from freshman ancient history to be Doric and not Ionic columns, and inside the sunny atrium. "We think of this home as the school's family room. Students are always welcome here." I'd never been inside the headmaster's house before. Had never even seen Charlotte Windsor. She was a reed-thin woman with perfect posture. Rumor had it that she lived on a horse farm in Virginia and flew up only to perform these wifely duties.

The house was all dark wood and red walls, the marble floors interrupted by bursts of gold carpets. A fire warmed the grand room, silver bowls shimmering atop the mantel. While parents clung awkwardly to their children, caterers sharked around the party with trays of cheese puffs. My father drank scotch and soda and kept sending me off to the bar to refill his glass while he held court, bragging to Tazewell's dad about the killing he'd made on the stock market crash, touting the strength of treasury bonds. "When you know what you're doing, even in a bear market, there's a fortune to be made."

It wasn't like my dad to talk about money. He was usually pretty tight-lipped and restrained, but the crash seemed to have brought something out in him. Maybe he needed people to know he was still on top.

Windsor also couldn't stop talking about money, shamelessly fundraising. The twin elms the storm had uprooted from Windsor's front lawn had been hauled away, but Windsor hadn't replaced them. He'd left the grass bedding raw, the soil exposed, and kept pointing out the window and asking parents for donations. "We've got to fill up the holes," he said. "We don't want any babies falling down and getting trapped." Kriffo's dad went outside and made a big ceremony of tossing a twenty-dollar bill into the deeper of the two cavities. As parents joined and left the party, a spirit of giving developed and more bills were added until both holes were covered in a fresh turf of green money. No one bothered to collect the donations. Maybe Windsor didn't want to be seen crouched down and literally money grubbing, or maybe he couldn't bring himself to trust one of the caterers to collect the cash.

The winds stirred, and soon the bills simply blew away, tumbleweeding across campus. For weeks afterward I saw tens, twenties, and fifties nesting in the lower branches of trees, clogging sewer drains. Even then no one from Bellingham claimed the currency. Earlier in the semester, Kriffo had told a story about Malcolm Forbes. "You know how rich that guy is? If Forbes was on his way to a business meeting and he saw a hundred-dollar bill on the sidewalk, it wouldn't be worth it for him to pick it up. In the time it took him to stoop down, he'd actually lose money." The story spread and found a captive audience. None of my classmates snatched up any of the stray dollars.

It was weird to see my classmates with their parents. Tazewell's father, Archwell, had a shock of bright white hair, a frail body. More like a grandpa than a dad. At one point Taze actually locked arms with his father, steadying him, guide-dogging his dad to the bathroom. I watched Race help his mother out of her coat. A sparrow of a woman, she stood beside Race, licking her hand and pressing down her son's red cowlick. She had a pretty face, a tiny nose, and thin pale lips, but she didn't seem to have any eyebrows. It looked as though her eyebrows had been singed off. Kriffo's dad was average-sized with a bald head and a barrel chest. However, his mother was enormous. Everything about her was big: her breasts, her hair, her voice. She looked like the world's scariest gym teacher. I heard her say, "My son is a champion."

It was strange to witness these guys with their parents, to see them as sons, to know that there were people in the world who would do anything to protect them. I had yet to ask any of these guys about the party, knowing how easy it would be for them to lie to me.

Through a window, I spied Yazid alone without any family in tow. Since Aidan's death I'd felt numb. I resented going through the motions of this social ceremony. Yazid saw me and grinned. I made my way out onto the veranda, hoping he might smoke me up and strengthen my numbness.

By the time I got outside, Yazid had been joined by an older man. The guy leaned toward one of the columns and pressed his ear against the white shaft. The stranger saw me and said, "Would you believe these are hollow?"

The man motioned for Yazid and me to place our ears against the column. He knocked lightly and we heard an echo.

"They look solid," Yazid said, "but you're correct. There's nothing inside."

The man had dark hair, a patch of gray skunked on his right temple. While the other fathers were all dressed in suits and ties, this man wore brown corduroys, a green plaid Pendleton. His chin bristled with black-and-white stubble. I didn't recognize him at first, but I'd seen this guy before. Diana's father.

"These columns." He tapped the wood. "Back when I was a student here, the seniors used to tie a sophomore to each column right after Winter Break. First snow. 'Getting shafted.' That's what we called it. We'd do it in the early morning so the headmaster could wake up and see those sophomores in their pajamas. You boys still do that?"

Yazid shrugged.

"I'm not sure," I said. "I haven't been here that long."

"It was good fun. Or maybe it was a crummy thing to do. Either way." He rubbed his hands against his chin, itching his beard, then he asked us if we knew his daughter. Yazid and I both told him what we figured every parent hopes to hear: that Diana was nice, sweet.

"Smart girl," he said. "But don't let her fool you. She's a tough one."

Yazid gave me a wink, then brought his thumb and index finger up to his lips, motioning that he was escaping to toke up. I started to follow Yazid, but Diana's father asked a question about night swimming. "Do you guys still swim after dark?"

"I did once," I said. "The water in the harbor stays pretty warm."

Diana's father told me about a farm his grandparents owned up in Vermont. "There's a lake, water's so damn cold and pure. Ruined me for swimming anywhere else. Diana hates it up there. Too quiet for her." He turned away from me and looked through the windows down into the party.

Diana was inside chatting with Archwell. She wore a blue kilt and white blouse, her hair pulled off her face with a black headband. She looked professionally pretty, not overly primped like a model but like it was her job to be worth looking at.

"You know, you try," Diana's father said, "to do everything for your kids." With that he walked down the colonnade, knocking lightly on each column as he went.

Chester's mother, Lorraine, had her son's curly eyelashes and soft voice. Together we strolled over to the dining hall for the Parents' Weekend banquet. Lorraine remembered me from Martha's Vineyard, and

I thanked her for sending Chester care packages. "Bet nothing at dinner will taste as good."

The Dining Hall had been transformed. The long tables covered in white linen cloths, formal place settings, glass bowls swimming with baby roses. Instead of the typical salad bar fare, the school had sprung for a buffet of raw oysters, crab claws, and shrimp cocktail surrounded by a fleet of ice sculptures. Carved replicas of tall ships with votive candles set around the glistening ice. I admired the sailboats as they dripped, melting away. Dad said, "Our tuition dollars hard at work."

The cafeteria staff had been forced into tuxedos and served us standing rib roast, creamed spinach, and potatoes au gratin. "You eat like this every night?" my father asked. "Hardly," I said. I looked around for Leo. He hadn't shown his face to me in days, and I'd begun to lose any hope that he might speak to the police. I thought of asking my father for advice, but he'd probably tell me to forget about Aidan, to put her behind me. That's what he had insisted on with Cal. I knew that wouldn't work. I thought about Aidan and Cal all the time. But they didn't live in my imagination. They were more real to me, more present in my daily life than my family.

I introduced Dad to Lorraine, and he was instantly smitten. Chester's father had stayed back in New York and my dad assumed the role of Lorraine's escort. He pulled out her chair and poured her wine. Reminding me of how he used to be with my mom. It was embarrassing to see him flirt, to be so brazen as to stare at Lorraine's cleavage. He asked how she filled her days, imagining her to be some perfect housewife, and was visibly surprised to learn that she was an executive at Kidder, Peabody & Co.

"Your crew is having a tough time," he said.

"We're built for it," Lorraine challenged.

Our parents discussed corporate takeovers, junk bonds, derivatives, and insider trading. They argued over some guy named Marty Siegel who was either a genius banker or a no-good criminal.

Chester asked me if I was going to the Halloween Dance that night.

"I wasn't planning on it," I said. "I don't have a costume."

"Just wear your suit," he said. "Say that you're an insider trader."

"Are you dressing up?" I asked. "Do people here do that?"

Chester told me that he'd been working on his costume for days and couldn't wait to unveil it. His mother leaned forward and said, "Halloween is Chester's favorite holiday. When he was little, he would dress up as a ghost. He was always so serious. It was a treat to see him have fun."

"Cool it, Mom," Chester warned.

Lorraine described one Halloween when she and Chester were walking through their neighborhood in White Plains. As she held Chester's hand and he swung his plastic jack-o'-lantern, he said, "I'm so happy. I'm so happy."

"He's won every tennis match he's ever played, but that's the only time I ever heard him say he was happy." Lorraine reached out and touched the scar on Chester's face.

"Here's to happiness," my father toasted.

Just then there was a loud crash. A few of us dashed out of our seats to see Tazewell's father supine on the floor covered in pink shrimp. The ice sculptures had thawed and, while trolling for shrimp cocktail, the old man had slipped on a puddle of melted sailboats. Dad ran right over to his friend and lifted him up, making sure that nothing had broken. Clearly embarrassed, Archwell allowed my dad to escort him out to the parlor. Tazewell was nowhere to be seen.

When my father returned, Lorraine was worried that he hadn't had any dessert. He deserved a reward for his good citizenship. She sent me off to beg for cheesecake. I went back into the kitchen asked a middle-aged woman who was scouring a large silver kettle if she wouldn't mind giving me an extra slice of cake. Then I said, "Is Leo working tonight?"

"Not tonight, not tomorrow night, or the night after that. Leo doesn't work here anymore." She couldn't tell me if Leo had quit or been fired. She handed me the cheesecake and continued to clean up the kitchen.

Dad was staying with Windsor, and I walked him over to the headmaster's house to say good night. He collapsed onto one of the Adirondack chairs that lined the porch and told me to have a seat. My dad had behaved better than I'd imagined possible.

"You were full of heroics today," I said.

"I loved prep school. Happiest time of my life."

I didn't know much about my father's childhood. I'd never bothered to ask and he'd rarely offered any stories. He'd grown up within blocks of our current apartment, gone to Kensington and then Princeton, working his entire adult life at the investment bank his grandfather had founded. I wondered how similar our paths would be. Mine had already diverged from his.

"Archwell is a kick in the pants." Dad slapped his knee. "Would you believe that crone is only three years older than me? He's been married four times, divorced four times. Each wife took a little more away."

It bothered me to hear Dad joke about divorce. I tried to remember the last time I'd seen my parents kiss or rub each other's shoulders. When I was little and they kissed, Riegel and I would cover our eyes, claim to be disgusted.

"That Lorraine was wonderful. How's her son?"

"He's a solid guy. Tennis star."

"Poor gal doesn't know she's about to lose her job. That's the rub of this crash. A lot of good people are getting sacked."

"Did you warn her?" I asked.

"God, no. Not my place. Never be the messenger of bad news if you can avoid it." Dad unbuttoned the collar of his shirt and pulled open his tie. "Everything working out for you here?" He stretched his long legs over the porch.

"There was some trouble," I said. "With a girl, a friend of mine."

"Windsor mentioned that you were part of some rescue effort. Said you were a big help."

"I wouldn't say that." I thought about describing the yachts being salvaged and flown overhead. My father would have appreciated the image, but the sight of all those flying boats, the beauty of that day, had been destroyed by the ugliness of finding Aidan. I played with the bracelet Tazewell had made for me.

"I've heard good reports on you all around," Dad said. "Your brother claims you seem like your old self."

I wasn't sure what that meant, who this old self might have been.

Was even less certain that I wanted to know. "Riegel took me on this wild-goose chase. I don't think you'd be too pleased."

My father looked at me. I waited for a nod, a sign for me to continue.

"Your brother," he said, "is blowing off steam. A final hurrah before he graduates. He knows I have a job waiting for him."

I tried to explain that Riegel had snared Ginger and Dill into some scheme, but my father reminded me that it was bad form to be a messenger or a snitch.

"Loyalty first, son. Your brother can come to me if he gets into any trouble."

We were both startled by a knock on the window. Windsor held up a bottle of Maker's Mark, his knuckles clenched around the red wax neck.

"Showtime." Dad got up and headed inside. "Have fun at your dance." He saluted good night. "Don't worry about Riegel. I have my eye on him."

On my way to Whitehall, I imagined Windsor and my father having a boozy time together reminiscing about their Princeton days. The kind of thing Cal and I would never have the chance to do. I was torn between going to sleep and coming up with a costume for the dance. Unlike Chester, I wasn't a fan of Halloween. I got to my room and stretched out on my bed staring up at the ceiling. A few days after Cal died, I'd heard one of the guys on the sailing team joke that if your roommate committed suicide, you got an automatic 4.0 GPA. "Prosper's one lucky bastard." No one laughed, but still, the comment made me furious. I'd threatened the kid, Donald Fisher, and he'd apologized.

Kensington had a real stiff-upper-lip mentality and no one thought I needed any counseling around Cal's death. Until I met Aidan, I'd never trusted anyone with my feelings or believed that talking about them could help. Cal had killed himself; Aidan had probably done the same. Full of self-pity, I thought, "Why not join them?" I knew I could fashion a sturdy noose without much effort, but there were no pipes in my room. Nothing to secure the rope around. Pills seemed too passive and unreliable. Slitting my wrists required privacy and a bathtub.

Stretching across my bed, weighing the various methods for suicide, I began to feel a strong pressure on my bladder. I had to piss. I started to get up and then it occurred to me that if I was serious about ending my life, if I was really that sick, then it shouldn't matter where I peed. I should just do it right there, wet my bed. The image of a nearly grown man pissing himself didn't strike me as sad or pathetic. It struck me as pure comedy. I got up and went to the bathroom.

There was still the question of a costume. After searching my room, I changed into a dark navy L.L. Bean Norwegian sweater with white Vs woven into the blue knit like bird's eyes. From there I pulled on some well-worn khakis and a pair of Sperry Topsiders. I stuck a notepad in my back pocket. It might not have seemed like much of a costume, but if anyone asked, I was *The Preppy Handbook*.

Back at the Dining Hall, an actual mirrored disco ball had been temporarily installed on the ceiling, sending prisms of light over the dark room. The ice sculptures remained, but the tables had been pushed clear so that students could dance. No one was dancing. Everyone was lined against the wall or sitting on sofas. Coach Tripp and the Spanish teacher, Ms. Alvarez, made a halfhearted show of chaperoning. The two were camped out on the stairs leading up to the girls' dorm. Coach Tripp kept taking sips from a red plastic cup and handing it to Ms. Alvarez.

A DJ played "Girls Just Want to Have Fun," while Kriffo and Stuyvie imitated Archwell slipping and falling. Tazewell worked a butter knife against the ice sculptures, skimming the frosty shavings across the dance floor.

All three guys had on the same dark sunglasses, black suits, and thin black ties. Diana sat on a sofa and watched. She wore black tights and a black leotard with a red paper heart broken into two halves pinned to her chest, a single teardrop painted in the corner of her eye.

"Who are you supposed to be?" I asked.

"I'm Misery." She pointed to Taze, Kriffo, and Stuyvie. "And they're my company."

Tazewell handed me a business card with THE COMPANY printed in the center. He kissed Diana's neck and said, "Misery loves company."

"Clever," I said.

Taze strutted out onto the dance floor and chest-bumped Kriffo.

"It was Aidan's idea." She spoke as though Aidan were in another room, watching. "Don't tell them," Diana whispered to me. "My little tribute."

"I saw her mother," I said.

"The drama queen. Aidan couldn't stand her." Diana got up from the couch and swayed, nearly fainting.

I helped her sit back down. All of the other girls were dressed in tight sequined clothes with lots of glitter on their faces. Sexy fairies, slutty witches. I saw Nadia in a pink tutu and tiara. Brizzey wore high heels and a polka dot bikini. She had a sash around her body that said in shimmering letters, MISS FUCKING AMERICA.

I wanted to ask Diana if she had been out on Powder Point that night, if she knew anything. She bopped her head to the music, her eyes rolling back. "Have you seen Chester?" I asked. "He told me he has a killer costume."

"Was that his mom you were sitting with at dinner?" she asked.

I told her that Chester's mother was nice and that my father seemed to have developed a crush on her.

"She's really pretty." Diana bit her nails. "Wish my dad hadn't come."

"I met him," I said. "He seemed pretty cool."

"He's a freak." Diana sat up. "At least he's given up on buying my love." She slouched back down again and asked, "Have you ever milked a goat?"

Diana mumbled something about her father leaving New York to become a farmer in Vermont. I couldn't tell what drugs she was on. She was too animated for pot, not quite amped up enough for coke. She slurred her words but didn't smell like she'd been drinking. My bet was that it was a combination of pharmaceuticals. Beads of sweat collected at her temples. With her teeth, Diana tore half of the nail from her pinkie. She stared at the blood rising off her skin. "Are you going to be okay?" I asked.

"Not for a long time," she said.

I wrapped a napkin around her pinkie and propped Diana up on the couch, then looked around for Chester, thinking he might be able to take care of her. She needed a guardian, someone to lead her away from the bad company she was keeping. I saw Chester across the room. He wore a jacket made out of a stiff, glittery material that shone in the strobe of the disco ball. Before I could reach him, Race walked up to me, wearing the same black suit and sunglasses as his buddies.

"Let's talk." He flipped his sunglasses onto his head.

"Not now," I said. "Diana's sick."

"Taking care of girls," he said. "That's your weakness. Heard you told Warr about the party. Pretty uncool."

After days of wondering what to do, how to confront my friends, I decided to simply be direct. "Was she there?" I asked. "Did you see Aidan?"

"Look." Race placed his open palm flat against my chest. "I can't keep track of everyone who comes to my house. It's possible she gate-crashed, but I didn't see her."

"Well, someone did."

Race lifted his hand from my chest. "So what if she was there? No one remembers her. Maybe that's why she killed herself."

We stared at each other until Race put his sunglasses back on and looked away. In that moment I wondered how easy it would be for me to tackle Race, pin him to the ground. I weighed the costs and benefits of this violence. The DJ segued into the Cure's "Why Can't I Be You?" I placed my own hand firmly against Race's chest. "I'm sorry," I said, "if I caused you trouble. But if you've got nothing to hide, you've got nothing to worry about."

"I've got college to worry about." Race removed my hand from his chest.

Before Race could say anything else, Diana let out a shriek. Race and I both looked up in time to see Kriffo force Chester into a head-lock, dragging him out onto the empty dance floor. Kriffo pulled at Chester's shoulders, tearing his shiny suit. I thought he might rip Chester's arms from their sockets. Before I could break them up, Kriffo lost his footing on the slick wet floor. Kriffo fell backward, torquing

Chester's body underneath his own, using Chester as a cushion. Even with the music blaring, with Robert Smith imploring, "Oh, why can't I, I, I be you?" I heard Chester hit the floor, heard a snap as Kriffo smashed the burden of his weight onto Chester's trim body.

Lorraine came to Whitehall the next morning. She needed to collect some clothing and belongings for Chester. The snap I'd heard was the sound of his humerus fracturing. "We're taking him to a specialist for surgery. He'll be in rehab for weeks, months, even."

Everything had happened so quickly. I kept trying to explain what I'd seen. How Kriffo had twisted their bodies together. "Will Chester be back?" I asked.

"I don't know," she said. "I hope so, for his sake."

Coach Tripp had been reluctant to move Chester. "Just stay still," he warned. Ms. Alvarez ran off to call an ambulance. I waited by Chester's side as the adrenaline surged through my friend's body, temporarily blocking any pain. I crouched beside him, promised everything would be okay. Diana stayed for a bit before leaving with Tazewell. I wondered if the fight had anything to do with her. Chester watched her leave, his eyes tearing up.

I said, "She's not worth it."

"She's worth it." He winced. "Just doesn't know that she's worth it."

Chester's coat, his costume, was made out of a weirdly textured material. I reached out and rubbed my fingertips along the hem. Sandpaper. He'd covered one of his sport coats in sheets of the stuff. "What is it?" I asked.

"I think my arm's broken."

"No, your costume. What are you supposed to be?" I felt the roughness of the sandpaper.

"Oh," Chester said. "I'm abrasive."

I carried Chester's suitcase down the stairs and out to his mom's car, explaining how I'd inspired her son's costume. Lorraine laughed and I was happy to see her smile.

Out by the Flagpole, Diana stood alone watching us from a distance. She had on a long white button-down and one of Tazewell's jackets, her legs bare, ballet slippers on her feet. Diana waved. I nodded at her, then said to Lorraine, "That's Diana. She's Chester's lamppost."

Lorraine looked at Diana and said nothing. In her silence, I once again heard the snap of Chester's arm. Kriffo had barely apologized. "He started it," he told Coach Tripp, the sandpaper from Chester's suit having scraped and bloodied Kriffo's cheeks and hands. "I was just defending myself."

Lorraine gave me a tight hug. Despite spending the night in the emergency ward, she managed to smell like vanilla, like cookies cooling on a rack. "Tell your father it was a pleasure to meet him." She wrote down a phone number. "It would be nice if in a few days you could call Chester and check up on him. He likes you. He hasn't liked anyone in a long time."

I was on my way over to speak to Diana when a station wagon with wood paneling pulled up in front of Astor. Diana's father slinked out of the car wearing the same corduroys and flannel shirt he'd had on the day before. Diana left the seawall and joined her dad. From that distance, I couldn't hear their conversation, but they didn't seem to have much to say. Her father opened the trunk of the car, pulled out a stack of empty cardboard boxes, then disappeared inside Astor.

Diana returned to the seawall. Her hair was greasy and mussed while her lips shone bright red from the cold. I could still see the faint tracing of the tear she'd drawn in the corner of her eye. She put me in mind of a fabulous hotel room some rock star had trashed. I sat down beside her and waited for her to say something.

She asked me about Chester and his arm. She too had heard the snap, knew instantly what it meant. How it might change his life. "Maybe it will help his tennis."

I said, "I don't see how."

"I used to do ballet." Diana flexed then pointed her feet inside her slippers. "My teacher was Russian. When she was little, someone broke her feet on purpose. It was supposed to strengthen the arch."

"That's crazy," I said.

Diana asked me if I had a cigarette. I didn't. She pulled out some ChapStick and ran the wax over her lips. "Maybe Chester will get stronger. You know, in the broken place."

I lied and said, "Aidan told me you really liked Chester. She thought you two made a good couple."

"When we were roommates, Aidan and I used to stay up all night. We'd talk about the stuff you can never mention during the day."

Her words sounded familiar, reminding me of something Chester had once said.

"Aidan was a good listener," Diana said. "No judgments, no interruptions." Diana leaned back onto the cement walkway. She put her arm over her face, kicked her feet against the seawall.

I took a chance and mentioned that I knew Aidan had gone to the party. "Were you there?" I asked. "Did you go to Race's that night?"

Diana rubbed her face, smudging her mascara, racooning her eyes. "My father," she said, "he came in his fancy red convertible and rescued me from the hurricane." She pointed to the station wagon. "Now he's tooling around in that shit box."

The water was glassy and calm. It wouldn't be easy to sail in this weather, hard to find wind that wasn't there. I imagined myself out on the water heeling my boat to leeward to fill the sails.

Diana's father came out of the dorm carrying a floor lamp and an enormous stuffed toy elephant.

"What's he doing?" I asked.

"Isn't it obvious?" she said.

Diana stood up, towering over me.

I took a chance and asked Diana directly, "Do you think Race and Tazewell had anything to do with Aidan's death?"

"I don't know about that." Diana rubbed her ballet slippers against the asphalt.

"What *do* you know?"

"Look." Diana blinked. "I don't know if Aidan made it to the party or not, but what I do know is that she was pretty upset about you. The last thing I heard is that she kissed you and you made her feel like a fool."

"It wasn't like that," I said.

"I'm not saying she killed herself over you. Aidan was pretty messed up all on her own. I'm sure it wasn't your fault."

Diana's father called out to her. Hoisting more empty boxes from the trunk.

"Shit," she said. "I have to go."

I stood up. "Can we talk later?"

Diana shook her head and laughed. "You won't want to talk to me. No one will. Soon, I won't even exist."

TWELVE

In the remaining weeks of the semester, I wrote an essay for Mr. Guy on the cold war and managed to earn an A– on a calculus exam. On my paper, Mr. Guy wrote, "Your hopes for perestroika are admirable if not a little naïve. We most likely will not see an end to these tensions in our lifetimes." I received a B– and was told I could rewrite the paper. When I didn't bother to hand in a revision, Mr. Guy stopped me in the hallway and said, "Jason, I'm disappointed. When someone offers you a second chance, it's rude not to take it." I no longer believed in second chances. Maybe that was my problem with Bellingham. For me, all of the second chances I'd been given had created opportunities for me to tell another lie about myself. At first, I'd thought of Aidan as a kind of second chance. A distraction from Cal. She'd turned into something else.

The question of Aidan's death overpowered me. Like Cal, she'd become a mythical, faithful companion. I feigned interest in my own encroaching future, but always I was thinking about Aidan, wondering what had happened to her. Most mornings, I imagined Aidan coming in through the window of Mr. Guy's classroom, standing up at the lectern and staring down Race.

The only time I really saw Race was in Mr. Guy's class. He'd arrive early, sit in the front, and complain about the sailing team. How he was stuck with amateurs. The SeaWolves had suffered their first losing season since Race had started at Bellingham, and he was happy to blame Coach Tripp for the losses. "Coach has no vision. If I could have him fired and replaced before spring season starts, I would."

Earlier when I'd complained about Race, Aidan had told me that she felt sorry for him. "We've got something in common," she said. "Neither of us has a father."

I'd pointed out that Race was lucky enough to have known his dad, and Aidan said, "That must be even worse. I never knew mine. Imagine how much it must hurt to have your dad taken away."

Often in the hours before curfew, I would drop in on Yazid and watch him get high. I didn't smoke much myself. Yazid loved playing video games and arguing politics. There was still some chance that the United States would start bombing Iran, and Yazid was convinced that any war would be unwinnable. While Yazid battled through the Legend of Zelda, collecting the eight fragments of the Triforce of Wisdom, I'd nod, sleepy from my contact high, as Yazid insisted that America was already a casualty of war. "This is not your United States," he would say. "Your Manhattan is my Manhattan. Real estate invasion. That's Saudi Arabia's war."

"I surrender," I said. "Just leave me a few blocks on the Upper East Side."

Every few days I called Chester. He was anxious for details about Diana. I told him that her father had lost everything on Black Monday. "Couldn't pay tuition." I tried to say this as though it weren't gossip, but what little I learned came filtered through Brizzey's rumor mill. "Di's mom bailed. Guess her dad's having a nervous breakdown. She's stuck on some farm in Vermont taking care of him."

"Should I call her?" Chester asked. "Could you track down her number for me?"

I told Chester I'd try to figure out a way for him to reach Diana. "Here's the latest sensation," I said. "Diana left a little something behind."

At lunch Brizzey had explained that she'd gone into Diana's empty dorm room the night her friend left. She bitched and wailed, "Di borrowed all these dresses. Norma Kamali. Promised she'd dry-clean them, but those fuckers weren't hanging in her closet."

Instead of borrowed dresses, Diana had left behind a sterling silver picture frame with an 8 × 10 glossy of herself. The photo had made its way over to Whitehall and was currently on display in Tazewell's room. In the picture, Diana stood in her dorm room posing with her back to the camera. Looking over her shoulder, throwing a coy smile to an unknown photographer.

"What's so crazy about that?" Chester asked.

"Well . . ." I was out in the hallway talking on the pay phone. I lowered my voice. "Diana's naked. In the photo you can see her ass, the side of her bare breast. She's standing by a mirror so you can see her front reflection too. It's something else."

"You're killing me," Chester said.

Chester and I small-talked about college applications. He hoped to get into Columbia but worried that he'd wind up at the University of Chicago, "Where fun goes to die." I'd already been wait-listed at Princeton but was keeping this news under wraps. I hadn't bothered to apply anywhere else.

Every time we spoke, I promised Chester that I would kneecap Kriffo for him. After a few weeks of hearing this, Chester joked that I was the procrastinating hitman.

"I'm just waiting for the right opportunity."

"It's okay," Chester reassured me. "Kriffo did me a favor."

As my father predicted, Lorraine had been laid off from Kidder, Peabody. Chester suspected that playing nursemaid had kept his mother from being depressed about losing her job. "Plus, I needed a break from training. I'm not sure I even like tennis. Not anymore."

Chester asked me if I missed sailing, and I had to stop and think about whether or not I did.

"Every day my body gears up for it. My muscle memory kicks in, then my body gets confused when I don't head out to the water. I miss sailing, but what I really miss is sailing with my friend Cal. I miss waking up in the morning and going out in the freezing cold and being miserable together. I miss how we used to stretch out across the bottom of the boat and just shoot the shit. I miss him a lot."

A month or so after Black Monday, Mr. Guy assigned our class an additional paper. He wanted us to compare the recent stock market crash to the big crash in 1929, but instead of a typical footnoted essay, he insisted we do some creative research on ourselves. Determine where our own riches came from. "Find out how your families were impacted by these seismic events. How your fortunes rose and fell."

It was a curious assignment, one I might have aced. I had my father and Riegel as resources. While none of us wanted the extra work, Race immediately launched a minor revolt. "That's an invasion of privacy," Race challenged. "He can't ask us to do that."

Race and Stuyvie conspired to send around a petition. I didn't take Race's outrage seriously, didn't put my name down on any protest. When Mr. Guy was late to our next class, I waited like everyone else, watching the clock. "Ten-minute bag rule." Stuyvie picked up his knapsack, ready to ditch, when his father, Dean Warr, strode into class. One of his loafers was missing its tassel.

The dean held up the assignment sheet Mr. Guy had given us for the Black Monday essay, fanning the paper as he spoke. "It's been brought to my attention that amendments have been made to your syllabus. While our teachers are entitled to alter assignments, they are not permitted to impose additional work, especially work I deem inappropriate." Dean Warr tore the sheet of paper in half. "No one has to write this essay."

Students cheered. Race smiled. That day's class was canceled. The dean dismissed us, told us to take a free period. He was about to leave when I raised my hand. "What if we want to write the paper?"

The entire class went quiet. I cleared my throat. "Mr. Guy gave us a good assignment. Think I can learn something from it."

The dean stood in the doorway. He looked me dead on waiting for me to blink. When I didn't, he reached into his pocket, pulled out a handkerchief. "Will someone help Prosper," he asked, "wipe off his brown nose?"

Nadia began shadowing me. Though I didn't mind the attention, I wasn't interested in leading her on. We ate lunch and dinner together, and when I learned that she studied piano, I showed her the special room in the library. We played Debussy, Elton John. Nothing too heavy. We didn't so much talk as chat, and I never mentioned Cal and rarely brought up Aidan. Nadia reminded me what it was like to be young. Maybe it was selfish, but I was desperate for any scrap of innocence, happy to steal scraps from others.

At Thanksgiving my mom visited and was annoyed when I invited Nadia out to dinner with us. "Doesn't she have her own family?" Mom was confused by Nadia's Southern accent. "I thought you were seeing some movie star from California?"

"Yeah," I said. "That didn't work out."

Though it was no surprise that Kriffo avoided punishment for his fight with Chester, I was stunned just before Winter Break when Stuyvie was suspended for a week. His mom had discovered the mud-covered jerseys we'd worn to play football. Stuyvie never bothered to wash them or sneak them back into the trophy cases. Instead, he'd stashed the dirty shirts under his bed along with a collection of empty beer cans. Tazewell came to my room one night to share the news. "Sucks for Stuyvie, but at least he did the right thing. Took the fall. Didn't squeal on the rest of us." Though I appreciated Stuyvie's loyalty, I was confused by Dean Warr punishing his own son. The suspension didn't amount to much—Stuyvie couldn't go to classes or play sports. Basically, he got to stay home for a week and watch TV. "Goes on his permanent record, though," Tazewell said. "That shit follows you around."

"Why do you think Dean Warr did it?" I asked. "Punished his own son."

Taze didn't have an answer. He shrugged his shoulders. "Stuyvie's one of those guys who doesn't quite know his place. His dad probably wanted to take him down a few pegs."

The semester was almost over and I was in my room one weeknight, bullshitting my way through a physics problem set, when there was a knock at my window. I thought it was Nadia. The more we hung out, the more I feared she might make some declaration of longing. But when I got to the window, I saw a girl in a fur coat. Brizzey breathed on the glass and drew a heart in the steam. I threw open the sash and let her inside.

"Just passing through?" I asked, as I helped her climb down and into my room.

Under her fur she had on riding boots, black leggings, and a white turtleneck. She wore her hair in a high swinging ponytail.

"I was sitting in my room painting my nails"—she held up her hands, flashing her gold fingernails—"when I remembered that we used to kiss each other. We've gone this whole semester without a kiss."

Heat blasted through the dorm, but it was freezing outside. Brizzey brought in a rush of cold air. We stood together in the spot where the cold and hot air met.

"The least you can do"—Brizzey pretended to chatter her teeth—"is warm me up."

Brizzey was sexy and I was just bored enough to be interested in playing this scenario out to its logical conclusion. I considered what Robert Mitchum would do.

"Have you really come to see me?" I asked. "Or am I just the first stop on your tour?"

"Oh, you're on to me," she said. "You're not even my first. I've already visited Wee House. Those boys live up to their name."

I reached out, petting Brizzey's fur jacket. It wasn't as soft as I'd hoped. The hairs were sharp, barbed, and itched my fingers. My mother had a rich full-length sable coat that her friends were always borrowing for some state function or gala event. The coat had a double lining with secret pockets. Mom had worn it on a ski trip to St. Moritz, our last great family vacation. Mom kept the coat on even during the return flight to the States. She wouldn't let the stewardesses anywhere near it. Back in New York, after we made it through customs, Mom proudly showed Riegel and me how she'd hidden cash from a Swiss bank account inside the secret pockets. Our mother the gangster.

I was about to tell Brizzey this story when she leaned in and kissed me. I kissed her back, took off her coat, and maneuvered her over to my small bed.

Brizzey wore a padded bra. The foam lining pushed up against me as I pressed my chest firmly onto hers. I didn't like Brizzey. Wasn't even attracted to her. Somehow that made me willing and able. We kept our clothes on, rubbing and pivoting against each other, my cock hardening against her belly. I gripped my hand against her crotch and held my fingers there as Brizzey wriggled back and forth. She bit my earlobe, and before long, she came, her face red, her legs twitching. "Goddamn," she breathed. I finished myself off pumping my body against hers.

Afterward, I held Brizzey, pressuring her head down between my neck and shoulder. She probably thought I wanted to keep her close, but in truth I didn't want to see her face. It was easier for me to be with a girl I didn't care about. Rubbing against each other was just a step away from jerking off, though somehow felt lonelier.

When she finally broke free, Brizzey went right to my mirror to straighten her ponytail. "In the future," she said, "we can have sex. I'm on the pill."

Brizzey's fingernails hadn't fully dried and I noticed flecks of gold paint up and down my pant legs. I felt the sticky come against my thigh, wanted to strip down and change my clothes.

Brizzey snooped around my dresser. I'd looked up the word Marieke had used, "reliquary," and decided to keep Aidan alive through objects. On my dresser, I'd placed the key to the piano room, the stolen library copy of *Sailing Alone Around the World,* the whale in a bottle, the apricot pit, and the tangerine, which hadn't rotted but rather dried, shrinking into a hard orange globe. Brizzey picked up the key before snatching the picture of Cal from the corner of my mirror. "Oh, my God," she said. "I haven't thought about him in ages." She sat back down on my bed holding the snapshot. "Fuck me, he was handsome." Brizzey laughed. "I mean you guys look alike."

"Believe me," I said. "I know I'm already past my prime."

"I never think about that," Brizzey said. "Getting older." She stretched her neck out and ran her hand across her tight skin. "In a way Cal's lucky. He'll always be seventeen."

I had to stop myself from tearing the photo away from Brizzey. She'd known Cal. Dated him just as she'd dated me, but I didn't want her remembering him. Her version of Cal was not something that interested me. Cal and I had both predicted that Brizzey would marry young, divorce, then elope with some European slob with a fake title. She was doomed to run around Greenwich, forcing everyone to call her "the Duchess."

"She's no dummy," Cal had said. "She could probably run a Fortune 500 Company what with all of her insights and evil."

"Remember when we went to the Gold and Silver?" Brizzey asked. "Back then, I liked Cal better, but now I'm not so sure."

She tried to kiss me and I moved away. "You should probably go," I said.

"And what if I don't?"

I looked at the photo of Cal. His face smiling, laughing at me, at the trouble I'd made for myself. The more I wanted Brizzey to leave, the longer she would stay. "Have you heard from Diana?" I asked. "How is she?"

"Who knows. It's embarrassing. I've never seen anyone fall so far, so fast, and so hard."

"So you haven't spoken to her. Your best friend and you haven't checked on her?"

Brizzey got up from the bed, put on her fur. "It's cold in here," she said.

It was actually quite warm. I felt myself getting sleepy like I always did after I came.

Brizzey sat back down on the bed, the fur itchy against my skin, and asked what it was she was supposed to say to Diana. "I'm not some expert on tragedy. Not like you."

In her endangered animal fur and riding boots she looked like a character from a Russian fairy tale, like a snow queen who needed to be set on fire.

"Cal was one giant tragedy." She smiled.

"Cal is off-limits," I said.

"What about the drowned girl? Didn't you have a thing for her?"

"You didn't even know Aidan. You shouldn't talk about people you know nothing about."

"I know she'd tried it before. Almost killed herself over some lesbo."

"Where did you hear that?"

"I read her diary. I do that sort of thing."

Brizzey leaned over and kissed me. This time I didn't stop her. Brizzey tasted sweet and metallic, like I'd bitten into a chocolate candy still encased in its foil wrapper. I pulled away.

"It's good," I said, "that I don't keep a journal. I wouldn't want you knowing my secrets."

"I love secrets." Brizzey stood up and opened the window, finally prepared to make her exit.

As she climbed out onto the fire escape, it occurred to me that Brizzey didn't have a single friend. She'd visited my room because she was lonely.

Brizzey leaned back inside. "I know one of Cal's secrets." She pulled her fur collar high around her face. A wolf ready to pounce. "Cal always suspected you were secretly in love with him."

Brizzey paused, waiting for me to respond. I could have raced to the window, pulled her inside, and made her take back her words. But there was no point in arguing with Brizzey. I decided in an instant that the only way to defuse the situation was to confirm all suspicions.

"Of course I loved him." I walked toward the window. "We were best friends."

"You know that's not what I meant."

"You don't know what you mean," I said. "Because you know nothing about love." I closed the window and pulled down the shade.

Right before leaving for Christmas Break, I checked my mail one last time on the off chance that Princeton had advanced me from their waiting list. Inside my mail cubby was a Season's Greetings card signed by Windsor and a cardboard tube. I opened the cylinder and pulled out a scroll, unfurling a long glossy photo, a color copy of the all-school portrait we'd taken earlier that fall. It had been sunny that day, our faces cast in a warm golden light. We were a good-looking, cheery group of kids, quick to smile on cue.

In her floral skirt, Nadia sat hunched over in the grass, a miniature garden fairy, while Kriffo reigned on the top row like some colossus. Chester stole a glance at Diana, who had blinked, a princess waiting to be kissed. In an accidental sight gag, Yazid's hair blocked the lower half of Stuyvie's face, making it seem as though Stuyvie had a werewolf beard. Brizzey dominated the center of the picture facing the camera head on, grinning and glamorous.

With their gaudy hula girl ties, Tazewell and Race had in fact beaten the clock, doubling their appearances in the photo. They grinned brightly on the top tier of the bleachers, then reappeared like bookends standing on the opposite side of the picture. I had to admit, I was impressed. They'd performed a clever magic trick, multiplying themselves, exerting their influence.

Finally, I searched for myself. I too was on the top tier of the bleachers, but there was an empty space between Tazewell, Race, and me. Unlike my classmates who stared happily into the lens, I'd been captured in profile with my back to the camera. I thought of that day, how I'd turned and watched Aidan fall out of sight. Tazewell and Race had performed another magic trick. They'd made Aidan disappear. She was that empty space between me and my friends. For those who didn't know her, there would be no official record of her at Bellingham. No lasting image. Nothing to remember her by.

THIRTEEN

At Christmas, I returned to my childhood: my collection of Hardy Boys mysteries, the red and gray plastic pieces from a lost game of Battleship, coins of white sand dollars, my varsity letter from Kensington. In the late afternoons, I wandered down to the lobby and chatted with the doorman, Max. He was teaching me how to play chess. I was hopeful that Chester might return to Bellingham, and I was willing to do whatever it took to maintain that friendship.

Mom seemed happy to have me reinstalled in our apartment. She'd dyed her hair a soft blond and I told her it looked pretty; I also noticed that she could have passed for one of my father's secretaries. Every morning she made me fresh juice, reaming the orange halves against a jadeite hand juicer, producing not much more than a few swallows. Mom wanted to know what my plans were for Winter Break, how I hoped to keep myself busy. When I was little she was very good at arranging playdates. That was how Cal and I had met when we were just four years old. Mom worried that I'd lost touch with my old friends, but Cal was the only true friend I'd had in New York. Everyone else had turned out to be a mere acquaintance. If I'd even bothered to venture just a few blocks away from the apartment, I would have been caught up in the bustle of shoppers and Christmas lights, but the Upper East Side had an attractive dullness and gravity. I was content to stay in the quiet of our neighborhood.

Mom had decorated a tree and the whole apartment smelled of

fresh spruce. On Christmas morning, Dad came over and the four of us had breakfast together with Dad flipping pancakes and Mom telling our housekeeper, Lotta, how to fry bacon. Dad had lost a few more pounds while Riegel had gained a tire of flab around his midsection. Mom patted both of their bellies, then Dad and Riegel crouched down into boxing stances and my father gently cuffed Riegel on his neck. Everyone agreed that the salt air had been good for me and even Lotta said, "The pink is back in your cheeks." I still hadn't told my family about Aidan and what she'd meant to me. I was secretly proud of my restraint, my stoicism. My ability to manage this pain all on my own.

As we sat in the kitchen eating forkfuls of syrupy pancakes and dry bacon, I felt grateful to my family for even the illusion of closeness. The apartment had seemed a little empty without Dad. It no longer carried the musky odor of an adult male. My mother and I weren't tripping over his enormous loafers or cringing at the sound of his booming laughter. My parents were on the precipice of their divorce, and it meant a lot to me that we could still sit down and share a meal together. After breakfast, Mom gave Dad a framed watercolor of our house in Maine. "I'm taking an art class," she said.

"You made this?" Dad held the small painting and smiled. "Pretty impressive."

Dad showed off the painting and I had to admit that it was good. The palette of pastel colors soothing. Mom had captured the rustic quality of the house along with the pretty rosebushes and dark shelter of pine trees. None of us had any idea that Mom could draw or paint or even see things in a beautiful light. I hadn't given her enough credit. Not ever. We each gave her a big hug, and Mom asked, "What's gotten into you all?"

Dad pulled me aside, confessing, "I didn't get your mother anything."

I hadn't bought my father a gift, but I had picked out an Hermès scarf for my mom. An orange-and-black silk square with a galloping horse in the center. I surrendered the scarf to Dad. He promised he owed me one.

Mom oohed and ahhed over her present while Dad claimed the bright colors complemented her new hairdo. I did the math on my generosity. The price of the scarf could have financed a ski weekend in Vermont. Still, allowing Dad to give his estranged wife a Christmas present seemed like the right thing to do.

Riegel gave me a Christmas card with a drawing of a reindeer peeing in the snow. "Ho Ho Ho" in neon reindeer piss. Inside he'd slipped what looked like pink and blue Monopoly money but what turned out to be five hundred dollars in U.S. treasury bonds. I thanked him and he said, "It's a sentimental gift. The treasury just stopped printing these bonds. You can't get paper ones anymore, only electronic transfers. Hold on to these babies."

Dad and Riegel argued about the stock market crash. Dad was convinced that high-speed trading was to blame, but Riegel felt that Black Monday was a combination of triggers. "Illiquidity and overvaluation," he said.

"Computers will destroy Wall Street." Dad insisted that the market had become too volatile. "The lesson learned is to cut back exposure."

Riegel belched and said, "Your problem, Dad, is that you're risk averse."

"How averse to risk can I be?" Dad asked. "I'm going into business with you."

I considered for a moment whether or not I would follow Riegel and work with Dad. One late night in Whitehall, Kriffo, Tazewell, and I had talked about what we wanted to do once we graduated from college. Tazewell wanted to be an heir. Kriffo planned on ruling over his family's sporting goods empire. "How about you, Jason?"

"You know," I said, "it's crazy, but I've never thought about it."

Kriffo spit out some tobacco juice and said, "That's because you've never had to."

But I would have to. And I wanted to decide soon while it was still my decision to make.

Our illusion of family closeness was short-lived. Dad spent most of my break away on business in Berlin and Hong Kong. "The world is shifting," he said. "Markets are opening. Soon we'll all be speaking German and Chinese." Mom went to Aspen. She invited me along, but she was going with a group of her divorced friends and some man, a mysterious Robert I'd never heard of before. After she mentioned Robert's name half a dozen times to Lotta, I began to fear that my mother was in the midst of a romantic distraction. Not something I wanted to witness.

Riegel was around for part of my break, but mostly he used our apartment as a crash pad. We went jogging together some mornings. Just like the old days. "Got a secret for you." Riegel wheezed and panted as we raced down Fifth Avenue. He told me that Dad had been right about computer trading causing the stock market crash. "It was Hiro," Riegel said. "Hiro was the snowball that started the avalanche." As we ran, my brother explained how his boss and a handful of other money jocks had nearly caused the world's economies to collapse. "The reason no one can figure out why Black Monday happened is that it started as a secret bet. These guys, Hiro's pals, wagered they could bring the markets to their knees. They started in Hong Kong, then swept through Europe. Dad got out before the real damage, but Hiro was trading so quickly, staying ahead of all the margins. He made a killing."

"I find that hard to believe. Sounds like Hiro is just pulling your leg."

"Trust me," Riegel said. "Hiro's part of a new breed. Those guys would short-sell their grandmothers."

"So it was a stupid bet?" My ears burned from the cold. "You know, my friend's mother lost her job."

"It may take awhile to recover," Riegel said. "But the markets are actually up for the year. I think Hiro did everyone a favor. Gave the world a wake-up call."

I shook my head. "Another friend of mine, her dad lost everything. What would Hiro think about that?"

Riegel brought up some phlegm from his throat, spat on the sidewalk. "People lose money every day," he said. "If it's your job to make money, it's your job to go out and make more."

Just as we were about to exit the park, I picked up my pace, sprinting ahead of my brother, finishing up strong. I heard Riegel breathing heavily, lumbering behind me, eager to catch up. I refused to let him pass me.

A few nights after Christmas, I had the apartment to myself. Hiro and Riegel had rented a mountain house and were entertaining investors up in Stowe. Riegel asked me to tag along, but I thought I'd take advantage of the solitude.

For my first dinner alone, I ordered kabobs and sour cherry rice from my favorite Persian dive and had a six-pack delivered up to the penthouse. Mom had left me a few New Year's gifts—gloves, a hat, a scarf—and I unwrapped them while waiting for my food to arrive. Every year mom bought me a cashmere sweater, and this year's model was a black V-neck. I pulled the soft light wool over my head and admired myself. Mom had good taste and the sweater fit perfectly. She'd tucked a tiny note card inside the sleeve, "You are my Sun. Love, your Moon." When I was little, on cloudy days, Mom would point up at the sky and ask, "Where is the sun?" And I would yell, "I am your son." It was silly, but I slipped Mom's card into my wallet when I paid the deliveryman.

I decided to have my feast in our formal dining room. My great-great-grandmother the only family member available to keep me company. I broke out the good china, the sterling silverware, and tore into some beef on a stick. The greasy meal tasted better than the Christmas prix fixe Mom had made us suffer through at the Rainbow Room. I raised my Heineken and toasted the Sargent portrait. For a moment I considered whether Riegel or I would inherit the painting. Mom believed inherited wealth was better than money earned. "We're a dying breed," she liked to say. "But we hold our place in history." It seemed to me that while my life would be comfortable, it might not be as comfortable as Mom's had been. With my cheap takeout, I was already exhibiting symptoms of the downwardly mobile. Every Prosper generation after mine risked being a little less prosperous. As much as she admired our ancestors' wealth, it bothered Mom that Riegel was so consumed by making money. "Your brother knows the price of everything and the value of nothing." Riegel had probably spent that very day avalanching down Mount Mansfield in pursuit of new investors.

For my own reasons I'd been angry with Riegel for weeks. If he hadn't driven me around during the storm, I might have spent the day with Aidan. She never would have gone to Race's. I'd asked Riegel how he'd done on his Melville paper, and he said, "I dropped the class. My professor had it out for me so I bailed."

My brother would always remain oblivious of the pain he'd caused. "Screw Riegel," I thought to myself. I pushed back from the table and went up to the Sargent, rubbing my greasy hands together. I took my thumb and pressed my shiny fingerprint into the corner of the painting, right above Sargent's signature. Marking it as my own.

I drank my third beer, feeling buzzed and considered going out. If I couldn't be with my family, I wanted to be with strangers. It was snowing lightly and I thought it might be nice just to go for a walk. I finished my meal, then left the dining room in a mess.

Outside, the cold air felt like needles in my chest. I'd thrown on my camel's hair coat and stuck a beer in either pocket, but I'd neglected to wear my new scarf, gloves, or hat. Even though I'd grown up across the street from it, I'd never crossed into Central Park at night. People were mugged, killed in the park. The previous summer, a guy named Robert Chambers had become famous, had actually been dubbed "the Preppy Killer." Riegel thought the nickname was ridiculous. "Chambers goes to BU. His mom's a nurse. Dude's a total scholarship reject. Not a preppy at all."

"Maybe," I'd said, "it's supposed to mean that he kills preppies."

I'd seen Chambers at Dorrian's, knew him a little. He was loud, a braggart. Whether or not he was an official preppy didn't interest me. The fact that he'd killed someone and seemed on the verge of getting away with it did strike me as something worth paying attention to.

Chambers was notoriously free on bail, probably partying in the city that very night. Dorrian himself had put up the money for Chambers's bond and I thought about heading over to the bar and having a drink, quizzing Dorrian on his generosity. I took long strides through the drifting snow, trying to remember the girl's name, the one Chambers claimed had begged him for rough sex, had tied him up with her own underwear, had forced him to kill her. The *Post* made her out to be a slut, claimed she kept some sort of sex diary. It scared me that I couldn't remember her name. She was a brunette, I knew that much, and also that she'd been found strangled in Central Park right behind the Met. Suddenly, I wanted to go to the actual scene of the crime, to pay her some respect. From the newspaper photos, I knew that she was a pretty girl.

Crossing Fifth Avenue, I walked swiftly, taking pulls from my beer, and soon found myself behind the museum by the obelisk. The massive shaft reaching out into the night. Cleopatra's Needle. The obelisk, the oldest thing in the park, more than three thousand years old, had been given to New York as some sort of Egyptian bribe. My mom was on the board of the Met and had chaired a few fund-raisers in its shadow. Mom told me how it had taken almost a year to transport the monument across the ocean and up Fifth Avenue like Cleopatra's own barge. The obelisk was older than the baby Jesus and somehow it gave me hope to think that something this old could last. Cal couldn't make it to eighteen, Aidan died without knowing her father, but this pink granite monument would stand watch over the city forever.

The air was cold and I was drunk, hearing suspicious noises. I swung around, checking behind myself. There didn't seem to be another soul in the park, but I kept hearing footsteps and rustling.

It occurred to me that I could cross all the way over to the West Side and crash in on Tazewell. I didn't even know for certain that he was in town, but I figured that maybe if we went out together a few beers might loosen him up. Maybe he'd tell me something about the night of the storm. It was still a long and even dangerous walk, but I was young and invincible. I stopped under a streetlight to finish a beer and noticed a man, the first person I'd seen in the park, standing a few feet away from me in the shadows. The man wore a black watch cap and pea coat. He lit a cigarette and I could see his face. "Want a smoke?" he asked.

The man held out his cigarette and I considered what would happen if I took it. He was a small guy, in his twenties. He stepped closer and I could see the razor stubble on his face. I imagined his rough skin abrasive against my cheek.

"It's freezing." He nudged even closer. "That's a nice coat you've got. This cigarette's the only thing keeping me warm."

I knew I could take down this stranger, use my height and reach against him, crack the neck of the beer bottle on the ground and flash my weapon. But he wasn't looking for that kind of trouble. Was this why I'd crept into the park? I wondered. Had I hoped to meet someone on this cold night? Would I bring him back to my empty apartment, pretend that he was Cal?

"A girl died here," I said.

"I don't know anything about that." The man exhaled, a wall of smoke forming between us.

"Her name was Jennifer Levin," I said. "She was only eighteen."

My lungs heaved with wintry air as I ran back up Fifth Avenue. "Cruising," I thought, that's what they called it. I'd grown up across the street from this action but never thought it had anything to do with me. But it was something men did, looked for sex in dark places.

I was almost at my apartment when I heard someone call, "Jason." A soft, motherly voice asked, "Why aren't you wearing a scarf?"

Cal's mother had aged, or maybe she'd simply stopped dyeing her hair. Though Caroline lived just a few blocks away, I hadn't seen her since the funeral. She was coming out of my apartment building and I wondered whom it was she'd been visiting. I leaned down to kiss her on the cheek and was surprised when she pulled her face back. She could smell the beer on my breath.

"You look all flushed," she said.

"Merry Christmas," I said.

"Yes." She smiled. "Merry Christmas." She held up her gloved hand to brush away the snow on my shoulders. I saw a silver glint on her wrist. "I was actually just dropping off your mother's fur coat. She let me borrow it."

I invited Caroline upstairs, but she told me her husband was expecting her at home. We just stood there together in the snow. I could see Cal in the way she nodded and crossed her arms. She asked me how sailing had gone that fall and was distressed to hear that I'd quit.

"Oh, that's not acceptable, Jason. What would Cal think? He'd be so mad at you. Promise me you'll pick it up again. Get back out on the water."

I saw that the Breitling, Cal's watch, was still on her wrist. I had to bite my lip to keep from crying, from collapsing at her feet right there in the snow. "I miss him so much," I said.

She opened her arms, and I fell into them. We both cried, not like we were hearing bad news for the first time or grieving soon after some tragic event. We cried like professional mourners, like people who had made it their business to grieve forever, to always be inconsolable.

"You must move on," she said. "It wasn't your fault."

Caroline had left my mother's sable coat with Max. He took one look at me, my face still flush from crying, and said, "Son, forgive me for saying this, but you look like hell."

Despite all the time I'd spent relying on Max's good company, I knew very little about him. "How many kids do you have, Max?" I asked.

Max shook his head. "Jason, I don't have any children. Thought you knew that."

"I'm sorry," I said.

Max removed his cap and rubbed his bald head.

"It's just that," I said, "you'd make a pretty decent dad."

"Get to bed, kid," he said and called the elevator for me.

I brought the sable coat upstairs, the fur warm and soft in my arms. I laid the coat down on my bed and slept on top of it that night. What Caroline didn't know was the very thing I'd been unable to confront. The horrible thing I'd done to Cal.

I awoke with Mom's sable coat wrapped around my waist. A faun, a half man. Though I wasn't one for remembering my dreams, away from Bellingham I'd had the chance to dream of Aidan. Vivid images of her swimming, treading away from me, her head bobbing like a buoy, the viscous water, dragging her down. Aidan strained to stay afloat while I stood on the shore watching.

Aidan had said that the two most important things in life were knowing what you wanted and understanding what you were afraid of. "Fear and desire," she said. "That's the key."

Though I resisted the thought, I knew it was possible that Aidan had killed herself. I wanted to believe that she hadn't. I feared that she had. I wondered what sadness might have convinced her to walk into the water. Wondered if it was the same sadness that had compelled Cal. I couldn't help but connect Cal's and Aidan's deaths. Together they were like a pair of binary stars, two lights so close and so bright they blended into one. Despite Caroline's reassurances, I understood that I was responsible for my best friend ending his life. It was my fault that Cal had lost hope. Losing Aidan made me feel as though I hadn't learned anything.

Just before New Year's Eve, my fake cousin Ginger called and left a message on the answering machine inviting me to a party downtown. I rarely ventured below Central Park South but, for Ginger, I decided to make an exception. I had to replay the message several times to get the address of the bar. She claimed that the place was a kind of speak-easy. That I would need to press a buzzer and when asked to identify myself, say, "I am the prince of Paraguay."

Ginger hadn't mentioned her baby, but I figured she'd already given birth. I was excited for her. Glad she had something to celebrate.

The bar was in the West Village, uncharted territory for me. I braved the subway, then stumbled around before finding the place, an old brick carriage house. Aidan had asked me about certain nightclubs, Tunnel and the Limelight, and was stunned to learn that I almost never went downtown. "That's another world," I said. "Not my scene."

Inside the speakeasy, boughs of pink and blue lights swung from the ceiling, low enough that I could reach up and touch the warm bulbs. I'd worn a jacket and tie, but most of the men were dressed in tuxedos with ironic glittery bow ties and matching cummerbunds. Women shimmied around the tight quarters in spangled cocktail gowns. It was an older postcollege crowd, and I was happy to be the youngest at the party. Making my way over to the mahogany bar, I saw Ginger swiveling on a stool and nodding at the bartender. Ginger wore a black beaded flapper dress with a silver slip underneath. When she saw me, she jumped off her stool, kissed me on both cheeks, and told everyone sitting at the bar that I was her Tiger. Her belly was gone and she toasted me with her champagne flute. I asked after her baby. "How's your little lamb?"

Ginger handed me a bottle of Perrier-Jouët, ordering me to have a drink.

All around us people were dancing, toasting, locking lips, declaring their resolutions, and scheming to get laid. It was the wrong atmosphere for what Ginger had to tell me, precisely why she'd chosen it.

Three weeks before she was due to deliver, Ginger noticed that her baby had stopped kicking. "Everything inside of me went quiet and cold."

She told me about the drive to the hospital, how Dill ran three red lights, how her mother, Miriam, claimed that losing the baby was for the best.

"The doctors couldn't give me a reason. 'Inexplicable.' But I wonder"—Ginger leaned in close—"what if I'm poison? What if my baby never had a chance?"

Ginger's face sparkled, the result of some cosmetic powder, but I told her that she was glowing and beautiful. "You're not poisonous," I said.

Ginger shielded her arms against her belly, still feeling the rupture, the missing life. There was nothing I could say to make her loss any easier to bear. "You're going to be a beautiful mother."

"You know they make you deliver the baby." Ginger rubbed her eyes, smudging her mascara. "Stillborn. That's what they call it."

Without thinking, I said something stupid, something I immediately wanted to retract. "Was it a boy or a girl?"

Ginger patted my arm and excused herself. It was noisy in the bar and I hoped that she hadn't heard my dumb question. She took her time and I grew anxious, but she returned with a fresh coat of pink lipstick and more of her shimmering gold powder. "Champers," she said to the bartender. "We need more champagne."

The bar filled with smoke and dancing bodies. Ginger knew everyone at the party. Men kept coming over to check on her and ask about me. Ginger told them that at the stroke of midnight she and I were going to board a catamaran and set sail out of New York Harbor. "Where are you headed?" one of the men asked. "Wherever the trade winds take us," Ginger said. She kissed these men on their cheeks and waved them away. At one point in the night, she leaned over and whispered, "Tell me if you see anything you like."

She wanted to hear how I was doing. I shrugged, said that I was okay, then surprised myself by telling Ginger, "I lost somebody."

I described how Aidan and I had sneaked in and out of windows. How we swam at night. "I haven't felt that close to anyone since Cal." I told Ginger that Aidan reminded me of her. And it was true. They shared a similar beauty and eccentricity. Ginger smiled. It seemed unfair of me to tell Ginger of my loss while she was still reeling from her own, but my story energized her. She wanted to help me. When I said, "I'm the one who's poisonous," she disagreed, pushing me on, eager to hear my theories about what might have happened at Race's. Ginger knew the type of guys I was talking about. "Reckless boys," she said, "and their reckless ways."

"You know," I said, "when you've done something terrible, something you regret, it gives you this special insight, like you can detect other people's bad behavior."

"Like you can tell when someone's guilty because you feel your own guilt."

"Exactly. Every time I see Race, I recognize something in him, something I feel within myself. Something rotten."

Ginger rubbed my shoulders. "We're quite a festive duo. I think we need a few spins on the dance floor."

We danced a little and drank a lot. Trying to forget the past year of our lives.

I was happy to hear that Ginger had left her mother's house and rented an apartment in SoHo. She was thinking of taking classes at NYU. "Second chances, fresh starts. That's what life keeps dealing me."

The night had come to an end, our new year about to begin. There were no taxis outside the bar, and I insisted on walking Ginger back to her apartment. Despite conventional wisdom, Cal and I always believed that we could see the stars at night in Manhattan. Ginger pointed up and said, "Orion will guide us home." Drunk and warm from champagne, we trundled along the icy sidewalks, the streets still filled with revelers. "I forgot to thank you," Ginger said.

"For what?" I asked.

"For convincing me to do that deal with Riegel. It's helping Dill.

He's working with that fellow Hiro, helping him amass his own art collection. Dill might even open up his own gallery."

"So Riegel came through," I said. "Go figure."

"I'm not surprised. All your dear brother has ever wanted is to turn a profit. Once when we were kids, my dad offered Riegel twenty dollars to rake the seaweed off our beach. Riegel took the money, then paid some local kid four dollars to do the actual work."

"Your dad must have loved that."

"He roared with laughter, then hunted down the local kid and gave him a hundred bucks."

I clutched Ginger's arm. "I miss your dad."

"We should take out his sloop this summer. Since he died, it's how I feel close to him. When I'm on the water, I can hear Dad in the wind, yelling at me to luff the mainsail."

The buildings were dark enough that I could see Vega, the brightest star in Lyra. I said, "I miss so many people."

"It's how we know we're alive," Ginger said. "We grieve the dead."

FOURTEEN

My second week back at Bellingham, we had our first snow. Several white inches accumulated by midmorning with the promise of an even heavier storm to follow. After lunch, I stood outside Astor packing snowballs and targeting underclassmen. Kriffo and Stuyvie joined me, and together we watched as the girls in their dress code skirts slipped, slid, and fell on the icy paths. We called out numbers rating their wipeouts. "Nice long johns," Kriffo joked. "Definite 8.5 on the Richter scale." Tazewell joined us, and I asked if they were going to haze any of the sophomores that night. None of them had heard about the tradition of tying sophomores up to the columns in their pajamas after the first snow. They all liked the way it sounded. "We've been too easy on the underclassmen," Tazewell said. "It's time we exert some senior privileges."

We made a loose plan to wake up early that morning and raid Wee House. "Do you think Race would be up for this?" I asked.

"Good call," said Stuyvie. "It's just his sort of thing."

Earlier in the day, during Chapel, Windsor had announced that Mr. Guy would be retiring at the end of the school year. I was surprised. Figured that Mr. Guy would hold on to the bitter end. That he'd heart attack while delivering a lecture on the Potsdam Conference. It occurred to me that Mr. Guy was still pissed about Dean Warr undermining his authority. I would have been. After the announcement,

Windsor encouraged Mr. Guy to say a few words, and all of us stood up and applauded as he made his hunched way up to the microphone. He thanked us for the ovation and said that after almost fifty years, he was finally ready to graduate from high school. It seemed like a terrible waste, to have spent an entire lifetime at Bellingham. What had he learned, I wondered, and what had the school given him for all of his trouble? When I first met him he had an almost invisible hearing aid. Now he wore bulky pink plugs that stuck out comically from both ears. The new hearing aids whistled as Mr. Guy returned to his seat.

Chester was not back yet, but he'd promised to return before Spring Break. We'd talked on the phone several times. His physical therapy had gone well and he hoped to rejoin the tennis team. He asked if I'd finished reading the book he'd lent me, *The Motion of Light in Water.* I hadn't even read the first page. I didn't want to admit this failure so I lied that I'd started the book and that it was really moving that his father's friend was clearly a great talent. "Glad you're liking it," he said. My comments had been so vague that if I'd been Chester, I would have quizzed me, forced me to reveal my lie. But Chester was happy to believe I was telling the truth. I tore through my room that night trying to locate the book. I'd outwitted myself. In the hopes of keeping the book neat and preserved, I'd put it in a special place that I had since forgotten.

As I searched through my desk and dresser, I noticed that my picture of Cal was also missing. It wasn't tucked in the corner of my mirror. This made me even more agitated. I went through all of my drawers, clothes, and sheets and tried to remember the last time I'd seen the picture. Brizzey, I thought. Brizzey swiped the photo. I was furious with myself for not noticing sooner.

Before sunrise, on the morning after the first snowstorm, I met Race, Kriffo, and Tazewell outside the Old Boathouse. I'd borrowed some nylon rope from the New Boathouse and was ready to get fancy with my knots.

"Where's Stuyvie?" I asked.

"He's sitting this one out," Race said. "Ever since his suspension he's gotten chickenshit. Sends his regrets."

Race wore a bright orange parka and mirrored sunglasses. He kept his hood down, his ears turning crimson from the cold. The knee-deep snow was topped by a crust of glassy ice. We trudged through the loud crunching snow blinded by the sun's early morning glare. Tazewell kept complaining about his nuts being frozen. When Kriffo offered him his scarf, Taze accused his pal of being a pussy. "What, are we playing dress-up now?" The slightest kindness a sign of weakness. Kriffo wore a puffy down coat, green ski cap, and purple plastic gloves. He looked as though he'd been inflated, his arms filled with helium. Frost glistened on the trees. I could feel my cheeks redden in the cold. Our breath made diamonds in the air.

The plan was to grab four guys from Wee House. Any four guys would do. "All of those kids are skinny fuckers," Race said. "I don't think their balls have dropped."

"Should we let them put their shoes on?" Kriffo asked.

"What are you, the fashion police?" Taze buttoned the top button on his pea coat. "The whole point is for them to get hazed."

Kriffo seemed concerned about frostbite. I explained that we'd be tying the boys to the column shafts and that they'd at least be under the shelter of the colonnade and not up to their ankles in snow. This put Kriffo at ease. Race handed out rolls of duct tape, unstrapping the silver adhesive and demonstrating how we might secure the boys' hands and feet. "We can tape their mouths shut first so they don't alert Mr. Snopes."

Mr. Snopes taught biology. A middle-aged man who had clearly stayed too long at the fair. He'd missed his chance to leave Bellingham for a better gig and now had to make due with his bachelor life. He coached the girls' lacrosse team and for this reason alone was considered a perv. Nadia planned on playing lacrosse in the spring. She told me that the girls on the team were always spreading rumors about Snopes giving them the eye or accidentally wandering into the girls' locker room. My bet was that he'd built up a tolerance, an immunity to their charms. That he'd spent so many bus trips listening to them gossip and complain that he'd long ceased finding teenaged girls attractive.

By the time we got to Wee House, some of us decided that it might be best to hijack two students. That four guys would be too much to wrangle. "Two is totally manageable," Kriffo said. "We each grab a pair of arms and legs."

Race was disappointed. He felt that two didn't make enough of a statement. Four was ideal but three at least sent a message. Three was a better spectacle. I agreed with Race. Deep down, I wasn't certain that I could manage even half a kid, never mind an entire fifteen-year-old on my own. I'd smoked a lot of cigarettes in New York and was already having a hard time just shoeing through the snow.

None of the lights were on in Wee House. Mr. Snopes lived on the first floor in the back of the dorm. We decided to hit the first two rooms, both doubles right near the entrance. It was Race's idea that we tape the boys' mouths first, then strap their wrists and feet. Right before we blitzkrieged the rooms, Kriffo whispered, "What if these guys have morning wood?"

"Why?" Race asked. "Would you like to fuck them?"

Taping someone's mouth shut turned out to be harder than I'd anticipated. My target popped the tape from his lips with his tongue and let out a yelp. I quickly placed my hand over his mouth only to have him bite my palm. As the kid fought me, I wound a tight band of tape around his entire head. Then I flipped the guy over and taped his wrists behind his back. Race taped his kid's hands in the front and seemed to regret it. "Your way is better," he said as we sneaked out of Wee House. Kriffo and Tazewell took longer and emerged with only one victim between them.

"What happened?" Race asked.

"The other one was naked," Tazewell said. "Even I have a heart."

Race seemed visibly disappointed. Kriffo was relieved that our three captives had all gone to sleep in thick wool socks. We cut a messy path through the snow over to the headmaster's house, like the world's most uncoordinated dog-sledding crew. From there, I made quick work of strapping each boy against a thick white column. I'd planned on using a fancy buntline and clove hitch, but in the end I settled for a series of tight constrictor knots. The four of us stood back and admired our handiwork. I didn't know any of the boys' names. They all had greasy hair and scrawny bodies. One wore camouflage flannel pajamas. "I can't see you," Race joked while slapping the kid's arms. The other two boys had on boxer shorts. One was lucky enough to have worn a Cornell sweatshirt, but the other stood shivering in a flimsy white T-shirt, CHOOSE LIFE printed in black block letters on his chest. All three looked terrified.

Tazewell complained that we didn't have a camera. He worried that we'd have no record of our masterpiece. I pulled out my Instamatic and the guys cheered softly as I snapped pictures of them modeling with their prey. "You guys got shafted," Race whispered.

The sun was coming up, and it seemed like a good time to haul ass. All three boys shook, a deep fear emerging in their eyes as they realized we were going to leave them. Running away, I looked back at the columns. I thought of Diana's father, who had introduced me to this tradition, wondered if he was getting any better. Then I remembered being bound up in a carpet at Kensington, remembered the laughter as my assailants rolled me down a hill. I wanted to explain to these three sophomores that there was a larger purpose, an actual point to this abuse. My hope was that Race, Taze, and Kriffo would begin to trust me, begin to feel bonded to me. I'd tied up three strangers in the hopes of building other ties.

Nadia had been especially happy to see me. Greeting me in the Dining Hall our first day back, she gave me a big hug, handed me a gift. "It's from my mother," she said. "A thank-you for being so nice to me." It was a tie, a Ferragamo tie. Pink sailboats on a field of blue. The sort of thing a banker would wear. It was a very thoughtful and expensive gift and without anything to give her in return, I kissed Nadia on the lips right there in the middle of dinner.

All around us people chanted, "PDA, PDA, PDA." I caught Brizzey looking visibly perturbed. I liked Nadia well enough. She was sweet and small. I liked the way she hummed as she played piano, how she'd look up from the bench and smile whenever she struck a dull note. It occurred to me that it might be in my best interest to date her to dispel any rumors Brizzey might attempt to erupt. I took off the blue-and-white Brooks Brothers tie I had on and knotted Nadia's gift around my neck, then held her hand and walked out of the Dining Hall with her.

The headmaster discovered the three boys tied to the columns soon after we left. He was not amused. After a rough fall semester, Windsor probably hoped to coast through the spring. An old sailor himself, Windsor untied my knots and welcomed the boys inside his home for some hot chocolate and blankets. One of the three boys was Officer Hardy's son. The one in the camouflage pajamas. Hardy had been lucky enough to win custody of his kid, luckier still to have the school offer his son a full scholarship, including room and board. James Hardy wouldn't need to worry about the stigma of being a townie.

I was impressed that the three boys held their silence, claiming ignorance as to our identities. The shafting grew into myth, and by early evening the official report was that at least a half dozen guys or more had been tied up naked. Kids bragged about being shafted, kids who had played no part in the prank. It became a special badge of honor and pride to have been singled out for this hazing, and all of the underclassmen who claimed to have been involved boasted that this meant they got to pull the same prank themselves the following year. Race, Kriffo, and Taze were thrilled. "We did it, Prosper," they said. "We're legendary."

After that first blizzard, the days got colder. The air stayed brittle, and when I stepped outside I feared my breath might shatter into a thousand icicles. In the mornings the guys on the top floor of Whitehall fled the dorm together, traveling in a pack, hoping the synchronized movements of our bodies would keep us warm. The temperature dropped so much that the ocean froze. Race swung by the dorm one Saturday afternoon and invited Tazewell, Kriffo, and me out for a drive. "The ocean is sheer ice. We could skate on it. Walk on water."

We packed into Race's Land Rover and drove down to the beach. I hadn't been back to that stretch of sand since Marieke's visit. Though

I thought of her often, Marieke remained a mystery to me. I couldn't imagine what it was like for Aidan to grow up listening to the jangling of those bracelets, smelling that musky perfume, standing always in the cold shadow of her mother's immense beauty, her ego. One of my biggest regrets was not being able to convince Marieke of her own daughter's happiness. Over break, I'd tried to rent the movie she'd produced, but every time I went to the video store the film was checked out. "That's a holiday classic," the video clerk declared. "Good luck finding it anywhere." On New Year's Eve I not only told Ginger about Aidan but I also mentioned Marieke. Ginger knew and adored the film. "My favorite tearjerker," she said. She had a copy of the movie in her apartment and we went back that night and watched it together as the sun came up. It should have been hokey, laughable, even—an old man and his cat on a road trip together. But when the cat died in the old man's arms, I found myself bawling. "Told you," Ginger said. "She might have been a crummy mother, but that woman made a great film."

At the beach, the sand was covered in snow, the sky a slate gray. Just as Race had promised, the ocean was frozen. Not a thin surface layer of slush as I'd imagined but a deep, hard, glacial block. The wind blew in ribbons snapping across our faces as the four of us in our dark parkas walked out several yards onto the ocean, sliding across the white surface. Taze wiped out, joked that he'd tripped on a wave.

"I didn't think it was possible," I said, "for salt water to freeze."

"The salt doesn't freeze," Race corrected me. "But the water does. The salt separates, gets pushed down below the water. Pretty cool, huh? Wish I had an iceboat. We could sail over the surface."

"Iceboat," I said. "They call them Skeeters, right? They've got those long-ass steel blades."

"Yeah," Race said. "My dad sailed one out on the Hudson. Saw him do it. Those fuckers fly."

Sunlight bounced off the white ice without being absorbed. I wondered how long it would take for this ocean to melt. Kriffo had brought along his hockey skates. He laced himself up and began cutting laps across the shoreline. Taze fell again, then stayed down, pulled out a joint, lighting up. "Look at me," he said. "I'm a chimney." Race and I kept walking, testing the frozen waters for weakness.

We were about a hundred feet from shore when Race turned to me. "Is there any chance you might want to sail this spring?" Race looked away after he asked his question.

Though I understood it took a lot for Race to make this offer, I didn't want to appear too eager. "On one condition." I breathed out a thick fog of air. "Tell me, what exactly is a SeaWolf?"

Race bared his teeth, growled, and smiled.

"We don't have to sail together," I said. "But if you're up for it, I wouldn't mind crewing for you."

"Truth is," Race said, "the only good day of sailing I had last semester was with you. Well, until you nearly killed me." Race laughed as though the whole thing was behind us now. As though we could joke about our past.

"I think together . . ." I smiled. "We'd be unstoppable."

We stood out on the frozen ocean discussing strategies, strength training, aerodynamics, the way an apparent wind could shift suddenly, violently if you were accelerating too rapidly. It wasn't the type of conversation I could have enjoyed with Aidan. Race and I shared an expertise, an intimacy that enabled us to speak in shorthand. We were insiders. It wasn't the same as talking to Cal, but it was close. I thought of how close our bodies would be, Race's and mine, when trimming the sails in light winds. Race and I would be right on top of each other balancing in unison.

I looked down at the ice. These frozen waters had swallowed Aidan. She really did swim like a mermaid. So strong, she would have fought the storm to stay afloat. My hero Joshua Slocum didn't know how to swim at all, insisting it was useless for a sailor to struggle in the open ocean. He sailed alone around the world without knowing how to doggy paddle. And when he died, he died out at sea sailing his sloop until it capsized, until the waters filled his lungs. Aidan prided herself on being unsinkable, but she'd been tossed around and broken. I was standing on a grave.

"So it's settled," Race said. "You're part of the team."

———

Yazid returned a month into the semester. "I abhor the cold," he said. "I'm allergic to it, or at least that's what my doctor's excuse claims." While the rest of us had suffered through blizzard conditions, Yazid had spent weeks sunning himself on the Mediterranean. We all agreed that he was the smartest person we'd ever met. Yazid's return was greeted with great anticipation. The Whitehall pot supply had dwindled to seeds and stones. Taze and I were disappointed when Yazid pulled out a bundle of leaves wrapped around red and green plant shoots. "These are fresh," he said. "I brought enough for everyone to try." He told us that the plant was called khat and that if we chewed the leaves and flower shoots we'd feel euphoric, buzzed. "You'll never want to sleep again."

In his room, Yazid had real adult furniture: a pair of comfortable brown leather chairs, a red-and-blue Turkish rug, tall brass floor lamps. He slept on a futon. The room of a very sophisticated dope fiend.

Yazid unwrapped the khat and showed us how to fold the leaves and chew on them to release the drug. The plant smelled like a mixture of oregano and mint. "It's like dip," Taze said. "Should I tuck it into my gum?"

Yazid explained that he'd been chewing khat since he was little. For him the drug was not much more than a cup of coffee. He cautioned that for us the khat might seem as strong as a bump of cocaine.

Tazewell wasn't used to stimulants. He couldn't stop chewing the leaves, green foam forming at the sides of his mouth, bits of leaf covering his perfect teeth. "I haven't been this high since the hurricane," he said. "We were crazy that night." Tazewell paced and played with the bracelets on his wrist. "I can't even remember her name."

"Whose name?" Yazid asked.

"The girl." Taze looked at me, his pupils like pinpricks. "The one on the boat."

I spit the leaves out into my hand. "You took a boat out in the storm?"

"Just a joyride." Tazewell smiled. "No big thing." Tazewell pointed to his bracelets and nodded to Yazid. "Have I made you one of these?"

Yazid shook his head.

"All this time," Taze said, "I've been smoking your dope and it never once occurred to me to make you a bracelet. I'm going to do it. Decorate your whole wrist." Tazewell got up and went to his room.

"Filthy," Yazid said. "He thinks I want his filthy embroidery."

I sat with Yazid for a while, certain that this new drug would keep me awake all night. Tazewell had allowed something to slip, *"I can't even remember her name."*

"Have you ever been to Race's house?" I'd never asked Yazid about the party.

Yazid said that he'd never been invited to anyone's home. "You'd think that one of these chaps would have invited me to one of your big American barbecues. When I was in London, my friends were always showing me off, introducing me to their families. I suppose I haven't made that sort of friend here."

I told Yazid that he had a standing invitation to stay with me in the city or up in Maine, and though I think he appreciated it, my invite couldn't help but feel like a consolation. "Are you sorry you came here?" I asked.

Yazid folded some green leaves and chewed slowly. The khat seemed to have an almost calming effect on him. "Bellingham," he said, "serves a purpose. Someone has to cater to all of these fuckups. Best of all, I've never once feared being kicked out. That's worth something."

Aidan had compared Bellingham to the Island of Misfit Toys, a sanctuary for the unwanted. But the problem, as I saw it, was that putting this many defective kids together only created more trouble.

I began to think of Tazewell, Kriffo, Stuyvie, and Race as "the Company." The new company I was keeping. When Chester returned in mid-February, he was annoyed to find me having dinner with Kriffo and Tazewell. I tried to play it off, but Chester was obviously hurt. That night he came into my room and asked for his book back. I had yet to locate it. Told him that I wasn't finished reading it yet. Chester showed me his latest scar, a smile that curved down his biceps and around his elbow. "Sixty-five staples. Nine inches long." The rough skin similar to the scar on his jaw.

"Impressive," I said. "Matches your other scar."

Chester clutched his chin in his hand. He took a deep breath. "Funny thing too," he said. "Same guy gave me both."

During Chester's junior year, Kriffo and Taze took up smoking cigars. "They didn't want to smoke in their rooms, so they turned mine into their own personal humidor. Back then, I had the only single, the best room in the dorm." Chester would stay in the library all night and return to find his place trashed, Kriffo and Taze sitting in their boxers puffing away on Montecristos. Even then, Chester didn't respond. Then one night, they just went after Chester. "They told me I didn't deserve such a nice room. Kriffo insisted I only got it because I was black." Chester let out a small laugh. "I let them know that they got lots of stuff, special stuff, every day just because they were white. Thought I was making a good point, but Tazewell held me down while Kriffo pushed the charcoal end of the cigar against my chin. Told me they wanted to brand me. That I was their cattle." Chester exhaled and asked me if I still had any whiskey.

I went over to my dresser and lifted up my dopp kit. Underneath, I saw a red cover and the words "Advance Copy." I'd found the missing book. There were two more bottles of Jim Beam and I gave one to Chester.

"I never told anyone how I got this scar," he said. "Not even my mom, and I tell her everything." Chester opened the bottle and took a small sip.

"I want to fix this," I said. "Make it right." I explained that I'd been courting the Company. "Do you remember Aidan?"

Chester offered me the bottle. "Sometimes I think I'm the only one who does," he said. "It's like somebody died and this place barely blinked."

The whiskey reminded me of the storm, of our first bonding session. I suddenly realized that while Aidan was at Race's, I was in the shower beating off. While Aidan was trapped on the beach, I was playing football. Though I'd mentioned our friendship, I'd never told Chester just how close Aidan and I had been. "I don't believe she killed herself." I made my suspicions clear to Chester. "At the very least those guys are hiding something."

Cal's mother had given me the order to get back on the water, to return to sailing as way of returning to Cal. Ginger had given me a very different idea regarding Aidan, the idea of becoming close to Race. "Make him your friend," she'd said, "and he'll tell you his secrets."

"I get it," Chester said. "It's like a bait and switch. But I'm sorry, I just don't think those guys will come clean. All they'll do is lie to you."

The entire sailing team stayed on campus during Spring Break, training, running drill after drill. Practicing boat control, trapeze techniques. For the past three years, the Tender Trophy had eluded Race, and he was confident that the two of us together could bring the award to Bellingham. Race and I shared the important love of a sport, and the more we won together, the more Race would want to seal that bond.

Nadia was upset that we wouldn't be spending Spring Break together. She'd invited me to Atlanta. Her family had a house on Sea Island. "It's totally exclusive," she said. "There's a guard and gatehouse. You can't even drive on to the island unless you live there or are somebody's guest."

Gates and private islands didn't impress me. I'd seen more than my fair share. It made me sad to hear Nadia smooth out her accent, dull her voice. Back in Atlanta she'd grown up believing that being sophisticated meant attending prep school in New England. What she wanted more than anything were postcards, snapshots of herself windsurfing, playing lacrosse, sneaking out to hotel parties in Boston. She was desperate to visit me in the city. "I'm the only freshman who's dating a senior," she confided. Our relationship hadn't progressed much beyond the kissing stage. I was afraid of touching her, harming her. She'd begun to ask me about Aidan, had developed a fascination with her and seemed to believe that we'd had some sort of tragic love affair. That Aidan had been heartsick and killed herself over me. Nadia was a sweet girl and it would have been unfair of me to compare her to Aidan. I'd managed to convince Nadia not to wear too much makeup, to keep her hair short, to play the piano with me. To be grateful for my attention. So far things had worked out between us, though I was beginning to sense that Nadia wanted more.

Spring Break. One morning the campus was teeming with students and the next morning it was as silent as an empty soundstage. It was strange to be at school when nearly everyone else was on vacation. Coach Tripp and I were the only two left in Whitehall. The dorm was always alive with music, animated with the sporty motions of young hyperactive males. It was nice to take refuge in the quiet hallways. No small talk, no bullshit. Coach Tripp continued to teach me about celestial navigation.

With the campus empty, there was nothing keeping me from seeing its beauty. I'd gotten so used to being at Bellingham that I'd stopped appreciating the ocean, the bracing smell of salt air. Waking up at five a.m. to train with the sailing team, I welcomed the morning into my lungs as if for the first time. I could feel the brackishness surge all the way down my throat and into my stomach. "Let's do this," I thought. "Get back out on the water."

I'd never sailed with a skipper as meticulous as Race. He had long thin fingers that moved with speed and accuracy as he checked our gear, making certain that everything was literally shipshape. "All-a-Taut-O," he'd call out when our boat was rigged. In turn, Race was impressed by my speed at tying knots, my understanding of when to use a particular hitch.

Race's mother had donated new training dinghies, 470s, the same type of dinghy Race would compete on if he made it to the Olympics. Speed machines, we called them. Elegant but demanding boats, quick to plane and charge through the water. I was happy to play crew, to harness myself into the trapeze and balance precariously on the gunwale, leaning back so far off the boat and so close to the water that it seemed as though I was literally pulling the dinghy through the waves. My power and gravity keeping us on a straight course. It was a breathless, exhilarating feeling to rediscover. Often, I felt compelled to close my eyes, surrendering to the excitement. I could die happy knowing that this was the last feeling I would enjoy. Then Race would call, "Ready about," and I would restore my concentration, focus on our teamwork.

Cal and I had always switched off, sharing the roles of skipper and crew. Believing that both were equal, neither subordinate, and that we should be equally great at both. Race was different. He needed to be in charge. I could hear it in the fierce tone he used to call out orders and see it in the way he threw his weight when we swung over to windward to steady our boat.

Race, like a lot of sailors, had his superstitions. He preferred wearing a wet suit instead of a dry suit, and though he could have afforded the best high-tech gear, he kept his lucky wet suit patched together with squares of duct tape. Before every regatta he listened to the same CD—a collection of Van Halen hits—and ate the same lunch—a roast beef sandwich made by his mother. Before a particularly challenging meet at St. George's in Newport, I'd watched Race check and recheck our lines compulsively. He hummed "Panama" and retaped each piece of duct tape, piling on four different layers. His mother had mistakenly packed a ham and cheese, and right before we were due out on the water, Race insisted that Coach Tripp drive him into town to a sandwich shop. "I've got a ritual going," he said. "I need to honor it."

I had my own superstitions. While Race wore thin leather gloves, I preferred to work the ropes with my bare hands. When I sailed, I needed to feel the ropes tight against my skin. I paid for this with blood blisters, wet, wrinkled fingers and palms. During the entire sailing season, my hands never dried. They stayed rubbery, saturated. No matter how much I warmed them, I couldn't get the salt water out of my skin, not without pulling off layers of wet calluses. I was convinced that my reaction time was faster, my raw peeling hands giving me a competitive edge. I used my blistered hands as an excuse not to touch Nadia.

Toward the end of spring training, Coach Tripp invited Race and me over to his apartment for pizza and a final strategy session. The most important thing for a skipper and crew was communication. Coach Tripp insisted that Race and I go for morning and afternoon runs together. He wanted us to keep each other company at mealtime and bond by watching Monty Python films. "Dinsdale," Race and I would call out to each other whenever our paths crossed on campus. Coach Tripp wanted us to be the Piranha Brothers. "It's a kind of courtship," Coach Tripp said, and when Race and I both scoffed at the idea of courtship, Coach explained that we needed to trust each other but we also needed to like each other. "Develop a sense of humor together. Have your own private jokes and soon you'll anticipate each other's every move. Finish each other's sentences."

After dinner, I invited Race to hang out in my room. I didn't see him around the dorm much. Like most day students, he had a complex about not really being part of the school. "Nice single," he told me. "I should invite you over to my house."

"Yeah. I guess I missed my chance to see it last fall."

Race picked up *The Motion of Light in Water*. I'd been reading it over break. Based on the title, I'd assumed the book was about sailing, but it turned out to be a memoir. The author, Chip Delany, was a science fiction writer and the book was his story of growing up in Harlem and being part of the '60s scene in Greenwich Village. Delany had met everyone from Bob Dylan to Albert Einstein, and he'd also managed to have a lot of sex. Revolutionary sex with women and men. Delany was gay, but he'd married a woman and had a child. The book wasn't at all what I'd expected and I wasn't sure what to say about it to Chester. Race asked me about the book and I told him that Chester had lent it to me.

"I'm impressed he came back to school," Race said. "That guy's got heart."

I nodded. "He's had a tough time here."

"You've got to admire a kid who just keeps his head down and takes his licks."

I doubted that taking his licks was something Chester wanted to be known or admired for.

I said, "Chester's stronger than all of us combined."

Race looked at me and nodded. "Maybe. I heard Kriffo tried to turn him into a human ashtray. Pretty shitty thing to do."

Race picked up the copy of *Sailing Alone Around the World* that Aidan had stolen for me and began to flip through the pages. "Can I borrow this?" he asked.

I didn't want to give it to him. My heart literally hurt at the thought of it. The book wasn't even mine to lend. By all accounts I should have returned it to the library, but Aidan had given it to me. "You've never read it?" I asked.

Race explained that he'd always meant to and that his father had named one of their sloops *Spray,* after Slocum's own boat. Race picked up the book and said, "I think I could do it. Sail around the world by myself. Think I'd actually enjoy it."

I told Race that he could borrow the book. "Just remember to give it back sometime, okay?" I knew I'd never see it again. But this was exactly the kind of bonding Coach Tripp had in mind. I needed to play along. Even if it meant losing a little more of Aidan.

"How tall are you?" Race asked.

We stood back to back in front of my mirror and were both surprised to discover that we were almost exactly the same height. From the first time we'd met I'd always thought of Race as being taller than me, believed we were incompatible as sailing partners because of this, but the truth was I walked around in a perpetual slouch. Our arms were the same length. I studied Race's reflection. He wasn't a bad-looking guy. He had clear skin and a muscular build, but he had the pinched face of someone who'd spent his entire childhood throwing tantrums in public places. I hadn't seen him with any girls. Hadn't heard him linked to anyone, not even Brizzey. Maybe he was too focused on sailing, or maybe he had an off-campus girlfriend. Race sat down at my desk and I leaned against the windowsill.

"Do you have a girlfriend?" I asked.

"Not while I'm training or competing. I don't want to deal with some girl whining at me about how I'm not spending enough time with her."

"You could date someone on the team." There were two girls on the team, Greta and Emmy, both sophomores, competent sailors who just needed more experience.

Race ignored me. "I should confess," said Race, "that I had a little thing with that girlfriend of yours."

"Nadia? Brizzey?"

"No, the other one. The crazy one." Race leaned back in my chair.

I focused on the raised chair legs and imagined knocking him over.

"What did we call her?" he scratched his chin. "Hester. That's right. Hester would show up at all my parties. Mostly just looking for drugs, but we hooked up. Said she liked me because I'm a redhead." Race smiled.

I felt my heart contract, quickening my pulse. "You two dated?"

Race looked away. "Dated? No, nothing serious like that. We passed her around, you know, for a good time." He smiled, still unable to look at me. "You didn't like her?" Race asked. "Not really, right?"

I shrugged my shoulders.

"Anyway," Race said, "thought I should clear the air in case you'd heard anything. Wouldn't want there to be more bad blood between us. I'm really glad you came around."

The whole time Race had been speaking, I'd been digging my nails into the windowsill. I didn't believe him. Aidan would have told me if she'd been with Race. As far as I knew, she hadn't been with anyone at Bellingham. I tried to relax, asked Race if he wanted to watch some TV. He said he needed to get home. "Do you ever wish you lived on campus?" I asked.

He shook his head. "I wouldn't fit in. I like my freedom, my king-sized bed. I like being able to lock my door."

Once everyone returned from break at the end of March, I stayed focused on sailing and completing my course work. My grades still mattered if I hoped to get in to Princeton. I had the second half of Mr. Guy's Modern U.S. History, along with another semester of calculus and English lit, but my other classes were all electives, classic senior slump fluff. Geology: Rocks for Jocks and something called The Great American Songbook, a class that consisted of listening to the chorus director's collection of vintage forty-fives and occasionally singing along to protest songs.

Race and I traveled to meets and regattas sometimes twice a week. I always liked the way the word "regatta" sounded. An old Venetian word. Cal had looked it up once in a mammoth dictionary. "Regatta" originally meant "to compete," but because Venice was such an empire, a city of water and gondola races, the phrase took on other connotations: "to catch" and "to haggle." But my favorite of all the alternate definitions was "to contend for mastery." I knew from Roland that "yacht" was the Dutch word for "hunt." When the two terms combined, I felt a special drive, a quest—the hunt for mastery. For most people, regattas and yachts didn't evoke much more than fancy boats and rich people, but I loved that idea of being the best.

The rules for any regatta read like they were drawn up by a team of idiot lawyers. It was easier to get disqualified than to understand the rules. This too was a source of great pleasure for me and for Cal. On the day of a regatta, no one from either team was allowed on the water or to view the course before the race began. This referred not only to team members and coaches but also family members. Cal's dad once got caught sculling on Lake Kensington before a big meet, thereby disqualifying our boat. Sailing—the sport of sticklers. Race was also a stickler for rules and was especially gifted at pointing out when our competitors faulted. Cal was the same way. He was the one who'd turned in his father for cheating.

It was hard for me to admit that I enjoyed sailing with Race. But when the two of us were side by side riding the waves, searching for smart winds, when he called out for us to tack or heave to, I was happy to follow his lead. Like any good skipper, he knew when we needed to reduce sail and when we could afford to hoist our spinnaker. Together, we understood our winds, recognized the difference between a header and a lift. On calm days we could turn a line of puffs into enough fuel to bring us first place. When the winds were fluky, we knew when to ease the sails and douse the jib. We still didn't talk much or laugh at the same things, but the water and air created enough of a language between us.

When I first saw the schedule of sailing meets, I knew that the toughest competition would come toward the end of the semester, when we traveled to Kensington. I hadn't been back there and had almost no intention of ever returning. None of my friends or coaches had bothered to stay in touch, and I'd been happy to seal off that part of my life. Coach Tripp had asked me if I would be okay. "I know you have some tough memories there." If I'd been honest, I would have requested politely to sit out the competition, but I was a member of a larger team, playing a supporting role, and so I asked Coach Tripp if I could address the entire squad, if I could tell the others what I knew from my own experience about sailing on that lake, how best to find the wind.

Lake Kensington was natural, glacial, and shaped like a lazy four-leaf clover. Half the shore was flat and level, while the other half rose into craggy cliffs that formed a rough canyon like the edge of a broken bowl. Thermals would drop down suddenly off the lip of the gorge. The differences between blue-water sailing and lake sailing are subtle and varied. The terrain around the lake shapes the winds in surprising ways, resulting in sudden gusts. I explained that we would probably find ourselves tacking more than we did out on the ocean. Making almost constant adjustments. Though the waves would be smaller, there would be more of them. A steady rolling chop. The lack of saline would also impact the weight of the wind and the movement of the water. Then there was the question of seiche. Because a lake was bounded on all sides, but still subject to barometric pressure, the water would often rise and pool on one side of the lake only to move rapidly without warning, surging like a runaway tide. "It's like the way water moves in a bathtub when you stretch back or move your legs." Lake Kensington was known for these sudden rolling tides, but if you checked the waterlines along the cliffs it was possible to predict a shift. In some ways, it was easier to sail on a lake, but because my team wasn't used to it, it would be harder for us.

During the entire drive to Kensington, I sang to myself, remembering all the songs I'd sung for Aidan. To add to my superstitions, I'd strung the key to the library onto a shoelace. I sailed every meet with the key beating against my chest. It wasn't always easy keeping my ghosts alive. But I tried. Sometimes it was enough for me to simply hold that dried tangerine in my palms, the waning scent still able to remind me of the first night I snuck into Aidan's room. With Cal, it was both easier and harder to conjure him. Easier in that all I had to do was set off with Race out on our sleek 470. Harder because I sometimes mistook Race for Cal. They didn't look alike or even sail alike. But they smelled the same, like fresh laundry. It was probably just the matter of their housekeepers using the same detergent, but often enough, when we tacked, as Race crossed over me, I would breath in the air scented with green apples and soap. I'd think Cal was sailing with me.

I was no longer sure that Race would confess to me. Tazewell had slipped up that one time in Yazid's room but was otherwise on guard. Taze busied himself playing center midfielder for the lacrosse team and scoring with freshmen girls—Lacrosse-titutes, we called them. Kriffo played catcher for the baseball team, still hoping to get into Princeton. One night at dinner, I'd mentioned Aidan's name to him, trying to draw him out, and he asked, "Who are you talking about?" When I reminded him about the girl who'd drowned, Kriffo said, "She told me I had a sweet voice. What do you think she meant by that?" Stuyvie didn't seem to trust me like the other guys. We never spent any time alone together. I'd replaced him as Race's sidekick.

When we arrived at Lake Kensington, Race and I sat at the end of the dock. His mother had made us both roast beef sandwiches and we ate lunch together while studying the water. The other team hadn't arrived yet and Race and I enjoyed the quiet. I was nervous, and I told Race that I was worried about competing against my old team. "I want you to know something," Race said. "Coach Tripp is a nice guy, but we're going to win this meet because of you."

The wind had blown through Race's hair and I had to stop myself from flattening his cowlick. "No," I said, "we're going to win because we're a better team."

We would be competing both as a team and for our own individual times. The meet consisting of two rounds of racing. After the first round we would return to shore and switch boats with the other team. It was considered poor sportsmanship to leave your challengers with a boat that needed to be bailed out. Race often left me to do the bailing.

I stood on the molasses-colored beach in my neoprene suit and watched the guys from the Kensington sail team arrive and rig their dinghies, debating whether or not I should go over and say hello. I recognized almost all of them. There was Jake Trotter and his caved-in chest, still terrified of being seen without a shirt. There was Mitchell Field who once challenged Cal to eat as many eggs as Cool Hand Luke. Cal won the contest, then spent two days doubled over, throwing up.

Donald Fisher, the guy who had cracked the joke about me getting a 4.0 because of Cal's suicide, saw me and looked away. He had on the exact same neoprene suit as I did.

Of all my former teammates, my favorite was Jonathan Porter. He was the kind of guy who would have made a great priest. Or maybe a monk. He had an angelic face and was always off studying how to raise bees or how to feed a village in Ethiopia for a month with just a bag of rice and a box of frozen fish. Jonathan and I sang together in choir. Jonathan, our high tenor, always taking the solo at lessons and carols, soaring through the high notes on "Once in Royal David's City."

These boys were safe, smart, and slightly above average. When I'd traveled among them, I'd taken them for granted. Cal called them "Team Beige." We were an arrogant pair, but Cal always felt that arrogance backed up with talent was just good self-promotion. I imagined that some of these guys had forgotten about me, but I knew that all of them remembered Cal. My best friend knew how to get people to root for him. When we won together, Cal was the guy they congratulated. Not me.

The last time Cal and I had gone sailing was on this lake. Not for a regatta, just a regular day of practice. Neither of us knew that it would be the last time we sailed together. We were barely on speaking terms but still sneaking into each other's beds. The winds that day were pure doldrums. We stalled out in the middle of the lake. Nothing to do but wait and wish for a pair of oars. Cal and I stretched out on the bottom of the boat head to foot, the two of us singing "Bridge Over Troubled Water." "Sail on silver girl," Cal and I bellowed. "Sail on by."

When we finished singing, Cal draped his arm over my thigh. We continued to bitch about the dead air as he rubbed my leg. Staring up at the sky, I hoped the wind would stay calm. I made a wish that Cal and I could be stranded there forever.

The Kensington coach gave me a quick salute but didn't bother to come over and find out how I was managing. He had a meet to prepare for, strategies to discuss, so I tried not to mind. Race approached me and said, "These guys look like a bunch of poofs."

"They're nice guys," I said. "But they're no match."

The lake had a clay bottom. The water so pristine and clear I could see the hull of our boat. It was a good swimming lake, and Cal and I had sneaked out any number of evenings and gone skinny-dipping. Kids would often dive down, pull out wet clumps of clay, clouding the water. Cal hated when anyone did this. It made him mad to see the purity of the water disrupted.

While Race and I made our way out onto the middle of the lake, our white sails like some giant's handkerchiefs, I noticed the sky darkening, the winds picking up. From the shore, sailing must appear to be a maddening series of tacking and jibing, backing and forthing, toing and froing. Though the maneuvers might have seemed arbitrary, the skipper orchestrated everything. "It's going to be a wild day," Race promised. I was prepared to work myself to near exhaustion.

The most exciting parts of any regatta are the timed starts and the close turns around buoys. I'd tried to explain to Aidan how sailors had to tack behind a designated area, jockeying for position, waiting for the signal to advance. "You can't simply park a row of sailboats in a line and fire a starter pistol." Cal and I had been masters at crossing the starting line right on cue. Though he was aggressive around buoys, Race was cautious with his starts, always worried about being penalized. When we crossed the imaginary starting line first at Kensington, I knew the regatta was ours to lose.

The weather on the lake that day was rough, the waves able to break our speed. Race and I knew we'd need to tack when the bow of our dinghy met the top of the smallest wave in a series. Each time the boat began to turn, I released the jib, positioning myself windward, trimming the sails. Race relaxed his body against mine, and though we shouted rallies of orders and agreements in urgent, curt voices, from time to time we'd catch each other's eyes and smile, as if to say, "Can you believe how lucky we are? Could anything in the world be as much fun?"

Everything tastes better after a day of sailing. My appetite would surge from all of the energy I'd expended. Sometimes when I sailed, I simply daydreamed about the meal I'd enjoy afterward, hoping to have a chance to reward myself.

I was in the middle of such revelry, when across our starboard side I saw Jonathan and Mitchell about to capsize. They were our only real competition, and if we beat them, we would come in first and most likely win the entire meet. It was hard to watch. We were sailing downwind. Jonathan and Mitchell should have been following a zigzag course, but they'd caught a wave and were traversing over it, catching speed. Seiche, I thought to myself. Unlike a surfer, a sailor never wants to tie his fate to a single wave. Jonathan and Mitchell stayed with their wave too long, bearing away, luffing the sails. Their bow dug into the wave, taking on water. I could hear Cal's voice reminding me, "Between winds and waves, a sailor needs to worry more about waves." Waves could toss a sloop up and bury it. It was like Cal was right there in the boat with me, shouting over to Jonathan and Mitchell to look out.

Jonathan and Mitchell began to jibe, and in the roughness of the wave, the boom glanced the shroud, snapping the wire and breaking the mast, the sails collapsing. It was like watching flower petals fold in on themselves after being shot at by a cannon.

I saw all of this in a flash as Race and I cruised by, confident that we'd won.

If Race and I had been better citizens we might have stopped to help the boat in distress, but we had our eyes focused on a larger goal. I looked back and saw Jonathan treading water. Mitchell clung to the boat, shaking his head.

Jonathan was pretty upset about the accident. "Freak of nature," I said. "What matters is you're both safe." A launch had towed them back to shore.

My old teammate kept repeating the story, uncertain what had happened. Jonathan was the type of guy who'd never broken anything, never even caused himself any harm. His wealth insulating him from danger and meanness. He didn't know how to handle bad things. "It's just a dumb boat," I said. "Entirely replaceable."

"But I destroyed it," Jonathan said. "It's my fault."

It comforted me to see Jonathan distressed and willing to take responsibility. Shame wasn't the scourge of cowards as Windsor insisted. Shame could be a good thing.

"Cal," I told Jonathan, "once ran my family's yawl aground. He not only destroyed the keel, he accidentally hit my face with the boom and broke my nose." I pointed to my crooked bridge.

"What did you do?" Jonathan asked.

"What else could we do? We laughed about it."

The losing team invited us to have dinner at the Kensington dining hall. I was grateful when Coach Tripp begged off. "Prosper," he asked me, "where should we go to celebrate?" I took everyone to the Starry Diner for burgers and fries. One of the doe-eyed waitresses recognized me and asked, "How come you don't show your face round here anymore? Did you forget about us?"

I'd never been so happy to be recognized, remembered. To be told that this was a place where I belonged. Cal had taken a part of me with him. Maybe all I wanted was to reclaim some small bit of that boy.

"Awesome burgers," Race said. "Taste just like victory."

It occurred to me that I had Race to thank for this good feeling.

I woke up the next morning still high from having won. On the back of my door, I'd taped up a calendar listing the sailing team's racing schedule, marking down our victories, making notes on our team's losses. Race and I had won all of our individual invitationals. Our recent conquest had qualified us for the Tender Trophy. I looked over the calendar, then noticed today's date. Exactly a year had passed since Cal's death.

There was a knock on my opened door. Chester, too polite to barge in. He held something up. "Score." He grinned, closing the door behind him. Chester had stolen Diana's naked photo from Tazewell's room. "I'm going to return it," he said. "To the rightful owner."

I'd forgotten how pretty Diana was. Her naked skin incandescent. Chester was embarrassed, but we both took a long look at the photo. The two of us imagining our hands cupping Diana's breasts. When Chester held up the picture, I noticed the photographer's reflection in the mirror. The image was fuzzy, a wild blur of hair, a squinting eye. Aidan had taken the snapshot. There was more between Diana and Aidan than I might have imagined.

I congratulated Chester, then said, "Since you're an expert, I need your advice." I had an anniversary to honor.

"We could break into her room," Chester said. "Or you could just ask Brizzey to return Cal's photo."

"She'd light it on fire," I said, "before she'd ever give it back."

Race stopped by my room that night. He'd sailed over from Powder Point on his father's Bermuda-rig sloop *Spray.*

"Up for a little night sailing?" he asked.

We cruised out into the middle of the harbor, the white jib and mainsail glowing in the moonlight. The sails snapped as we dropped anchor. Race opened two cans of Coke, poured some of the soda out into the ocean and splashed some rum into the cans. "Yo ho ho," he said, handing me a drink. "Let's plan our attack."

Since we were seeded first for the Tender Trophy, we'd have a home water advantage.

"The key," I said, "is just knowing our own waves and rocking the course."

"Yeah," Race agreed, "but I'm worried about Coach Tripp. That dude has zero strategy. He's the hole in our boat."

"He's not so bad," I said. "He's only twenty-three."

The nearly starless sky was black and cloudy. We knocked back our rum and Cokes, the fizzy drink spicy, sweet. I convinced Race to play a game Cal and I used to love. We'd see who could come up with the most common words, sayings, and clichés that came from sailing. "Batten down the hatches," "give a wide berth," "taken aback," "aboveboard," "true blue," "high and dry," "hand over fist," "know the ropes," "three sheets to the wind," "walk the plank," "catch my drift," "on an even keel," "loose cannon," "miss the boat," "chew the fat," "let the cat out of the bag," "no room to swing a cat," "beat a dead horse," "shake a leg," "slush fund," "cut and run," "close quarters," "deep six," "scuttlebutt," "chockablock," "the cut of your jib."

"Aloof," Cal once said.

I challenged him to explain.

"It's from *a luff,*" he said. "To sail to windward. To keep your ship distant from the shore."

"We should make up our own phrase," I suggested. "Add our own contribution to nautical lore."

Cal thought about it for a while and then said, "How about, the starboard sea?"

"What?" I asked. "Like the sea on the right side of the boat? That doesn't mean anything."

"No," Cal insisted, "it means the right sea, the true sea, or like finding the best path in life. It's deep. I'm telling you, it's going to catch on. By this time next year, everyone will be using it."

Race did his best to play Cal's game. More for my benefit than his own. He saw that the game made me happy.

"Hard and fast," he said. "It's another way of saying a ship's beached."

"Did you see those boats last fall?" I asked. "The ones the helicopters winched and flew."

"Yeah. They brought them to our shipyard. Total loss. Real shame."

"I appreciate being out tonight." I stretched out over the bowsprit. "It's been a rough day."

"How so?"

"Anniversary. My best friend, he died a year ago."

Race didn't say a word. I could smell his clean laundry smell.

"My sailing partner, Cal," I said. "You probably competed against him."

Race nodded. "Taze mentioned something about him."

I told Race about Cal, then explained that Brizzey had stolen my photo of him. "She swiped it after we fooled around."

"What a klepto," he said. "That's how she wound up here, you know. Stole her roommate's Rolex. She came to my house once and made off with all my best CDs. Someone should lock her up."

Race promised to get my picture back. Told me it was the least he could do. "At this point," he said, "I owe you. You're the best crew I've ever had." Race looked out over the water. "No one reads the wind like you. It's like you can actually see it."

"Everything I know," I said, "I stole from Cal."

The boat cradled us, lulling me to sleep. I located the Great Bear,

Ursa Major, and found her binary stars, Mizar and Alcor, the horse and rider.

"Which one's the rider?" Race asked. "That's the one I want to be."

I told him I wasn't sure. "It's funny," I said, "how a really bright star can actually be two stars. How your eyes can't separate them or tell them apart."

"What's really amazing," Race said, "is that all those stars are dead. But we still see their light."

Race was right. The stars we were watching, the ones Cal and I had used so often to guide ourselves into and out of storms, were actually extinct, their brightness long extinguished. Cal and Aidan, my binary stars, both dead.

"We could stay out here tonight," Race said. "My mom would vouch for us."

I took a sip of Coke and stared at Race, our faces inches apart. I said, "I owe you. After Cal died, I never thought I'd sail again. Figured I was bad luck. Means a lot that you trust me."

"You're not bad luck." Race reached out, planting his hands on my shoulders, his fingertips digging into my skin. "Or maybe you are." He laughed. "But maybe I'm bad luck too. Two negatives make a positive, right?" Race held on to my shoulders, rubbing them briefly before letting go.

A moment passed between us. Race said, "My dad died out on this harbor, you know. We were fishing when he had a heart attack."

I did know this story, but I listened as Race described how he'd had to motor back to shore alone, captaining the vessel while his father faded away. "The whole time I was piloting the boat, I kept thinking that if we never made it back to shore, maybe he'd stay alive. Doesn't make any sense, I know. But when we got to the pier, that was when he stopped breathing for good." Race took a long chug from his soda. "You would have liked my dad. He made beautiful boats."

"Do you really want to sleep out here?" I asked.

Race surveyed the sky. "Looks like it might rain."

Instead of sailing, we powered back. I wondered what might have happened if we'd stayed out there together. Race was growing more and more relaxed. Willing to share his thoughts, his feelings with me. This was more than simple camaraderie. Race and I had actually become friends.

"Would Cal have liked me?" Race shouted over the engine's thrum. "Would he have thought I was a good sailor?"

Suddenly, I saw Cal and Race together in the same boat. Cal would have thought that Race was too much of a grind, too practiced and studied a sailor. He would have seen through Race's egotism into the heart of his insecurity. "He would have thought," I said, "that you were aces."

Race dropped me off at the pier. We said good night just as it began to shower. The soft rain sounding like a conspiracy of voices.

"Be safe getting home," I said. "Don't drink and sail."

"I'm not going home. Going to pillage the ladies of Astor. Celebrate our victory and claim our reward."

"The booty master of Astor. Good luck to you."

Race invited me to join him, but I didn't feel like visiting Nadia. More than anything, I didn't want to climb through Aidan's old window. We said good night again. Race punched me on the shoulder and said, "I mean it, man, it's like you see the wind."

I didn't sleep well. Thrashed around sweaty and confused. Thinking about Race and his father. Feeling guilty for our friendship. I dreamed of water: black waves, fiery rain. I thought I heard someone in my room singing over me. When I woke up the next morning, I could hear the distant sound of machinery. The foundations for Prosper Hall and Windsor House were being poured and I could hear the dormitories, my legacy, taking shape. I was about to head off to the shower when I noticed a padded bra on my bureau propping up my picture of Cal.

At Chapel, Windsor announced that Race and I would be vying for the Tender Trophy. Race actually jumped up out of his seat, urging me to do the same. We stood there as our teachers and classmates applauded. Soaking in their thunderous approval. Afterward, Tazewell congratulated me and said, "I've never seen Race so happy. You're a good influence on him. It's like he's had a personality transplant."

Though hosting the Tender Trophy was a big deal, the day of the regatta was a full day of competition at Bellingham. Chester had his own championship finals and Nadia had her final lacrosse game of the season. Everything was happening on campus staggered at various times. I hoped to have a chance to see Chester and Nadia play. At lunch, I asked Nadia whom she was competing against.

"Miss Lilly Tate's School for Young Ladies. Have you ever heard of a sillier place?"

I had just enough time before my meet to catch Nadia in her miniskirt and mouth guard. She played attack wing, rifling her stick like a marksman, feeding the ball to the offense. I stood on the sidelines and listened as the Lilly Tate girls complained to their coach, Colin Florent, that he'd forgotten to fill the water bottles. Florent, a stocky, thick-armed man, called out to a woman snapping photos with a fancy Leica, "Hannah, can you run and get some water?"

Watching Hannah Florent, I thought of what Marieke had said about Bellingham's beach, how ordinary it was. Hannah's rich chocolate hair was coarse and streaked with gray. She had the creased, freckled skin of a woman who had spent too much time in the sun. I watched her struggle to collect the stray water bottles and saw how the girls on the lacrosse team ignored her.

"Can I help you?" I asked. "Want me to show you where you can fill those up?"

Later Nadia would complain that I'd left the field and missed her big play. I told Nadia that I was sorry, I hadn't meant to bail on her. What Nadia couldn't understand was that I didn't want to lose out on a chance to meet the woman who'd caused Aidan to break all those windows.

I carried the water bottles for Hannah and made small talk, but I didn't introduce myself. Hannah kept taking deep breaths, hungry for the salt air. "This school is so beautiful," Hannah said. "You must love going here."

"It has its advantages."

Hannah wore a white tank top and linen pants. Her arms were sleek and muscular. She looked less like an artist and more like an athlete.

"Our girls are always thrilled when we play co-ed schools."

"What do you teach?" I asked.

She told me that she taught art and I mentioned that my family owned a Sargent, a Miró, a Calder. Showing off. Hannah nodded and told me that I was lucky and that she was always amazed by her students' art collections.

"People mostly buy art," I said, "to feel like they've escaped the middle classes."

Hannah laughed, a rich, sonorous laugh that shook her entire body. "You're a funny one, aren't you?" she said.

I brought Hannah to the Athletic Center and together we filled up the bottles, methodically, efficiently. "We're quite a team," she said. "We could be professional water boys." We brought the bottles back to the sidelines and looked out over the field at the girls playing lacrosse. Warriors in skirts and elbow pads. I pointed to some of the storm damage, showed Hannah where the Baraccuda's glass fin had been mended and glazed.

I was running late for my sailing meet. Race would be worried. Before I left, Hannah thanked me and said, "I never caught your name."

I don't know why I said what I did. Maybe I wanted Hannah to remember something, or maybe I wanted to test her, but when she asked me my name I didn't even pause. "My name is Aidan," I said. "It means fire."

Just before the regatta, Coach Tripp pulled the sailing team together for a pep talk. He had on a red baseball cap, a Bellingham sweatshirt, and plaid Bermuda shorts. Coach had his own superstitions, and after we won our first regatta, he decided to quit shaving. His beard had come in all patchy and orange, but it made him seem older. We stood around in a circle waiting for instructions, but Coach didn't say anything at first, just stared at all of us. This made me listen even harder. "Sometimes," he broke the silence, "when we're huddled like this, it scares me. I feel so powerful, like whatever I say might actually matter." He took off his baseball cap. "Sailing is the art of asking questions: Where is the wind? How will it come to me? High pressure, cold and sinking. Low pressure, warm and rising. Isobars joining areas of equal distress. Forming closed concentric patterns. I plot weather systems on maps and they are as good as stories to me. Detailed notations of where I've been. The best days of my life have been spent on the water."

Coach Tripp was known for getting carried away. I looked over at Race, ready to share a smirk, but Race was dead focused. He wanted to win this meet more than anything else in his life.

"I don't want this journey to end," Coach said. "I wish we could keep winning together. I hope all of you will continue to be the best at everything you do. I hope you'll always think of me as your coach."

Of all the days I spent sailing at Bellingham, the day of the Tender Trophy Regatta was the least challenging and, in many ways, the least memorable. On a mild, sunny afternoon in May, Race and I cruised around the harbor, besting our best competition. We'd sailed nearly perfect meets, master classes in mastery. Anticipating each other's moves, making each other better with every tack. When our times were announced, Race and I dove off the pier and into the water. Both of our noses were sunburned, our bodies in almost identical muscular shape, our hair highlighted in similar shades of red and blond. We could have been mistaken for brothers.

The only thing left to do was celebrate. Race had planned a blowout party that weekend, just a week before graduation. Our time together was running out.

Chester finished his spring tennis season with only two losses. He'd hoped to go undefeated, but he told me that he'd actually learned more from losing those two matches. "I figured out some of my weaknesses," he said. "Turns out losing can be good for you."

"I don't know about that," I said. "I think losing is only good for the winner."

Chester had been accepted to the University of Chicago and was still hoping to hear from Columbia. We were playing chess in his tidy room and I asked him if he would come to Race's party with me. He thought about it, weighing the upside and downside as he did with every chess move. "Can you guarantee my safety?" he asked. "I'm dead serious."

Though I promised to protect Chester, I knew I couldn't guarantee anything. "Aren't you at least curious to see Race's house? Consider it our going-away party. Our last blast."

"Is that what this is about? Having a good time? What about your friend Aidan? What did you find out about her? Or did you forget? Were you having too much fun winning?"

Chester slid his knight across the board and explained to me that the game was over. He was four moves away from checkmate. I left, ran back to my room, and returned with the book he'd given me to read. "I read this," I said. "I read it for you because you asked me to."

"I appreciate that." Chester rearranged the pieces on the chessboard. "But I'm not going to Race's. I need to protect myself. Jason, as much as I'd like to believe that we're friends, I know I can't count on you."

"That's not true," I said. "If it came down between you and them, I'd throw you the life jacket every time." I thought of all the people who'd been unable to count on me, and I began to understand just how important to me Chester had become. "Look," I said. "You're right, you shouldn't go to the party. It wasn't fair of me to ask you, but please know this: I'm your friend."

Mr. Guy had insisted on meeting with each of his students individually to discuss our final projects. I walked over to his home, the little brick house near the beach. My final project was a consideration of the INF Treaty, an agreement between the United States and the USSR to eliminate all intermediate- and short-range missiles. Mr. Guy was fascinated by my optimism regarding U.S.–Soviet relations. He continued to call me naïve. "Well," I said, "a little hope is better than mutual assured destruction." We sat in his modest living room in wingback chairs. He served me black currant tea and a cinnamon-flavored cookie that he said his friend Paul called a snickerdoodle. The name seemed to delight Mr. Guy.

The walls of his living room were decorated not with candid photos of grandchildren but rather formal photographs of men in military uniforms. "Are any of those your students?" I asked.

Mr. Guy had graduated from the Naval Academy at Annapolis and one photo was of him in his uniform, another of his friend Paul, and then several more of students from Bellingham he'd sent there. I watched Mr. Guy in his three-piece suit and bow tie admiring the photo of himself as a young midshipman.

"I heard you're an old salt." Mr. Guy winked. "We should have recruited you as well. Though I don't imagine you'd care to spend much time on a battleship. Certainly, I suppose, you could be an astronaut. We could rocket you off on a spaceship. I think you'd quite like that."

Relaxed in his home, Mr. Guy was an entirely different character. "You've done good work for me this year," he said. "Wish I'd gotten to you sooner. You came to us from Kensington?" Proud of himself for having remembered this.

"Seems like a long time ago," I said. "Another lifetime."

We talked about my paper, and Mr. Guy confided in me that he was dubious about the cooling tensions between the United States and Russia. "There's still too much money to be made on war. Perhaps they'll determine a new configuration, what with China and the Middle East ripe for conflict."

"If you graduated from Annapolis," I said, "you probably worked in military intelligence. Bet you know where all the cold war bodies are buried."

He smiled and rubbed his hands together. "Now you're on to me. All of that's for my memoirs. But I will tell you this: Where the government is concerned, never believe the official story. It's always a cover. The truth: unattainable."

We sipped our tea and ate our cookies and talked a little about Mr. Guy's retirement. When I asked him why he was finally calling it quits, he said, "Because I'm a relic."

Mr. Guy kept showing me periodicals I should read, arguing over Reagan and Gorbachev. Finally, when I told him that I had to go, he searched around and handed me a manila folder filled with notes for a paper that seemed to focus on the influence of *The Grapes of Wrath* on the lives of migrant farmworkers. "What's this?" I asked.

"Your friend Aidan," he said. "Her independent study. I felt her insights were always keen but she needed to work on her organization. These are her notes. I gave her mother most of her other papers, but I found this file when I was cleaning out my office. I'm taking a chance that you might want it."

There was Aidan's round, looping handwriting. The notes were in fragments and though I could decipher individual words, I had a hard time reading full sentences. But the real reason Mr. Guy had given me this file was that in the corner of one of the pages, Aidan had sketched a cartoon of a boy with curly hair and a cleft chin holding a bird. She'd labeled the figures "Sweet Boy" and "Seabird."

"That was an awful business," Mr. Guy said. "Completely mishandled."

I held the file against my chest. "Aidan thought you were great."

"I'm hardly great." Mr. Guy drank his tea. "But I was bothered"—he paused—"by a lot of things."

I nodded. The bird Aidan had drawn was small, like a starling. "Is there anything you can tell me?" I asked.

"There were times in the past when I was asked to secure certain favors, but I can assure you that where Aidan is concerned, I have been left in the dark." Mr. Guy shook his head. "I have no facts for you, just gut feelings. When the police chief's son is suddenly given a full scholarship, it sends a certain message." Mr. Guy got up to refill his teacup, pacing and agitated. "I'm right to retire. The teachers here no longer run the school. Students do. I might as well be a butler following you lads around with a dustpan, sweeping away your dirt."

Before I left, I asked Mr. Guy, "What will you remember about this place?"

He paused for a moment, took a sip of tea, and said, "I used to believe having a good memory meant being able to remember everything in perfect detail. Now I believe having a good memory means being able to selectively forget. It's not what I'll remember, Jason," he said. "It's what I'll forget that matters."

Nadia's birthday was coming up and she wanted me to take her virginity. "I know I can trust you." She offered to sneak into my room at night. I argued that it was too dangerous for her to sneak out. "What about early in the morning?" Nadia suggested. "We could wake up at four a.m., pretend that we were going running, and just meet up. I've heard guys prefer having sex in the morning."

I wasn't sure where she'd heard this, though I imagined Nadia and the Astor girls had done their share of plotting around this matter. "I've never taken anyone's virginity before," I said. "It's not something I want to do." It was scary having that sort of power over a girl. You could hurt her in ways you might never understand. "Okay," I relented. "On your birthday."

There was a mattress set up in the Old Boathouse and that was where Nadia wanted to have sex. Among the paint cans and retired crew shells. She went over to scout out the space right before her birthday and brought blankets, scented candles. "Can you buy the condoms?" she asked.

I walked to the Gas Mart. A familiar blue Chevy Malibu was parked in front. I hadn't seen Leo since the fall, and I wondered if he'd gotten a job at the convenience store. I braced myself to see him. When I went inside, Leo was busy buying a jug of milk. He was dressed in a white polo shirt with GOODWYN MARINA stitched in blue over his heart. Leo didn't say anything to me. He didn't have to. I waited until he'd left the store to buy the condoms.

The first time I had something that could be mistaken for sex was with Ginger. It was summertime and we were staying at her rambling mansion. My father hadn't made the trip. It was the last time I saw Ginger's father, Roland. I'd been so excited to sail with him, to show him how far along I'd come, but he couldn't take me sailing because he kept having to walk along the beach with my mother. At some point during that weekend, Miriam took Riegel and me grocery shopping and left us at the store. My mother was furious.

It was hot that summer and the house had no air-conditioning. To stay cool, Riegel and I camped out on army cots up in the tower's screened-in sleeping porch. A swarm of Japanese beetles clawed at the mesh screens, and I wondered if they'd eat through the wires and attack me. Suddenly, a door swung open and Ginger climbed into my bed. Riegel was sleeping just a few feet away. I thought maybe she'd made a mistake and meant to curl up beside him.

"Are you awake?" she asked.

"I was having a dream," I said. "About beetles."

Despite the heat, I had a sheet wrapped around me. Ginger lifted the sheet, swung a leg over my body, and straddled my waist. She held the sheet over her head, making a tent. She was seventeen. I was twelve. Her blue cotton nightgown transparent. She wasn't wearing any underwear. I remember being confused by the stickiness of her crotch. Though I'd had wet dreams, I'd never considered the actual mechanics of sex. I had purple giraffes on my shorts. Ginger pulled them down and kissed the tip of my penis. I was too young for this. I would have preferred it if Ginger had sneaked into my room and asked me if I wanted a bowl of ice cream. This was my fault, I feared. I kept wondering if I'd sent some signal to her, if I asked to be misread. She kissed my stomach and before I could stop myself, I came. I remember wincing, drawing a hand over my face. Ginger didn't move. She stayed on top of me. For as long as I could recall, she had been like a sister: kind, loving, a bit of a terror.

Afterward, she told me that she'd wanted to be my first. Wanted to take care of me in this way. I didn't know what to say to Ginger and so I said, "Thank you."

"You're just a boy. Aren't you?" She pushed the hair back from my face, kissed my forehead, and said, "Let's go up to the observatory. See the stars." We left one tower for another. I felt ashamed. Ginger must have wanted to make everything right between us and so she taught me the one poem she knew and said that it was ours. That William Blake had written it for us.

I thought of this as I walked back to campus, wondering if I should share it with Nadia. It wasn't that Ginger had messed me up. I realized that most guys would have been grateful. But she had taken some not-small thing from me. Nadia was fifteen and she wanted to have sex. I wanted to do her this favor. Hoped that I wouldn't mess her up for life. We were all pretending we knew what we wanted to do with our bodies.

Race had invited almost everyone from the sailing team and most of the guys from Whitehall to his party. Instead of driving us over the causeway and onto Powder Point, Race picked Kriffo, Stuyvie, Taze, and me up at the Bellingham finger pier not in his Boston Whaler but in a vintage Chris-Craft, the mahogany hull a rich toffee brown. "Taking you guys over in style," he said. All he needed was a white captain's hat to complete the allure.

The Tender Trophy was a trophy in name only, but Race's mother had had an actual sterling silver trophy cup made with Race's and my name engraved on the body. As Tazewell steered the Chris-Craft, Race poured several cans of Miller Lite into the large silver cup while Kriffo and Stuyvie chanted "Tastes great, less filling" over and over again. A joke that for them would never get old. Race hoisted the trophy and Stuyvie and Kriffo changed their chant to "Jason's great, Race is better, Jason's great, Race is better." We each took long chugs from the trophy, the beer tasting of silver polish.

We cruised over to South Side, and I finally witnessed up close all the stone mansions Leo and I had blindly driven by so many months ago, their imposing hedges blocking any roadside view of their opulence. The mansions opened their lawns, their arms, to the ocean. Race's house was large, though not nearly as impressive as Ginger's rotting family home. I'd seen bigger estates, but I'd always imagined myself living in a stone house by the sea. Fine Italian masonry work that would withstand the elements and time. Round gray stones that would keep me cool in the summer. I resented Race a little for having my chosen home. More than anything, I resented that I'd no longer be able to think of my dream house without Race wandering into the picture.

Docking at sunset, the sky streaked with orange and purple, the air calm and sweet. Before any of us could disembark, Race said, "Hold on a minute. I want to remember this."

Race led us up the path to his home. Kriffo found a basketball on the lawn and challenged Stuyvie to a game of one-on-one. Tazewell and I followed Race inside the house. The entryway was crowded with dirty clothes and sailing gear.

"My mom just left. We've got free rein." Race picked up a duffel bag and walked upstairs. "She cancels the maid service when I'm here alone. Trying to teach me a lesson."

Taze disappeared through the kitchen's swinging door. I held back and admired the living room. High cathedral ceiling with wooden support beams. A few of the interior stone walls were exposed, but most had been covered over with plaster. Standing in the middle of that living room, I tried to imagine Aidan in this house. A coldness ran through me. A ghost passing through a living body. This was the last place Aidan had visited before her death. I wondered if Race heard her spirit at night. Through the window, I saw Kriffo and Stuyvie shooting hoops, unaware of just how lucky they were to be alive. At times, I felt haunted.

There were several ornately framed oil paintings in the living room. Still lifes and seascapes. A picture of an old man in a wooden bateau seized my attention. The image resembled something I'd seen months ago at the Whaling Museum. I went up close to the canvas, trying to discern the artist's signature.

"None of the paintings are real." Race stood behind me. "We own all of the originals, but Mom keeps most of them locked up in a vault." Race pointed to the old man on the boat. "This one she lent out to a museum. Crazy tax break. She had some artist paint these copies just for show."

"People do that?" I asked. "Own originals of something but then display copies?"

"Embarrassing, right?" Race blushed a little. "I'm honest about it, though. Since Dad died, Mom's always afraid someone's going to break in and steal everything."

I didn't see the point of having an original work of art if you kept it locked up. It was like not owning the original at all.

Race handed me a beer and a box of pizza. He'd ordered dozens of pizzas, some of them decadently covered with chunks of lobster. "My creation," he said. Kriffo and Stuyvie came in from playing basketball and clicked on an enormous TV.

"Check this out," Kriffo called to us.

He'd landed on a news show. I recognized Robert Chambers from the times I'd seen him at Dorrian's. A reporter chattered on about a recent video he'd uncovered of Chambers partying with a group of girls dressed in lingerie. We sat on Race's soft sofas and watched Chambers pretend to choke himself while the trashy girls giggled. He held up a Barbie doll, twisted the plastic head. "Oops," he said. "I think I killed it."

We laughed. All of us. Out of nervousness, perhaps. Laughing made the acid from Race's pizza rise up in the back of my throat. Stuyvie picked up the remote control and turned the channel.

"It's too bad," Tazewell said. "Chambers was primed to get off. Now he's fucked."

By midnight the party was in full swing. The entire Bellingham campus had emptied out onto Race's lawn. It was a Friday night, late enough in the semester that Dean Warr had eased up on monitoring weekend sign-outs. I was certain he knew about the party. His son was doing beer bongs a few feet away from me. There were also plenty of kids I didn't recognize. In the summer, while everyone was away, Race probably hung out with his townie friends, dropping them all once the school year picked up again. A shitty thing to do. Tazewell played DJ, blasting reggae and passing joints. I stayed sober.

I worried about enjoying myself around these guys. Worried about turning into one of them. From a distance, I watched Skinner and James Hardy toss shiny beaded pillows and leather seat cushions through a window and out onto the back lawn. Race saw them too and didn't seem to mind. A few weeks back, I'd bumped into Officer Hardy in the General Store. Heard him charge his groceries to Race's mother. He didn't notice me, though at one point, we were standing in the same aisle.

I left Race's house and wound up back down at the dock where Race had parked the sloop *Spray,* the Chris-Craft, the Boston Whaler, and a sleek red cigarette boat that looked like a fantasy, a cartoon of speed. Kriffo was sitting in the cigarette boat, smoking a cigar.

I waved and Kriffo invited me aboard, offered me one of his Montecristos. I took it and had him light it for me. The cinnamon smell of cigar smoke reminded me of sailing with my mother and Roland, but it also reminded me of those times in my childhood when my father had missed some important event only to stumble into my room late at night to wake me, kiss me on the forehead, and find out how things had gone. On those nights, Dad always smelled like cigars, like he'd been out enjoying himself.

"It's nice here," I said. "Race has a good setup."

Kriffo agreed. "I'll be sorry to graduate. There's nothing like this in Syracuse." Though Tazewell had been accepted early, Kriffo and I both had yet to hear any update from Princeton. He'd shown me the orange Princeton sweatshirt his mother had given him for Christmas. "My mother fucking cursed my luck."

One of the things I'd noticed about Kriffo was his weakness for nostalgia. For the past month, every night in the dining hall he'd wax poetic about that evening's dinner. "This is the last time we'll have tacos," he'd say. "The last time I scarf down this shepherd's pie." I'd come to think of Kriffo as an endearing giant even though I knew how easily he could crush or harm. Even though I understood how much he'd hurt Chester.

I said, "I've been taking a survey. What are you gonna miss most about this place?"

Over the spring, Kriffo had bulked up, expanding his already expanded girth. He looked uncomfortable in his body, like his muscles were a costume he'd put on wrong and couldn't shed. He thought about my question and said that he'd miss his friends. "You guys, of course. I'll miss knowing that there are all these great guys who one hundred percent have my back."

I agreed. "We've taken good care of one another."

"For a long time," he said, "I was pissed at you for tackling me in front of everyone. But you turned out to be all right."

Kriffo spat over the side of the boat. I couldn't tell if he was drunk.

"Have you ever been out on this boat?" I asked. "These are real monsters."

"Just that night of the storm," Kriffo said. "You know, the thing with the girl."

Kriffo had convinced himself that I was there for the hurricane party. That I was part of whatever they'd done. I said, "Yeah, that was pretty wild."

"It was mostly an accident." Kriffo nodded. "I mean when you look at it that way, it's really nobody's fault."

"We did the best we could to save her. Right?"

"Maybe not the best." Kriffo sucked on his cigar. "We had to cut her loose. We could have died out there."

My shoulders began to shake. I made a fist to calm myself.

"I don't know how you and Race charge around on the water." Kriffo shook his head. "Those waves scared the hell out me."

I left Kriffo with his cigar and his guilt and ran back up to the house to find Race. There was no way for me to ask Kriffo questions if he thought I was actually there that night. I would have already known the answers.

Race stood alone on the third-floor balcony, drinking beer, looking down at his guests, the smell of marijuana, a mixture of fresh shit and mown lawn wafting up from below. "My Piranha Brother," he said and bumped my chest. "You have everything you need?"

I thanked him for the party.

"That trophy cup is yours, you know," he said. "My mom had one made for each of us. I didn't want to say anything in front of the guys. It's not like we're pussies, but I think it's good to have a little hardware for our hard work."

"I should start a bragging wall."

It was a nice gesture. Filled with his mother's kind thoughts. She'd been there that afternoon when we won, waiting on the shore for the results. It was hard to view a regatta even when you were out on the water yourself—even if you knew where to look. Beautiful to watch but not exactly a spectator's sport. Race had more or less banned his mother from watching him sail. "She knows I don't like it. Makes me nervous." But there she was, and when we emerged chilly and soaked after our celebratory water plunge, she greeted us with thick fluffy towels. She told Race how proud his father would have been.

Race and I looked down at his party together. Brizzey and Stuyvie were bobbing and weaving trying to dance to Peter Tosh. I asked Race, "Who looks good tonight? Who are you planning on celebrating with?"

We ranked the girls at the party from "unfuckable" to "fuck yeah." Race was interested in a junior named Carmen. A brunette with long feathered hair. "I like a girl with an overbite," he said.

I said, "Aidan had just a hint of an overbite."

"I wouldn't know." Race smiled.

"But I thought you said you hooked up with her."

Like any bad liar, Race had forgotten his lie. "Oh, yeah. That's right."

"I was wondering if you could clear something up for me." I rubbed my face. "See, that night of the storm, I thought Aidan came out here looking for me, but maybe she was still interested in you."

Race was past the point of denying that Aidan had gone to the party. He'd given Leo a job to make this truth disappear. "What happened then?" I asked. "Kriffo said you took her out on your cigarette boat."

"Let's not do this," Race said. "Things are good between us."

"How did she drown?" I asked. "We won our trophies. Just tell me."

"Why do you care? She was nothing."

I pushed Race against the balcony. In one swift move, I raised my arm, gripping his throat in my hand. My heart lurched inside my chest as I imagined what might have happened to Aidan. "What did you do to her?" I demanded. "Why did you hurt her?"

I was choking Race so hard that he couldn't answer. Race tried to push me off, but I used the full force of my body against him. After all our hours on the water together, all my self-control and determination to find the truth, and yet I still wound up with my hands around my enemy's neck. As I felt myself ready to squeeze the life out of Race, I considered what had brought me to this moment, this confrontation. I understood that this moment wasn't only about Aidan. My skin warmed. Flush with the memory of what I'd done to Cal.

"I get it, Race." I loosened my hold. "We're not so different. I did something awful once too." I let go, releasing my grip.

Race sucked in air. I expected him to take a swing at me, but he didn't. He just stared at me and breathed in heavily.

"You don't have to tell me anything," I said. "I'm pretty sure I know what you did. Certain I can guess."

The night before Cal died, I came back to our room late, found Cal bare chested, his skin slick with sweat. He'd been lifting free weights in our room. His arms and chest muscles taut and sinewy. He had on gym shorts that I was certain belonged to me. The front of his hair was soaked with sweat, while my own hair was wet with rain. I was wearing a hand-me-down, my dad's ancient green trench coat. The coat had epaulets and brass buttons and made me feel like a soldier in Napoleon's army. I'd been spending as much time away from Cal as possible. Resisting temptation and punishing myself—for what, I didn't dare admit.

That night I'd walked into town for a cheeseburger. After dinner, I went to a pharmacy to read magazines. I flipped through a bunch of sports and sailing magazines, and I probably would have left without buying anything, except this anemic kid behind the counter kept looking over at me. I stared back, then turned away. He approached me and asked if I needed any help. The kid was my age, but he didn't look like anyone I knew. He was thin, with pale, bloodless skin, black spikes of hair, and thick, rubbery lips. His fingernails looked bruised at first, like he'd slammed his hand in a car door, until I realized that he'd painted his nails black. He smiled at me. "Find anything you like?" he asked. He wasn't creepy. Not really. But up until that point, I'd thought that whatever existed between Cal and me was separate and distinct from the rest of the world. It hadn't occurred to me that a stranger could sense and recognize something so private.

I asked the anemic kid if the store sold *Penthouse*. He bit his black nails and tilted his head. He told me that they carried *Playboy* and something that he thought was called *Big on Top*. The store kept both behind the counter. I asked to buy a copy of *Playboy,* paid for the magazine, and left.

I walked back to campus in the rain, went to the chemistry lab, and tried beating off to the *Playboy* in the bathroom of the Science Wing. The women in the issue all had frizzy, bleach-blond hair, small tits. I could get hard, but I couldn't stay hard enough to come. When I returned to our room, I was pretty worked up.

Cal rubbed a towel across his chest and asked me to listen to him. He'd been doing a lot of careful thinking and had reached certain conclusions about our friendship. Mainly, he was confident that we hadn't done anything wrong those times in the dark, wrestling on the floor and in bed. He shook his sweat-soaked bangs away from his eyes and forehead, then in a clear measured voice, he explained that he loved me as much as he ever expected to love anyone. More, even. We were young together. We'd always be young to each other no matter how fat, bald, and blow hearted we became to the rest of the world. He said, "It's simple, really." When I didn't respond, didn't clear my throat or blink, even, Cal reached his arm out and touched his hand to my shoulder. When I still didn't respond, Cal turned away, nodding his head and saying again, "It's simple, really."

I thought of the kid at the pharmacy and the naked ladies in the magazine. I was sad, but I was also angry. I lunged at Cal. Hurled myself on top of his slick and sweaty body, razing him down onto the wood floor. I smashed my closed fists against his ribs. Cal tried to push me off at first but slowly made less and less of an effort to defend himself. He went limp. Maybe he thought I was playing a new version of our game. I punched his chin, slapped the sides of his face. When I couldn't stand the sight of him any longer, I flipped him over. It *was* simple, really. There was something I could do to put an end to the matter. Something final. The violence aroused me. The close proximity of our bodies turned me on. It was nothing for me to force myself onto Cal. To keep him pinned down with my knees on his legs, my hand around his neck. I could fuck him knowing that he'd never want me again.

All of the lights in our room were on, the door unlocked. I was still wearing my trench coat and the material fanned out over us, covering our bodies. If someone had walked through our unlocked door, he might have had the mistaken impression that I was on my knees, praying for strength. With one determined blow, I destroyed everything that was beautiful in my life.

I rolled off of Cal and left him curled up on the floor. I cleared my throat, spat in a wastebasket, and told Cal that I was switching roommates, changing sailing partners. It was over between us. He didn't move for a long time. I undressed and got ready for sleep. Finally, before turning off the light, Cal pushed himself up from the floor. I tried not to look at him. His face was red, swollen. He held his arms around his rib cage. Had I simply offered him a cold cloth or helped him to bed, I could have begun to make things right between us. He stood for a moment, not looking at me, then bent down and picked something up off the ground. "This yours?" The *Playboy* must have fallen out of the inside pocket of my coat.

I didn't speak to Cal again. Before we went to sleep that night, Cal said, "Don't worry, Jason. You can pass. No one need ever know. Your secret will end with me."

On our last night together, I told Aidan this secret. She listened, nodding. Afterward, she was quiet, absorbing the hideous weight of my confession. I could feel her trying to summon the right words. "What you did," she said, "was awful. What it led to, even worse." She held my hand. "You can't change what you did, but if you honor Cal, maybe a time will come when you'll be ready to forgive yourself."

Race played it cool. He told me I could leave or stay. He didn't care. "I'll call you a cab," he said. "Or I'll pour you another drink. It's all the same to me."

I leaned over the balcony and looked down at Race's fake paintings. "My brother Riegel works for this Wall Street big shot. He told me the stock market crash was caused by a bunch of traders who'd made a dumb bet. They wanted to have some fun, create mayhem. I figure you guys, Taze, Kriffo, and Stuyvie, you all had some sort of bet to see who could hurt Aidan the most."

Race said nothing. Carmen with her overbite and low-cut T-shirt joined us on the balcony and told Race that his party kicked ass. Race was happy for the interruption. He had something he wanted to show Carmen and he steered her away from me and down the stairs.

I was in a room full of happy, young people. I'd never felt older. Never felt more alone.

FIFTEEN

Nadia and I woke up early on her birthday, sneaked out of our dorms, and met at the Old Boathouse. Both of us dressed to go for a run. The boathouse smelled of paint and varnish but especially of mold. A row of high windows ran along one wall, but the sun would not rise for several hours. Nadia had arrived first and lit up wide pillar candles that sent the aroma of fake strawberries and vanilla bean through the small, enclosed space. We took off our sneakers and flopped on the mattress she'd already covered with her own soft blankets. We kissed and she went right for my groin. "There's no rush," I said. "We've got your whole birthday to celebrate." Nadia began taking off her tank top, and I said, "Did you ever do that thing when you were a little kid where your parents balanced you on their feet?"

"Like an airplane?" she asked.

I stretched out on my back and bent my knees and Nadia leaned over and squared her chest against my feet. Straightening my legs, I balanced Nadia. She was so light. We both made funny zooming noises as though she were careening through puffy clouds. Looking up into her face I saw her perfectly shaped mouth, smelled her saccharine tooth-paste, noticed where she'd forgotten to tweeze a hair from a small mole on her chin. I also saw myself as a child, the broad grin on my father's face as he balanced me in the air.

"This is fun enough," Nadia said, "but you can put me down any-time you like."

Nadia was just humoring me. The airplane trick a bad idea, a poor distraction. I sat up and said, "Once we do this, you can never take it back."

Nadia took off her tank top. She wasn't wearing a bra. Her left breast was larger than her right, and her nipples pointed out in different directions. Her arms and legs were tan but her torso was pale white. She slid off her running shorts and stood before me in just a pair of white lace panties. "Take them off for me," she said. I brought her down onto the mattress. Hooking my thumbs around her panties, shucking them off in one clean move.

Without much thought, I stood up and took off my T-shirt, my sweat pants, and then my boxers. Nadia stared at my body. She'd never seen me naked, barely seen me with my shirt off. After all the sailing and training, my body was lean, strong. I'd never been overly proud of my physique, but I was aware of the muscles along my abdomen, the tension in my calves, the thickness of my thighs, the definition of my pectoral muscles. This was as good as I would ever look. Nadia's eyes widened, first with a kind of frenzy, a desire, then suddenly her eyes dampened and she began to cry.

"What's the matter," I asked. "What's wrong?"

Nadia looked at me not with desire but with resentment. "You're so much better looking than I am."

I told Nadia that she was the prettiest girl at Bellingham. I hugged her and kissed her neck.

"You're just doing me a favor." She pulled her face away.

There was no right thing to say. If I told Nadia that I did want her, she would hear the lie in my voice. She was a smart girl.

"I've just been kidding myself, haven't I?" She pulled her tank top back on. She couldn't find her panties, but she reached over me and picked up her shorts. "You're still in love with Aidan."

She didn't say this in a mean or accusatory way. She wasn't speaking out of spite. And she was right that I couldn't stop thinking about Aidan.

While Nadia tied her sneakers, I sat naked on the mattress staring at the dark windows.

"Did you have sex with her?" Nadia asked. "Did you sleep with Aidan? Are you worried I won't be as good?"

That night on the *Swan,* after I told Aidan my horrible truth, I expected her to reject me. To run away, even. But she seemed to understand that I needed comfort. Aidan knew what it was like to have your love turn to rage, to hurt the one person that you cared for above all others. "You need," she said, "to find a way to trust yourself again." The last time I'd been physical with a person, with Cal, I'd lost control and turned violent. I hated knowing that there was a violence within me that could mix so easily with sex. I was afraid of hurting Aidan. And Aidan was afraid of something else. "I used to try," she said, "to have casual sex." She sat up straight on our bunk. "But then I realized I'm not a casual person."

We laughed. I ran my hand over her back. "Well, sex," I said, "shouldn't be a casual thing. Not if it's worth having."

And so Aidan and I did all of the private things we could to each other's bodies, holding back that one last thing. Believing that there would be a time in the not too distant future when we would share everything with each other. Maybe we were beginning to fall in love, maybe we were just nursing each other back to health. For so long, I'd feared that I was hanging on to Aidan, on to all my thoughts and memories of her because of how our night together changed the meaning of all my nights with Cal. But I understood now that that it didn't change anything. I loved them both. I'd opened my life up to each of them. I wasn't worthy of either. If asked to choose between them, I wouldn't.

I couldn't salvage things between Nadia and me. I stayed naked as Nadia dressed. "I care about you," I said. "The last thing I want is to be a disappointment."

Nadia left, and I sat there for a little while among the old crew shells, the cans of dried paint. After Race's party, I'd gone to Chester and told him how I'd confronted Race. How Kriffo had called the whole thing an accident.

"They lied to her mother." Chester couldn't stop shaking his head.

I begged Chester to come forward about the hazing, the harassment he'd put up with for years. "There's got to be enough to get at least one of those guys kicked out. We could go after Kriffo. Say that he broke your arm on purpose."

"You really don't get it," Chester said. "Aidan was killed. Windsor looked that girl's mother straight in the eye and said 'suicide.' No one cares about my arm or the scar on my face. No one cares about a skinny girl from California."

I picked up a paintbrush covered in a thick coat of dried white paint. I thought back to the night we'd painted the roof CLASS OF '88. We had only a few days left before graduation. Not much time, but I realized that there was something I could do. I needed Chester's help.

When I explained to Chester what I had in mind, I knew that there was a good chance he'd say no. But he liked my idea. "That's clever," he said. Together we sneaked out of Whitehall, climbed up onto the roof of the Old Boathouse. I'd gathered some unused brushes, some half-filled cans of white paint. Working quickly, cleanly, we managed to paint our message before the sun came up. When we finished, I jumped off the roof, then helped Chester down, careful not to hurt his arm. We sat on the wet lawn, our white message radiant in the dark.

"What made you so sure those guys hurt Aidan?" Chester asked. "How'd you know?"

"Because I loved her." I peeled white paint from my hands. "And because I did something terrible once, something I'm ashamed of. I'm not so different from those guys."

Chester didn't ask me what I'd done and I'm not sure I would have told him if he had. Instead he told me a story about another black student who'd gone to Bellingham. "His name was Shawn. Everyone here loved him. He was from Chicago, well built, played football, basketball. The white kids tripped over themselves just to hang out with the guy." Chester and Shawn were never friends. "He was older than me. First time we were alone together in the gym, he told me to keep my distance. It wasn't like I thought we'd be friends just because we were both black. But Shawn saw me as some kind of threat. He'd figured out a way to make a place for himself. Didn't want me to ruin it for him." Chester's eyes began to water. He wasn't crying exactly. "My allergies," he said, "they're killing me."

"So what happened?" I asked. "With Shawn?"

"It was stupid," Chester said. "I went into his room when he wasn't there, crumbled some of my mother's cookies and brownies all over his floor and closet, his bedsheets, even in his sneakers. His room got infested with ants." Chester sniffed. "Later, I heard these seniors talking about how Shawn was 'dirty.' For a long time, I hated myself."

I told Chester I knew what it was like. To hate yourself for what you'd done.

"That book," I said, "the one you lent me. It scared me a little."

"How come?"

I ran my hands over the wet grass. "The way the writer went back and forth between men and women. I've felt that way. I'm not sure what it makes me."

Chester nodded. "Doesn't make you anything."

In the East, the sun cast a brilliant red light on a distant, developing storm. "Red sky at morning," I said. "Sailors take warning."

"Let's go." Chester stood, offering me his good arm. I took his hand and allowed him to help me up.

I made it clear to Chester that I would take all of the blame. "We're in this together," he protested.

"If there's any heat," I said, "I'll take it."

Our message lasted that morning almost through breakfast. The grounds people had been ordered to drape the roof with a tarp, but the winds were heavy and the tarp kept blowing off, revealing our indictment: THE CRIMES AND COVER-UPS OF THE CLASS OF '88. By lunchtime, the entire roof had been painted over in red, but then the rain came, rinsing the red paint away, the white letters showing through. It would take several more coats of paint to cover up our accusations of a cover-up.

At dinner that night there was all sorts of speculation. I sat at a long table with Kriffo, Tazewell, and Stuyvie. We ate fried chicken and chocolate pudding, Kriffo lamenting the fact that it would be for the last time.

"Who do you think did the paint job?" Kriffo asked. "What do you think it means?"

"It doesn't mean shit." Taze smelled like he hadn't bathed in days. The great unwashed WASP.

I smiled. "I did it. You guys inspired me."

All three of them exchanged looks. Wondering what I meant.

"I didn't want you to think"—I pushed back on my chair and picked up my tray—"that you'd gotten away with anything."

For the first time since I'd been at Bellingham, the headmaster asked to see me. I went to his office ready for a fight, knowing that in many ways I was almost as untouchable as Race. Windsor wasn't wearing a jacket or tie. He looked as though he'd just strolled off the golf course. His pants were decorated with pink whales spouting green water out of their blowholes. Windsor told me that he'd tried to reach my father but that my father seemed to be away.

"He travels a lot," I said. "Works hard to honor all of his charitable donations."

"I'm sure you know why I've called you in here."

Windsor leaned back in his cushioned seat and I leaned back in my hard chair. Neither of us said a word. I noticed the spidery red veins on his nose and cheeks. He probably saw a look of contempt flash over my face. We were at a stalemate. Windsor couldn't kick me out without losing his dorms.

"So how are we going to settle this matter?" Windsor asked. "I have a mind to send your father a bill for the cost of repainting the roof. You can tell him what you like. Create your own little cover story."

Windsor looked like a man who was angry not because someone had stolen his car but because someone had scratched the paint with a key. His was a vibrant, intense anger.

"The one thing I can't figure out"—I tore some skin from my rough, blistered hands—"is how you managed to write that fake suicide note. The one you passed off to Aidan's mother."

"I assure you," Windsor said, "I have no idea what you're talking about."

I left Windsor's office invigorated, high, even. Running out into the Fishbowl where students collected between classes and free periods, I searched for Chester, hoping to tell him what I'd said to Windsor. A crowd of students were busy Scotch-taping sheets of paper to the wall across from our mailboxes. Almost everyone was laughing. Yazid stood by the mailboxes and watched.

"What's going on?" I asked.

"Wall of Shame," Yazid said. "The rejects are posting their rejection letters."

Yazid and I admired the memorial of denial. The embossed letterhead alerting Brizzey that she would not be attending Vassar. Skidmore's red stamp of rejection negating Stuyvie. I didn't see any correspondence with Race's name. Kriffo had posted his own note from Princeton so high on the wall that it was hard to read. It was nice, comforting, even, to see someone say no to my classmates.

Yazid was headed back to England to study at Cambridge. He asked where I was going.

I still hadn't heard from Princeton. Still didn't know if I was off their waiting list.

"Check your mailbox," Yazid said. "Maybe you'll have your answer."

The envelope was thin. I hesitated before opening it. Told myself that either way, acceptance or denial, it didn't matter. I'd be fine. I ripped through the envelope, tearing the message informing me that I'd been removed from the waiting list. My formal acceptance would appear shortly. I'd made it. I was in. A member of that exclusive group of men within my family.

The night before graduation, I bumped into Stuyvie at the General Store. We ignored each other, but when I left the store, he was waiting for me outside, drinking fruit punch. Though he kept wiping his face with the back of his hand, he still had red stains on the sides of his mouth.

"All of you guys get to leave after graduation," he said, "but I'm stuck here all summer. It's not fair."

"You could visit Brizzey," I said. "She seems to like you."

Stuyvie shook his head, rolled his eyes. "As if."

I started down the sidewalk. Stuyvie followed. It occurred to me that Race and Taze might suddenly appear and jump me. I wasn't looking for any more trouble.

"Just thought you should know," Stuyvie said, "that not everyone got off scot-free."

I stopped walking.

"You didn't think that I got suspended for some dirty jerseys. Trust me. I caught all sorts of hell over your girlfriend. My dad didn't let me get away with anything. I'm going to fucking state college. Zoo Mass."

"Sorry." I shook my head and backed away. "I can't help you."

Later on, I thought about what I should have said to Stuyvie. How I should have pointed out that his punishment, his week of watching television, the black mark on his permanent record, his future at a state college, was nothing compared to Aidan losing her life. I understood that Stuyvie's dad had done what any father would try to do—protect his son. But in doing so he'd only done his son more harm.

On the morning of graduation, Chester came to my room to tell me some good news. He'd seen Diana on her way to the headmaster's house. "Brizzey was wrong about her not paying tuition. Diana's been doing correspondence courses. Dean Warr arranged it." This seemed like a nice thing to have done. I didn't want to become so cynical that I couldn't believe in bad people sometimes doing good things. Diana was going to march with all of us and receive her diploma. "She looks beautiful," Chester said. "She's like glowing. Totally luminous."

For graduation the girls wore white dresses and the boys blue suits with red ties. The ceremony was held on the waterfront, and as I walked over to line up for the procession, I saw Diana standing on the front lawn of the headmaster's house. There was a small gathering of students and faculty, and I stood off to the side while Windsor dedicated two maple trees. Diana had donated them both to replace the elms that had fallen in the storm. The trees were still saplings, but Windsor spoke haltingly of how their red leaves would bring shade and comfort for generations to come. The trees were dedicated to Aidan. "They're from our farm," Diana told me.

Diana had on a simple white sundress, her hair pulled back off her cleanly scrubbed face. When she saw me, she broke out into an unexpected smile. We were supposed to line up for the ceremony. Our parents were already seated, the brass quartet warmed up and cued up, but Diana took me by the arm. "Let's make them wait for us," she said.

I asked how she was doing, and she told me that she'd taken up horseback riding and dressage. She couldn't afford her own horse or even lessons, but she'd begun volunteering at a stable. "I shovel horse shit," she said. "And they let me ride for free." She wasn't going to college, not yet. "My dad still needs me around. I might take some classes, but I'm happy just staying close to home." Her father had lost their money, but somehow Diana seemed stronger, nicer, even.

I told her that I'd spent months worried, confused over Aidan's death. "Doubt that I'll ever know what really happened at that party," I said.

It was warm, but Diana shivered. She looked at me with her pale eyelashes and said, "There was no party, Jason. There was never going to be any party."

Diana explained that Tazewell and the others had come up with a scheme for getting back at me for Race's sailing accident. "They were going to haze you. They wanted you to feel what it was like to be caught hanging underwater." Tazewell had bragged to Diana about the plan. The guys had invited me out to Race's and me alone. "They wanted to hurt you." Diana had seen Aidan that Saturday morning right after I'd left with Riegel. She'd told Aidan what the Company had planned for me. "My bet is that Aidan went there to protect you."

When I didn't show up, when there was no one to torment or torture, they did to Aidan what they'd planned to do to me. Just when you thought you had an approximation of the truth, there was another truth underneath.

"What bothered me," Diana said, "was that thing with the suicide note. But Aidan used to read me passages from her journals. Crazy depressed stuff."

Before Diana could finish her thought, I made the leap for her, following her suspicions. "You think someone tore out a few pages from Aidan's journal? Passed them off as something they weren't?"

"It's possible. After Aidan died, I know Windsor and Warr searched her room together, rifled through her stuff. Guess they needed something to show Aidan's mother."

The white sail of Diana's dress blew around her in the wind. She'd obviously thought about contacting Aidan's mother and wondered how something like that would play out. Chester called over to us. The graduation procession was about to begin. Diana said, "Windsor and Warr will just stonewall. They'll turn Aidan's mother into the crazy woman who can't get over her daughter's suicide, who blames everyone but herself for her child's death."

For the next few hours, I sat under a big white tent and listened to the graduation speeches, and even as I crossed the stage to shake Windsor's hand and receive my diploma, I kept thinking, "Aidan saved my life." If not for her, I would have drowned. If she hadn't gone to that party, Tazewell and Race would have simply rescheduled my torment. But Aidan had hoped to save me and they had dragged her from that boat and left her to die out in the harbor during a storm. I felt like I was being pulled up from the bottom of a well. Out of the darkness and into the light. I finally had my awful answer.

I asked Diana why she hadn't told me this. She'd known at least part of the truth that day we sat out by the Flagpole.

"I wasn't sure about anything. Couldn't get Tazewell to admit the truth. Still can't." Diana looked out at the water. "Plus, I was caught up in all my own troubles. I'm a selfish girl. I was mad at Aidan. Mad that she was gone. That she couldn't listen to me or help me anymore."

Diana pointed out that she had asked Aidan to warn me. "My first instincts were to protect you." Her ultimate loyalty was not to Tazewell but to Aidan and the people Aidan cared about. "She was crazy over you," Diana said. "She kept this list of all the snacks you brought her. All the songs you played. I told her she was really lucky. Not one of those boys ever gave me anything."

Only my mother made it to my graduation. Riegel had already started working for our father, the two of them traveling together. "Your dad sends his love and regrets," she said. "He's going to buy you a very fancy car to make up for it all."

Nadia asked to say hello to my mother, and I reintroduced the two of them. They both had on similar green dresses and my mother complimented Nadia on her good taste. The whole time Nadia stood with us, I could see my mother looking over her head waving at the other parents, so many of whom were her friends. Sensing that she'd been dismissed, Nadia hugged me and said good-bye. I thought my mother had been rude and I told her so.

"Is she your girlfriend?" my mother asked. "She's perfectly welcome to come to dinner."

As we packed, Mom told me that she and Dad had reconciled. There would be no divorce. No splitting of assets or parting of ways. "It's for the best, really," she said. "We need each other."

This news neither surprised nor comforted me. I took a long look at my mother. She was a pampered woman. One of that rare tribe of individuals who could truly claim never to have worked a day in her life. My mother had relented, had changed her mind about the divorce. Her fear of being alone was the only thing holding our family together.

After dinner, I showed my mother the waterfront. Wanting her to see where I'd raced. I wasn't as eager to leave campus as I'd expected. I described all the different buildings and trees the storm had damaged, pointing out the places that had been repaired. Mom and I stood by the seawall, and I finally told her about Aidan, described the first time I saw her. "She looked like a bird," I said. "Like a cormorant."

"Roland taught you that," Mom said. "How those birds dry their wings in the sun."

She was right. He had taught me that. "You loved him, didn't you?" I said. "That's why you two were always walking on the beach together."

"Oh, if I had any romance left in me"—my mother crossed her arms over her chest—"I would say that he was the great love of my life. You don't get many of them, you know. Most of us are too foolish to realize when we're in the midst of one."

My mother had her own lost love, her own private sadness that had led her to make too many compromises. I worried about her happiness.

Mom and I would spend the night at a hotel in Bellinghem before driving up to Maine to begin our summer. I told her I still needed to say good-bye to a few friends.

"Take your time," she said. Then she added, "I'm sorry again about Nadia, but I don't like encouraging that sort of behavior. She may think she's your girlfriend, but I know better."

I shrugged my shoulders and began to turn away, but Mom reached out, cupping her hand against my neck.

"Last week I ran into Caroline." She lifted her palm up to my face. "Told her you were graduating. She was thrilled to hear that you were back sailing. We both agreed that we'd never seen two more perfect partners. You and Cal out on the water together. You have no idea how beautiful the two of you looked."

She reached out and rubbed the side of her thumb over the cleft in my chin.

"Where is the sun?" she asked.

"I am your son," I said.

I'd already said good-bye to Coach Tripp, Chester, and Yazid. Coach Tripp surprised me with a gift. A sextant. "It's just plastic," he said. "I know it's not fancy, but I figured it would be a good start."

It was one of the nicest gifts anyone had ever given me. Coach Tripp told me that he was leaving Bellingham. He'd been recruited to sail some rich guy's yacht around the world. "Looks like we're both graduating from this place," he said. "Or at least leaving it behind."

I told him that his new job sounded like a dream.

"Thanks for all of those star lessons," I said. "You taught me well."

Chester had been accepted to Columbia and we planned on seeing each other when we could. His was the one friendship I knew I would keep. He didn't blink when I told him how I felt about Cal and Aidan. I would always be grateful for that quiet moment of acceptance.

All around me students were leaving, packing up their old lives, preparing for new ones. Come fall, I'd find myself at Princeton, with Tazewell lurking always in the background. I'd seen him that morning in the bathroom, brushing his teeth, a towel wrapped around his thin waist. "Someday," I said, "I want you to tell me how you managed to get away with it all." Tazewell spat into the sink and said, "It was easy. I come from a long line of pirates."

Maybe what separated us and made me different from the Company was that I didn't aspire to get away with my crime.

Years from now, I would attend an opening at Dill's art gallery and be forced to air kiss Brizzey on both cheeks. I might travel all the way to New Zealand for a regatta only to find myself competing against Race. I'd receive newsletters and updates about Kriffo's sports injuries and Stuyvie's big plan to replace his father as dean. I would remain steeped in all their glories.

I found myself near the once forested area where we'd had the groundbreaking for Prosper Hall. Somewhere there was a picture of my father, Windsor, and me smiling our ceremonial smiles as our shovels cut the earth. Trees had been cleared, construction begun, the dimensions of the new dormitories made clear with cement and rebar. I wondered who would live in these quarters, boys or girls. Would there be a fire escape, or would the windows be sealed to prevent anyone from sneaking in or out? I'd never really thought about having children, but any son or daughter of mine would be a legacy at Bellingham, would have a home named after him or her. A home borne of a father's desire to hide his son's shame.

Just one last time, just to say good-bye, I walked down to our beach. As I trudged across the familiar sand, I stripped off my suit, leaving my clothes on the shore, and dove into the cold Atlantic.

The wind was picking up. I scanned the harbor for yawls. For one I might steal and sail across the equator, past the horse latitudes, down to the Southern Hemisphere. Hoping to find myself under Argo Navis, the ship of stars. The boat that ferried Jason and his Argonauts to their Golden Fleece. The constellation, once the largest in the sky, had been broken up, separated by astronomers. Where once there had been a single constellation, now three smaller groupings of stars glittered. Carina, the keel; Vela, the sails; Puppis, the stern.

I wanted to sail under our shattered constellation. Aidan and Cal my fellow privateers. The two of them giving off more light, more warmth than I deserved. Cal would teach Aidan how to work the lines, her red hair fiery in the moonglow. She would whisper to Cal how sorry I was. Convince him to forgive me. It was only because of Aidan that I had begun to forgive myself and only because of Cal that I had learned to care for Aidan. The three us part of some larger whole.

I wanted to swim until the dark water and navy sky were one. I felt myself rising, soaring away from this school. Hunting the sky for yachts. Believing that it took those three extravagant boats and those sturdy helicopters to chariot Aidan and Cal away from me. The tide was coming in, the waves gaining strength, but I felt buoyant, triumphant, even. I ducked my head underwater, held my breath, lengthening the keel of my body. Swimming closer to the rocks, I heard the waves and wind creating their own siren's song, the soft voices of my lost friends. I flipped over, floating on my back and leaning into the starboard sea. The night descending, stretching above me like a map promising instruction, direction.

I would spend the rest of my life searching for guiding stars.

ACKNOWLEDGMENTS

I am grateful for the generous support I have received from The Iowa Writers' Workshop, Vassar College, Emerson College, the University of Houston, the Bread Loaf Writers' Conference, the Sewanee Writers' Conference, and Inprint. I would also like to thank my colleagues at Rice University, Justin Cronin, Marsha Recknagel, Susan Wood, and my colleagues and students at Agnes Scott College.

For his incomparable wit and careful reading, I extend my deepest gratitude to the brilliant Ethan Bassoff, a man who works tirelessly and dreams brightly. I am in awe of my editor, the radiant and wise Daniela Rapp, and forever grateful for her luminous vision. Thank you to all the good people of InkWell Management and the sainted souls at St. Martin's Press. Much adoration for Lindsay Sagnette, who first gave me shelter. Cheers to Cynthia Merman for her thoughtful and elegant copyediting.

Thank you to my family for their warm, open hearts. Big love to: Amy, Gerry, and Joseph Heroux; Jared, Heather, Jasper, and Dashiel Dermont; Johanna and Kathy McCarthy; and Catherine McCarthy and Stella Dermont.

A special blessing to Megan Bloomfield for the meaningful conversations she had with me about running before the wind.

I am honored to have studied with the dear departed Frank Conroy and Barry Hannah, whose early readings and encouragements kept me writing. For their invaluable lessons, I am indebted to Ted Weesner,

Andre Dubus III, Robert Boswell, Edward Hirsch, Roxana Robinson, James Alan McPherson, Mark Doty, Antonya Nelson, Marilynne Robinson, and Claudia Rankine.

I would like to thank the following individuals whose friendship and love continues to inspire: my fellow seafarers, Holiday Reinhorn, Andrew Porter, and Jonathan Blum; my matinée idol, Mark Jude Poirier; my great blessing, Amy Margolis; my dream girls, Jericho Brown and James Allen Hall; my dear poets, Michael Dumanis and Cate Marvin; my sweetness, Justin Quarry; my mosquito bite, Christopher Borg; my stars, Sabrina Orah Mark and Reginald McKnight; my ideal, ZZ Packer; my graces, Laurie and Paris Watel; my friends for always, Maribel Becker, Tanya Ceccarelli, and Victoria Allen; the exquisite Connie Brothers; my sage, Michelle Wildgen, and my long-lost Susan Gildersleeve.

And finally, I offer my deepest love and thanks to my parents, Joseph and Joanne Dermont, who gave me an ocean, a library, their love. I am so lucky to be your daughter.